FOREST
BORN

ALSO BY SHANNON HALE

THE BOOKS OF BAYERN

The Goose Girl

Enna Burning

River Secrets

Forest Born

Princess Academy

The Book of a Thousand Days

FOREST BORN

SHANNON HALE

BLOOMSBURY

LONDON BERLIN NEW YORK

Bloomsbury Publishing, London, Berlin and New York

First published in Great Britain in July 2010 by Bloomsbury Publishing Plc
36 Soho Square, London, W1D 3QY

A CIP catalogue record of this book is available from the British Library

ISBN 978 1 4088 0861 0

FSC
Mixed Sources
Product group from well-managed
forests and other controlled sources

Cert no. SGS-COC-2061
www.fsc.org
© 1996 Forest Stewardship Council

Printed in Great Britain by Clays Ltd, St Ives plc, Bungay, Suffolk

1 3 5 7 9 10 8 6 4 2

www.bloomsbury.com

For Magnolia Jane,

who has heart-speaking

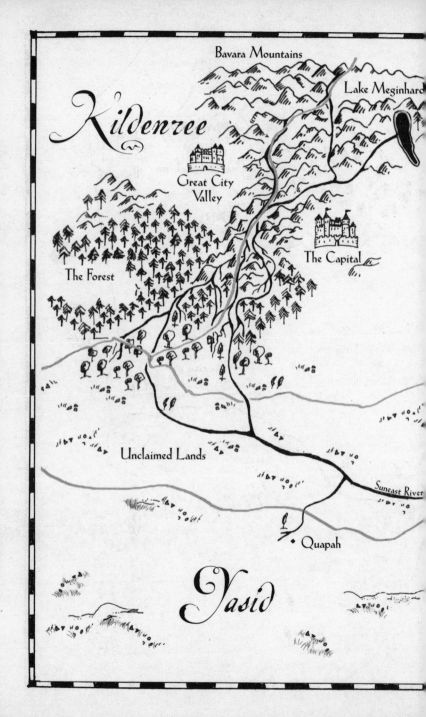

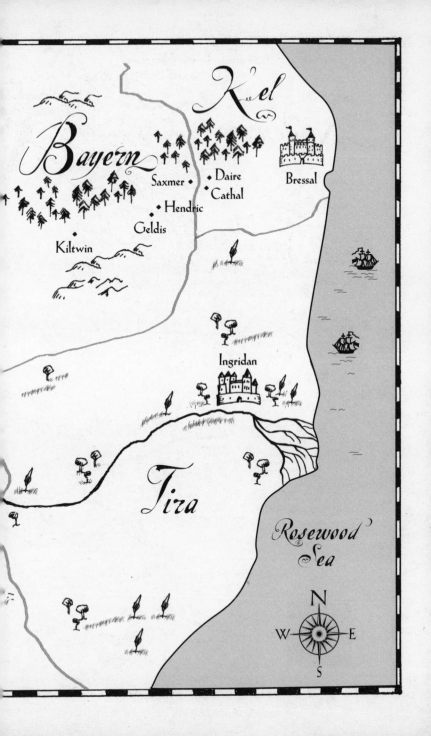

Part One

The City

Chapter 1

Ma had six sons. The eldest was big like his father, the middle boys were middling. By the time Razo was born, all the family's largeness must have been used up. The brothers called him runt and made him feel that word. He spent winter nights longing for a younger sibling, someone he could call runt, someone he could push and pinch.

Ma was longing too, but for a girl to share thoughts with, a daughter cut and sewn from her own soul.

When Razo was almost five, he and Ma both got their wish. The baby girl was born on a night so hot the wind panted and the summer moon blazed like the sun.

"Rinna," Ma named her.

"A girl," said the father.

"Rinna-girl," said Razo, peering over the side of the cot.

The baby blinked huge dark eyes and opened her mouth into a tiny circle. All desire to push and pinch hushed right out of Razo.

He bent closer to her ear and whispered, "I'm going to teach you to climb trees."

Ma did not allow her baby girl into any timber, though Razo, with a trembling kind of impatience, looked her over each day to gauge if she'd grown big enough. The dark-haired baby cried if Ma put her down, so Ma did not put her down. She did chores with her daughter strapped to her side.

One spring morning when Rinna was two, her father went hunting in the deep Forest. Three days later, Ma sent her older boys to look for him. They found his pack and some bear prints, a reminder not to wander far.

That night in the one-room house built of pine, the brothers stared stiff-eyed at the darkness, the unfamiliar sound of their mother's sobs spooking them into wakeful silence. No one moved, except Rinna.

"Ma," she said. "Ma sad."

She crawled off her mat at the foot of her parents' cot and lay down by Ma, fitting into the curve of her body.

"My peaceful girl," Ma whispered. "My tender Rin." She kissed the top of her daughter's head and sighed before falling asleep.

Rin sighed too. She slept with her nose touching her mother's shirt, her dreams laced with the scent of the juniper berries Ma loved to chew.

Rin learned to crawl on moss and walk on pine needles, and by the age of four she could climb a fir as easily as fall into bed. That was thanks to Razo, who never had worked up a reason to push his little sister. When Rin was not clinging to her ma, she was running after her brother. She talked some and laughed some, but mostly she watched—the faces of her brothers, the sway of the trees. She watched the world the way most people breathed air.

"That girl sees the bones inside birds," her ma would say. "That girl can see your soul."

It was early autumn, after Rin's seventh birthday, when Razo, who was almost twelve and old enough to earn real coin, announced he was going to the city. Rin had never insisted on much from her nearest brother—she'd never had need. But now she flushed with indignation. Why should he go someplace so distant and horrible that he could not take his sister along on his shoulders? She would ask him that, she would demand he stay. But she did not have the chance. Razo left during the soft side of day while Rin still slept. He did not say good-bye.

Four days had clomped by, pulling a knot of anger tighter in Rin's belly, when Ma left too, called off to help a neighbor birth a baby.

Rin stood by her ma's house, her arms dangling at her sides. Never had she been without both Ma and Razo, and she felt like a fledgling perched on the rim of its nest. She stared first into the deep Forest, then back toward the city where Razo had gone—both directions frightened her.

Her niece Nordra was sitting on a log, her long black

hair tied at the back of her neck. She was eight, one of several nieces and nephews who were older than their young aunt. Nordra hummed a tune, and Rin's heart cringed. Why was she just fine there, playing alone with no Ma or Razo, and why couldn't Rin be fine too? It was not fair. Rin hated how she felt, weak and forgotten and so scared. Her blood flashed hot in her face and drums beat at the insides of her ears.

"I want that," Rin said, pointing to the stick Nordra was using to twist holes into the dirt.

Nordra shook her head. "I'm using it. Go get another."

Rin's cheeks blazed. With Ma and Razo, Rin rarely had to ask for anything. She looked hard at Nordra, her thoughts skipping toward an idea of what she could say to make her niece relent.

"If you don't give me that stick, I'll tell Ma you took it from me, and she always believes me." Rin could see Nordra knew it was true. "She loves me best, and she'll wallop you with her wooden spoon. So you better give me the stick."

Nordra gave up the stick, though her chin trembled.

Rin felt amazing, big as her brother Brun and powerful as Ma. So she demanded the doeskin boots Nordra's da had made, and the bright red cloth she used to hold her hair, and her doll of wrapped sticks. Nordra gave each thing over, crying pitifully all the while, and with each new treasure Rin felt bigger, stronger, better.

"Rin! Rinna-girl, what're you doing to make Nordra

cry?" Ma bustled through the clearing, her black hair shot with white frizzing free from her blue headscarf. She pulled Rin to her feet by the back of her tunic.

"I just asked her for the things and she gave them to me," Rin said, though the doll and boots felt treacherous in her hands.

"Then stop asking for things that aren't yours. You just shut that mouth and keep it shut unless you have something nice to say. I'd never guessed you had such a bad core to you! I'm ashamed of my own daughter, making little Nordra cry. I'm right ashamed."

Rin had seen Ma's face red with anger before, but never when she was looking at her daughter. Rin's bones shook. She wanted to flee from her body and claw her way into the sky to hide in the clouds where no one ever went. But Ma's stare pinned her like a bug under the point of a twig. At Ma's order, Rin gave everything back and apologized.

Ma looked at Rin once more, shook her head, and walked away.

That was when Rin ran. She ran because she hurt as if red coals glowed inside her chest. She ran until the trees swallowed the sight of her mother's house. Always before when there was pain or sadness, Ma hugged or hummed it out of her—but this time Ma had walked away.

Rin stopped in a mess of unfamiliar trees, turning around, hurting so much, shaking and confused and not knowing where to go. She was bad. Her ma thought so. Home was lost somewhere in the trees, Razo was gone, Ma had turned her back. The coals in her chest blazed, the pain fierce and white hot. Desperate, Rin stumbled into a fir tree and hugged it as she would have hugged Ma.

"I'm sorry," she whispered. "I'm sorry I'm bad. I'm sorry."

She listened, wishing with a childish hope that her mother's voice would find her there in the Forest and say it was all right, that she was not really bad, that she was forgiven and should come home. She listened harder, trembling with a desire to hear. A space inside her opened.

No mother's voice. But something else.

Not a sound, not a smell, not even a feeling. If it had been a color, it might have been green. If it had touched her ears, it might have sounded rhythmic, like the creak of a rocking chair or drone of a bee. If it had a scent, it might have been sweet and drowsy, like fresh pine on the fire.

The place in her chest that had ached with panic now felt warbley and sweet, drowsy and green. Her heart cooled, her breathing slowed, her jumbled thoughts sorted themselves. Calmed now, she understood that Ma would not be angry forever. And Rin worked out her own fault: telling Nordra what to do, demanding what was not hers. It was true what she'd told Nordra—Ma did love her best. But she'd spoken those words not because they were true, but because it would hurt Nordra. And Ma's love was sure to change if Rin stayed that insistent girl who took Nordra's stick.

In the future, she would not demand anything; she would keep the harsh words inside. She felt sure she could do this, a peaceful confidence shushing the tremble from her limbs.

And suddenly she knew which way was home, as if the trees themselves had pointed the way.

Ma scowled at Rin over supper, but that night she made room on the cot. Ma's warmth stilled her fears, and Rin found she could sleep. But that night she had a dream that would stick to her in years to come—a huge worm curled inside her middle, and when Rin opened her mouth, dozens of tiny worms crawled free, dripping from her lips, covering Razo and Ma and her entire family in wriggling slime.

The next morning, the dream clutching at her head, Rin crawled out of her shared cot and tripped away from the house to the nearest grouping of aspens. Her cheek against the papery bark, her small hands gripping the slender trunks, she closed her eyes and listened again for that calming green. It was not really *listening*, not with her ears, but she did not know how to explain it to herself. Peace sluiced through her, and again she made the promise to keep in the hard words, to demand nothing, to be her ma's peaceful Rin.

She returned to Ma working over the morning stew, unsure how to act or what to say. It had been so easy to hurt Nordra and almost lose Ma's love. What if she did that again?

Ma is good, Rin thought. *Ma knows what to do.*

Rin had always watched her mother, so it was not hard to try to be like her. She felt her body take on Ma's sturdy stance, her hands ready to work, her eyes watchful for who needed a hand.

"I can finish the bread," Rin said, working the dough Ma left on the table.

"There's my girl."

When Razo visited from the city a few months later, Rin trembled anew. She had not been Rin-with-Razo for so long that she could not remember what that girl did and how to keep that girl from being bad.

Razo's good, like Ma, she thought. So she mimicked him, finding herself more talkative, eager to explore and wonder, always moving, always near to grinning. He did not seem to notice any change in her—rather, he seemed delighted. But when they were with the rest of family, she felt overwhelmed by all the voices and ways of being, and curled up quiet.

Trying to be like Razo or Ma helped some, but that unpleasant agitation only released her when she was alone listening to the trees. She never thought to ask Razo if he too made a habit of relaxing against a tree's bark and drawing in its calm. When the disquiet began to roar, it just felt natural to turn to the trees.

Soon the trees affected not only her mood but her understanding. Each year a trunk put on a new ring of growth, and within those rings she found the tree's own story. She listened to the scent of it, the feel, the sound, and her mind gave it words—*soil, water, sap, light . . . and before, night and rain, dry and sun, wind and night . . . the drowsy stillness of leaves in a rainfall, the sparkling eagerness of leaves in the sun, and always the pulling up of the branches, the tugging down of the roots, the forever growing in two directions, joining sky and soil, and a center to keep it strong . . .*

There were times when the trees' lives felt more real than her own.

Razo left again for the city, and Rin felt his distance every day. Ma seemed farther off too, since Rin no longer fit on her lap. Ma's family kept growing, with five sons married, and Rin stayed busy. She was the most helpful girl, the children's best caretaker, and Ma's shadow. Her mother discovered Rin had a talent for reading the lie in a person's face and called her any time one of the young ones made questionable claims.

When Rin was thirteen, her brother Deet's wife died birthing their first child. Deet had no end of family to comfort him, but he sought out Rin. For weeks they took slow walks or sat peeling roots together, Deet talking, Rin listening. She never said much, but in a couple of months he began to smile, and the following year he married again.

And Rin kept on listening, never asking, never demanding. Until Wilem.

Wilem had only one brother, who preferred sleeping to anything else. But Wilem liked to dirt wrestle with the Agget-kin, as Ma's children and grandchildren were known, and so made the twenty-minute walk to visit several times a week. Once he wrestled Rin when she would not say no to a challenge, and after, victorious though sweating hard, he said, "Sisters might not be so bad if they're like Rin." His teeth showed their points when he smiled, reminding Rin of a fox.

The idea of Wilem entered her like a pleasant sliver she did not want to pluck. She considered him quietly until the day she spotted him climbing a tree alone. She shirked the wash duty to follow and pretended surprise at finding him up there, but stayed, and they threw pine cones at the nephews and laughed into their elbows. She felt a peculiar freedom in the top of that tree, hiding from work and becoming giddy from the scent of his skin. They were straddled between two branches, forced to lean together. The spring breezes were still salted with the chill of winter, and Wilem's warmth felt wonderful. She was fifteen years old, but it was the first time she'd been alone with a boy outside her family.

"You're wild, Rin," he said.

No one had called her wild before. She was Ma's shadow. But she wanted to be wild now, for him. Wild seemed more enticing than a bowl of berries.

She relished how she felt when she was imitating his careless, confident manner, falling into his quick pattern of speech, jumping from silence to silliness. He seemed to enjoy living. Wilem was someone she could stay with for a long time and not grow weary.

Ever since she'd made Nordra cry, words of appeal or demand were thick wool in her mouth. But she was intoxicated by wild, she was tipsy with living that brief life as a new Rin. So when Wilem climbed down the tree to go find her nephews, she felt as if her last chance to be wild Rin, to be desirable Rin, would run away with him.

She asked him to stay. She dared him to kiss her. She felt his warm, trembling lips against hers, and she wanted more, felt the want like a grumble in her belly, a sharpness in her chest. He was not going to kiss her again, so she spoke, saying anything she could think of to keep him close. And he did stay, for a while. They held each other awkwardly there under the tall pine while she talked to him and he clung to her. He kissed her again when she asked, and though his lips were soft and her middle thrilled, she could feel he did not mean the kiss.

They were not laughing anymore. The thrill cooled, and Rin was exhausted from trying to keep him. It was late when he left for home, his head bowed and shoulders stooped, and she was certain he'd never kiss her again.

The next morning she felt wrong, as if day had dawned only partly made, as if Wilem had taken half of her away with the kiss. She touched her lips. What had she said? She shuddered, an ache and a twisted stomach suggesting she had said too much. Something was wrong. She'd spied her older nieces sharing kisses with neighbor boys, and the next day they were full of sly smiles and giggles, not aches and shudders.

Coals burned inside Rin, hotter and hotter, while she dressed and helped Ma with the morning chores. She did not understand why she burned, but she wanted to cry from the pain.

As soon as she could get away, she ran, falling into the arms of a fir tree.

Take it away, she demanded silently. *Take whatever's wrong, cure me, make it right.*

She tried to throw herself into the soothing thoughts of the tree and seize its peace, but she could not forget Wilem. What had she said? She did not want to remember. The harder she worked to shut that out, the more twisted and dark her feelings became. Had she simply outgrown her connection to trees? Or was it possible the trees were shunning her for what she'd done? After making Nordra cry, her mother had thought Rin was bad and turned her back. After kissing Wilem, it seemed the trees did the same.

Rin ran to another tree, leaned against it to listen, and was accosted by a dizzying darkness. She fled to the aspens, and in place of green calm she felt clutched at and pulled down. She sat on the forest floor with her arms over her head, too lost and confused to cry. If the voice of the Forest was simply silent, then she should feel nothing at all, not this loathing—as if all the trees spat hate and disgust at her. Her stomach turned, her head felt hot, her arms were too weak to lift. She wished she could die.

When evening came and she still had not died, Rin stood up, brushed off her skirt, and went home. It would not be too hard to hide her misery. Lately, no one took much notice of Ma's shadow.

Chapter 2

pring gusted into summer, and every day Rin
ran. She ran over pine needles that snapped and
moss that hushed. She zigzagged and changed
paths, bolted through sunny clearings and back into
cool shade. She sweated to exhale the tightness in her
chest, to hide from a world that felt crowded, hostile,
and too dense to breathe.

The exertion helped some, but today guilt cut her
run short—Ma had need of her, and her brothers and
their wives too. She took one look toward the deep Forest, longing to test its promise that she might lose herself entirely in its echoing silence. Someday perhaps.
But now she veered toward home.

When she reached the clearing of the homestead, she
rested her hands on her knees, waiting for her breathing
to slow. There stood her ma's house, one room built of
wood, shutters wide open in the summer afternoon, fir
boughs on the roof turning brown. Dotting the small
clearing were five other houses, built by her big brothers

for their own families. Everywhere children wrestled and shrieked and chased. The whole place bustled, motion constant, the family like a huge beast with a thousand parts.

Rin spotted Ma, a sobbing grandchild on her hip and a long wooden spoon in her hand. Rin's mother was nearly as wide as she was tall and looked sturdy enough to face down a root-ripping storm.

"Brun, your Lila there is making a ruckus that'll scare the squirrels into winter," she shouted as she crossed the clearing, sounding loving even as she scolded. "See to her or I will. Gren, don't you knock over that pot I just filled if you want to live to supper! Jef, you sack of bones, get back to work. I didn't raise you to nap like an overfed piglet. Look at you children—what pretty needle-chains you made! Now don't go scratching each other's eyeballs. Tabi, let go of your brother! He's not a branch to swing from."

Rin followed Ma through the clearing and to the fire pit on the far side of the little house. When Ma began to stir the pot hanging over the fire, Rin took the spoon from her hand.

"Rin, there's my girl, only sensible person for leagues. Keep the stew from burning while I patch up Yuli's knee, will you? I can't think what those children meant by . . . now wait just a minute." Ma peered at Rin's face. "What's wrong?"

Rin tried to smile. "Nothing, Ma."

Ma sat Yuli on a bench, his sobbing more habitual than urgent, and put a hand under Rin's jaw. "You sure? You've been quiet lately . . . but it's not so much the quiet as something inside the quiet."

Rin shrugged, though her insides were turning to ice. Had Ma noticed these last months how often Rin ran off? Could Ma see that she was shaking inside? Would she speak the words, would she pronounce the problem and then make it right?

Ma felt her forehead, her cheeks, made her stick out her tongue, prodded her belly, listened to her elbows for creaks, pulled down her earflaps to look for rash. "Seem fine. You not feeling fine?"

Rin shrugged again. She'd never bothered anyone about the spiny things in her heart. It did not seem right to complain, especially not to Ma, who worked from the moment her eyes opened until she groaned as she lay down at night. Maybe everyone felt knotted like that but it just was not something spoken aloud. Or maybe only Rin was all wrong. If so, she'd never speak it, especially not to Ma.

"Could you . . ." Rin stopped.

"Ask me, Rinna." Her mother rarely told her what to do. Rin was the child who never needed scolding, who heard what her mother wanted before she'd even finished speaking. But Ma commanded her now, with fists on hips and eyes almost angry, daring her daughter to stay quiet. "Ask me."

And so Rin was surprised into saying exactly what she was thinking. "Could you hug me?"

Without hesitation, Ma pulled her in close, hugged her as if she were a tiny baby scared to be in the open world. Rin's head pressed into her mother's warm shoulder, and she breathed in wood smoke and juniper.

"My girl," Ma mumbled against her daughter's head. "My treasure. My perfect girl. How I love you and love you."

Rin wished she were six and could fit on her mother's lap, and every bad feeling or big scary terror could be drowned out by that ferocious love. There inside her arms, Rin's ache soothed a bit, but the snarled unease did not untangle. Rin had not believed one embrace could fix what was wrong, but she'd hoped enough to try.

"Thanks," she whispered.

Ma hugged her firmer still and smattered her head with kisses before letting go and returning to Yuli, whose cry had become offended.

"Anytime you want a hug, my treasure, you just blink," Ma said over her shoulder as she wiped Yuli's knee with a wet cloth and gave him a heel of bread to chew. "Can't think what's the matter with me if my little girl has to ask for love."

"I'm all right," Rin said, eager to hide it again. "Maybe I'm just feeling lonely for Razo."

"Yes, I bet that's it. That'll be it."

Rin scraped the bottom of the pot to keep the stew from

burning and tried to lose her worries by concentrating on the sounds around her—Yuli's shaky breaths, Ma's comforting mumbles, someone chopping wood, hollers from the children's game of owl and mouse. And the constant murmuring of the trees—wind in the high branches, pine needles clicking together, the soft knocks of cones, the creak of wood. But she could not shy away from the same thoughts grinding in her head: *hide yourself, try not to be who you are, you don't belong in this good family, even the trees think you're all wrong, you've got to go away, away.*

But where would she go?

In the yard everything quieted, then silence burst with hollers and calls of greeting. Could it be Wilem? He had not returned to the homestead since that night four months ago. Many times when she'd been running, Rin had almost turned toward his home. For what purpose? She did not understand why she'd felt so desperate for him to kiss her or why the trees now kept their peace to themselves. But surely nothing she could say would fix it.

Rin tiptoed around the side of the house. In her nervousness, her hands rose to cover her mouth.

A couple dozen members of her family gathered, her Ma squealing and administering hugs. In that sea of dark heads, Rin caught sight of orange. Her heart beat harder. There was only one person in all of Bayern with hair that color—Dasha, the ambassador from the country of Tira, and her brother Razo's girl. That meant Razo was here too.

Rin could hear Dasha saying, "It is a pleasure to return to the homestead again, Mistress Agget."

The Tiran girl had taken to referring to Ma as Mistress Agget, a formality that actually made Ma blush. All the folk known as Agget-kin called her Ma, including her grandchildren, who referred to their own mothers as "my ma" to avoid confusion. Even the nearest neighbors called her Ma. Only Dasha would stiffen things up like that. Apparently she was wealthy, her home in Tira a palace. "Isn't it wonderful how she's so comfortable here too?" Rin's family often said. But early last spring when Dasha had first arrived at the homestead, Rin had detected shock in Dasha's expression, even a little disdain. So why had Dasha stayed with Razo? That was what Rin wanted to know.

At last she glimpsed her brother, just exiting his mother's embrace. Razo looked the same—he was the youngest and shortest of the brothers, his cropped dark hair sticking straight up. Just the sight of him made her want to giggle. He was her best friend. And she had been his best friend—until Dasha.

Rin smiled, straightened, and waited for Razo to look for her, because he always did. She was usually standing a ways back, and he would call her Rinna-girl and push everyone aside to hug her or wrestle her or challenge her to a race or just knock his forehead against hers and smile.

His glance was roving. Her stomach tingled in anticipation. Then their eyes met, and in that moment before he could speak, a shock split her as she realized, *I can't tell him either.*

All these months she'd been planning what she would say on his return. "Razo, how can you stand to be away from the trees in the city? Or don't you feel anything from them? I used to think with them, through them, and feel calm. But not anymore." If she said that much, she'd also have to explain. "But then I kissed Wilem, and the trees changed toward me. I must be really bad if even the trees want me gone, and maybe if Ma knew me inside instead of out, she wouldn't love her girl anymore." If she could explain, perhaps he could help her make sense of it and fix it.

Only now did she understand that she could not admit it, even to him. He would not know how to mend her or the trees, and she could not reveal her secret ugliness, not without the risk of losing his love. That comprehension knocked her as if she'd fallen back-first out of a tree.

Razo waved. "Rinna-girl!"

She put her hands over her face and cried.

Everything went quiet. She could hear one of the children whisper, "Is Rinna crying? Why's she crying?"

"Uh . . . ," said Razo. "Um, Rin? Did I—"

"What's the matter with our girl?" her mother asked the general gathering. "Does anyone know?"

"Kif, did you and Len do something?" Ulan asked her oldest boys.

But for the slamming pain in her chest, Rin might have

laughed. It was ridiculous, her family looking dumbfounded while she cried without reason or sense. She would have tried to shrug it off and pretend that she'd stepped on a sharp rock or something, but the sobs kept pulling out of her chest, stuck to each breath like pine sap on her fingers.

Dasha spoke in a casual voice. "Rin and I are dying to take a walk together. It's been months! We should be back by supper."

Dasha's arm hooked Rin's and she walked her away from the homestead, whispering directions. "Don't trip, there's a big rock on your left. Duck under this branch. Let me help you hop over this fern." By the time Rin dried her face and looked around, they'd left her family far behind.

"Is this the way to that sunny clearing with the aspens?" asked Dasha. "The one we went to last time I was here?"

Rin just nodded. Dasha was such a happy, bouncy kind of person, and Rin did not have the energy to try and reflect her mood.

The clearing was much smaller than the homestead, but wide enough that daylight streamed through the canopy. Aspens sunned themselves, leaves turned up and quaking. It used to be Rin's favorite place in all the Forest. The last time she had pressed her forehead to an aspen trunk here, instead of soaking in their green calm, she had jerked back from the heart-battering ugliness.

Dasha sat on a rock and sighed. "Now, shall we just sit or would you like me to blather?"

"Blather please."

"With pleasure."

An hour flowed by as Dasha recounted her first sea voyage that previous spring, traveling north from her home country of Tira to a port in the kingdom of Kel.

"Razo made friends with the whole crew, as you can imagine, and they had him climbing ropes and hoisting sails. He learned seafaring songs, a few he wouldn't repeat."

Dasha described Kel, the green slopes around the seaport, the charming hats the Kelish ladies wore, and meeting King Scandlan. "He was odd, really. Perhaps I expected all kings to be as warmhearted and gallant as Bayern's King Geric, but Scandlan was distant. Razo noticed it too, though he did not find the king's behavior as odd as I did."

Rin could not resist adding, "Razo probably felt sympathy for the king, figuring he was plagued by an itch that he couldn't decently scratch in public."

Dasha laughed. "Razo *would* think that!"

She went on with the story of their horseback ride into Bayern, where Dasha had come to replace her father as ambassador from Tira. Rin stretched out on a bed of moss, her chin in her hands, thinking about faraway places and ignoring her ache. *Maybe Dasha is a good sort after all, just like everyone says.*

She imagined asking Dasha, *Does everyone secretly feel lost? Sort of shoved into a corner alone? Do you feel something different when you're close to trees? Did they ever turn away from you? Do trees care if you begged a boy to kiss you? Have you ever felt like your home wasn't home anymore? If you were me, where would you run?*

Soon the shadows were thick, crossing the clearing as if fleeing to the east. Dasha stared at the sky soaking up a darker blue.

"I could stay here all night," she said casually, without looking at Rin as if not to pressure her. "Or we can go back. Whatever you like."

Rin squinted toward home. She was not eager to face her family, but the day was quickly exhaling into night. She sighed. "If we head back now, we'll get there before dark."

Be nice to her, Rin reminded herself as they walked home. *For Razo.* She tried.

"Thank you. Sometimes being around family is best, and sometimes it's not."

"Those are true words," Dasha said, her eyes on the path. "I love my father, but it is nice being in Bayern without him. He is not like your mother. He is rather . . . hard. But I imagine even with a large, loving family, sometimes it would be good to get away."

Dasha took Rin's hand, a sisterly gesture. Rin did not want to hold her hand—she wanted to banish her back to Tira and have her brother all to herself.

"There you are!" Razo jogged up, slightly out of breath. "Everything all right, Rinna-girl?"

"What? Oh, you mean earlier?" Dasha said before Rin would have to explain. "Oh yes, she's fine, that was nothing."

"Oh. All right. So, while you were gone, I challenged the brothers to a slinging contest. They're still bandaging their egos."

"You're the best in the world." Dasha kissed his cheek, and Razo shrugged to hide his gratified smile.

Rin watched him, aware more than ever how he had changed in the past couple of years. There was a confidence in him, as if he were always dressed in armor from helmet to shielded boots. She did not know what had caused the change—his adventures in Tira, or getting out from under the shadow of five older brothers. Or Dasha.

Razo was looking into the canopy, and he asked, "Is it going to rain tonight?"

Dasha turned her face up, considering. "No, not tonight."

"Excellent. We can sleep out."

Rin wondered why Razo would ask Dasha that, and why Dasha would know the answer, but she was not in the habit of asking many questions.

That night at the homestead, all six houses emptied their inhabitants onto the forest floor. Rin, Razo, and Dasha lay their bedrolls on a patch of moss between two fir trees and stayed up with the moon, whispering stories and laughing into their pillows. On his previous visit, Razo had told his sister all about his year in Tira, but Rin wanted to hear it again. She enjoyed her brother's attempts to keep his expression unaffected while he described how he'd bested two companies of soldiers at a slinging competition or discovered who had been plotting to restart the war between Tira and Bayern.

As Dasha watched him, her smile grew so ardent her nose wrinkled. She would reach over to touch his arm when she thought he deserved some comfort; she would giggle when he said anything the least bit amusing. And when Razo looked back, he seemed ten years older. This orange-haired girl from Tira was altering Rin's favorite brother, spoiling him for other company, the way a night left out on the table changed yesterday's dinner.

Razo did not seem aware of anything but Dasha until he asked, "Rinna-girl, are you really all right?"

She shrugged, then sighed, then buried her face in her arms. She felt stripped and beaten and completely out of lies. "I don't know."

"What's going on?"

She shook her head. "You'll think I'm odd."

"Too late."

"Ha." But she was too afraid and confused to try and speak the whole truth, so she said, "I don't feel right here anymore. I've been..." No, she would not admit how often she'd run toward the deep Forest and yearned to keep going. She'd seen the hollow sorrow that still lay on Razo's face whenever he remembered their father. "Sometimes I want to just...go away."

Dasha clapped her hands together. "Of course! You will return to the city with me and Razo."

"What? No. I . . . I can't go to the city. What would I do in the city?"

Rin had never been to Bayern's capital, not even for market day with her brothers. She imagined it as an enormous beast crouched behind a wall, and when she walked through the gate, it would catch her in its spiked teeth.

"You could get work in the palace, Rin, or be a waiting woman perhaps."

Rin expressed her doubt with a snort, and Razo said, "Rin a waiting woman? That's a laugh."

Rin did not see Dasha elbow Razo in the gut, but she heard his grunt.

"Don't you know who you are?" Dasha asked, her fists on her hips. "You are sister to Razo of Bayern's Own, the most important group of soldiers in the kingdom. He also happens to be the chief personal guard to the Tiran ambassador." Dasha inclined her head. "Not to mention that he's dear friends with Bayern's king and queen. Apparently it doesn't occur to your brother that he has handy political connections and might use them, but politics is what I do. If you want to live in the city, in the palace, and be a waiting woman, then good gracious, girl, use your connections and do it."

Rin blinked. "But . . ."

"You should definitely come," Razo said. "It'll be good

fun, you'll see." And he launched into an exhaustive narrative of all the city's charms, mostly involving apple cakes, sausage vendors, and palace banquets.

Soon the idea was firming inside her. Leave the Forest, go to the city. Keep moving. Like with swimming. Last summer some Agget-kin had dammed the stream and made a pool. They discovered pretty quickly that if they did not keep moving in the deep spots, they would sink. Whenever Rin was alone, the world still, nothing to do but think, she felt that sinking sensation in her middle, sure her head would go under and she would drown inside her own self.

Keep moving, she thought. The trees no longer relieved her, and running far and flirting with the deep Forest helped a little but cured nothing. She had to go farther, do something different.

When all three began to yawn more than talk, Rin settled onto her bedroll and closed her eyes. As soon as her thoughts were her own again, she felt that gray panic rush through her, gnawing her bones crooked.

I am going to the city, she thought hard at herself to bolster her spirits. *I'll go before my family notices anything's wrong. I'll get away from trees that loathe me. And I'll be all right.*

The idea of leaving the Forest felt like standing on the rim of a well and willing herself to fall in. But she could not stay home, not as she was, not with the piercing disquiet, the wrongness that clung to her like wailing children who never sleep. She needed to run farther. She needed to go out into the world that had changed Razo and ask it to change her too.

Somewhere a mouse squealed inside the talons of an owl. Somewhere a dry leaf cracked under an animal's step. Everywhere the trees sighed. It was a long time before Rin could fall asleep.

Chapter 3

hen Razo and Dasha took leave of the family four days later, Rin stood beside them, wearing her good tunic and boots and dangling the small sack of her possessions over her feet.

Everyone was gathered before the main house—Ma, the five oldest brothers, their five wives, and the twenty-three children. They patted Razo's back, engaged in last-minute wrestling matches, and gave Dasha timid cheek kisses, since she was too foreign and fancy for common handshakes and slaps.

Then one of the little ones said, "Why's Rin got her pack too?"

Everyone went quiet. A bird called out from a tree, shrill and insistent. For only the second time in her life, Rin found herself the focus of her entire family. She kept her eyes on the shadow of her bag swishing over her boot.

Dasha cleared her throat. "Rin's coming with us. To the city. It might be nice for her to have a change of scenery. Work in the palace. That sort of thing."

No one spoke.

Dasha cleared her throat again. "I'm sure she will be back before long."

"Rin's going? You're going?" Rin recognized her brother Jef's voice, though she did not look up. "You're teasing, aren't you?"

"No," said Razo. "You just open your ears when we say, Rin's coming with us and don't make a fuss."

Her oldest nephew Meril said, "Don't believe half of Razo's stories about the city. It's not as nice as he makes it out."

"It's a dirty, smelly, crowded——," her brother Brun began.

"There are people who'll hurt you for no good reason," Brun's wife Sari interrupted. "They'll knock you down, they'll spit on you, not care a spoonful of mush about——"

"Ma needs you," said Ulan, Jef's wife. "And who'll help me with the little ones on wash day? Come now, this isn't like you to run off and leave us all——"

"Don't give her a hard time," said Razo. "She wants to come for a bit. No harm. So, bye now!"

Razo took a few steps as if hoping for a fast departure, but Rin could not make her legs move.

Coward, she thought. *You coward.*

Each time Rin had been about to tell her ma, her ma would look at her with eyes full of sweetness, and that expression that said Rin was her beloved girl, her most precious one. Rin could not bear breaking that. She felt fresh sympathy for eleven-year-old Razo sneaking away at dawn so he would not have to say good-bye to his baby sister.

"Rinna?" said Ma. "You're going to the city?"

Rin glanced up and then back at her boots as quickly as she could. Ma looked so confused, Rin's heart cracked. She was betraying her. But to stay and keep pretending that she belonged in the Forest, that would be a betrayal too.

"I am, Ma," she said. "Going for a bit."

One of the children started to cry, softly at first, but when her mother tried to hush her, the cry broke into a wail of despair that reached up through the canopy and seemed likely to pierce the sky and make it rain.

"What's happening?" another child whispered.

"Rin's leaving," someone whispered back. "She's going to the city forever."

"Forever? Rin's leaving forever?"

More crying voices joined the first, and the wail was so loud, no one could hear Rin mutter, "Not forever. I hope."

It was all Rin could do not to join in, let her voice rise up to the treetops and crack the sky. She nearly said, "Never mind. I'll stay and everything will be normal." Maybe it was for the best that she struggled to speak in crowds.

What good was she to her family broken? She could not keep pretending to be the same Rin, the never-fail Rin, the helpful Rin, not when she was about to break apart like burned-through wood. The trees had changed for some reason, and she was no longer welcome in the Forest.

So at last Rin shouldered her pack, met her mother's eyes, and said under the hubbub, "Bye, Ma."

Rin turned and walked away before she could cry. The protests silenced behind her. Razo and Dasha soon outpaced Rin, her steps slowing. She needed to shut herself in that moment. Hurting was the least she could do for the offense of leaving her Ma.

She glanced back once, and a few members of her family lifted their hands in halfhearted waves. Her mother had not moved, her hands still clasped together, her weight on one foot, her face nearly expressionless. But when she caught Rin's eyes she sprinted forward, and her blue headwrap slipped, setting free loads of kinky black and white hair. Rin waited, her heart squeezing painfully.

Ma seized Rin and squeezed her, pulling in her arms and her head, as if afraid the girl would fall apart. The whole world became Ma's warmth, her hands, the smell of juniper, the thud of her heart.

She released Rin to look her in the eyes, anxiously smoothing her daughter's dark hair away from her brow, straightening her tunic. "I never thought you'd leave. Of course you might, but I just never thought . . . Razo's always had half his mind elsewhere, so that boy coming and going feels as natural as the turning of the seasons. But not my Rinna-girl, not my baby girl." She took Rin's hands, rubbing them between her own. "You've not been yourself of late. And I know if you'd wanted me to know why, you

would have talked to me about it long ago, so I don't a̲
But I tell you this—go out there and find whatever's floated
out of you and then come back to us right quick. Some folk
is made for wandering and being in the open world, but you're
a Forest girl, Rinna. I can't help thinking that the longer
you're away from your family and your trees, the more you
just might wither away. So come on back and be my sweet-
eyed tender girl home in her Forest again. Right quick. You
hear me?"

"I will, Ma. I'm sorry. I'm really—"

Rin shut up, her voice hooked to tears now. Her mother
was right about the withering. She already felt dried-up and
half-dead, and it hurt so much she actually looked to see if
her limbs were splitting.

"I'll miss you every moment until then. My baby girl, my
peaceful Rin. Go on and catch up with Razo, I won't keep
you. Just you know I'll be hoping for you each day."

Rin nodded. She had not intended to run, but when she
turned her back on her mother, her body wanted to collapse, and running seemed the only way to stay upright.
Dasha glanced at her when she caught up with them, but she
did not ask why Rin had been fleeing as if for her life. They
walked in silence for a time. And Rin did not look back
again.

It was good she was going. It was. Living with her family,
letting them believe she was her ma's shadow, that was a lie,
and the kind that would build into a storm to blow her

down. It *was* good that she was leaving, so why did she feel like a straw doll that had lost all its straw?

They traveled for two days, the hum and click of the Forest sweeping past Rin in a blur of green. Emerging from under the canopy to join a main road, Rin had to gasp at a sky that grew bigger and bigger till she thought it might swallow the whole world. Eventually she had to admit the sky was greater than the Forest, a thing she had never before imagined.

An escort waited at the city gates with two spare horses for Lady Dasha and her chief personal guard. Rin rode on her brother's horse, her arms seizing his chest in case the beast took a fancy to flinging them off. She did not trust horses. They were so large and they moved in unexpected ways. People were one thing—Rin enjoyed trying to guess a person's thoughts. But who knew what a horse was thinking? Rin looked into the huge round eye of the beast beside her and decided that she did not want to know. It most likely involved eating its rider, bones and all.

The city was everything that the Forest was not. A wall ten men high kept the trees out and the people in, boxing in the clanging and whirring and cracking and whacking. So much noise that Rin wondered how the people could stand it. She startled constantly, confused by the commotion, imagining she kept hearing someone call her name. Her heart was tired from stopping and starting, and she wanted to cover her ears and yell at everyone to just hush up.

Dasha said, "Soon it will all sound like wind in the leaves to you—just noise you find yourself ignoring."

"You don't notice the noise anymore?"

"Not so much."

Rin considered. "If there was a dog standing on your pillow barking in your face every night, do you think you'd eventually get used to that too?"

"I . . ." Dasha smiled. "I hope to never find out."

It seemed to take all day to ride up the curving streets, but at last they reached the topmost swell and faced what could only be the palace. It was as huge as the city-dwelling beast of Rin's nightmares.

"Oh no," she said aloud.

"Did you say something?" asked Dasha.

Rin did not care to admit, "I'm feeling fairly alarmed at the moment and I suspect if I go inside that thing, it'll chew me up and spit me out," so she said, "It's big."

Razo snorted. "That's the truth. Just wait till you see inside—it's full of *Rooms*."

He dragged Rin through corridors and galleries, court-yards and antechambers, pointing out the absurdity of the palace finery with a tone that attempted derision but sounded proud. "Vases everywhere, as if all the tables weren't enough. I mean, what's the point of having all those little tables if

you have to go and find vases to put on them, and then find
something to put in the vases? Hundreds of vases, nearly a
thousand. And you'll know I'm not exaggerating if you count
sometime. I have."

His fervor made Rin smile, which was a distraction from
her lingering dread. At least the palace had not actually
turned into a monstrous beast and chewed her up. Yet.

Rin could not tell much difference between a stone wall
and an inlaid wood wall, but she said "ooh" and "wow" so
Razo could believe she was properly impressed. He greeted
everyone by name—kitchen staff, chamber ministers, guards
and courtiers and maids alike. Everyone hailed Razo in
return, and no door seemed closed to him.

"My sister," he'd explain in passing. "Here from the Forest. I'm showing her all the *Rooms*."

And the sentry would nod and let him pass.

"You're important here," Rin told Razo, knowing that
would make him puff up and gloat, but she could not resist.

"What do you mean *here*?" he said, but he was so delighted, he took her to the kitchen next. "Best place in the
palace." She soon agreed. The storeroom alone took her
breath.

The rest of the day rushed past like a spring-fattened
stream. They ate; they found Dasha, who had secured Rin a
post as a waiting woman, whatever that meant; then Razo
and Dasha bid her good night.

Another antechamber. This one full of beds and

wardrobes and screens for undressing. This one was apparently her new home. It came with three waiting women who talked. And talked and talked. And sometimes expected a response.

So Rin tried to do as she'd always done, patterning her style of speech and attitude after another, trying to fit into their mood. But one girl talked quickly, the other slowly, and one was quiet, then given to sudden bursts of energy. And they spoke of things foreign to Rin, other towns and families, castles and gowns, music and dancing. She did not know whom to imitate or what to say, and the dizziness of so many *Rooms* and the feeling of being buried inside a stone beast was overwhelming. Rin ended up shrugging a lot until she finally just lay down on her bed and shut her eyes.

She missed the breeze moving over her skin. She wished she might look up and see stars popping through a canopy of pines and feel nothing but the chill goodness of a night forest, the warmth of Ma at her side, the slumber breathing of her family all around.

Instead she heard whispers.

"Relative of someone important, I gather, or why else is she here?"

"Do you think she's dim-witted, how she hardly speaks?"

"Undoubtedly."

"Her Majesty's never had more than four waiting women. This one's unnecessary."

"It'll be nice to have an extra hand till Cilie comes back, though I could wish she wasn't yet another rough girl."

"How did Cilie secure her post? I never heard."

"She's from one of the east provinces—a poor girl. There was some sad story involved, and you know how the queen crumbles for the sad stories."

"I could wish Her Majesty had a little more backbone, to tell the truth."

"When does Cilie come back? Perhaps she knows the new girl."

"Oh, I doubt the new girl is from the east. If I had my guess, I'd say she's Forest born."

ver the next few days, Rin saw little of Razo and Dasha, and had the extraordinarily odd experience of spending most of her days under a roof. Waiting women served the queen, but Rin only glimpsed Queen Anidori coming and going, while she had her fill of the other women.

They seemed competent, though they spent a tremendous amount of time talking before performing any duty, asking another's opinion how to do this or that, or ought they do this instead? And did anyone else catch a gander of that new chamber minister with the broad shoulders? And wouldn't another night of music in the grand chamber be just the thing?

Rin watched and listened, and found ways to be useful.

"Look at that spot! She'll never complain, but I know this is Her Majesty's favorite dress."

Rin took the dress back to the laundry-mistress.

"Tomorrow's the queen's riding day, and that stable-master hasn't replaced the left stirrup yet, I'll wager."

Rin went to the stables and watched the stablehands at work, and when no one noticed her, she fixed the stirrup herself.

"Where's that button? I swear I had it right here. Look at that, just about to sew on a new button and it up and walks away."

In Rin's vast experience as an aunt, no object ever walked away but it had help from a child. She slipped into the adjoining nursery, where the queen's son, Tusken, played with pale wooden blocks. He had a mass of wavy fair hair tumbling around his face, and cheeks so round and kissable they seemed like peaches ripe for plucking.

"Hello, Tusken," she whispered, kneeling beside the prince and kissing his cheeks a few times because she could not help it. He was nearly two years old but still wonderfully chubby, and her heart strained for her little ones back in the Forest.

She held up both of her hands. "How many hands do I have? Let's count. One, two. Now let's count yours."

He held up his hands and no button fell out, but he kept his mouth curiously shut.

"Good boy. Now let's count teeth."

She opened wide her mouth, and he did the same. Inside his cheek, something gleamed. She scooped it out with her finger.

"Oh dear, you could choke on that. Buttons aren't food, lamby. We only put food in our mouths."

She helped him stack his blocks and cheered when he

knocked them down. Then she returned to the other ladies, placing the button on the table.

"Hello, there it is! Where'd you find it, Rin? Eww . . . why is it wet?"

Rin decided she'd keep a closer eye on Tusken.

Summer was lingering out of doors, the days long and sweet as if sucking on a honey stick. Rin watched it through a glass pane. She was continually flinging open windows, leaning out, smelling the air that tingled her nose with scents of flowers and horses. She longed to be the one to escort Tusken on his daily romps in the garden, but she was being especially cautious. *Don't ask for anything, make no demands, keep the hard words inside.*

Finally one of the others suggested it, a pale girl named Janissa who sported scratches and an angry welt across her cheek from chasing Tusken through shrubbery.

Although Rin had taken charge of a dozen children at a time, this one little boy felt as important as a hundred. She took Tusken's hand and led him past staring servants and observant sentries with an apprehension that made her squeeze her eyes shut.

It was a relief to be in the gardens, crawling through bushes, making "soup" in a castoff helmet with water, flowers, dirt, and leaves. The few trees were squat and ornamental, but where the gardens merged into the stable yard, a massive elm held court, looking as out of place as a roughly clad giant would in the palace's throne room.

Stablehands came and went, soldiers and pages, and no one slowed to touch the tree or even look up to admire its lush crown.

They must not need trees, she thought. *They must not feel any more from a tree than from dead wood.*

She'd wondered the same about her own family in the Forest, but now it seemed true. People would not be willing to live in a city if they needed trees as Rin did. As she had.

Rin accompanied Tusken outside all week, and on the seventh day at last she dared. She brought Tusken to the elm, where he sat in its twisted roots, breaking sticks into tiny pieces.

Rin stepped closer. *Maybe it's only the trees of home, maybe they're what's wrong and I'm all right . . .*

She pressed her cheek to the ropy bark and closed her eyes. Trembling, she opened herself inside, as if she were listening hard, though not with her ears.

Please, she thought, hoping for a trickle of that familiar peace to work inside her. *Please.*

She gasped and flung herself away, filled with a creeping nausea that pressed against her throat and made her forehead sweat.

Tusken hopped to her, and she pulled him close.

"It's not the trees," she whispered, though he would not understand. "It's me, Tusken. What can I do about that?"

"Tick," he said, waving a stick near her face. "Tick. See tick?"

"It is a beautiful stick."

Tusken nodded.

Rin did not sleep well that night. Early, before the waiting women awoke, Rin crept out into the dark blue morning and ran as if from death itself. The air tore out of her lungs, her feet hammered on the ground. There was no running away here, with a wall enclosing the gardens and stables, and sentries by the gates. No illusion that she could keep on going until she ceased to be. But at least while she moved, the piercing disquiet did not undo her.

Rin washed her face and arms in a bird bath and sneaked in just as the others began to stretch and awaken.

That afternoon, Cilie, the fifth waiting woman, returned from her visit home and declared she was nearly expiring from eagerness to have some time alone with Tusken.

"I'm happy to keep taking him out myself," Rin said.

Cilie sat before a mirror, redoing the complicated coil of her hair, which was long and brown and lush, the most striking feature of her otherwise plain appearance.

"Let her do it, Cilie," said Janissa. "He seems to like her. She's had more success than the rest of us."

"That won't last," said Cilie. Her eyes were small and a little close together, reminding Rin of a pig. "There's no pleasing the little prince, spoiled to the bones he is."

Rin very much wanted to say, "There's something in you I don't like. Not a bit. You have the look of a dog who's eaten its master's meal and is ready to bolt. And you have pig eyes. So don't you complain about Tusken in my hearing." But she stuffed the words inside and did not argue, taking Tusken by the hand without waiting for permission.

In the gardens that day, Rin and Tusken discovered fat snails, a rainwater-filled hollow teeming with water insects, and once, Cilie crouching behind a shrub.

Rin strode right up, her fist on her hip, a mannerism that was all Ma. Cilie startled and ran off. Some time later, she spotted Cilie by the stables, arguing with a man Rin did not know.

"Something there I don't like . . . ," Rin muttered.

The next day Cilie was waiting for Rin beyond the arch that led to the flower garden, a spot hidden both from the nearest sentries and the gardeners working beyond in the sun. She smoothed her glossy brown hair away from her forehead, making sure every hair was in place.

"It is my turn to watch Tusken. I love him and miss him desperately after so much time away."

Cilie did want to be with Tusken, but not because she loved him. There was some other purpose in those pig eyes that Rin could not read. Rin tried to walk around her.

Cilie grabbed her arm. "You're not clever enough to care for this boy. The queen doesn't trust you. She wants me to take him from now on."

Rin was afraid to speak with all the hot anger rising to her throat. She pulled her arm free, gripped Tusken's hand,

and started away, saying, "Well, Tusk, shall we hunt frogs today?"

Cilie darted in front of Rin and shoved her hard in the chest. Rin fell back, hitting the flagstones. Cilie tried to pick up Tusken, but he spun away in an oblivious dance. Rin scrambled to her feet, putting herself between Cilie and the boy. She held up her hands in fists and glared. Razo had taught her how to throw a punch. He'd let her practice on his flattened palms, and she'd laughed so hard she'd gotten the hiccups. But she had never actually hit anyone. Now, facing Cilie, her fists trembled with eagerness. Even more insistent were the words building inside her like a mouthful of stones.

"Leave him alone." Rin was as startled by her words as Cilie seemed. Telling others what to do was her ma's business. Shame burned in Rin's cheeks, but she did not apologize or turn away.

Cilie took a step back. "How dare—"

"I see you." The passion in her words made Rin feel warm and bright as the sun. "No one else does, but I do. I see you're hiding something. And if you hurt Tusken, I'll kill you."

Cilie stumbled a few more steps back. Rin could see she believed the threat but still did not flee, her own intent greater than her fear. So what was Cilie's intent? Could she truly mean Tusken harm?

Yes. Now that Rin looked, she could see that clearly in Cilie's face. Secrets, dark designs, murderous thoughts, and desperation. And all of it focused on Tusken.

Rin's anger washed away as quickly as it had flamed to life, replaced by clammy fear. She swooped at the boy, flinging him into her arms, and hurried into the garden. Footsteps slapped behind her, and Rin ran faster, casting her gaze around for safety.

"Finn!" she called to a large soldier with dark, longish hair, one of Razo's closest friends and a fellow Forest born.

Finn left his group of soldiers, his eyes darting to Tusken's face, then around for signs of an enemy. His steps quickened into a run. "What's happened?"

Rin glanced back—Cilie was already gone. She took a breath and discovered she was trembling so hard she could no longer hold Tusken and handed him over to Finn. What had that woman been up to? Perhaps nothing serious, perhaps Rin had overreacted. But she still itched with fear.

And it was not just the altercation that set her feeling like a bag of chattering bones—it was speaking those words. She could feel them in her head still, rolling around, clanging into her thoughts. *Leave him alone. I'll kill you.* In truth, Rin could not bear to finish off a pigeon she'd downed with her sling, but the threat had felt so real.

And she felt bad. Wrong. Sick with herself. Certain that if her ma had heard her speak those words, she would have turned her back. Rin had sworn to herself that she would never speak like that again, not as she had to Nordra all those years ago. Living in the city was dangerous—so many people, so many chances to slip up.

After a few moments in patient silence, Finn asked, "Do you want me to stay with you?"

Rin nodded, got on her knees and hugged Tusken, whispering to him of all the spectacular insects they were going to find today. Tusken patted the top of her head and said, "Win," finding the *w* sound in her name. Then, "Finn. Win, Finn, Win, Finn," marching around to the beat of his rhyme.

Finn stayed by them all afternoon. She'd always felt a certain kinship with the large soldier, who wasted no words, and once her trembling subsided, she found it easy to reflect Finn's quiet nature.

When they were ready to go in to dinner, Finn escorted them to the queen's antechamber.

"Do you want me to stay?" he asked.

Rin shook her head. "No, I'll be all right. Thanks, Finn. Thank you."

Cilie was inside, whispering angrily with two of the waiting women. Rin overhead a few words: "... completely crazy ... attacked me ... Tusken shouldn't ..."

Rin passed them without a second glance, taking Tusken into the nursery.

She was teaching Tusken a song when the queen appeared in the doorway, tall and slender, her yellow hair braided and hanging in a simple loop.

"Mama!" Tusken yelled and waddled to her. She picked him up and swung him around.

"Hello, my most precious. Oh, it's good to see you. I was so busy this week, but our visitors left today and now I'm all yours."

"Mama busy."

"That's true, but no more. Were you playing with Rin?"

"Pway Win," Tusken said, tugging on the blue stone necklace at his mother's throat.

Rin closed the door between the nursery and the antechamber. In the four weeks since she'd come to the palace, she had never spoken to the queen, and it took a few moments to muster the courage. She kept her eyes on Tusken's dangling bare feet so she would not lose her nerve.

"I don't trust Cilie," Rin said in a small, shaky voice.

There was a pause before the queen replied. "And you think I shouldn't trust her either?"

Rin was still anxious from her words of demand that morning, quaking inside like aspen leaves in a windstorm. *Be careful*, she shouted at herself.

She took another breath. "I don't trust Cilie with Tusken."

The queen's arms tightened around her son. "Do you know anything specific? Has she made threats or hurt him?"

"No, I don't know anything. She's . . . I'm sorry." Rin almost turned and left then, sure she was behaving as no waiting woman should. But she remembered the look in Cilie's close eyes and summoned more courage. "She was acting oddly, insisting she be with Tusken. And something in her . . . expression . . . made me not trust her."

"Do you think she plans to hurt him?"

Rin shrugged helplessly. "I don't know anything, but I feel afraid for him."

The queen studied Rin's face. "Thank you, Rin. I'll take your warning very seriously. If you discover or even suspect anything else, please come to me."

Rin believed her. Everything in this woman, every part of her face, every movement of her hands, spoke of truth. Rin watched the queen as she spoke to Tusken, instinctively positioning her own body in a similar attitude, feeling how much more confident she felt with her shoulders pressed down and back like that, how naturally her left arm hung at her side, how pleasant her lips felt in the attitude of almost smiling.

"Come on," the queen said, placing Tusken on her other hip. "Your da will want to hear the new song you learned. Let's go see if we can hunt him down."

"Dada hiding?" asked Tusken.

"In a crowd of ministers, no doubt. We'll save him. Thank you, Rin."

"You're welcome, Your Majesty," Rin said, imitating the warm, low cadence of the queen's voice. It felt nice.

The queen paused at the door. "I knew your brother before I was a queen. He was, and remains, a friend truer than sun in summer. I like that he calls me Isi. I know all the 'your majesties' people ply me with are out of respect for the crown and I should take my due. But when we're alone, Rin, I'd like it if you'd call me Isi, too."

Rin tried the words. "Thank you, Isi."

Rin stared at Isi's back as she left the room. A chill in her blood spoke of fright, though she was more curious, the kind of curious that thrilled and stung. While she'd been with Isi, the constant squeezing in her chest had eased some. For the first time in months, maybe years, she had not felt like a stranger.

That's who I want to be, Rin thought. *If I had to be someone forever, I'd choose her. There's something different. There's something about our queen* . . .

Not that she wanted to be queen of Bayern, she told herself. She just wanted to feel like that, to move through each moment as easily as a fish through clear water. She wanted to see good everywhere, as she imagined Isi did, to have confidence in her shoulders and truth in her face. She wanted not to be the girl who had to trick Wilem for a kiss, who fled toward the deep Forest, who ran from home.

She'd heard rumors that the queen was friends with the wind, though she did not understand what that meant. Razo had never said much about her, but perhaps Razo did not notice Isi the way Rin did because he had no need to. He was at home in forest or city, cottage or palace, Bayern or Tira. When he left the Forest, he'd been moving toward something good, not running away like Rin was.

For the next two weeks, Isi made certain there were two soldiers flanking Rin and Tusken on their bug-hunting adventures. Cilie was released from waiting woman duties and sent to report to the chief steward as a maid, but occasionally when Rin looked up from where Tusken had discovered an impressive beetle or a stone shaped like a chair, she would notice Cilie in the distance, watching.

si! Isi! Rin, is she in her rooms?" Enna, a black-haired woman of twenty years swooped into the queen's antechamber, her arms loaded with bolts of silk in red, yellow, and blue. Finn remained on the threshold, one hand on his sword hilt, as if expecting someone to burst in and threaten Enna's life.

Rin sat up straighter, energy rushing into her limbs. She'd known Enna for years as a fellow Forest girl and loved reflecting her manner. It made her feel strong and significant—though it was tricky too, since Enna tended to toss out demands as easily as hellos.

"She's out," Rin said. "Caught in a net of meetings, I'd guess."

"The poor thing. I'll stick around. She's bound to be back soon if Tusken's here." Enna plopped into one of the cushioned chairs and put up her feet. "I swear, this entire palace is teetering on the edge of insanity. And, Rin, you're one of the only ones around with any sense. How do you feel about that?"

Enna gave dark looks to the queen's other waiting women darning hems in the corner. The waiting women returned quiet glares.

Enna sighed, arranging the bolts of cloth on her lap with a look that begged inquiry, so Rin asked, "What's all the fabric for?"

"My gown. I refuse to get married in drab white, of all the ridiculous colors for a wedding day. The thread-mistress wants to make my wedding gown, 'And now, and in a hurry,' says she, 'so pick your fabric if you want to be married this summer, or if you dawdle I'll tell you quick as my tongue can fly that you won't be getting your dress in time and then that moon-eyed young man of yours,' (that's what she called you, Finn) 'that moon-eyed young man of yours won't get his wedding and he'll come blame me. But I'll tell him sure as I'm telling you how can I make a dress without the fabric? I ask you, how?' And on and on she goes as if I had all day to listen. I tell you, some people don't know when to just snap it shut."

Enna looked over her shoulder at Finn as if for his opinion, and he smiled at her, and they smiled at each other in silence for so long that when Enna looked back to Rin again, she had a dazed expression as if she'd just woken up.

"What was I saying?" asked Enna.

"Snap it shut," said Rin.

Enna's eyes widened.

"Oh!" Rin laughed, her face burning. How easy it was to say such things around Enna. She needed to be more careful. "I meant . . . not you, I meant that was the last thing you said."

"Oh. Right. You have a good memory. Well, I need Isi's opinion, of course. What do I know about fabric for gowns and weddings in palaces and such? I'm still not sure this big hullabaloo in the city is the best idea anyway."

Finn's smile deepened. Apparently he knew, as Rin suspected, that Enna did indeed prefer a big city hullabaloo of a wedding to a quiet Forest party.

Razo popped his head around the door and exhaled when he took stock of the room's occupants.

"Here you are. I went looking for you two down in the thread-mistress's chamber, and when I asked her where you were . . ." Razo blew out his cheeks.

"Say no more," said Enna.

"Sure enough, that woman had enough to say for all of us. Hello, Rinna-girl." Razo knocked her with his shoulder. "I never get used to you in these prettified clothes."

Rin smoothed the blue light wool tunic over her skirt, feeling the prick of sweat on her skin underneath. She'd sneaked out earlier in her old Forest clothes to run off the raw panic that was creeping over her again, and had thrown on the fine clothes only moments before Enna arrived.

Razo poked at her skirt with one finger, as if it were an animal only feigning death. "Almost want to call you some other name . . . I'll have to think on that. Rinna-lady, maybe? Naw, you don't have the lady look."

"Razo . . . ," Enna said, scolding in her voice.

Rin tried to echo Enna's chastising stare.

"What? It was a compliment! Rin doesn't want to look like a lady, do you? Can't climb a tree in a fancy skirt. And I can't imagine you at home in any place where there aren't a thousand trees to climb at a moment's notice."

It was an innocent comment, but he'd unknowingly struck her right in her pain. Rin felt a frown dig into her forehead before she turned and pretended busyness with Tusken.

"Rin," Enna said, her voice concerned, "now what's—"

Before Enna could finish, Isi swept in, picking Tusken off the floor and sitting with him beside Enna.

"What a morning," she said, kissing her son's cheek. "I'm glad you're here, Enna. Great crows, but what a morning. Hello, Rin, thanks for watching my boy. Was he good?"

"Always," Rin said.

"Always," Isi repeated. She buried her face into his neck, making eating noises, while the little boy laughed his rough, gravelly laugh. Isi was still smiling at Tusken when she said, "Bad news from the east."

"Ugh." Enna covered her head with a bolt of yellow silk.

"I know, I'm sorry, Enna, Finn. It does look as if the wedding will have to be postponed. But hopefully just for a week. Finn, Geric needs you."

Finn had been sitting on the edge of a table by Enna, one hand on her knee, but now he stood, half-turned to the door, ready to go at command. "What's happening?"

"Oh, probably nothing serious," said Isi. "But after Tira and the war and everything, the ministers clamor to respond quickly to any hostility. A village near our border with Kel was attacked. It could be bandits—though I thought we'd rooted out all the serious banditry that erupted after the war. It could just be a bad tavern quarrel, for all I know. The message was oddly unclear."

"Come on, Isi," Enna said. "You're not going to cancel my wedding for a tavern brawl? Just send one of those those overeager cousins Geric seems to have by the dozens."

"The fact that it's near Kel . . ." Isi glanced at her waiting women, and Rin wondered if she was thinking of Cilie, who was from a border town. "Something is going on in Kel. They sent our ambassador packing, explaining King Scandlan was feeling under the weather and wouldn't be holding court for some time. But the dismissal was suspicious, and given that this new trouble is so near Kel, Geric wants to get there quickly and make sure all is well. He's taking Bayern's Own."

"Really? All of us?" Razo peeked up from where he'd been lounging on the carpet, fiddling with a loose nail on the underside of a table.

Isi barked a surprised laugh. "How long have you been there, Razo? I guess I should know to check under rugs and tables for you. Yes, Geric wants all of Bayern's Own who are currently in Bayern. No time to send for Talone and the rest in Tira, of course."

"Just as well," said Razo. "I was getting bored. I mean"— he shot a glance at Enna, who was still draped in cloth—"not that Enna and Finn's wedding preparations aren't *thrilling*. I guess I've never had such a good time in my life as Enna's discourse this morning on which style of slippers are most— *ow!*"

Razo was interrupted by the slap of Enna's slipper against his head.

"You're not going anyway," said Enna. "You're the Tiran ambassador's personal guard now, and that trumps your other duties."

"That's right," Razo said, knuckling his forehead. "Finn, promise me you'll have an extremely boring time—no adventures whatsoever."

"None whatsoever," Finn said.

"That wasn't convincing at all." Razo turned to Isi with a pleading expression.

"He's subtle, isn't he?" Isi said, looking over her shoulder at Rin.

Rin nodded. "From birth. As a little boy, he was known to scream 'Smell me!' whenever he—"

"That'll do, baby sister," said Razo. "No one wants to reminisce."

"You can go if you like, Razo," said Isi. "I'm sure Geric

would be grateful for your eyes and your sling, if the ambassador gives you leave."

"After some well-placed compliments, she'll be clay in my fingers. Just wait and see."

"I'll wait and see just how eager she is to have a break from you," said Enna.

"I should report to Captain Brynn," said Finn. "He'll want to leave in the morning." He held out his hand to Enna, helping her stand, letting the cloth tumble to the floor.

"Sorry," he whispered.

Enna shrugged, though Rin could see she cared quite a bit. "As long as you didn't invent the trouble to get out of marrying me."

Both Isi and Razo made doubtful noises.

Enna leaned back to look at Isi. "Am I going too?"

Isi shook her head. "Don't bother, Enna. It doesn't sound dangerous. You may as well stay and get everything ready so you can marry that troublesome scoundrel the instant he gets back."

"He's some trouble, it's true, but he's only a scoundrel when I ask him to be."

"And only when she asks nicely," said Finn.

Razo covered his head with his arms. "Ugh, save me from the sauce of their loveyness."

Isi laughed, but Rin frowned, still going over Isi's words in her mind. She'd implied that if the situation had been more dangerous, then Enna would have been asked to go.

Why? No one else in the room had seemed surprised by that exchange, except perhaps the other waiting women, their faces bowed over their darning, the window light at their backs hiding their expressions.

Enna's arms were around Finn's neck. "You be careful. I've already had you fitted for your wedding clothes, and it'd be a nuisance if you went and lost a limb."

Finn whispered something in Enna's ear. She half-laughed, half-sighed, and he kissed her cheek and then her lips.

"All right, all right," Razo grumbled, pulling himself off the floor. "If it's going to get all sticky around here, then I'd best be off to find Dasha and do my duty. She's bound to get grumpy if she doesn't get her fair share of farewell kissing."

"That's so *noble* of you, Razo, to make the sacrifice," said Enna.

"That's me, all sacrifice and nobility. And charm. Don't forget the charm." He kept talking as the three left the room. "And we'd better stop by the kitchens to get our own supplies. They never pack the right kinds of food . . ."

At dawn the next day, King Geric rode out with thirty of his personal band of soldiers, Bayern's Own, Finn and Razo among them. The king was taller than Finn, though not as broad. Even dressed in the same subdued colors for travel as his men, he had something about him that reminded Rin he was the king. Confidence, perhaps, boldness, and an awareness of everyone around him. He shouted to his wife, "No worrying, now!"

Captain Brynn rode beside him and made his own farewell salute to the queen. He was fair-haired by Bayern standards, and though captain of the king's hundred-band, he had the clever and anxious look of a scholar. Rin could not see Isi's face, but it must have betrayed her worry, because Brynn shouted, "I'll protect the king's life on my own, my queen. I swear it!"

"Thank you, Captain," said Isi. "You all come back to me as fast as sparrows!"

Rin held a very sleepy Tusken. She'd pulled him from bed to see his father off, and he still had not so much as squeezed open an eye. His ability to sleep like the dead through all that clamor amazed her, and she wondered if she had ever felt so completely content, even as a small child.

"I always worry," Isi said to Rin, watching her husband ride through the palace gates. "But they'll be fine. Of course they will."

The chilly calm in Isi's voice made Rin take a second look at the departing figures, searching for a head shorter than the rest, his hair standing straight up. Razo was her favorite person in all the world, besides Ma. Her other brothers treated her like a smaller and quieter version of their mother. But Razo . . . he wrestled her and let her face get dirty, put a sling in her hand, and showed her the gut-tickling satisfaction of a well-played prank. Each time he'd left the Forest, she'd felt a slap of grief that she'd kept quiet and close. But he always returned a little braver, a little smarter—even a little taller.

She spotted his head there among the dozens, almost too far away to see. Instead of filling her with loneliness, this time his leaving made her afraid.

Chapter 6

en days after the departure, a messenger burst through the doors of the queen's antechamber.

"Your Majesty! Your Majesty, news from the king's expedition." The messenger's voice cracked from thirst. Isi arose from her seat, clutching Tusken. Dasha, Enna, three waiting women, the prime minister—all were standing, waiting for him to speak.

Razo, Rin was thinking. *Razo, Razo . . .* The tension hurt her skin like a fever burn.

"We were northeast, a day's ride from Kel." He coughed, his dry throat refusing words. Rin shoved a jug of water into his hands, and he gulped it down, gasped, and continued. "The king was attacked. Your Majesty, should I deliver this news in private?"

Isi took in the room's occupants, then asked her other three waiting women and two sentries to step outside. Rin observed Isi's stature and pulled herself a little taller.

The messenger spoke again as soon as the door was

shut. "Rumor led us to a village called Geldis, torched to its timbers. The king ordered a search of the area. As soon as we fanned out, the attack came. Fire out of nowhere. Brynn was killed right off, the king and others wounded."

Who was wounded? Who? Rin stared at Isi, willing her to ask.

"Brynn. Oh no, poor Brynn. He was engaged to be married." Isi pressed both hands on her chest as if against a great pain. "He swore to protect him—that was the last thing he said to me, that he would protect the king with his life. How . . . how seriously was the king hurt?"

"I don't know, Your Majesty." The messenger wiped his nose and frowned. "Burned, but alive when I left. The camp-master took him away, and I jumped on a horse to bring the news. I'm sorry. We couldn't see where our enemies hid—or how they were lighting things afire, if you understand me."

"I do." Isi's eyes were cold, intense. "Do you know the names of the wounded?"

The messenger's face filled with regret, but he managed to keep his eyes on the queen. "I don't, Your Majesty. I'm sorry."

"Ma," said Tusken, pulling on his mother's sleeve. "Mama, this. Mama, this." He stuck out his tongue and made a long, wet noise.

Isi rubbed his head. "You are so clever," she said, trying to keep her tone light.

Enna said, "Let's go after them! Right now, I'm ready. Isn't that right, Isi? If Talone were here, he wouldn't dilly-dally. Who's in charge with Talone in Tira and Brynn gone? Ratger, isn't it? I want him here immediately. You, messenger, whatever-your-name-is, draw a map of exactly where you left the king's party." Enna opened the door and shouted into the corridor, "You, waiting women, stop waiting and get parchment and food, find Ratger, and get the stable-master and the prime minister . . ."

Isi's face was pale, and Rin was reminded that the queen had been born across the Forest and over the mountains in Kildenree, where most folk had fair hair and fair eyes and skin that burned easily in the sun. She stayed seated, her breathing stiff and slow as if she were forcing herself to stay calm.

In moments, Enna had given everyone assignments and sent them away, leaving Enna, Dasha, and Isi alone with Rin and Tusken.

"We'll leave in the morning," said Enna. "I wager Ratger will bring five hundred-bands."

"An attack on the king is an attack on Bayern," said Isi. "Close the city gates, call up the reserve guard, send messengers to warn the border towns. And send an advance party so he—so they know we're coming."

"I'll tell Ratger. But we both know . . ." Enna paused, glancing at the room as if checking for lurkers. "We both know that one good fire-speaker could rout a battalion."

"You think you and I should go alone," Isi said flatly.

"Of course I do. We've the best chance out of anyone to find the fire-speakers and . . . and subdue them before they hurt any more people. A little whoosh-whoosh with the wind, a few well-placed fires, and we could wrap it up and send everyone home."

Isi opened her mouth as if she would argue, then shrugged. "You're right. If they hurt Geric, they might try to kill him next, and others besides."

"Nightmares, but what a scene. I thought we were going to have some rest before my wedding."

"I'm sorry, Enna."

Enna shook her head. "Please. Brynn is dead and Geric is hurt—but not dead. You hear me, Isi? He's not dead. You think he'll retreat to Kiltwin, hole up at his cousin's castle?"

"No, he'll make straight for home. Straight for me and Tusken."

"I will go too," said Dasha.

"That's not necessary, Ambassador."

"Please call me Dasha, and I think it is. Since coming to Bayern, I've met countless people who lost family members in the war my country started. Every day I'm mindful of that horrible suffering. I don't want to stand around, being a statue in honor of Tiran cheerfulness. If I go with you, perhaps I can help prevent more suffering. Besides, if the king is hurt, what of Razo? And Finn—"

"Finn is fine," Enna said.

"But—"

"Razo is fine, Finn is fine," Enna said with so much heat in her voice Rin almost believed it was true, though surely Enna had no way of knowing.

"And what would happen to our currently amicable relationship with Tira," said Isi, "if the Tiran ambassador was injured or even killed in Bayern?"

"I just won't get killed then," said Dasha. "And I think I'll avoid injury too while I'm at it."

"That's a good idea," Isi said.

"Thank you, I thought so too."

"Dasha's getting pretty good with fire," Enna said, with some reluctance in her voice. "And she does have the water part that we don't. Might come in handy."

Rin's skin began to tingle. *Fire-speakers. The queen's wind. Razo asking Dasha if it would rain. Fire. Water. Wind.* They spoke casually, as if, perhaps, they assumed Razo had explained it all to her. Curse him.

Isi glanced her way and Rin remembered herself, thrusting her attention back to Tusken, who was clambering on her back. She was a waiting maid, there to watch the child, not take part in the queen's council. But her thoughts still churned like leaves in the wind. Everyone knew that in the war between Tira and Bayern, a so-called fire-speaker had burned a tenth of the Tiran army, turning them back from invading the capital. A fire-speaker who could send attacks of fire, burning from a distance. That had been Enna, Rin now guessed. And the rumors about the queen and wind . . . So, both Enna and Isi could control wind and fire, and Dasha too. No, with Dasha it would be fire and water.

Rin felt like half a girl, a scrap of a person, sitting at the feet of these fearless women who were confident, wise, grown. With a hunger and a hope that felt bigger than her body, Rin yearned to be like them. Especially the queen. If only she could stay close to Isi, listen to her, watch her, perhaps she could learn how to be. Perhaps she could become someone new, someone fixed and good, someone who could go home again.

Chapter 7

Rin woke to the morning drum making rounds through the palace corridors, calling out those who were to leave on the expedition. It did not call for Rin, but she sprang up anyway, sneaked past the sleeping waiting women and ran down to the horse grounds. She'd slept in a travel tunic and leggings, even in her boots, and her leather knapsack was already packed with a hunting sling, a cloak, a change of clothes, a leather waterskin, and bread left over from supper.

The grounds were crowded with wagons and horses and men with weapons. The quaking calm of early-morning bustle surrounded her, the intensity and hurry jarring with the dark sky and sleepy light in the east. She eyed a wagon and considered crawling in and covering herself up with feed sacks. Instead she stood beside it, trying to look bold but feeling pathetic.

Her unease had been bad enough of late, but worry for Razo seemed like to kill her. She needed to know that he was all right. *Keep moving. Stay with the queen,* that was what she had to do.

"Rin?"

Rin startled, her limbs running with cold. Isi was dressed in a brown tunic with leggings for riding, her hair in one long plait down her back, unadorned. She did not look royal. But for her yellow hair, Rin thought she might have fit right in at the homestead.

"Did Enna ask you to come?"

Rin's heartbeats scrambled in anxiety. "No. I'm ... worried about Razo, and—"

"Majesty." The chief steward rushed to the queen. He had slicked hair and a nose so tiny he seemed to be always sneering. "Majesty, the girl Cilie you sent to me ... she didn't return to quarters last night."

"I asked you to get her out of the palace while I'm away."

"And I would have, Your Majesty, but she never checked in after chores. No one knows where she is."

Rin felt sick. She'd assumed Tusken would be safe in that big palace surrounded by soldiers, but perhaps not with Cilie slinking about.

Isi was already running back toward the palace, and she shouted over her shoulder, "Rin, come with me."

Soldiers stood guard outside Tusken's nursery. Janissa was asleep at the foot of the prince's bed, and she startled when Isi and Rin entered. Tusken lay curled up in a ball, mouth open, chest rising and falling. Rin bowed her head with relief.

The queen was all focused energy. "Rin, take him down for me? Janissa, help me gather his things."

"Down?" Rin asked.

"He's safer with me and Enna out there than he is alone in a palace with a missing girl who might mean him harm."

A roundish soldier with kind eyes escorted Rin and offered to carry the prince. Rin shook her head. She was not a large girl, but her child-carrying muscles were as strong as pine branches. She set the sleeping boy against her chest and gave him a little squeeze, his heart pressing closer to hers. Warmth gushed through her.

"I love you, Tusken," she whispered.

He moaned in his sleep and stubbornly did not wake even after she clambered into the back of the wagon and the company began the bouncy trek down the city streets. He slept for hours, giving Rin time to think as dawn broke into day.

Keep moving, she thought. Back home, fleeing into the deep Forest had been a temporary reprieve. Escaping to the city had not cured her either. It seemed she was the problem, not the trees. She wished she could run away from herself.

Tusken's wagon stayed in the center of the small army, flanked by Dasha, Enna, and Isi. Rin knew Isi would not casually risk her son's life, so he must be safe with those three women. Everyone must be safe with them somehow. Even Rin. Hopefully Razo too. What a big open world they rode into, how many strange dangers—not the kind she knew, like unexpected falls into Forest ravines or cuts that did not heal. But fire coming out of nowhere, people who wanted to kill. It made no sense. She wrapped her arms around Tusken and imagined how her mother might have felt when she embraced her little girl.

Isi and Rin took turns in the wagon, keeping Tusken entertained or holding him while he napped. When Isi sat with her son, Rin rode the queen's horse.

I'm going to die, Rin thought, *and when Razo hears it was because I couldn't stay upright on a horse, he'll be laughing too hard to mourn.*

In truth, the horse was gentle and walked so carefully, her balance never wavered. But he was a *horse*, a large beast with unfamiliar movements and no expressions to read except the undoubtedly murderous thoughts in his huge eyes.

The third day of travel, they met the king's company as it retreated toward the city. Geric was riding at the head. That he was on horseback seemed an excellent sign, but from a distance Rin could see the bandages. She was standing in the wagon, straining to spot Razo.

Isi cantered her horse forward and Geric set his dappled mare to meet her. They dismounted, Isi throwing herself off her horse, Geric climbing off gingerly. Isi's hand wavered over her husband's bandaged face, white strips of cloth wrapped around half his head and covering one eye, extending over his right shoulder and arm, down the right side of his body. She kissed his left cheek.

"Da!" Tusken was shouting. "Dada! Win—Dada."

Rin helped Tusken out of the wagon and they ran across the field toward Geric and Isi, Enna and Dasha keeping close beside them. Razo was suddenly there, Finn too, unsinged and smiling. Rin discovered she was smiling too, so much that it hurt, and hard dry sobs shook out of her chest.

"Razo, you're all right," she said.

He scoffed. "Of course I am. Who could hurt me?"

"Make camp!" shouted Captain Ratger at a nod from the king. There was a squeaking of leather saddles as riders dismounted, horses nickering at the lift of weight, muffled thumps as packs were dropped. Isi and Geric stood together, talking, a moat of solitude surrounding them. So intently did they look at each other, Rin wondered if anything in the world could have called them out but Tusken.

"Dada!"

"There he is!" Geric scooped up Tusken with one arm.

"What dat? What dat?" Tusken reached for the bandage on his father's face, grabbing a handful of cloth. Geric groaned and pulled back.

"Ooh, careful, Tusken. Da's hurt. Here..." Isi took Tusken from his father, and Geric half-sat, half-fell to the ground, his left eye squeezed shut. A physician was at his side at once, feeling his forehead for fever, touching his pulse, calling for water.

Tusken wriggled out of Isi's arms and squatted by his father, patting his good shoulder, his expression mimicking an adult's seriousness. "Sowy, Dada. Sowy, sowy."

"It's all right," Geric said in a croaky voice. "Everything's fine."

All around, cooking fires were being built, horses unsaddled and brushed, bed rolls prepared. The late-afternoon sky was limpid, blue and cool, no need for tents. Dasha and Enna sat on low stools by the king, Razo and Finn at their sides. Rin stood behind them, expecting to be asked to leave, but no one addressed her.

". . . out of nowhere," Geric kept saying. "Just, *whoosh*— fire, all at once. I fell backward off my horse. The worst of it caught Brynn, who was no doubt rushing to save me—a stupidly brave thing to do. The rest got my horse. Poor Springer. She was hurt, and they had to . . ." He cleared his throat. "In moments it was over. The attack wounded eight others, but only Brynn was lost. He died quickly. I'll be thankful for that at least, though I've wished every moment since that I could at least face Brynn's murderer with a sword in my hand." Geric grinned bleakly. "Good time to be clumsy, eh? If I was as skilled a horse master as my wife, I'd be dead."

Isi laughed once, hard, and it made her eyes water.

"They attacked as we approached the village of Geldis. It had been burned completely, its inhabitants taking refuge in Hendric to the east. Sudden fire, and then nothing. I left five men in the vicinity to try and track them. The size of our battalion was a disadvantage when facing this kind of danger. I'm eager to return to the capital and get aid sent to that village. We left supplies in Hendric, but the people of Geldis will need help rebuilding their homes."

"The men you left . . . do you think they're fit to root out a fire-speaker?" Isi asked.

Geric shook his head helplessly.

"Well, you all know what I think we should do," said Enna.

"I can guess where this is going." Geric squinted at Isi. "I don't suppose you're expecting another child, my dear, as you were the last time you ran off on a mission without me?"

"Not at the moment, my dearest. I'm quite fit to travel."

"So you plan to—"

"To track them down, whoever is burning villages and trying to kill you. Enna, Dasha, and I will find them and stop them."

Rin heard Razo whisper to Finn, "Told you they wouldn't let us go."

"Blast, this is not what I want!" Geric seemed to want to stand, but he glanced at his bandages and stayed down.

"I know," said Isi. "I'm sorry. I almost can't bear to think about it, leaving Tusken, leaving you. But I have to."

"You don't have to——," Geric started.

"You think I'm going to let itchy-skinned fire-speakers come into my country, attack my husband, and hole up somewhere only to attack again? You think I'm not going to hunt them down and burn every hair from their heads and make sure they're too scared or too dead to ever come near you again? If you think I'm that kind of a woman, then you don't know whom you married, King Geric."

She huffed an angry breath. Geric smiled mischievously.

"Stop it," Isi said with warning in her voice.

"What did I do?" said Geric. "I didn't do anything."

"But I know what you're thinking, and just because you're all bandaged and in terrific pain and looking pathetic doesn't mean I'll let you get away with those little knowing smirks."

"What's going on?" asked Enna.

Isi sighed. "Nothing. He just likes to see me get angry."

"I don't just *like* it," said Geric. "I——"

Isi gave him a warning look. "Not another word, Your Majesty."

"I'll go." Finn spoke to Geric but his eyes strayed to Enna.

"That's right." Razo straightened up. "If there'll be a hunt for fire-speakers, you're going to want me along."

"I should go too . . . ," Geric began.

"Oh for all the silliness," said Isi. "Half your head and arm are burned, you can barely stand up. And when unknown fire-speakers are trying to kill the king, that's when the king needs to get behind a very tall wall. Besides, someone has to stay at the palace to take care of Tusken and everything else. Yes, I can see that you're prepared to argue with me some more. Good luck."

Geric groaned in defeat.

"So it's settled," said Razo. "The five of us go."

"Sorry, Razo," Isi said. "Our party should be as small as possible, so we can be quick and inconspicuous, and I don't dare bring anyone along who can't face down a fire-speaker. I'm feeling quite stubborn about it. Brynn is dead, my husband was nearly killed, and I'm not in a good mood. You know what damage a fire-speaker can do—and there may be more than one. Enna and I . . . and Dasha . . . we're the best hope for ending this quickly. You all know it's true."

Finn was frowning, but he did not argue.

Geric sighed. "You're right. I don't like it, but you're right." Tusken plopped down on his father's lap and began to click two stones together.

"Keep close watch on Tusken. Cilie may mean harm, and she's disappeared." Isi heaved a sigh as she sat beside him. "I'm just so relieved you're alive!"

Geric rubbed the back of her neck with his left hand. "I'm sorry I made you worry," he whispered.

She cut her eyes at him. "Whoever started that fire— that's who will be sorry."

"Ooh, are you going to get angry again?" He grinned with half of his mouth, and she rolled her eyes.

A physician lifted Geric's arm to remove the bandage. Geric clenched his jaw and shut his eyes, his face turning red with the effort not to scream.

"Sorry," he said through gritted teeth. "Should. Take care of this."

Isi held his uninjured hand while the physician peeled back the bandage. The sight of Geric's raw, blistered skin made Rin's own arm throb in empathy.

To give the king his privacy, Enna departed with Finn and Dasha with Razo. Rin stayed nearby with Tusken, chasing him around and around to get out the cramped energy. Soon Isi called for Tusken, and he ran to his mother and father. He did not look back at Rin, and neither did the queen, her thoughts no doubt with her husband. Rin hesitated but did not think she should follow if they did not call.

She felt forgotten, alone and left with the night. It was what she had been dreading. Nothing to distract her now.

Just beyond the road, a wood beckoned. These were not the trees of her home—their shapes were almost disturbing in their unfamiliarity. She ducked between trees and felt a subtle relief wash over her, brief and distant. For the moment, she just felt glad to be near living things that demanded nothing of her.

She placed a hand on the bark, longing to feel more than pale relief. Her heart cramped with homesickness for that calm that used to root her drifting soul. But the memory of the elm stopped her—no peace, no relief, just a nauseating wash of slick black hopelessness. She moved her hand away, afraid to try, and sat on the ground.

The air changed with the nearness of night, blowing damp and cool, as if the oncoming darkness were a wave rolling in from Kel's ocean. Rin shivered and tried to take comfort in the fact that good things like night still existed.

Alone, aimless, her thoughts tumbled around her. What did she want? To be all right with her own heart. To lose the dread and disquiet that gnawed at her chest. To go home to her ma and play with her nieces and nephews, and eat bread hot from the oven pit and roast pine nuts and just lie back and feel home again.

But she could not go back where her mother still believed she was a good girl, where family barely noticed her, where Wilem hung his head. The city was so many walls and roofs and talking faces. The only place lately she had felt at home was with Isi. And now Isi was going where neither she nor even Razo or Finn were allowed to follow. Sitting on firm earth, Rin felt as if she were sinking.

Through the trees, she spotted three girls. Their hair was hidden in Forest women's headwraps, but Rin was certain that underneath the cloth, one had yellow hair, one black, and one orange. They were walking to the far edge of camp nearest the wood with Razo, Finn, Geric, and Tusken, making farewells. The fire sisters—that was how Rin had begun to think of them. Three girls who could speak the language of fire. She had no place with those girls, but she ached to. Rin stood, hesitated, tripped forward, and finally ran. Maybe Isi would let her come, if she asked. No, she could not ask, but if she followed . . . By the time Rin emerged from the trees, the girls were lost to the light of campfires, swallowed up by night.

Rin dragged herself back to camp. Both sorrow and relief warred in her chest, and she slumped against a wagon, startling when she realized what was inside. A body covered by a blanket, one scorched boot peering out. Brynn. She remembered when he'd promised Isi to guard the king with his life, his aspect anxious and curious. His hair had been a paler shade of brown, his face long, his build . . .

Something glittered on the edge of her memory, and she looked up into the stars as if for help recalling. Rin had seen him before the day of departure. In the stable yard. In the distance. The man arguing with Cilie. That had been Brynn.

Rin backed away from the wagon, her fingers and toes tingling. Cilie had wanted to be near Tusken, but not because she loved him, as she claimed. She and Brynn had argued together. Over what? Now Cilie had disappeared and Brynn was dead. Were those events connected?

Rin ran for her pack, her heart thudding in her chest, in

her ears. She had to tell Isi . . . well, someone should tell Isi. But now Rin had an excuse to follow, and she seized it like the last hold on the edge of a cliff.

The queen had brought her to watch Tusken, and she could not abandon him.

But he's with his father and an army of soldiers, she reasoned. *And I'm not good to anybody half-crazy.*

Still, she cramped with guilt and worry at the thought of leaving the boy. So she would not leave him without a caretaker. Her pack on her shoulders, she ran toward the edge of camp where she'd last seen Razo, finding him ambling back alone, his hands in his pockets.

"Whoa there, Rinna-girl, what's your hurry?" His gaze roved over the pack in her hand, her boots, her hood. His eyes narrowed, an expression meant to convey wariness, but on Razo it looked comical. "What're you up to? Something sneaky."

"I'm in a hurry, but I need—"

"Uh-uh. Just you remember that I'm your big brother, even if you're as tall as me, and . . . hold on, you're as tall as me! I thought I'd outgrown you last year. How did that happen?" He checked her boots. "You're not stuffing extra socks in there to boost you up? That *would* be sneaky."

"I need a favor. I need you to keep an eye on Tusken from now on, until Isi gets back."

"And does this mean that my baby sister is planning on leaving us?"

Her eyes flicked again to the edge of camp.

Razo caught her arm. "Why're you being so mysterious? What's cooking in that head of yours? Hey, is your hair puffed up higher than normal? Is that why you're taller? I bet it's your hair. That'd be triply sneaky if you puffed your hair just to be taller than me." He patted her head, testing for unnecessary puffiness.

"Please, Razo. You're more experienced with children than half of these soldiers combined and far better at keeping someone safe than I am. Just promise you'll watch Tusken."

"Uh-huh, and if I do that, you're bound to do something silly like go chasing after Isi, aren't you?"

She looked at him sharply. He picked dirt from under his fingernail.

"If you're not going to talk I'll have to figure it out myself, and I'm not half as slow as our brothers would make you think. Not half. Only about a quarter as slow and twice as charming."

He smiled at her. She smiled back against her will.

"So why would you be following those girls? You just miss Dasha, do you? Or wait, you've been hired by our enemies to kill the queen."

She snorted.

"Yes, I'm afraid that's it. My sister is an assassin. That's why she's so tall. She's hiding a sword in her boots and poisoned darts in her hair. Look, I'd like to go too, but Isi thinks they'll do best alone, and maybe she's right. Besides, Ma would scalp me clean if you got hurt."

"And then you'd be even shorter."

He glared in an attempt not to smile. "You might want to rethink your plan anyway. No chance you'll catch up now, seeing as how they're riding."

Horses. Rin had not considered they'd use those cursed beasts. How was she going to keep up on foot?

"Rin, what's going on?"

Rin sighed. "Cilie, the waiting woman that was? She and Brynn knew each other, though she was from the east and rarely talked to anyone. I saw them alone by the stables, arguing. I don't know what it means, but I think Isi will want to know. And you should tell Geric."

Razo rubbed his chin. "That is too suspicious to ignore. Why don't you tell Geric, and I'll run and tell Isi?"

"No! I need to go. It's not just the telling that matters. I need to keep moving . . . I need to stay with those girls." She shuddered, feeling helpless, but pulled all her energy together to make one last plea. "Razo, please? Will you watch Tusken for me and let me go?"

He stared for a moment before grabbing her and hugging hard.

"Rinna-girl taking after her brother, sneaking around and making plans that'll get her into trouble? I'm so proud of my little Rinny . . . no, that nickname doesn't work. How about Rinna-minna?"

"Razo, they're already gone. I need to go quickly."

Razo stared at the black and exhaled loudly. "Fine. Just be careful. I can't afford to lose my scalp."

Rin blinked, her face tingling with the heat of surprise. She had not expected him to agree.

He jogged off toward the line of horses and came back so quickly she'd only had time to stare at the wood and sigh. He was leading a dappled horse, still saddled.

"This is Gladden. She's nice and easy and was only ridden this past hour, so she's fresh. I put her brushes and stuff in the saddlebag. You know how to brush down a horse? And saddle her?"

Rin nodded impatiently. She had no idea, but she'd figure it out later. She had to go now. Fear was seizing her, and she was sure she would die if she did not stay with those girls. Irrational, unfounded, but the fear still felt as real as the night. Razo helped Rin mount and tossed up her pack.

"You'll watch over Tusken?" she said.

"Not a problem. Children are easier than frogs. I had a frog in Tira, and I had to keep pouring water on it all the time and finding worms, and if I didn't it would make these noises all night, like *graaak, graaak, graaak*—"

"Razo . . ." The fear in her turned icy, the heat in her cheeks replaced by gray cold. She leaned down, grabbed his arm, and spoke with all the urgency she felt. "Keep Tusken safe, here and at home, until his mother returns. Promise me?"

Razo's eyes widened, surprised by her tone. "Of course I will, Rinna-girl. I swear it on my own life." His briefly serious expression softened with a smile. "What do a bunch of soldiers and waiting women know about children compared to a fellow like me with twenty-two nieces and nephews?"

"Twenty-three."

"Twenty-three?" he muttered as he wandered back to camp. "When did that happen? I leave the Forest for a few months and everyone goes off and has babies . . ."

She nudged her horse. The beast made a dry wheezing sound before starting a slow walk, and Rin imagined the mare was laughing at her ineptitude. On foot it was a simple task for her sneak around, but on a horse, she felt exposed, naked, as easy to spot as a full moon.

The floor of the wood was damp from yesterday's light rain, and she followed hoofprints all through the night, clinging to her horse's mane and telling herself, *It's not as bad as leaping into a well. Not as bad as that.*

Part Two

The Wood

Chapter 8

 in rode through the night, afraid to lose Isi's trail, and even more afraid of dismounting and not being able to get back on the beast again. But near dawn she worried Gladden was as tired as she, so she slid onto the soft earth, still clenching the reins.

She fumbled at the strap, sliding the saddle off and nearly toppling under its weight. Then she tied the horse's reins to a tree and brushed its brown coat before curling up on the ground, the saddle as her pillow.

She slept fitfully, dreaming of the horse bucking her off, of finding the girls only to be sent away, of a yellow snake that dropped from the trees and tightened its smooth body around her throat. She woke for good when a shaft of morning light cut through her eyelids.

Another hour wasted while she tried to saddle the horse. Eventually she managed to lift the heavy thing onto Gladden's back and strap it on, but when she clambered up, her weight made the saddle tilt to the side, the mare prancing uncomfortably. After climbing a tree and dropping onto the saddle, she'd ridden only a few minutes before the saddle leaned even farther over. The horse stopped fast, and Rin was dumped onto the ground. She scrambled for the horse's reins, but no doubt tired of sliding saddles and girls jumping out of trees, Gladden trotted off and was gone.

Tears of frustration made a haze of the trees, and that horrible dead ache in her chest grew so heavy she thought it would stop her heart. She was lost. If she made it back to the road, the king's camp was sure to be gone, and she'd have to walk to the capital on her own. That could take weeks. Worse, she would not be able to find Isi and the others now.

She leaned against a tree and let sorrow rise up to her ears like flood water. Her cheek pressed against bark, she closed her eyes, and for a moment she saw her anxious fretting as if watching it from a distance.

"What am I doing?" she said. "Of all the pointless . . ."

She shook herself, found the hoof tracks, and followed on foot. That path crossed with another set of multiple horse prints, and she followed the new set for a few hours until she heard voices.

Rin sneaked forward. When a girl wanted to be alone in a family of dozens, walking around undetected was an extraordinarily useful talent. Also, if a girl wanted to climb a tree and dump a bucket of wash water over a certain brother's head, quick and quiet movements were paramount. Rin had years of practice. So she shinnied up a tree, perched near the trunk where branches would shield her from view, and listened.

"I think we should keep to the wood until we're closer to Geldis."

"We would move faster on the road."

"But I'm concerned about watchers."

That voice was definitely Isi's.

Out of habit, Rin mused over the good pranks she could play, hidden as she was in the wood. She could wait until they were asleep and drag Enna and her bedroll off, so she woke up alone and disoriented—that trick was an Agget-kin standard. Dozens of times she'd seen one of her brothers hauling his bedroll back home in the morning, muttering, "Very funny," while the guilty parties snickered out of Ma's hearing.

Dasha spoke again. "Isi, but what about—you said someone had followed us into the wood."

"Yes, but I know who that is now." Isi's voice raised, shouting directly at Rin's tree. "Would you care to join us?"

Rin felt made of ice from her toes to her fingertips. Discovery was an unfamiliar and uncomfortable sensation, and she wondered if Isi had help from the wind. Rin grabbed a branch with her hands, swung out of the tree, and dropped to the ground.

"Rin!" said Enna. "Were you doing an imitation of an enormous squirrel? Honestly, I thought you were the sensible one in your family, but you're half Razo after all."

"That's odd. I was actually expecting..." Isi scanned the wood behind Rin. "Did you come on a horse?"

"It ran off. I—"

Isi mounted her black stallion bareback and rode into the trees, her face intent as if listening.

Enna sat on the ground and began sorting through a bag of food. "I give her six minutes to find your horse and come trotting back with it in tow."

Dasha was embracing Rin. "Look at you! What in the— Why are you here?"

Rin shrugged helplessly. Dasha laughed in her pleased way, her nose crinkling in pleasure. "She follows us in the dead of night through a wood full of sticky brambles that leave burrs on your tunic, jumps out of a tree like a hopping bird, and when I ask her what she's doing, she shrugs. Rin, you are darling!"

Isi returned, just as Enna predicted, with Gladden following behind. Isi did not even have the horse's reins—it just trotted after the queen's stallion like a puppy after its master. The saddle was dangling off the horse's side.

"Have a little trouble with the saddle, did you, Rin?" There was humor in Isi's voice, which relieved Rin immensely. If something was still funny, then perhaps everything would be all right.

Enna laughed. "I'd bet twelve slippers that horse was saddled by a Forest girl. Your horse ran off indeed. Can't wait to tell Razo."

"Your Majes— Isi," Rin said. "I came because there's something I thought you should know. I once saw Cilie arguing with a man, which was odd because she never spoke to anyone besides the waiting women. And I only just realized who it was—Captain Brynn."

The girls waited, looking at Rin, as if expecting more. Rin flushed.

"And . . . that's all. It just seemed odd that Cilie disappeared and then Brynn died."

"That is odd," said Isi. "Was there anything else? Is Tusken all right?"

Rin's face burned hotter. "He was with his father when I left. And Razo swore to protect him. With his life."

Isi nodded. "A great promise." If she was worried, she made no more sign.

Dasha showed Rin how to saddle her horse and they rode all day, Rin expecting every moment that Isi would send her away. But when the blue in the western sky mellowed into gold, the queen still had not ordered her home.

They soon stopped for night. Enna cleared a space of leaves and twigs and piled a heap of dead branches. *A Forest girl should know better than to try and start a fire like that,* Rin thought. *Enna should begin with kindling, then add twigs before—*

"Oh," Rin said, gaping as the pile of branches suddenly blazed, though no one had touched it. *So that's how it works.*

Enna glared at Dasha. "It was my turn to start the fire."

"Oh," Rin said again, realizing it had been Dasha, not Enna.

"But you said I need the practice," Dasha said demurely, stirring the fire with a stick as though it were soup ready for tasting. Her eyes flicked to Enna and then back at the fire. "How did I do?"

"You did fine, as you well know." Enna pulled a bag of provisions off her horse and began working on supper.

"I just wondered . . . if there's anything else you can teach me. I mean, I still can't do as much with fire as you, can't make big fires or keep creating them as long as you—"

"Nor are you ever likely to. No one can." Enna sat beside Isi, putting an arm around her waist and tugging as if trying to get her to smile. "Isn't that right, Isi?"

"No one burns like Enna."

Rin wished they would explain more, but Enna returned to her cooking. Isi's eyes flicked to Rin's face, and she seemed thoughtful.

After a dinner of boiled potatoes and travel jerky, they lay down, but there was only a moment of silence before Enna groaned.

"I'm too jittery to sleep. How about a tale before bed?"

"Maybe something familiar would be nice," said Isi,

"since we're far from home. Will you tell about the three gifts?"

"No, no, that's yours. You tell it."

Rin kept her eyes on the canopy, where the breeze-lifted leaves raked the sky, and listened to Isi's voice untangle the darkness.

"When the creator made the world, everything had its own language, and all could communicate freely—tree to wind, rock to snail, flower to honeybee. Last of all, the creator made people, and they strode over the land, speaking strong words and taking control. They broke the balance, and one by one knowledge of the languages was lost, leaving creatures deaf to any but their own.

"But as moons rose and fell and days and nights did a spinning dance, different sorts of people were born in the crannies of the mountains and wilderness. Born with a first word on their tongues, they could hear and learn new languages. As they found one another and taught one another, three gifts were named—nature-speaking, animal-speaking, and people-speaking. Though rare, now there were people again who could understand the language of fire and wind, of bird and horse, and of people too. The last, however, proved the most dangerous."

"I've never heard you say that before," Enna said, her voice soft and sleepy. "The part about people breaking the balance, being the cause that the languages were forgotten."

"It's just my own telling." Isi sighed, her blanket rustling. "But it makes sense to me. People move through this world unlike any other thing. When someone has the knowledge of only a single language—like fire, for instance—it overcomes them unless a balancing language is learned. But I've never seen anything that rots a person like people-speaking. It is a gift unlike the others, bound for destruction." Isi sighed. "Well, that wasn't a very good tale, was it?"

Enna yawned. "It'll do in a pinch."

But Rin was spinning with those ideas—everything had a language, and there were people who could learn them. Marvelous thought, mystifying thought.

"Rin," said Enna, "Isi and I already know each other's stories, and I suspect Tiran stories are boring . . ."

"What?" Dasha interrupted. "I—"

". . . so why don't you tell one?"

Rin did not feel capable of entertaining three such girls with anything out of her mind. But she glanced at Isi once for confidence, cleared her throat, and chose her words, like picking berries from a thorny bush.

"There was a girl who was friends with trees. Whenever she was sad or lonely, she sort of listened to the trees in a different way and could not really hear them but sort of could. Then she did something different than she'd ever done, wanted something for herself, and the trees stopped being her friends. And she didn't understand why. So she ran away." Rin realized she needed an ending. "And she found someone who figured out what was wrong with the trees, or with her, and made it all better."

There was a long pause in which Rin became aware of the painfully high chirp of a night bird, then Enna laughed. "Rin, that was a really pathetic story."

Rin smiled sheepishly. "I know. About halfway through I was hoping that you'd all fallen asleep."

"Not bad for a first try," Dasha said, patting Rin's arm. "Think about it some more and tell it again another night, will you?"

Enna and Dasha yawned in unison, and the girls cozied into their blankets. By the time Enna and Dasha's breathing went from restful to dead asleep, Isi was still staring up at the twisting canopy.

"I liked your story," Rin whispered.

"Thanks. I told it for you."

"You did? Thank you, for taking the trouble." Isi must have guessed Rin had not understood their conversation about fire-speaking.

"Did you tell your story for me?" Isi whispered.

"Oh." Rin's chest seemed to be full of breath. "Maybe I did."

"I've never known anyone with tree-speaking before, though I always suspected it was possible."

Tree-speaking. The word felt like fire in Rin's mind.

"What's it like, Rin?"

"I don't know. I don't think I have—uh, had—tree-speaking. I just listened, sort of, and I would feel different. It's . . . I can't explain."

"Do you mind if I guess? When you were younger, perhaps, some need led you to first hear the trees. You were listening in a different way—and it's not really like listening. Or feeling or smelling, is it? But something else, a different sense."

"Is wind like that too? And fire?"

"In a way. What do you understand from the trees?"

"Just . . . calm. It's easier to think, to feel all right. But I don't . . . the, uh, the *tree-speaking* doesn't work for me anymore. I . . . did something. Maybe the trees didn't like it and they turned away from me."

Isi moved onto her side, propping her head with a hand. "I can understand some bird languages, and horse too, and I've learned that animals mostly don't care what people do or think. I can't imagine trees would note the way a person acted, let alone punish you for it. Do you?"

Rin exhaled. "No. I suspected that much. But then I can't figure why they changed. Or maybe I changed?"

"I don't know. Will you tell me when you work it out?"

Rin wished now more than ever that she could hear the tree's calm again, just to have something she could share with Isi. The losing felt as tragic to her as Isi's story, when the web of languages connecting the world snapped. She felt the mystery of that loss around her, ragged ends of broken webs teasing her skin.

"May I stay with you?" Rin whispered.

"It might be dangerous what we're doing."

"I'd still like to stay with you. Isi. Please. I'm better around you."

Rin was feeling stripped and cold and confused, and she could not find the energy to say anything more, so she curled up tighter, letting her eyes close. The firelight bled through her lids, and she watched swirls of orange and gold collide as she heard Isi say, "Stay with us, Rin, but be careful. Please be careful."

hey traveled under the cover of the wood for four days. Kiltwin, a large walled town, lay just beyond the trees to the south, and Isi wanted to avoid it. She might be recognized there, slowing them when speed and stealth could be vital. So they kept moving east through the trees, Isi depending on the wind to guide them.

"The wind carries with it images of what it has touched," Isi explained to Rin. "It's constantly muttering, though it takes some understanding to puzzle out what it means."

So when Isi listened to the wind, she knew of things that were out of sight. She could also send the wind any direction she chose, all from understanding its language. Rin gazed at the passing trees and wondered what else might be possible.

Isi brought them out of the wood near what had been the village of Geldis. It was just debris and embers, heaps of ash. Enna kicked blackened timber and glared at the horizon.

"Where are you? Are you here? I'm here now. Come out!"

Despite the chill icing her gut, Rin did wish those burners would come running at them, and let the fire sisters end it right then. A bird lit at her feet, then flew off; a breeze ruffled loose soil. Nothing else moved.

"Now what?" Enna asked.

"The villagers of Geldis went east to Hendric," Isi said. "So do we."

Hills rolled away from the wood, open farms changing to wooden homes sporting pens of pigs and donkeys. By evening buildings clustered into the town of Hendric, clapboard homes and shops clinging to a crossroads.

The inn was a large rickety structure, the rooms upstairs balanced over an enormous common room, the roof thatched with straw that wriggled and whimpered with mice.

Before leaving the wood, Rin wrapped her hair into a cloth common among Forest women so she would not stand out in her own party. Isi and Dasha felt around their foreheads and necks, anxious that no strand of yellow or orange hair escape to draw attention. Enna blackened their eyebrows with a piece of charcoal.

In the common room that night, Enna and Isi made polite conversation with travelers and locals alike, trying to steer the topic to what happened in Geldis, hoping to find a trail to follow. Rin wanted to help, but there were so many people—eating, drinking, singing, laughing, pushing, shoving, yelling, weeping. She sat in a corner, her arms around her chest.

A droopy-eyed farmer cornered Enna, droning on about how the king was to blame for Geldis. When the hearth fire surged unexpectedly, Isi pulled Enna to a table against the wall.

"We can't draw notice."

"He was an arrogant cow," Enna said, tearing a piece of bread into crumbs. "You can see I showed restraint, since he still has all his hair."

"Truly you are a diplomat," said Dasha.

"I don't see you talking to anyone, Ambassador."

"Because my accent—"

"Lovely excuse. Go on. Take a risk."

Dasha rose dramatically and moved to the next table beside a man with long black and white hair.

"Good evening, sir," said Dasha. "I am stopping this night at the inn and was hoping to find news of the kingdom. May I sit beside you?"

He rolled his head on his neck, shifting his gaze from his ale to her face. "You . . . your voice sounds funny."

"Oh that, well . . ." In her nervousness, her Tiran accent became even more pronounced. "I have a cold." She sniffed.

The man rubbed his own nose. "I've had a cold for years. Ale's the only thing that helps." He sniffed—a wet, grating sound.

Dasha winced. "It doesn't seem to be helping very much."

"You should see me the rest of the time."

"I'm very sorry for that. It must be uncomfortable to be sick, and with unrest about. Sir, you have the face of one who has a deep sight."

The man's crumpled face transformed with a grin. "A deep sight, huh?"

"Indeed. That's why I had hoped to speak with you of all these people. I'm concerned about what happened in Geldis."

"Who isn't? I talked to Geldis folk. They were attacked at night, burned right out of their houses, and no one saw the attackers. Some people say the king himself went to take a look and was killed dead. But a traveler came through last week"—he leaned closer to Dasha to speak low—"asking questions about who'd stopped here lately. My cousin said he had an accent. Tiran, maybe. You ask me, I say those stinking Tiran burned Geldis, weakening us up before they invade again." His voice grated even lower, his eyes shifting. "Tiran might be in disguise here in this very room. You'll smell them before you see them—they're fouler than skunks."

Dasha stood up quickly, humor battling solemnity on her face. "Thank you, sir. You have been so helpful."

"Don't be so hasty. I'm here alone. I don't suppose . . ." He looked up at her through his eyelashes and gave a short, pathetic sniff.

She shook her head and mumbled, "May your cold improve," as she walked out of the inn. Rin and the other girls followed, and when the inn door shut behind them, Dasha threw herself against the side of the building, coughing out the laugh she'd been holding back. "I love being in disguise! This is fantastic!"

Enna sighed. "Razo's bound to be disappointed at first, but eventually he'll understand that you've found true love."

"Yes, Sniffles and I planned a furtive meeting later by the woodpile, if his da will let him off chores."

"It was impressive," said Enna, "how he identified that peculiar odor all of your countrymen share, as if you've been stewed in vinegar. He didn't smell it on you, but that lapse could be explained by his tragic cold . . ."

Two men and a woman, laughing loudly, came down the street toward the inn. The four girls silenced and moved to the far side of the building.

"People say the king is dead," Isi whispered. She sat on the ground, her back against the inn. "We need to resolve this as quickly as possible."

"Isi, this cannot be Tira's doing," said Dasha. "Last Razo and I were in Ingridan, all was well. The Assembly was confident that peace would continue, the general opinion toward Bayern was positive. I just can't believe the Assembly would send groups to attack the king, let alone burn a little village like Geldis."

Enna snorted. "No, Tira would never march into Bayern like that."

"In the past," Dasha said patiently, "but not anymore. I believe that."

Rin did not know what to think. Razo now lived half the year in Tira, and he seemed to trust them. But just two years before, Tira's army had invaded Bayern without provocation and killed thousands.

Isi looked up sharply just before the two men and a woman appeared around the side of the inn.

"You there, you girls." The man's words sloshed, suggesting he'd been familiar with some ale that night. His cheeks were ruddy and his long black hair clumped together. "You. One of you anyway." He put his arm around the woman and they laughed in each other's faces. "We want to dance! And my friend lacks a partner. So one of you . . ."

"No thank you," said Isi.

"One of you dance with him." The man's gaze landed on Rin's face. "You. Come on, one dance."

Rin's hands flew to her mouth, and she looked to Isi for help.

"She's not interested in your kind offer." Isi stood beside Rin, a warm hand on her shoulder. "But thank you and enjoy this fresh summer evening."

"One dance." The man reached for Rin, grabbing her arm.

Enna shoved the man's hand away. "She said she's not interested."

"I didn't hear her say anything, but you'll do just as well." He put his arm around Enna's waist and hefted her up, dragging her toward the inn.

Rin felt tied up and helpless. Fire would start now, or wind or water, and everyone at that inn would know what secrets the fire sisters kept. She wished she could do something, say something, but she just kept her hands over her mouth and backed away.

Enna was kicking and hollering. The ruckus caught the attention of the inn dwellers, and the doors opened, spilling music, firelight, and people into the street.

Isi and Dasha were on the man, pulling his arm, trying to set Enna free. Isi's expression was desperate. She was not afraid of the man, Rin could see, but of what Enna might do if the man did not back down.

"One dance," the man kept saying. "Don't be so shy!"

The woman laughed at the to-do and the man's friend was so enthused he joined in, pulling Dasha and Isi back, laughing into his beard in a bewildered way. Rin rocked back and forth on the balls of her feet, her hands fluttering around her chest. She'd been trying to imitate Isi's way these past days, but Isi was so bold, shouting commands. Rin did not dare. Her hands returned to her mouth.

"Stand down!" came the shout as a new figure entered the fray. He shoved the man's friend to the ground, pulled the man from Enna, and twisted his arm behind his back.

"Finn!" Enna shouted, surprised and angry and thrilled at once.

"You don't push me!" The friend lurched to his feet, his belly pulling his weight forward. He yanked his sword from a leather scabbard and took steps toward Finn. "Try that again, boy."

Finn shoved away the clumpy-haired one and drew his own sword, positioning himself between the weaponed man and Enna. "Very well."

From the unwavering point of his weapon to his unshaking legs, there was no question Finn was a soldier, someone who knew his sword and could use it. His opponent looked him over, his sword tip wavering, dipping. He glanced behind him as if for an escape route.

"Sheath your weapons and walk away," said Isi.

Her voice was so sure, so full of right and command, Rin was surprised no one was dropping on knees in acknowledgment of the queen. Even not knowing who it was they obeyed, the two men backed away, giving Finn a wide berth. Their woman friend had stopped laughing, and the three of them headed into town, apparently no longer in the mood for dancing.

Isi sighed, glancing at the small crowd leaning out of the inn doors. "So much for not drawing notice."

"Do you think we should move on tonight?" Dasha whispered.

Isi shook her head. "No fires were set. Hopefully this will seem just an ale-inspired brawl. But let's get off the street."

With his sword sheathed, Finn lost all his menace, his shoulders slumped and face long, his eyes on Enna. She turned away.

They followed Isi through the crowded common area and up the squeaking stairs to their room. The innkeeper raised his eyebrows at Finn as he followed the four girls inside. Finn shrugged and grinned.

"Oh, Finn, don't give them more to talk about," Isi said.

He was last in the room, and he shut and locked the door behind him, seeming to take as long as possible. When he turned to face them, his expression was sheepish.

"I wondered when you were going to show up," said Isi.

Enna started. "You knew?"

"I suspected. In truth, I didn't need to hear the wind whispering about a man alone in the wood to figure out Finn would try to follow you."

Enna put a fist on her hip, and Rin thought to be glad that hot gaze was not directed at her.

"Did you think I'd need you to protect me?" Enna asked.

He shrugged. "Maybe. You never know when you need a sword at your back."

"You thought I couldn't handle myself."

"No, I—"

"I'm not talking to you, Finn," Enna said.

They readied themselves for the night in silence. Finn faced the wall as the girls undressed into shifts and cozied into their cots, Dasha sharing with Rin, and Isi and Enna on the other. Finn took a spot on the floor, laying his body before the door, his head on a bedroll.

Enna yawned. "A tale before bed?" It had become custom their four nights in the wood. Rin had even practiced her own story till Enna had cheered with approval.

"A song would be nice," said Isi. "And nicer still if you'd sing it."

Enna glanced once at Finn and quickly away again, keeping her eyes on the window while she sang.

She had a high voice, higher than her speaking voice, but it slipped out of her throat soft and simple. Her song was of a carpenter's daughter who lay in the branches of an oak tree as if cradled in a lover's arms and would love no other. Her father discovered her hopeless passion and taking pity, he cut down the tree and carved it into the shape of a man. But to the girl it was no kindness. The tree was now dead, and she wept for the loss of her love. Rin had heard the song before. The way some sang it the story was funny, and she recalled laughing at the girl's silliness and the father's inept compassion. But in the dark, with Enna's voice reaching up and around, there was no humor. Only loneliness.

Dasha rolled over and placed an arm around Rin, a gentle touch, a gesture of friendship. Rin flinched, but the touch made home seem real again, Ma beside her, her tunic wafting wood smoke and juniper, and everything safe for the night.

"Try not to wake us, Dasha," Enna whispered, "when you leave to meet your beau by the woodpile."

"I shall pour all my efforts into a stealthy tiptoe," she whispered back.

Still woozy from the crowd and noise of the inn, Rin slumped into sleep so fast she felt as if she'd been hit over the head.

After a time, her sleep became light, wakefulness and dreams tugging back and forth until wakefulness won. She opened her eyes. The dark was pulsing with remembered images—Dasha daring to speak up while Rin sat in a corner; Isi and Dasha rushing to help Enna, while Rin stepped back, her hands over her mouth.

She squeezed out of bed and padded to the window and the dim view of town. Ma had said, "The longer you're away from your family and your trees, the more you just might wither away." Rin did feel like half a thing, like a dried-up root. But then again, she had often felt that way. Dasha's vigor for life, Enna's passion, Isi's love—those girls were as full of energy and joy as the members of Rin's own family. And then there was Rin.

Tree-speaking, she told herself. She did not think trees had a language in the same way wind seemed to, or horses and birds. Surely trees could not empower Rin, as fire did for the others. What a strange idea, and she would have tossed it away like a cone empty of nuts, but that Isi seemed so sure. Tree-speaking. Is that what made her feel different, what separated her from everyone else, what crowded her inside until she wanted to scream and flee from her own ugliness? Even before Wilem she'd felt that way. But now she could not go to the trees for comfort—now the wrongness clung to her viciously, weighing her down more and more with each day.

Rin searched for the dark smudge beyond the town that was the wood, strained with her eyes and then with her heart. At least back home she'd been useful to her ma—but what did she have to offer someone like the queen of Bayern? Rin's chest felt like a knot too solid to unpick. Tension buried any hope of sleep, so she focused on the distance where the wood waited, trying to remind her body what it felt like to commune with trees, to hear the sap moving through the limbs, a breeze lulling the leaves . . .

Calmer, quieter, Rin became more aware of everything. She could almost hear Enna exhale before the sound reached her ears. Her skin tingled as if the night was just about to get hotter. Something was strange—something about the air. Rin backed away from the window and leaned over Isi's bed.

"Isi?" she whispered. "Isi? I think—"

There was a noise like wind howling or a voiceless scream. Then the straw roof was blazing.

in fell to the floor as blistering heat stormed above her head.

"Wake up!" she shouted.

Isi was alert at once, upright with eyes wide. A second rush and the wall was boiling with orange and gold flames. Rin grabbed Dasha and pulled her hard, onto the floor as their bed caught fire. The room was engulfed in tearing flames. The heat was so intense Rin could not open her eyes. No breath filled her, the air eaten away. She covered her head with her arms and hoped she would die quickly.

Then wind gushed through the window and blew a hole through the roof. The flames pulled into themselves and extinguished, the heat from those flames bursting into new and harmless fire through the hole and into the sky, leaving a bright streak of smoke. She did not know if it had been Isi's or Enna's work, or perhaps both. When the rafters and walls beaded with water, Rin guessed that much was Dasha, gathering the moisture from the outside air and dousing the embers. Finn was at the door with his sword, scanning the hall for an intruder.

The girls gasped at the air that gushed in through the window, cool as water. From elsewhere in the inn they heard a scream.

In the corridor, the roof began to blaze. People in night-clothes wailed as fiery straw fell on their heads, the corridor so jammed no one could get out. Isi was shouting orders at Enna and Dasha, and Finn fought to stay beside them. Rin was getting pushed back. The wailing, the smoke, the people, all choked her with panic.

The crowd shoved, and Rin fell before the open door of a sleeping chamber. The straw roof sizzled and spit, rolls of flames turning the room gold. A young woman had climbed atop a stool with a baby in her arms. Trembling, she put one leg through the window to climb out. They were three stories up.

Rin ducked under arms, shoved between backs, and flung herself into the room. She grabbed the woman by the hem of her tunic and yanked her back to the sill.

"Let go!" the woman screeched. "We're going to die! I have to save my baby, I have to—"

"We won't die, not unless you throw yourself out that window. Come down."

The woman turned, and her eyes were frightening, wild

and dangerous with fear. "My baby will burn, my . . ." She began to weep and clawed at Rin to break free.

"The fire will stop," Rin said, coughing from the smoke.

"We'll burn!"

"Listen to me, the fire will stop! It will stop. Come down here now, come down with your baby and you'll see. The fire will stop."

The woman gasped, as if Rin's words were a pocket of fresh air inside the smoky room. "The fire will stop?"

"It's already out, see?"

The hysteria cleared from her eyes and she clutched her baby to her chest, blinking and looking around. Smoke tickled their eyes, blackened straw dusted their shoulders, but there were no flames, no heat.

"I've never seen . . . but it's gone. You said it would." She stared at Rin, dazed and desperate. "What do I do now?"

"You grab your things and take your baby outside. You can do that?"

The woman nodded. "I can do that."

Rin watched her go. The frenzy in the corridor had quieted with the fire's demise. She could hear Enna shouting something, Finn directing people downstairs.

"The fire will stop," Rin whispered. Feeling like an empty grain sack, she sat down and sobbed into her arms. That mother and her child would have died from the fall. It was a good thing to help them, it surely was. So why did she feel like a very bad girl due a wooden spoon beating? Guilt and confusion and sorrow gnawed at her, and running away sounded so promising.

Isi wouldn't run away, Rin thought.

She heaved herself to her feet, collected their things from their room, and trudged down the corridor, passing empty rooms full of charred and damp wood. The stairs shuddered beneath her feet.

The girls and Finn stood in the road, staring at the blackened inn as it groaned and leaned to one side. Dasha and Isi were retying their headscarves over their conspicuous hair, but none of the dazed travelers in nightclothes looked their way. Gathered in small groups, they whispered and cried, never letting their eyes stray from the ruined building.

"That could've been my grave right there," someone said. "I sleep like a tree most nights. Good fortunes, that could've been my grave."

"That fire started pretty suddenly, don't you think?" Enna whispered. "Spread quickly too. Funny that."

Other townsfolk on the crossroads were opening windows, creaking doors, blinking into the night, judging whether what they were missing was exciting or dangerous.

Rin still felt spooked, her muscles tense, begging her to run. *Be calm,* she told herself. She inhaled, drinking in night—her favorite time, when the world was scrubbed of edges and hardness—and tried to remember how it used to feel to lean into a tree, hear its deepness with her own.

While seeking that stillness, she looked around, taking in the moment.

Everything seemed slowed, easier to see. And in that stillness, she noticed a figure. Every other person either stood before the inn as if they'd just escaped its smoky ruin, or in the doorways of their homes afraid to emerge. But one man rushed away, no protective home around him, no sign of ash on his clothes. Even from a distance, she could spot that no-good look of a man with something to hide. She exhaled, letting the moment go. The seeming slowness fell away, and she decided she had imagined it.

"I bet he knows something." Rin gestured to the figure now bolting toward the cover of trees.

Isi nodded. They all ran, ducked between two cottages, and emerged facing the wood, no one in sight. Isi paused, her head cocked, and Rin guessed she was feeling something tangible in the air, listening to what images the wind brought her.

"Another house, through the trees. He's in there."

"Let me go first," said Finn.

"Not a chance," said Enna. "You stay with Isi."

She ran ahead, her white shift outlining her form against the night. Rin had stuck on her boots but still wore only a shift too, the cool air creeping up her legs and bringing out goose bumps. They followed Enna through trees and tree shadows until the darkness peeled back and the gray outline of a roof poked through the gloom. As one they slowed, creeping as they neared. Rin could make out the little house now—wood, no windows, one door in front. Enna moved faster than the others, and Rin suspected she was determined to put herself in front of Isi in case of danger. Finn did the same, walking now between Isi and Dasha and slightly ahead.

That's what I should do, thought Rin. *That's what Razo would do. Be brave, run into the fray.*

Rin quickened her pace, gaining on Enna.

"Rin," Dasha said with warning.

The sound of her whispered name tingled through Rin, made her whole body more aware of the danger. That man might be the one who tried to roast them in their beds, and he might burst through that door and burn them like Geric, like Brynn.

Better me than the queen, Rin thought. *Better me than the Tiran ambassador. Better me.*

She stepped from heel to toe in fluid motion, balancing herself from her pelvis outward, mindful of twigs and leaves. Her passage nearly silent, she aimed to get to the house first. Perhaps she was not powerful like Finn, Enna, and Dasha, but Rin yearned to show Isi that she was worthwhile in some way so she could stay with the fire sisters. If she got to the house first, she might warn Isi if the man was truly inside and if there were others.

Rin moved faster, but Enna would not be left behind and broke into a jog. Enna's foot came down on a stick.

The crack seemed to make the entire wood tremble. Rin froze. They all did, breaths held, feet midstep. The door did not open.

Enna exhaled softly and started to whisper, "I think—"

The door slammed against the house and a bolt fired from a crossbow. Rin felt a shout heave from her throat as she raced forward. Wind howled. Fire burst in the air, lighting the scene in a brief, eerie flash of orange. The man hollered and dropped the crossbow before he could reload, the weapon ablaze in his hands. Then Finn was upon him, yanking both the man's hands behind his back. Rin glanced down at her own body, at the other girls—no sign of the bolt. She had a nudge of instinct to look high to her left, and by the light of the burning crossbow she saw the bolt stuck in a tree where the wind must have blown it off course.

"Back into the house," said Enna.

"We won't hurt you," said Isi.

"I don't think we can promise that exactly. But we won't unless we have to."

"We just have some questions," Isi continued as if Enna had not spoken.

Finn pushed the man inside. Rin followed, last this time. She looked back at the bolt, stuck deep into a solid trunk. The wood was quiet and so dark. There could be others out there in the trees, pointing loaded weapons at her even now. Rin had never realized that the world was so full of sharp things, and how many people were eager to use them.

She turned her back on the night and hurried into the house, pulling the door fast behind her.

A small, mean fire sputtered in a hearth so full of ashes, Rin wondered the flames did not suffocate. By the half-hearted light, she could see the man's face—he was old enough to be a grandfather, though she could not imagine that haggard face ever kissing a child. His hair was probably white, but so greasy it turned a mottled gray, and his beard grew patchy across his jaw. If he'd been a dog, Rin would have assumed he had the mange.

"Have a seat, sir." Isi pointed to the room's only chair, and he took it roughly, sitting down so hard the wood complained. Finn stood behind him. "I believe you aren't the one who set fire to the inn tonight—"

"Ha!" said the man.

"And I also believe you know who did. Who was it?"

The man spit on the floor. Enna shoved her way between Isi and the man.

"She asked you a question, and we're not leaving until we get a good answer. So tell her, what do you know about the burning?"

He spit again on the floor, marking the hard-packed dirt with a splatter of wet.

"You just keep at it," Enna said, folding her arms. "Spit all night and all day too. I don't have to live in your slimy house."

The man gathered more saliva in his throat, taking his

time with it, making an unappetizing grinding sound before he pointed his lips at Enna's face and spit. Before the spittle could reach Enna, wind flew between them, smearing the wet glop over his own face.

"Argh!" he yelled, scrubbing his cheeks with his soiled tunic.

Enna laughed, a surprised, ecstatic laugh that bounded out of her belly, and she exchanged pleased looks with Isi. Rin guessed that both of them had sent wind.

Then Enna was in the man's face, holding his tunic by her fist. She stared straight into his eyes, and he blinked for the smoke. Because smoke was twisting out of his tunic above the spot where she grabbed him, curling into his face. Unease made lines around his mouth.

"I could fizzle your little abode into ash in the time it takes you to spit again. And I'd enjoy it. Are you starting to comprehend your situation?"

The man blinked rapidly, the gray plumes drifting through his lashes.

"I think you know that I don't care two eggs for you or your saliva-strewn home, and the only reason I'll leave it standing is if you give me a more interesting direction to go. So tell me—where?"

Rin could see the man was both angry and afraid, but he shrugged in an attempt to pretend indifference. "Doesn't hurt me to tell you. She'll want to see you, way I hear it. Go on to Kel, then. Go north across the border from Saxmer, that's where her boys came from. You're bound to find her. Or she'll find you, the way I hear it."

"She?" Isi frowned. "Who is she?"

"Who? The one who'll fry you up for breakfast."

"Not ringing a bell," said Enna.

He spoke slowly, as if they were hard of hearing. "The queen of Kel. Imagine not knowing who it is wants you dead."

"We're being truthful with you, sir," Isi said in her most regal voice. "I expect you to be the same."

"I think he believes what he's saying," Rin whispered. It was one way she could be useful.

Isi gave Rin a curious look.

Enna leaned her hand on a small table, her attitude unimpressed. "And just how do *you* happen to be chummy with the queen of Kel?"

He coughed as a tendril of smoke tickled his nose. "Don't know her myself. But I met a couple of her boys—they'd been staying in town, though they're gone now, I'll wager. They gave me gold to keep an eye out—didn't know there'd be five of you, said there'd probably be two, and when I heard you were poking around last night at the inn, I told 'em. They made you a little wake-up present, did they? Wakey-wakey, little girls!"

The talking brought back his gall, and he laughed in Enna's face, spit flying at her eyes. She blinked, and the small wood table beside her exploded into flame so hot it crumpled and died into a heap of cinders. A pool of water curled around the spot, cooling the remains and slicking the floor with ash. The man's eyes widened, and he swallowed.

"If you follow us," Enna said darkly, "or let her know we're coming, that black greasy clump will be you. We have ways of knowing." Rin could tell Enna was lying about that last part, but the man seemed convinced.

Then Enna smiled brightly. "Good evening to you, fine sir!"

The five of them walked toward the inn, Finn and Enna keeping an eye on the house until they were out of sight. Isi fell in next to Rin.

"You believe he was telling the truth?"

"He thought he was. I'm pretty sure." Rin shrugged. "My brothers play a bluffing game, but a few years ago they stopped letting me join in, 'cause I never lost."

"I wonder . . . do you think there's something about tree-speaking that gives you a talent for seeing others more clearly?"

"I . . . I don't know. I thought about what you said, how animals don't care what people say and do. The same would be true of trees, I think. Why would they care or notice if a person lied?"

Well away from the house, they paused to pull clothes from their packs and dress. Isi sat on a fallen log, Dasha and Enna on either side. Finn positioned himself behind

Enna. Dasha made room on the log for Rin, but she leaned against a tree, tucking herself in between its thin branches. There was a hollow comfort standing like that, and while the others spoke, Rin thought of the crossbow bolt. Of the whoosh and sting of wind and fire heat and the man who would have killed her. Of pushing in front of Enna. Of almost dying. Of home and Ma and being farther away than the lands in tales, and maybe never going home. Of standing by a strange tree in a faraway wood with girls who spoke the language of fire. Of a queen of Kel who wanted them dead.

The girls talked. Rin listened and thought about the crossbow bolt.

"I think my tactics worked rather well," Enna was saying.

"Diplomacy might have been more efficient," said Dasha. "And spared us some of the spitting. People appreciate it when you take the trouble to flatter and understand—"

"People like clumpy-head back there appreciate exactly two things—their own smell and the fear of an immediate and uncomfortable death."

"Perhaps next time we could try my way. Is that all right, Isi? We might take turns with our various approaches and so perhaps avoid having to wash our boots after each encounter?"

"My questioning got at who's behind all this, at least."

"Actually, we still don't know much," said Dasha. "You see—"

"There is no queen of Kel," Isi finished.

"I knew that. I was just . . ." Enna sighed. "Never mind, I didn't know that."

"Rin says he believed what he claimed," said Isi, "so either he was lied to or things in Kel have changed quickly. It's only been a few months since our ambassador was dismissed from Bressal. I wonder what is happening there, what King Scandlan is doing . . ."

Enna picked up a stick and began to dig at a root. "I couldn't care less for Kel or her queen. But someone who *claims* to be the Kelish queen is sending fire-speakers out in the night to burn Bayern villages, and that makes me grumpy. So I'm all for tracking down this 'she' and telling her, very politely, that in Bayern, burning down inns just isn't good manners. And then char every hair from her body."

Finn smiled behind Enna's back, enjoying every word.

"So you think that the burnings were caused by cultural impoliteness?" said Dasha. "Interesting. You will notice that there are several buildings in this quaint little hamlet, and the one we happened to be sleeping in was the only one marred by fire."

"You noticed that too, did you, Ambassador? Well, Isi, I guess I'm going to have to take back some of the things I said about Tiran lack of observation."

"Wonderful. My real concern right now, not an hour after someone tried to murder us in our sleep, is what you think about the perception skills of my countrymen."

"Thank you, girls," said Isi. "That will do. What do you think, Rin?"

Rin startled. She'd been feeling invisible all night, a stranger lurking on the edge of big events. Isi's attention pulled her from the shadows and surprised her thoughts out of her.

"I think that Enna and Dasha don't really dislike each other as much as they pretend."

Enna and Dasha both made surprised noises in their throats, something like, "naw" and "yee."

Isi smirked. "Indeed. What I meant to say is, do you think we're being targeted?"

Rin had thought about this too. "First a village was burned. That brought the king. He was burned, though not killed. That brought the queen. Then the inn was burned, though again, you weren't killed. Either they're trying to kill Bayern royalty and they're failing, or the point of the attacks is to provoke you. To do something. Maybe to go somewhere?"

"The Tiran," said Enna. "They're trying to restart the war."

"Enna," Isi said with warning.

Enna rolled her eyes. "Or I guess it could be Kel. Maybe they're using the tension between Tira and Bayern as an excuse to spark a conflict with us. See, I don't always jump to the Tira-is-evil conclusion."

"Kel doesn't usually tend toward belligerence," Finn said.

Isi nodded. "Their navy is formidable, protecting them from a Tiran sea invasion. Their most serious threat would be a Bayern ground attack, but the rough terrain isn't hospitable to an invading force—bogs, woods, crags. And they've always been eager to make treaties and be a valuable trade partner. Why would they suddenly stir up trouble? It doesn't make sense."

"So it *is* Tira," said Enna. "See, I knew they were evil."

Dasha made a noise of annoyance.

"I was kidding, I was kidding!" Enna said, then she added in an undertone, "Mostly. Anyway, we don't know if Isi was the target in the inn. I'm the one who burned a tenth of Tira's army. If anyone's looking for vengeance—"

"If we are coming up with reasons people might want us dead," said Dasha, "I think I can play that game. I am the ambassador of Tira, responsible for thousands of deaths and injuries during the war."

Enna looked at her blankly. "You killed and injured thousands of people?"

"I meant," Dasha said through gritted teeth, "that my country's army caused the damage."

"Oh, because that's not what it sounded like. I would've thought that, being a well-versed diplomat, you'd know how to speak straight."

Dasha threw up her hands at the sky.

Enna sat down and started to laugh so hard her body shook. "I'm sorry, it's just that we were almost burned alive tonight, and someone's hunting one of us down and is not afraid to kill anyone who gets too close...and I haven't slept well in a week, and I'm supposed to be married by now and...and..." Her voice squeaked as she tried to suck in more breath through the laughter. "And Dasha said she killed thousands of people...and..." She took two deep stuttered breaths, wiped her eyes, and looked up at Finn, who stood behind her, touching her hair. She flexed her shoulders as if about to shrug him off, but then just sighed. "And I forgot what was funny. I wish something was funny. Nothing's funny." She looked at the queen. "Sorry, Isi."

Isi shrugged. "I have an unreasonable hope that things will be funny again soon."

"Promise?" Enna's voice was soft and pleading, a tone Rin had never heard from her before, making her sound like a small child in need of comfort. Finn squeezed her shoulder.

"We'll figure this out and get you and Finn married in a few days," said Isi. "And then we'll laugh for hours."

Enna put her hand on top of Finn's and looked at the huge darkness before them. "All right. All right. That's all right. A few days."

"Finn?" said Isi. "What do you think we should do?"

"Go to Kel," he answered without hesitation. "Cross the border by Saxmer, like clumpy-head said."

"That could be this so-called queen's intention all along," said Dasha. "To herd us into Kel."

"I worry about that," said Isi, "but it's our only indication where to find these burners. I don't want to see another village razed like Geldis, another victim like Brynn or Geric. And sadly I think that will be our last inn on this journey. If we're attacked again, I don't want to be around others who could get hurt too."

Finn was looking over Isi's small map. "If we cut through this wood, head north by northeast, we should get to Saxmer in . . . maybe four days? We'll have to go on foot. This isn't a path for horses."

"And so we lose ourselves in the wild," said Dasha.

"Right." Enna stood, brushing off her skirt, and her manner was so *Enna* again, Rin questioned her memory of the girl's momentary insecurity. "I can help with the losing ourselves part, but as for surviving in the wild on these meager provisions"—Enna shook her bag—"I'm one Forest girl who never cared for straying far from my bed."

Dasha hooked Rin's arm. "So what do you say, Rinna-girl? Think you and Finn can keep two city-bred noble ladies and a home-fond Forest girl alive in all these trees?"

Rin's eyes went wide. She whistled a note that plunged from high to low, and she said as Razo might, "City-bred is half-dead."

Finn snorted.

Since they would be going on foot, someone needed to return to town and arrange for their horses to be sent back to the capital. Enna's gray Merry was virtually her pet, and the queen was very attached to her black stallion Avlado.

Finn volunteered. He'd been carrying the packs Rin salvaged from the inn, and he set them now at Enna's feet. She did not acknowledge him, though he waited for a few moments before turning toward town.

"Wait, Finn." Isi's hands clutched together, suddenly nervous. "I . . . I didn't want to do this, but Geric should know. He needs to know where we're going, that there's a rumor of a queen in Kel, that she wants us dead. He should know soon."

"Send a message with someone in town, Isi." Enna stood up, a touch of panic in her voice. "Write a note and send it."

Isi shook her head. "I don't trust a message to be kept safe, or fly with the speed we need. Finn, I'm sorry, I've got to send you back."

He stepped forward as if he would argue, but checked himself, nodding.

"Rin," said Isi.

"Please, no." The thought of being sent away created eddies of panic inside Rin.

Isi considered, then nodded. "Rin, you stay with us, but be careful, no more rushing ahead of everyone." She gave Finn some coins. "Give three to the innkeeper to help with repairs, the rest are to get you back. I doubt you'll be able to buy supplies in Hendric tonight, but it's not far to Keltwin, and there is a little food and water in our saddlebags. Don't kill yourself or the horses, Finn, but go quickly."

He nodded again, then his eyes went to Enna. She

moaned sadly, came forward, and melted into his arms. He lifted her up and squeezed her hard, sighing as he did, his face relaxing. He pulled back to kiss her, three long farewell kisses, then left without another word.

Enna watched him go till he was out of sight. Then she sighed, and the look on her face left no doubt in Rin's mind that Enna loved Finn more than the moon and the night.

She whispered, "I'm going to have to have a little chat with the queen of Kel."

Chapter 11

No one felt sleepy, and the night was chilly enough that the thought of sprawling on hard earth made walking on preferable. Near sunup, they snuggled into cloaks and rested for a few hours, waking to glare at the late-morning sun as it slanted into their eyes.

"I hate them," Enna said. "Whoever is responsible for making me sleep outside without pillows, I hate them."

"Mmm-hmmm . . . ," Dasha said. Rin had noticed that the Tiran girl often had trouble remembering how to speak in the morning.

"If Finn were here," Enna continued to mumble as she rewrapped her head cloth, "he'd let me rest my head on his chest at night. Or leg. Or arm. And then he'd find whoever was responsible for the whole sleeping outside with no pillows situation and hold him while I kicked him in the shins."

"Hmm . . . ," said Dasha.

"In the shins. Hard."

"Just don't you let go of that lofty dream, Enna,"

said Isi. "Four or five days to Kel, where we just might have time for some shin kicking."

They set off in silence, Isi in the lead, and Rin could see the worry in Isi's face, thick as a rainy sky.

"Something troubling you?"

"What isn't?" Isi rubbed her head as if to get at an ache. "I can't shake the coincidence that we're dealing with fire-speakers again."

"I've been musing that over too," said Enna. "Before me, there were only those fire worshippers in Yasid, and they kept to themselves. Then I learn it and suddenly . . ."

"Fire-speakers in Tira," said Dasha. "And now in Bayern, leading us to Kel."

"Fire wants to spread," said Enna.

"You have a point," Isi said. "It seems to be the easiest of all the speaking gifts to learn."

"But not to master."

"No, you're right—easiest gift to learn, hardest to master. Except maybe people-speaking."

"Blegh," Enna said, as if trying to rid her mouth of a sour taste. "Don't call it a gift. Curse, maybe."

Isi nodded. "All the people-speakers I've known were—"

"Evil," said Enna. "Dark-souled, likely to chew their own grandmother's eyeballs—"

"I was going to say, corrupted by their gift." Isi blew hair out of her eyes, her gaze rising from the deer track they walked to the shifting trees. "It's sad really. You'd think people-speaking would bring the speaker closer to people, as wind-speaking does with wind. But instead it dooms people-speakers to separation and self-destruction. I think people-speaking is the most dangerous gift to have alone, with nothing to balance it."

"Even more than fire?" asked Dasha.

"I think so anyway. I've known three people-speakers, and two died young. I wonder if a person can exist long with such a burden. My mother—she must have something else balancing her, maybe without knowing it. Because she was difficult, but not as bad as some."

"Sileph," said Enna. "Selia."

"People-speakers?" asked Dasha.

"Yes," Isi said. "They're both dead."

There was a smile in Enna's voice. "Nice to have something out there more dangerous than fire. Makes me feel like a tame kitten."

"Watch out!" Rin said.

The three girls stopped short as a snake startled across their path. Rin was carrying a forked stick for just such an event, and she jammed it against the neck, pinning the creature. Dasha gasped.

All three girls were staring at her in horror. Rin winced, and her face flushed.

"It's . . . for dinner, you know. Snake meat. So we don't run out of food."

Still, she did not move to pick it up, staying as far away as the stick would allow. Isi and Dasha took several steps back, gaping at the green squirmy body in pale silence before Enna sighed.

"Fine, I'll skin it." She grabbed it by the neck and with a quick twist the squirming ceased. Dasha emitted a trembling little moan, which made Enna grin.

They roasted the meat that evening, along with a rabbit Rin had downed with her sling. Rin had eaten snake before—she'd also eaten boiled ants, roasted slugs, snails baked in their shells, and grasshoppers relieved of their spiny legs and warmed on a stick over a fire. Often in the thin of winter, she'd munched pine bark, and one memorable spring, a handful of maggots. But she did not think it necessary to turn over logs for dinner just yet. It was late summer, so fallen nuts and bright berries were tangled in the brush. She showed the girls how to spot edible mushrooms and stew a broth of grass and pine needles, chewing on the tangy needles to boost their spirits between meals.

Rin had been sure that a few days without silver flatware and servants would turn Dasha into a blubbering baby. But Dasha sang as she tromped through thickets and bragged about the collection of burrs she sported on her leggings.

The first time Rin gave her a cattail root for dinner, Dasha took a bite and exclaimed, "It *is* food!"

Enna was staring. "What did you think?"

"Well, I know you said it was, but who knew that food can just grow from the ground like that outside a crop field?"

Enna was still staring. "You make it really easy, Dasha. I don't even have to say anything."

Dasha took another bite and giggled. "Rin, you're amazing. It's all so amazing. I *love* the wild."

Enna leaned to Isi and whispered loudly, "I know I promised you I'd be better, but I just have to—"

"No," said Isi.

"But she's practically begging me to mock her, and I just thought of—"

"Shush, Enna."

"But—"

"Eat your root, fire girl."

"Fine. But it was going to be funny."

Rin never got tired of hearing Enna talk, and Dasha too—marveling at how they spoke without thinking first, seeming so relaxed, untroubled. Isi was different. Perhaps that was part of being queen? Rin guessed Isi was constantly aware that everything she said and did might affect not just herself but all of Bayern. No wonder she often seemed weary with caution.

Maybe that's why I feel best mirroring her, Rin thought, for while Isi took care with words, she also had a confidence, a sense of place that Rin lacked. If Isi's queenship explained her caution when speaking, Rin did not know where her own came from. Ever since the inn burned, Rin had been dreaming again of the gray worm curled in her middle, stretching.

Sometimes they traveled through grass-tangled meadows and streams with wide sandy banks. But whenever they were deep in trees again and could not see the sun, Isi would ask Rin the direction, and Rin could point and say, "North-east."

"How do you know?" Dasha asked with an awed smile.

"Moss grows on the north side of the trees and rocks."

"But that rock has spots of moss all over it."

Rin did her best not to laugh. "That's lichen."

"Oh. But what if there's no moss and it's high noon?"

"Most trees lean south."

Dasha squinted. "I don't see them leaning anywhere. Huh. You are so smart, Rin."

It felt odd to hear that from Dasha—the ambassador of Tira, a noblewoman, a girl who could read books and do numbers. Rin was finding it difficult to keep resenting her. Pretending Dasha was a friend of Isi's who had nothing to do with Razo made walking beside her and sharing her blanket at night much less trying.

With the grudge in abeyance, Rin noticed just how spec-tacular Dasha was with the water-speaking—leading them to drinking water, encouraging stream fish into a trap, and even keeping them all dry in a rainstorm.

One evening lightning flashed, for a dazzling moment

revealing the white skeleton of the world. The image stayed in Rin's eyes after it all went dark again. She shivered. In the buzz of hot light, everything had seemed made of bone—pale and hard, standing on shadows. She thought of cross-bow bolts and queens who burn crowded inns.

"Rain," Dasha warned.

The four girls clustered together, and when the clouds sighed and released the torrent, the rain bent away as if an invisible roof peaked above their heads, sending the drops out and down on either side. Dasha laughed, as pleased with herself as a child learning a new trick.

Dasha's water-speaking had proved essential, Isi's wind-speaking brought word of game to hunt or people to avoid, and the fire-speaking lit their fires at night. Watching the fire sisters work their own talents, Rin felt even sharper regret for losing her communion with trees.

This wood was different than her own Forest of creaking pines and crackling aspens, where the thick canopy kept the ground tidy. This wood was wild, slashes of sunlight lancing the air, a disarray of brambles and ferns and bushes. And it felt so alive it seemed to be crawling outward, expanding its roots, lifting into saplings. The trees were constantly pulling themselves down and sprouting anew, keeping the whole wood young, throbbing, hissing with life.

New trees, vibrant trees. How would she feel inside their thoughts? At home, succumbing to a tree's green sounds had lifted her anxiety momentarily. Was it possible that these trees could change her, make her a new Rin? The desire was like the constant itch of a bug bite, and she feared scratching would only make it worse.

The third evening after Hendric, while the fire sisters prepared dinner, Rin crept just out of sight. She approached a slender tree rich with glossy leaves and imagined closing her eyes and falling into that half-sleep where the ground seems to lift and then sink, where Rin became not herself, not the thinker, but a figure seen from a distance, a character in a story someone else was telling. No real thoughts, no worries, just the steady, nearly silent hum of water and sap moving out through the branches, twigs, into the veins of each leaf, the feel of that pulse making her calm and sleepy as a well-fed baby wrapped in blankets.

Tree-speaking. Ever since Isi had named it, Rin missed her closeness with trees like she missed her own ma. And maybe if she could get it back, she would discover new things, understanding empowering her as fire and wind strengthened Isi.

Rin's forehead touched bark, she closed her eyes and opened herself inside to sense, to hear, to feel . . .

And was blasted with a sensation of loathing, filling her like maggots bursting from an animal corpse.

She recoiled, her whole body shaking, and hurried away from the tree.

Never again, she told herself. *I'll never try again.*

The decision felt as final as death.

Isi glanced up as Rin stumbled into camp. "You all right, Rin?"

"I'm fine."

A lie. Maybe a harmless one, but it stuck in her mouth, tasting bitter, and she could not shake a feeling that she'd forgotten something important.

I lied to Wilem too.

Rin shuddered. It was a thought she'd been fleeing from, and she refused to think it now. Running into the world had not changed her, as it had Razo. She'd stayed close to Isi and tried to be like her, but she was still just Rin—lying, broken Rin. And these fire sisters knew her no more than her family back home. They were only fooled by her, charmed by her seeming sense, when all she did was try to reflect them back to themselves.

I'm the sheen on water, Rin thought. *I'm a looking glass. I'm not real.*

But she seemed to have no choice—she had to keep moving. Was it the tree-speaking that made her feel so wrong? Or perhaps the peace that had once come with tree-speaking had temporarily numbed the truth—that Rin herself was rotten at the core, bug-eaten and damaged, a diseased tree with shallow roots, a hollowed trunk with yellowing leaves.

Rin kept listening to the girls, her eyes on Isi, studying

how to be wise, noble, unafraid. How to be less like Rin. She watched, but the lump of hopelessness hardened inside her. On they walked. And Rin felt farther and farther away from herself.

si kept them in the wood past Saxmer, emerging from the trees to join a trade road leading from Saxmer to the Kelish village of Cathal.

"Cathal hugs the border, and trade with Bayern is common, so folk there should speak our language as well as Kelish. Let's pass through Cathal and see what we can learn."

The road to Cathal was battered and only one wagon wide, with swells of hard earth where mud had frozen during cold and rainy seasons. Enna tripped often, and cursed each time she tripped, until Dasha said, "Enna, you might watch your language."

Enna grimaced. "I was. You should hear my thoughts."

Cathal lay on the base of a gentle hill bright with yellow-green grass. Rin could count thirty wattle-and-daub houses. The older homes near the road were stone with thatched roofs that might keep out the rain of spring but not the cold of winter. But it was a summer night, warm as a breath on the cheek, and the fields were full of the slow movements of cattle. It was much simpler than the Bayern towns Rin had seen, with no visible inn or market, no lord's house, no wall or town center or row of shops. But it seemed lovely to Rin's eyes, surrounded by the hope of healthy animals and meat for winter. To build so many houses so near together seemed like an amiable thing to Rin, people who chose to live close as if they really did enjoy the company. So Rin was shocked when she was near enough to see their faces—depressed, full of gloom and heartache.

"What's the plan, Isi?" Enna asked in a whisper. "Doesn't seem likely we'll find an inn hidden in this stack of shacks."

"I don't dare sleep here and make it a target for fire-speakers anyway," Isi said. "But I'm hoping we can stop for dinner and learn whatever we can about this queen of Kel. It's Kelish custom to offer hospitality to travelers by placing a lighted candle in the window."

Dasha nodded. "Inns are rare in Kel, even in the cities. They consider it good luck to house travelers." Her eyes scanned the town's windows, shutters open to the humid night, windowsills lightless. "But perhaps not in Cathal . . ."

On they walked, no candles in sight. The villagers' eyes flicked over the girls, taking note of their Bayern tunics, skirts, and leggings. The Kelish men wore long tunics in white, gray, or yellow, with sleeves that dangled from their forearms down to their knees. The women wore the same tunics with dangling sleeves, and over the tunics, sleeveless dresses laced at the bodice. Both men and women sported caps with thick bands across the top of their head, the women's hats rounded in back, holding their hair in a sack at their necks.

"See the ladies' hats?" Dasha whispered to Rin, smiling as if nothing was wrong in all the world. "Didn't I tell you they were darling?"

An older woman swept out her little house, gray hair tucked into a yellow cap. She had a square face and a build that must have been daunting before age sloped her back. A man sat in a chair beside the door, sword strapped to his side, smoking a pipe into the summer evening. He coughed, but not from the pipe. Behind his back, the woman was deliberately sweeping dust in his direction, gusts of debris swirling up into his face. There was an honest look to the woman's face, besides the glee she seemed to take at the man's hacking. The man, on the other hand, had an expression of . . . Rin could not name it, but she was certain he deserved worse than a lungful of floor dirt.

So when Isi said, "Rin, keep an eye out for anyone who seems a trustworthy soul," Rin gestured to the sweeping woman.

"She might tell us the truth."

Isi asked the woman a question in a language Rin did not understand, though the sounds of it pleased her. The woman glared at the back of the man's head before going inside her home and sticking a lighted candle on the windowsill. The man sprang to his feet and shouted at the woman, and the woman shouted back until he stalked off.

Isi spoke again in concerned tones, and the woman waved her hand dismissively.

"I know of the western tongue," said the woman, her accent pinched and sweet, as if she spoke with her mouth squeezed together. "You are Bayern?"

Isi nodded. "We are. We don't want to cause you trouble."

"I am ready with the trouble." The woman shook her broom in the air. "If someone was not coming now, I was for hitting him already." She smiled to show she was teasing, though Rin could see she almost meant her words.

She gestured the travelers inside, where the smell of bread drenched the air. Rin spied the lumps of new loaves covered by a cloth, and her stomach gurgled, reminding her how many days it had been since she'd eaten bread. That was the smell of home, and her ma, and the warm cottage when rainstorms seethed outside. It was a hard, hard thing to lose a home full of bread and Ma.

"I have dinner. You are hungry?" The woman sat the four girls on various stools and perches around her one-roomed home, handing out carved wooden bowls heaped with well-cooked beans and meat. The food was thick and well salted, but Rin's attention kept straying to the bread.

Isi introduced them all and explained they were travelers with business in Kel. "Mistress . . ."

"Mistress Mor," said the woman.

"Mistress Mor, if I may ask, who was that man? Your son?"

Mistress Mor cackled, and Rin could not help smiling at the lively sound. "Not my son! My son is skinny and nice. That was"—she leaned out the door to spit—"soldier. How you say, soldier for no loyalty, soldier is paid?"

"Mercenary," said Dasha.

Mistress Mor nodded. "Like ants they are crawling all in houses. We are ordered for putting them in homes and giving them to eat. And they are no nice boys."

"King Scandlan ordered you to take in mercenaries?" Dasha asked.

"Maybe he. The order coming from Castle Daire. Daire is home to Lord Forannan and Lady Giles, but lord and lady now are gone. They were for being good to us. Now Castle Daire is home of queen."

There was a shout in Kelish, and they all stood, Dasha dropping her bowl in alarm. The soldier had returned with another, this one wearing a chain-mail vest and iron helmet. He pointed at Mistress Mor when he spoke. She met him at the threshold and spoke back, her voice taut and angry.

"What'll it be, Isi," Enna asked, glancing at Dasha. "Diplomacy or action?"

Isi stood between Mistress Mor and the soldier, placing a gentle hand on the soldier's chest, and spoke in Kelish.

The new soldier spoke back, and now the language did

not seem so sweet to Rin. His eyes roved over the girls, taking in their clothes.

"You do not belong here," he said in a hard accent.

Isi, still calm, said, "Neither do you."

The soldier shoved Isi aside and threw a chair at Mistress Mor. She cried out as the chair struck her. Before she'd even fallen to the ground, his sword flamed red hot, and he screamed as he dropped it.

Rin rushed to Mistress Mor's side. The old woman clutched at her ankle, muttering something in Kelish.

The soldier yelled, and more soldiers came. But the villagers were gathering too, in the square opposite Mistress Mor's house.

"Rin, stay with her," Isi said, pulling Dasha and Enna out into the road.

Villagers with their draping sleeves hefted rakes and shovels, brooms and sticks. Soldiers in leather or chain-mail vests eyed the villagers. The soldier who lost his sword was still hollering in Kelish, pointing at Mistress Mor's house. The three girls stood like guards before her threshold.

"You're hurt?" Rin asked.

Mistress Mor winced, shaking her head. "Just . . . the ankle. Just the ankle." Then she said something in Kelish. Rin felt pretty certain it was a curse. She helped Mistress Mor to her feet, supporting her as the woman hopped back into the house and lay on her bed. Rin placed a rolled-up blanket under her calf to support the leg.

The noise outside continued. Rin's middle felt like a winter pond. Isi had told her to stay back. It was exhausting, this wishing to be Isi but being trapped in useless Rin.

A sudden shout made her run to the door. Perhaps two dozen mercenaries stood facing the girls, their swords waving. The villagers huddled together, some yelling back.

"Tell me what happens," said Mistress Mor from the bed.

With anxiety clawing at her chest, Rin could barely think, let alone speak. She took a deep breath. "The mercenaries and villagers are shouting at one another. But my friends will take care of it. Don't worry."

Rin worried.

"How many soldiers? How many you seeing?"

Rin counted. "Twenty-one."

The old woman shook her head. "There are more in Cathal, and they are not for liking this."

A cry pierced the silence, as fierce and desperate as a starving crow. Enna's eyes flashed toward the far side of the village. Rin could hear her say, "Isi, there's fire."

Enna ran off, leaving Dasha with Isi. When the mercenaries moved forward, the ground under their boots was suddenly muddy. Wind raged around them, the mud slippery beneath their feet. When they fell down, the hilts of their swords burning, Isi and Dasha ran after Enna.

Rin crossed the room to peer through a shutter on the back wall. She could see smoke and hear shouts and the sounds of metal striking metal.

Here I am, she thought, *watching again.*

A sensation like a dark sludge pouring moved inside her and made her want to be sick.

Rin sat beside Mistress Mor on a low stool. She stared at a chip in the daub and listened to the cries, running, curses, and sometimes gaps of silence. One altercation seemed to be nearby—a woman's voice shouting, a man's voice answering, a strike like wood on metal, and a scream. High and soft, the call of a small child. Then silence. Rin's blood chilled.

Someone began speaking in a whisper so stiff and urgent it quivered like a tent rope. It was a woman's voice. Rin looked at Mistress Mor. Her face was white with pain.

"Did you hear that?" Rin asked.

Mistress Mor nodded. "My neighbor, Aileann, I think. She is saying, 'Please, please.' Aileann has little girl."

Rin half-stood, hesitated. "Will you be all right?"

"Yes, yes, I am fine enough. You are going. Go."

Rin nodded and fled through the door. She followed the sound, sidling between two houses and stopping in a shadow.

There was a wild-haired woman facedown on the ground, one hand pressed palm to dirt, the other reached out and up, pleading toward a mercenary. Her face was streaked with dirt, clean lines where tears ran, and a bruise was swelling the side of her face. Beside her lay the pieces of a shovel, its wooden shaft broken in two. The mercenary was short and thick like a big toe, his wide nose wrinkled in a sneer, and his eyes were crazed. His arm squeezed the neck of a child of about four years. She squirmed and cried, flinching away from the short sword he held across her belly.

The mercenary's eyes flashed, half-mad with fierce amusement, and the way he spoke to Aileann, Rin guessed he knew her well, perhaps had been housed with her. The little girl was surely Aileann's daughter—they had the same stormy hair that stuck up and around, half-covering her face. Rin could not see the girl's eyes, but she could see the worried mouth, the chin that trembled.

Aileann repeated that same word over and over, *please, please, please.* It seemed to be all she could say between terrified sobs.

That little girl. She was about the same age as Rin's niece Genna, she had the same hair color as her nephew Incher, the same round, simple face as Tusken. Little Tusken. No one should hurt a child. And yet there was someone with a sword, someone who did not care about another's pain, someone who might kill. Rin looked around, desperate for help, but the girls were nowhere near.

Ma would never allow a bully like that mercenary to hurt a child. But she was so far away, Rin could not think what her mother would do. Isi would use her fire to burn the sword out of his hand and the wind to blow him off. Rin held no weapon. All she could do was speak. The idea sent waves of nausea pulsing through her, but there was no time to worry.

Rin stepped out of the shadow and into moonlight. The mercenary's eyes found her at once.

He began to speak in Kelish, but Rin interrupted.

"Do you understand me?" He did not answer, but she could see he did. "Please don't hurt the girl. Listen to me first." Her teeth were chattering, she was so angry and so scared, and so unsure what to say. Since the age of seven, she'd trained herself never to tell anyone what to do. Doing it on purpose felt like trying to forget how to walk.

"If you hurt her, you'll regret it powerfully, you'll wish you'd just slit your own throat. So don't. Just don't."

His eyes were wild, open and darting from Rin to Aileann to the houses around them. His sword trembled. "Are you to stop me? Ha!"

The little girl moaned, soft and tired now, as if she had no more voice to cry. Her mother wailed with new terror, her hand still reaching in hopeless desperation.

"Shh," Rin hissed at her. The man was so twitchy, she was afraid a loud noise could set him off. Anger boiled her bones and made her feel hot and dangerous, though her teeth were chattering so hard now that her slamming jaw shook her vision.

She studied his face, remembered the way he had looked at the little girl, as if she were a mangy cat, barely worth notice and good for nothing but casting aside.

Rin moved toward him, as slow as a shadow inching with the sun. She opened her hands, showing she had no weapon.

"I can't hurt you," she said.

"You are for hurting me?" His voice boiled. "She was putting milk in my boots this morning. She is trouble every day I am on this village. She is no girl, she is demon. You keep closer and I am eating her for supper!"

"Not yet," Rin said, her voice shaking, her throat nearly closing off. But somehow the words vibrated with ease and confidence. "First I want to tell you a story. About her. About the little girl. She loves to run so fast she imagines her hair turns into wind. And she loves to climb trees and eat pine nuts out of the cones. When she's six years, and ten, and twelve, sometimes her mother will let her curl up on her lap like she still does now, and they'll rock by the fire, humming together. She loves her ma so much."

Rin meant to attack him with words, challenge and demand and tear away his confidence, as she had with . . . A memory flashed behind her eyes of the night with Wilem, the things she'd said. She clamped it down. *Never mind that. Never mind.* But attacking did not seem right for the mercenary—attacks could anger him and get the girl hurt. Calming is what he needed. She wished she could make him feel what she used to feel when at home with her aspens.

"She has older brothers, but her ma loves her best. Loves her like her own self. When she gets older, she'll worry that her ma loves a stranger." Rin swallowed, but her tongue was dry as bark. She kept her eyes on the little girl and forced more words out. "When she's fifteen she'll go on a journey, because home just won't feel right anymore. The journey will be hard, and scary, but she'll meet people who are like her and can help. She'll worry sometimes about her ma, worry that she won't ever get to go home and that will break her ma's heart. But in the end, she'll change, like an apple gets rosy in the sun, and she'll go home again, and this time it will *feel* like home. This time she'll stay forever, and her ma will be so happy."

The mercenary was frowning. The sword in his hand lowered, just an inch. Rin kept talking.

"Someday when she's grown with children of her own, she'll still love to run so fast she'll think her hair is turning into wind, and she'll still climb trees as long as her knees can bend. And her whole life will be long and good too, because you let her live. Because of you."

While Rin spoke, she kept moving forward, very slowly, and the armed man's feral eyes stayed on her. The girl still hung from his arm, tears leaving streaks on her dirty cheeks, just like her mother's. Aileann had not moved, though she gasped and sobbed with her mouth open.

The man seemed confused. He looked at the girl again, as if he did not know what kind of beast she was after all.

"How . . . how you are knowing?" He sounded as though he believed Rin, every word.

"I *know*," said Rin, then she was close enough to touch

him. Her hand reached out, but her eyes strayed to his blade, held there inches away, sharp enough to swipe through her wrist in one stroke. She trembled all over. "She needs to keep on going. She's got running to do and a boy to meet someday, and children waiting to be born. You should let her go run so fast her hair can turn into wind. Let her go. Fast as wind."

Twice Rin hesitated, but finally she placed her hand on the man's arm. She used to soak in the calm of the trees when she was touching their bark, breathing in the exhale of their leaves—perhaps she could offer this mercenary some calm in her touch. Perhaps she could be his tree.

"Nothing wrong in all the world," Rin said softly. "No need to make a fuss. Let her go running, let her grow up to be a ma—a ma like your own, who cuddled you close and kissed you fast. No fuss at all."

His eyebrows furrowed, and he looked at the girl, then down at her mother.

Please, the mother said once, her voice exhausted and final.

The mercenary let go.

The little girl yelped as he dropped her. She scrambled into her mother's arms, and they sat on the ground, gripping each other and sobbing, their eyes shut.

Rin began to back away very slowly, not wanting that mercenary's attention to return to her, not with that sword in his hand. He was staring at the child and shaking his head.

Another mercenary ran past, heading north of town. He saw his companion and stopped, asking him a question in Kelish.

The squat mercenary looked at his friend, half-dazed. "I was . . ." Then he pointed at Rin and spoke in Kelish, sounding confused and half-asleep.

The new mercenary growled. He came at Rin so quickly that she spooked and fell backward, striking her head on the ground, the sweep of his sword cutting the air just above her. Her tongue was salted with the taste of blood. Dizzy, she searched for sight of the mercenary's sword—there above her. He was swinging for another strike. She covered her head with her arms.

Sorry, Ma, she thought. *Sorry, Razo. And Wilem too. Sorry.*

in hid her face, her whole body tense as she waited for the sword to slice her. But nothing happened. She heard a gurgle and peeked. The mercenary's face was red, and he dropped his sword, his hands flying to his neck. The gurgle was coming from his throat. He fell to his knees, tearing at his shirt, slapping at his lips. When he leaned over, water poured from his mouth, but still he choked, scratching at the earth and coughing. His wet hand reached for Rin, and she scuttled back on her hands and feet.

"Go away!" Rin pleaded. "Go away!"

The squat mercenary grabbed his comrade around the shoulders and ran away. Rin could hear the man heave the last of the water from his lungs, gasp and breathe at last. But they did not stop running.

Aileann and her child had fled too. Footsteps hurried toward her from behind, but she did not flinch, guessing who it was.

"Are you all right, Rinna?" asked Dasha. "Come on

now, let me put my arm around you, that's right. Let's go back to Mistress Mor's, shall we?"

Rin wondered why Dasha seemed to be trembling harder than an aspen in a windstorm. After a few missed steps, Rin realized she was the one still trembling.

Inside the cottage, Isi was kneeling beside the bed, wrapping Mistress Mor's leg with strips ripped from the queen's cloak.

"Good luck for opening home to travelers," Mistress Mor was muttering. "Good luck break my bone."

"Mistress Mor—," Isi began.

"No, no, it *was* good luck. You gave us reason for ridding of pests. They come here months ago, leave sometimes, always come back and eat as if no winter comes. Sometimes slap women, sometimes push children." She sucked air in through her teeth at the pain and began speaking more quickly, adding occasional Kelish words in her haste. "I go to Castle Daire for complaining. I go with some men, but I did no trusting them to be smart, so young and stupid for carrying swords, *du konish*. Many soldiers at castle now, and they no letting us by gates. Some woman say queen in Kel orders soldiers to our town and say no for talking to us. Banner flying in castle tower, *mom pinken*, yellow lily, banner for queen. If King Scandlan married again, he no for telling us."

"Which is strange." Isi rubbed her eyes. "Is the king even aware that a so-called queen resides at Daire and is amassing an army of mercenaries?"

"I am wanting for going to Bressal and for talking at King Scandlan. Not with this ankle now, *limish tom, lim fartik* . . ."

Enna came through the door, wafting a strong whiff of smoke—some wood smoke and some not, announcing other things had burned. It was not a comfortable scent.

"All's quiet, and the fields are full of fleeing villains," Enna said, dropping onto a stool. "The cowards. They love a midnight attack when there's no one to fight back, but one little push and they run away. They make me want to spit in their eyeballs."

"And the villagers—," Isi began.

"None dead," said Enna. "But not for lack of trying. Those goat-faced pigs went crazy as soon as the villagers started fighting back. This would've been a slaughterhouse. I saw women setting up house for those whose roofs were burned through. I think they'll be all right, Isi, if you're thinking we should scurry after a certain queen."

"That's where the mercenaries are headed. We'd be wise to go on, finish this before she can send more soldiers in retribution."

Mistress Mor eyed the girls. "You are . . . *yunik fam* . . . how do you say?"

Isi smiled. "Odd?"

Mistress Mor nodded. "Odd, yes. And dangerous too." She laughed with her head back, and seemed pleased to do so. "My son will come soon for seeing me. You go."

They were at the door when the woman gestured to the table where the loaves of bread sat under a white cloth. "And one bread for taking, please."

All four girls sighed with relieved delight, then giggled at their joint sigh.

"I would politely decline," said Dasha, "if that amazing smell hadn't been teasing me to near insanity."

They thanked Mistress Mor, Isi placing something in her palm that most likely was round and gold. Then they jogged to the edge of the village, each tearing into a chunk of the bread. The crust was crisp and thin, the inside nutty and dark, and Rin could not remember ever enjoying food so much. It smelled like home, but it tasted different—new and strange and full of hope. She let the first bite mellow on her tongue, let the softness dissolve until the flavor changed.

"Enna, did you find any signs of horses we might buy?" Isi asked.

"There weren't many to begin with, and the cowards took those as they fled."

Dasha sighed. "It will be a long walk to Daire."

Rin was secretly relieved. She felt tilted and quavery from her encounter with the mercenary, and she wanted to feel herself moving, use her walking muscles, not clutch to the saddle of an uncertain beast.

Enna began to trudge northeast. "There weren't any fire-speakers in the village tonight, near as I could tell. Those fires were started by cowards with torches, punishing the villagers for fighting back. Filthy-fingered, litter-born, rancid—"

"I can't fathom what is happening," said Isi. "A queen in Kel, a secret queen, who attacks Geric, attacks us, houses mercenaries on the border with Bayern. Whatever the reason, we have to stop her—or whoever is behind these attacks."

"We are in Kel now," said Dasha. "Shouldn't this be King Scandlan's matter?"

"When fire-speakers burn houses and attack people, that's my matter," Enna said. "And if the burners are hiding behind a queen in Kel, that's where I'll go."

"You're right, Dasha," said Isi. "We're stepping into dangerous diplomatic territory. But our ambassador in Kel was dismissed, and Scandlan has been unresponsive. If we go to Bressal first, it could take weeks to find safe paths through the bogs of Kel. We need to act quickly before more people are hurt."

"Still," said Dasha, "this seems risky."

Isi nodded, her eyes sad. "But I think it's a risk I need to take. Dasha, if you are at all concerned about being involved—"

"I am concerned," said Dasha, "but I still want to be involved. You're right that something is amiss in Kel, and by virtue of our talents, we are bound to help."

"Thank you. We'll need to get inside the castle and take

down the fire-speakers as quickly as possible. Wind can push back fire attacks, but with your water, Dasha, you might be able to stop them cold."

"I am ready."

"Good," Isi said. "I want to lock up whoever is behind this for Scandlan to judge. Let's always keep in mind that we're in Kel, and if we trip up, Scandlan might feel it his duty to declare war on Bayern. Especially if this person really is his wife and the rightful queen. So we tread carefully."

"Carefully," said Enna, her eyes focused on the way before them. "We can do that. Absolutely. And then we'll do whatever it takes."

"Carefully," Isi warned.

"Right." When Enna spoke again, her voice was so soft, Rin had to strain to hear. "I don't want to hurt anyone. I swore I never would again. But you should know, I will if I need to, Isi. If I need to keep Bayern's queen safe, I will kill."

Rin could see Isi's profile as she looked at Enna, lines of sadness in her face, torment almost, and Rin expected the queen to declare that Enna need never go back on her promise. But then Isi raised one eyebrow.

"As if you could."

Enna stared at Isi so intently she tripped over a rock. "Excuse me?"

"You talk so big, *I'll kill if I have to*, but you couldn't even kill me."

Rin and Dasha gaped. Enna sighed and waved a hand as if trying to sum up a lot of information quickly. "One time I tried to kill her and I failed. It wasn't . . . I didn't mean . . . it was a long . . . well, anyway, after that, there was nowhere for our friendship to go but up."

"I can depend on Enna for just about anything," said Isi, "but I could never make her a court assassin. She'd fall flat on her face."

"Ho there now, my queen, I can slay with the best of them. If you just weren't so good at defending yourself—"

"No excuses. You can set fire to an army, but when it comes down to it, you're really bad at individual murders."

"Fine."

Rin watched Isi closely. There was a tightness in her voice, a sadness in her eyes. Despite the teasing, the queen cared very much whether her friend killed again.

Isi did not just like Enna, Rin considered. She needed her, and not just for Enna's talents, her protection and power. The queen needed to hear a second voice, to have someone she trusted always on her side. Rin thought of her own mother, surrounded by people, all family and no friends. The homestead was frantic with people, but they were all people Ma fussed and sweated and cared for. Who cared for Ma?

"If it's possible that this queen of Kel has been trying to herd us to Castle Daire, then why are we . . ." Dasha gestured with her chin toward the direction they walked.

"I know," said Isi. "It's an uncertain road. But I can't imagine she could kill or even capture us. Enna alone can hold off an entire battalion of soldiers or a handful of fire-speakers." She hooked arms with Enna at her side, and Dasha put her arm through Rin's. "This queen of Kel thinks she can defeat us? Ruffle our feathers? Make us flinch? Ha, I say."

"Ha!" Enna echoed with enthusiasm.

A loud, contented *moo* echoed Enna's laugh, startling Dasha to scream. Rin realized they were walking through a herd of cows sampling the damp grasses of the night field.

Recovered, Dasha held up her head as she tromped on. "That's right. Ha to that burning queen, and *moo* too. There's a good deal of water hanging in those clouds up there that is eager to meet her fire-speakers."

Rin put her arm more firmly through Dasha's, breathing in the good feeling of being with friends. And not just any friends. Joined with those three girls, she felt as insurmountable as a mountain, as solid as a forest of trees. It made her feel bold, almost as good as them, almost as strong.

"Have you been to Daire before, Isi?" Dasha asked.

"No, I believe both the castle and its town are small. Last year Geric and I traveled to the coast and took the sea route to Bressal to meet with the king. Scandlan was reserved but gracious, so his current silence troubles me. We stayed a couple of weeks, taking Tusken with us. He loved the sword dancing and drumming. Geric loved the roast boar and fishing with nets in the ocean. I loved the tales."

"You've never told me any Kelish tales," Enna said.

"Haven't I? They're . . . strange, in a wonderful way, but they don't make good bed tales. I've wondered why the Kelish stories are about humanlike animals, as if in order to see the story it has to be a bit removed from what is actually real."

"So go on, then," said Enna.

"All right. So. The boar, the stag, and the eagle met on the last craggy peak of the world, looked down, and sighed at what they saw. The boar was a king, and he said, 'There are not enough people.' The stag was a poet, and he said, 'There is not enough beauty.' The eagle was a cleric, and he said, 'There is not enough mystery.' Then the wolf, arriving late, looked up instead of down and said, 'There is not enough hunger,' and promptly ate them all." Isi cleared her throat. "And . . . that's the end."

"Oh," Dasha said. "I see."

Isi laughed. "The Kelish enjoy the unexpected endings, especially ones that involve death. All Kelish tales are questions, and this one asks, if the boar was king, the stag was poet, and the eagle was cleric, then what was the wolf?"

"A woman," said Enna.

"Unkindness," said Dasha. "Brutality, selfishness, people

who play life like a game and kill to win. What do you think, Isi?"

"King, poet, and cleric are all professions, so maybe the wolf represents a profession as well, like a warrior. Or perhaps it's something less tangible, like . . . time." Isi shrugged. "It seems like a riddle, but then I think, maybe there isn't one answer. What do you think, Rin?"

Rin still had not said a word since yelling at the mercenaries to go away. She cleared her throat and was about to agree with what Isi had said, but a different thought seized her. "Maybe the wolf isn't a person or a thing. Maybe it's something inside—inside us." She imagined the wolf poised in her own chest with maw open at her heart, a beast that could eat her from the inside. The girls did not answer, and Rin cursed herself for speaking her thoughts.

"Huh," said Dasha. "Well, I like the tale. It is sort of dreadful, but so is this night, and the distraction is constructive."

So Isi told another, and another, as they walked forward and up in the night of a hidden moon. Rin listened but only barely, because she kept asking herself, *What is the wolf?*

A solitary tree lurked on a hilltop, its branches reaching high and wide. It was a perfect outline against the starlit sky, perhaps the loveliest tree shape Rin had ever seen, and it filled her with wonder for the beauty in the world, even here, so far from home that people spoke a new language and told animal tales that asked questions more confusing than dreams. It was not until they passed beneath it that Rin realized the enormity of the thing, and she held her breath in awe. She was reminded of the ancient elm in the palace yard, and marveled again at what a tree could become outside a forest. Isi, Dasha, and Enna had all left home and family, and they were doing fine. Rin had hoped that she too could bloom away from home, but passing beneath that tree, under a foreign night sky, she felt even tinier than before, a mote of dust that could be lost in the merest huff of wind.

On they marched, the hour moving through them and past them so quickly, Rin was not tired by the time they reached Daire. They halted at first sight of the castle, in a rocky field dotted with trees. The wind troubled the leaves and stirred them into a fluster, chattering and nipping at each other like kits. The moon revealed itself, leering over the castle battlement. In its shadow, the queen of Kel was waiting.

Part Three

The Castle

he moon lit the castle from behind, scratching its jagged outline across a blue-black sky. Much smaller than the palace in Bayern's capital, this border fortress was built of connected towers with toothy tops. Rin could hear the occasional bawl of cattle, for Kel was as seemingly full of cows as the Forest was of squirrels. It was a comforting sound, a reminder that there were creatures who did not know about crossbow bolts and fire-speakers, and were just happy to smell late-summer grass.

Just beyond the field, Rin felt the pull of trees. A wood. A place to hide. She began to veer that way, hating the open plain where anyone might spot them by the garish light of that white moon.

Dasha's arm was still in hers, so Rin pulled the Tiran girl along.

"This does seem too open, doesn't it, Isi?" said Dasha.

Ahead stood three dark figures. Rin startled and

Dasha made a dry scream. How had Isi's wind not given warning? Then Rin noticed their huge height, their stillness. Three pillars of stacked stones, standing three men high, side by side as if guarding the wood.

"They're cairns," said Isi. "Built both to honor the gods in the wood and to keep them there."

"Why?" asked Enna.

"Gods in the wood are good luck. Gods roaming free get involved in people's lives."

Rin could tell from Isi's voice that she did not believe in sacred cairns or gods in the wood, but as they passed by the third pillar, Enna's face was full of curiosity and reverence. Rin herself felt something peculiar just seeing the cairns, as if she were looking at the body of someone she used to know.

"I think the cairns are the way of the clerics and the people to say, we know there is something more, but we don't know what," Isi went on. "So we give it shape, and that shape may be the wrong shape, but it's there to remind us of what we can't see. The wrongness of it is what makes us think. The error in what we made will bring us the truth."

"That makes me think of the sea . . ." Dasha sighed, a sound of longing. "We see the surface, blue or silver or gray, and waves hitting the shore. But we know there's so much we can't see, so what we love about it becomes in part what we imagine it is hiding."

Isi stopped. The other girls halted just as suddenly,

waiting for whatever news Isi heard on the wind. Isi began to turn, looking for a source.

"They're staying downwind, but I got a glimpse. Armed men. Over . . ." She pointed vaguely to her right, then behind them. Enna's hands were in fists.

"The wood," Rin urged. She used to love night, when the worst thing hiding in the darkness was one of her brothers tiptoeing to pull a prank. Now night was full of burners and swords and bolts, and Rin's skin ached for trees to shield her. Enna and Isi turned as they walked, scanning the darkness.

"They could pick us off with arrows," Dasha said, her voice trembling.

Isi shook her head. "No, they're too far behind us. Enna, do you hear anything?"

"Wait." Enna stopped. "They're ahead of us, too."

All stopped. Enna and Isi were listening—not with their ears, Rin knew, but in some other way, sensing wind and heat. The lurkers must have been close, because Isi or Enna pulled a wind to circle around the four girls. Rin hoped it was thick enough to toss away arrows and protect them from fire.

A moment later, a group of soldiers came running from the wood, swords raised.

"Enna, heat their weapons out of their hands," said Isi. "I'll take their breaths. Dasha, can you sink them where they stand?"

Dasha nodded.

"I'm going to release the wind now."

The circling wind died, and Rin could feel light vibrations of wind and heat; then the soldiers were dropping swords and gasping as if the air had been pulled right out of their lungs. While they gasped and stumbled, the ground beneath their feet was getting wetter, deep ground water rising up through the dirt and soaking it through, mud as deep as their knees seizing the soldiers' boots and holding them fast. When the breeze stilled and the men could breathe again, they found themselves stuck in mud, unable to take a step.

"None of them are fire-speakers," Enna said, apparently able to tell from a distance.

"Who sent you?" Isi's voice was hard. "Tell us now or worse things will happen than muddy boots. Who ordered your attack?"

Isi repeated her demand in Kelish, but they did not answer. Perhaps the soldiers guessed that it was an idle threat, or perhaps the threats of their own leader were more dire.

"Isi," Dasha said. "It seems likely that whoever burned the inn would know we could handle this many soldiers."

Isi looked toward the castle. "She's planning something."

Enna turned her back to Isi, facing the other direction, and Dasha the same, the fire sisters forming a triangle, scanning the horizon for coming danger.

"Rin, take cover," Isi said.

Rin wanted to stay. She did not feel in danger with those girls—stepping away from them and into the darkness, that seemed riskier. So she did not go far, just a couple dozen steps to the nearest cairn, putting the massive stack of stones between herself and the castle. Her boots were coated with Dasha's mud, and she scraped them off with a rock.

"Maybe we should——," Enna started.

A bonfire of wood blazed so suddenly, Rin had no doubt a fire-speaker had done the job. She peered around the edge of the stones. There, where the outer wall of Castle Daire touched the wood, a fire burned beneath a massive tree. A metal cage dangled from a branch, high enough that the flames did not touch it. But if the cage slipped, it would fall directly into the fire.

Two people were in the cage. A boy holding a child. And Rin knew them. She knew the shape of them, the size of them. She wished she was mistaken, wished so hard her head ached.

"Who . . . ," Dasha began to ask.

"No," Isi breathed. "No. No. No."

Isi knew. And so, with a sickening drop of her stomach, Rin was certain too——the boy in the cage was Razo, and the child was Tusken.

Isi took one step forward and the bonfire died. Wind whipped up, knocking down anyone standing between Isi and the cage. Rin half-expected the entire castle to explode in flame, but before Isi could do anything more, a voice cut through the wind and night. A woman's voice, her accent neither Kelish nor Bayern. A pleasing voice.

"Now please stay calm. There's no cause for an ado. All will be well. I will not hurt you. It would benefit everyone if you would listen for a moment. I know you are curious to understand why you are here. You want to end this peacefully, so it is wise to listen before you strike."

Out of the shadows, a slim figure walked forward. Her face was not yet visible, but Isi gasped.

"Get away, all of you," Isi commanded. "Enna, Dasha, go. Go now!"

"No, don't, please. It would be better if you stayed."

And they stayed. Rin felt turned to wood. More than anything, she wanted to hear that voice again. And the figure kept advancing. She moved in such a way that Rin was sure she was aware of her hips and liked them a great deal. Her robes were made of a loose pink fabric that clung to her curvier parts. Her pale hair, silvery in the night, hung loose over her shoulders, and made her appear tall, lean, almost luminous. In all, she seemed the most beautiful creature alive. It was easy to watch her and forget about Razo and Tusken in the cage.

Do something quick, Rin thought, though she did not move. Neither did the fire sisters. Dasha's expression was curious, Enna's was rigid as if she were in great pain. Isi's was stiff with horror.

Isi spoke one word. "Selia."

Chapter 15

Here I am!" said the woman, lifting a hand as if to present herself. The bonfire blazed anew, and Selia was lit from behind in orange and gold, as grand and unearthly as the stone pillars, but sinuous as a snake.

She kept moving forward. "And overjoyed to see you. Truly. I've been simply breathless to— Now, Enna, be calm. Terrible things will happen if you burn me. Terrible things. I think you believe me, don't you? Yes, you do, poor thing. I am awfully convincing. There is really no choice but for you to listen. Calmly, politely. Unclench those fists there, Crown Princess." She'd reached Isi, and she picked up Isi's fist and smoothed her hand straight. There was no hesitation in her fluid motions, no fear in her face. "That's better. As I was saying, I am completely overjoyed to welcome you to my kingdom. You are the honey cake for my feast. And I cannot wait to eat you up. Easy now, Anidori. Just stand there, harmless please. If you hurt me, your son loses his head at once."

Rin glanced around, trying to find some evidence that this claim was true. How could it be? Tusken was in that cage, and she had seen what these fire sisters could do. In moments, surely they could take out all the soldiers, and this Selia too, before anyone got close enough to pluck a hair from Tusken's or Razo's head. Did the girls believe Selia's threat? Why did they not act? *Now, hurry, now.* And yet . . . why did Rin stand still as well? Just listening to Selia's voice, her whole body relaxed. Not the same as when she allowed herself to feel the peace of trees—that peace came from her core and flowed out. This calm seemed to fill her head like smoke fills a room. Her body was separate from her, a different being, and her thoughts were too hazy to make it move.

Besides, why bother? Selia said there was no way to save the boys, and surely she was right. And her voice was so reassuring. The more Rin listened, the more the delicious sound of Selia's words crept inside, roosted in her like a flock of sleepy birds, happy to be home. Rin almost smiled at the thought. She liked birds. She was feeling cozy and safe, like birds at home in their trees . . .

"A word of advice? The next time you take it in your head to execute someone, dig up the courage to do it yourself. You can't trust anyone these days, can you? It takes courage to kill, Crown Princess. Real courage. Time and again, you've proven that you don't have it." Selia put a hand under Isi's chin and whispered, "But I do." She kissed Isi on the lips, like a little girl might kiss a precious doll.

Enna hissed and fire burst at Selia's hem, making her take two steps back in surprise. But in an instant the fire was gone, as if sucked away by a fire-speaker, and Selia shook the smoke out of her skirt. She smiled tenderly at Enna. "No more of that, Enna. Be a good girl." She pressed her cheek to Enna's, whispering something in her ear. One of Enna's eyes leaked a tear, but she did not so much as push Selia back.

This is people-speaking, Rin thought. This was the curse, as Enna called it, the one gift that corrupted everyone it touched. This was more dangerous than a sword, more than wind, water, and fire. Rin was still hidden behind the cairn, and Selia had not seen her. She should do something. But she did not. Under Selia's voice, Rin felt like an ant in a flood.

"I think I will take you all back to my castle—yes, *my* castle." Selia's eyes were triumphant, hungry even, as her gaze returned to Isi. "Did you think I would never have my own?"

"Selia," Isi said, getting three slow syllables out of her name. Her breathing was heavy, she blinked slowly. "You—"

"That's enough, Crown Princess," Selia said in a voice meant to soothe. "Please don't tax yourself. You are to be my very special guests, and I want you in the best of health.

We'll have a fortnight of celebrations before the big ending. Oh, the things I have planned for your amusement! Such a collection of barrels and nails and wild stallions to please a boatful of royalty! I know what fondness you have for such things, so I've spared no expense. But don't be alarmed. If you play by my rules, no one need be harmed, not even a squealing piglet."

Selia was going to take them into the castle. Into a cage. Like Tusken, like Razo. Rin took a step backward, another, but she was shaking so badly a small stumble brought her to the ground.

"It really is wonderful to see you. We haven't been alone, just to chat, in years. The last time we were in a forest and I was admiring one of your gowns, but you did not want me to touch it. Rather petulant of you, I thought at the time, but you never did know how to be royal and yet behave royally. Do not concern yourself about that now. After all, not everyone is born with social grace, and I long ago pardoned you for your stinginess with clothing. Speaking of clothing, don't you adore this dress?"

Selia spun around, the soft pink fabric flipping up and wrapping her legs. "Imagine it without the scorch marks—that was unfortunate, but you see how forgiving I am to look past it, as I know Enna cannot truly cause me any harm. This dress is the latest Kelish fashion, but I added the lace on the sleeves myself. As soon as Scandlan and I announce our marriage and I make appearances at court, you will see all the Kelish women add lace to their sleeves. People look up to their queen—when their queen has substance to offer. That will all happen soon. My husband the king wished to announce it at once, of course, but I thought it wise to take it slowly. He is so indulgent. He loves me tirelessly. You just can't imagine how thrilled he was to make me his queen.

"Look at me! I just talk and talk when you'd think I'd be a proper hostess and take you back to my palace for refreshments in our commodious dungeon, but I see you and realize how long we have been apart. I have so much to tell you! First of all, I want you to know that the little boy is safe and healthy." She looked up at the cage, smiling distractedly. "Such a find. Such a treasure. I can't thank you enough for bringing him out of the palace yourself. Cilie just didn't know how she was going to manage kidnapping him from under your nose, even with the distraction my hearth-watchers started to get Geric out of the way. This convenience was much better.

"I'm thinking of raising him as my own. A child can be a charming accessory for any noble lady, and it will save me the trouble of having to go through the unpleasantness of bearing one myself. He already passed the bawling baby stage and is conveniently mobile, and so will do nicely."

Isi's jaw flexed, and she leaned forward as if preparing to take a step. Selia laughed, so light and fresh it was as if the moonlight sang. She rubbed a consoling hand on Isi's arm.

"There, there now, we can still talk about his fate. Nothing is decided for certain. I will appreciate your input greatly. You see, Crown Princess, how reasonable I can be when you play nice? I will save your child. I won't wring his tiny little neck and toss him to the hounds, but only so long as you don't cause any trouble. You want him safe more than anything. Oh yes, you do, I can see the power of your desire wetting your eyes and quivering your adorable little chin." Selia stroked Isi's chin with her finger. "You will do anything to protect him. No need to say it. And I *will* protect him, I swear it. I will keep him safe as long as you and your friends are good girls."

Everything inside Rin was screaming, *No, no, no! That's Razo up there, that's Tusken. Stop listening to her. Stop!* She clung to the rocks in the cairn and tried to stand, but her legs ached with shaking, and everything seemed too hard. The effort exhausted her muscles, and Rin slumped back to the ground, the lulling of Selia's voice soothing the anger from her blood.

"It was easy to coax Tusken away from those soldiers. They were at camp. Geric was in a tent with a physician, and twenty men were guarding one little boy. He was so darling! Overjoyed to see a fair-haired lady just like his own mother. He was eager to come, and that short soldier only too happy to carry him for me. I left my men and hearthwatchers in the wood. They never had to use arrows or fire. Sweet of you to raise such a compliant child."

Rin wanted nothing more than to curl up and go to sleep. Still on the ground, she lay on her side, extending her arm to rest under her head. Her hand brushed something hard—the exposed root of a tree, arching up out of the dirt like a bent knee. *A tree.* She crawled, following the root to the tree. The cairn now completely blocked all sight of the girls and Selia.

Rin leaned against the trunk . . . *please, please* . . . aching for the escape of trees. She did not dare open herself to the tree, but her skin crawled with Selia's voice and she was desperate for relief. Just to be near the tree helped a little, just to try and remember how she used to feel inside that uncomplicated stillness. *Green and buzzing, drowsy and sweet*, she reminded herself, and she almost heard that murmur in memory. Heard it in a different way than she heard the urgent rasping of crickets spilling out of the wood or Selia's voice from the other side of the cairn. Heard it through her skin or deep in her chest.

". . . I will make sure Tusken never wants for anything . . ."

Stop, don't listen. Rin pressed herself closer but still kept herself from opening her senses to the tree. She wished she could plant her feet in soil and grow thick bark, let her arms trail through breezes and twist toward the sky. That promised safety. Trees did not care about what people said, did not understand. Just the slow throb of sap, the quiet stretch of roots, the sleepy crackle of leaves feeling a breeze . . .

Rin shut her eyes and insisted that her body relax. *Remember the rhythm of sap, leaves tasting wind, trunk a fortress of memory, bark thick, limbs strong . . .* Selia's voice slithered back into her consciousness.

"I really hated it when the king of Bayern died and you became a queen before I could."

Rin put her hands over her ears, but it did not matter. Even blocking out the sound of Selia's voice, the feeling of the words continued to roll around in her mind until Rin yearned to hear them again. Her hands dropped.

"But one can't rush into things—no, plans must be carefully laid, and sometimes that takes years. Oh, we have so much catching up to do! Or at least I do. Why am I always catching up to you, when I can run faster and think faster? Do you know? It is irritating. Still, I will always be sure that . . ."

No.

". . . and Tusken will be as happy as an otter in . . ."

No.

". . . his very life depends on . . ."

No! Stop listening to her. Remember the trees. Relax. Rin breathed, filling her lungs, her center. *I am nothing. I am part of the scenery, a fallen leaf, a scrap of bark. No danger, no time, no rush.*

Her trembling slowed, and her thoughts cleared as if the wind had swept fallen leaves from her mind. Before she could lose the stillness, Rin gripped her hands into fists and left the shelter of the cairn.

The first few steps were the worst. If anyone looked her direction, they would see a girl moving toward the wood. So she went slowly, no motion worth drawing notice, no sound to provoke a turn of head.

When hunting, silence was essential. But sneaking past people required seeming casualness as well. No exaggerated tiptoeing or fleeing from tree to tree. Back home, no one bothered to look at Rin much, and she was practiced at keeping quiet. She could stroll behind one of her brothers and lift the meat out of the sandwich in his hand without drawing attention. That trick always made Razo laugh.

Razo. The thought of her brother kept her moving through the night, slow but persistent, and she was reminded of a root, seemingly still yet always digging, always moving. She entered the deeper wood in order to skirt Selia and her guards, then swing back to the cage. Keeping one hand up, she touched trees in passing, just to remind her of the steady peace she was trying to maintain, the voice of trees flowing through her, the drowsy hum of sap and water, the wistful murmur of leaves on wind.

The green world, she named that place where she could hear trees. It had been like a second surface to everything, a soft barrier she could lean through. When completely submerged in green, she was immobile. But if she could barely touch it, lean half in and half out, perhaps she could gain some of that clarity and slowness and still keep moving forward.

This was not like sneaking with Razo. She quivered with the strange and yet familiar impression that she was different somehow. Air filled her in a new way, thick and cool and fluid, like water filled a fish.

Wonder at what she was doing was distracting. She pushed aside her thoughts, focusing on balancing herself in that place where Selia's voice did not matter, where panic could not turn her into a useless, quivering animal. She forced herself to relax in order to maintain the nearness of the green world, physically trembling with the effort. What she tried seemed impossible—struggling to slow, fighting to be calm, laboring for rest. She might as well scream for quiet. As she thought it, she realized how absurd it really was, and in that moment the stillness crumbled. There was no calm, no control. Selia's voice slammed back into her head.

". . . could just chat with you all night it seems! I have a particular fondness for words. I suppose you know that, Crown Princess. This has been a true joy, but the night grows chill and we should retire indoors."

Rin was alone in a foreign wood, vulnerable, confused, anxious to run away but stuck to the spot with fear. Her heart pounded as if it wanted to escape from her chest, her vision wavered, her whole self seemed to be thudding away with the heartbeats, and she gasped just to breathe.

"Stop it," she told herself in a haggard whisper. "Stop. Be like Isi, like Razo. Fearless and just fine. Do it."

She rested against a tree, still not daring to actually listen, sweating as she fought for the courage to be calm. The greenness seemed closer, so she shut her eyes and bid herself slip toward it, almost hearing the tree's low rumbles, almost tasting that tranquility. When she was no longer aware of Selia's voice in the distance, she walked on.

Though she moved as slowly and casually as a deer nosing for greens, the effort made her muscles warm. Razo and Tusken were in a cage, Isi and the others trapped by that voice, and if the soldiers noticed Rin they would kill her and Razo and Tusken too because Selia had said she would kill them if the girls did not do as she said and stay still and . . .

No. Think about Razo. This was just a game. She was playing stealth. She'd stolen Jef's sandwich and was sneaking away, that was all. To go laugh with Razo. She could do this.

She was just a tree.

It seemed she would never reach the spot, then suddenly she was there. An oak tree, large, ponderous. The cage was lashed with ropes to one of its thick base limbs, hanging above the lapping fire. Selia was heading back to the castle. Isi, Enna, and Dasha were following, flanked on all sides by soldiers. The fire sisters were not bound. They would go willingly or not at all.

Most of the soldiers were moving toward the castle. Even those stuck to their knees in mud had managed to dig themselves out. Only about ten remained. They would return their attention to the cage and take Razo and Tusken back to the castle too. Rin did not have much time.

She pulled a knife from the pack on her back and gripped its blade with her teeth while she climbed. She lay flat on the branch holding the cage and pulled herself closer. Razo was watching, eyes unblinking, terrified and hopeful too. Tusken was asleep in his arms. At the rope now, high enough that the fire below was just gusts of warmth and wind-battered smoke, she pulled the knife from her teeth to show Razo her only weapon. He pointed to a fat, intricate knot securing the rod in the latch, then he made a sawing gesture in his hand. Rin cut at the rope, the effort making the metal cage creak. Her heart blasted with each beat. Razo shut his eyes, his lips muttering something that looked like, "Please, please, please." Just as Aileann had in Kelish. The echo gave Rin chills.

At last her knife hit the metal rod, and Rin pulled the rope loose, opening the door. Relief poured through her like warm water. She stuck the knife in the ropes for Razo to pick up and took Tusken from his arms. The sudden weight almost threw her from the tree, but she gripped the sleeping boy and bade her trembling legs to hold her steady. She inched along the branch to the trunk, Razo behind her. Tusken moaned softly in his sleep, and even in that moment of terror, balancing for her life, scraping her legs on the bark and barely able to move, she could not help pressing her lips against his damp brow. He smelled of road dust and Razo's own sweat. Her heart yearned for him and she thought, *I'll protect you, lamby. I'll die for you.*

She felt the moment when she passed from the bare branch to the curtained privacy of the tree's foliage, felt it like a sigh. Razo was just behind her. That was when they heard the shouting.

"They've seen the empty cage," Razo whispered. "We've got to run, now."

"Just climb a little higher and they won't find us."

"Rinna, come on, we—"

"We can't run fast enough. They'll catch us on the ground. The tree will hide us."

Razo's eyes darted wildly, trying to see the soldiers through the leaves. "I'll drop first, then you give me Tusken and—"

"Climb up, Razo," she said. "They'll look for movement, they'll look on the ground. They won't look up. People rarely look up, rarely notice trees at all. Listen to me and climb!"

Razo hesitated. Rin did not talk like that to Razo. This journey was pulling words and demands out of her, and she feared she'd done wrong. When she spoke again, it was in the barest whisper.

"Please. I know trees, and I know people. This will work."

Razo looked with longing at the ground, but he nodded and took Tusken from her arms.

The boy was so completely asleep he did not even moan as Razo propped him on his shoulder, holding him with one hand and climbing the tree with the other. They went up two more branches to where the leaves were thickest.

Razo was staring down, scratching nervously at his hair, and glancing back at Rin with an "Are you sure?" expression. She nodded. If the soldiers stood close to the oak's trunk and looked up, they would most definitely see three people huddled there. But she believed they would not look.

Rin sat next to Razo, sharing a branch, the three of them squeezed between two other limbs. Razo's breath was coming in fast huffs, from the exertion of climbing with one arm, but also, Rin guessed, from fear. Voices darted their way, shouts of confusion and anger at the cage hanging empty. Now the soldiers would search the wood.

She needed to stay still, stay quiet. But Rin's heart was thumping again as if to break free, her limbs shaking. Selia had said she would kill Razo and Tusken. Surely she would now that Rin had set them free. And kill Rin too. All of them, in retribution for what Rin had done. The fright and effort burned, and hot tears oozed down her cheeks. Fear was everything and everything hurt so much, she wondered if she might die.

Calm. Please, be calm.

She was too terrified to remember that greenness into herself. She felt ravaged by her memory of Selia's words, ruined, sure that death was imminent for all of them, and it was her fault. The fear and guilt was white-hot pain. Her trembling shook Tusken, and he murmured. What if he woke and cried out? The searchers would find them in an instant. Razo seemed to be shaking as much as she. They needed to calm.

Inside the tree, water flowed like blood in a body, keeping the branches strong and the leaves alive and green. So sleepy, so content with its roots in the wonderful dampness of deep, deep soil, with the sun down and the leaves at rest. Rin put one of her arms around her brother's shoulder, and between them embraced Tusken, still fast asleep.

Razo's eyes met hers, startled and unsure.

"Try to sleep," she mouthed silently.

Razo grimaced, his eyes saying, "Are you crazy?"

She took a deep breath to show that she was trying, then closed her own eyes. Hoofbeats and shouts from the searchers made her heartbeats scatter and her legs ache, but if she could absorb the calm of the tree, perhaps Razo and Tusken would feel it from her.

She knew that if she listened to the tree, she was sure to encounter that nauseating wrongness. That fear was nothing compared to her terror of Selia and her searchers. Shouts raised goose bumps on her arms, but she clung both to the tree and to the idea of the tree. She could feel her brother start to relax beside her, his breath slowing almost to the pace of Tusken's calm inhales and exhales. The nausea was creeping around her, the loathing filling her limbs like water in a jar. She welcomed it now, ready to greet that horror over the reality below. Her stomach rolled, her bones shuddered, but she did not let go.

Still half-aware of the danger outside their house of leaves, Rin plunged herself through the sickening dread into oak-bound memories until the present was a distant idea . . . and then, just gone.

in's mind was falling through rings of memory, rains and drafts and seasons of early cold, days of clouds and days of sun, circles and circles, back and deeper, protected inside a hide of bark, tender roots buried deep, fragile leaves lifted high.

She'd grown up plunging into the thoughts of trees, but this felt new. Perhaps she experienced it differently because she had a name for it now—tree-speaking. Or perhaps in her desperation for escape she submerged herself deeper than ever before. She let all these possibilities pass through her like water through roots, without stopping to consider. Still her mind fell.

It was not a dream—time still moved in dreams, things happened in order. This was a moment with no comprehension of time, like a circle has no beginning or end. Rin met herself there, saw herself in a way without seeing—a girl who listens to trees.

The slick wrongness poured over her, coated her. But she did not try to flee, still aware that the terror that existed without was worse. She needed to keep Razo and Tusken resting and quiet, and she needed to hide from searchers, from Selia.

Alongside the tree's own memories of rain and sun and storm, Rin met her own memory, the one she'd been fleeing from for months—*Wilem is beside her in a tree, leaning near, and warmth rushes through her whole body as she realizes, I can make him stay.*

Rin jolted, almost waking from the tree sleep. Stumbling across that memory was like tripping on a hidden root and falling flat. She became aware of cicadas screaming in the forest night, the crackle of leaves rubbing in the breeze. Rin's heart slammed into her ribs, and she felt sleeping Tusken stir and heard Razo moan.

No, Rin. Calm. Peace. If embracing the memory of Wilem was the only way to maintain the tree's calm, then she would face it. That spinning wrongness clutched at her, but she clenched her jaw and submitted to the memory—not the thin, scrubbed thing she'd toyed with these past months. The truth of it, all of it.

∞

For the first time since Nordra's stick, Rin desperately wants something for herself. Razo was her best friend, but he's gone off into the world, and the homestead has become just a place for him to visit. Besides, he has Dasha. Who does Rin have?

For one afternoon, she has Wilem.

He comes over to wrestle and run with the Agget-kin, and mostly with Kif and Len, two of Rin's older nephews. She likes the way Wilem looks, black eyes and black hair that is so long in front he has to push it out of his eyes. His eyeteeth are especially pointy, and when he smiles they peek below his lips and give him an exciting, feral look. She finds it easy to fall into Wilem's pattern of speech, his careless but thoughtful way of seeing the world, easier than anyone besides Razo and Ma. It is a pleasure to emulate him, to feel as he must feel.

They sit in a tree all afternoon, hiding from work and tossing pine cones. And leaning closer to each other. The smell of his skin . . . That treetop afternoon seems like the life of a different Rin. She is as carefree as Razo, has some of that pretty sauciness that Ulan does when she tosses her hair and laughs, some of that sweet girliness that Genna does when she bats her lashes. Rin does not worry about all the chores she is missing and making sure the little ones are fed and readied for bed—for the first time, she feels not like Ma's shadow, but like her own girl. A girl who might be worth knowing. She feels extraordinary.

She takes deadly aim at her brother Jef's tousled head and pegs him with a pine cone. He looks around wildly, but not up. People rarely look up, she realizes.

Wilem laughs. "You're wild, Rinna. You're dangerous."

She's never wanted to kiss someone before. But now as she leans against Wilem, she imagines how it might be—like how she feels when her hair is freshly washed and a warm breeze blows it back from her face, like when her belly is full of roasted quail and fresh bread. Extraordinary.

Dusk settles around them in great dark folds, and the nephews come looking for their friend.

"Wilem!" they shout, not knowing which tree is his perch. "Come on, we've got a prank planned. Are you still here? Come out!"

Without a word to Rin, Wilem begins to scramble down the tree. Rin feels all the air go out of her, all the girliness and prettiness and possibilities. She climbs down after him, faster than is safe. Her only thought is, If Wilem goes away, the wild Rin goes too. And she wants to keep that Rin so badly, she wants to cling to her and not return to being Ma's shadow— silent, harmless, forgettable.

She's nearly climbed to the Forest floor when in her haste, she slips off a branch and into Wilem. He catches her. And he doesn't let go. Her heart bangs against his chest, a sensation that's pleasantly painful, and with barely a hesitation, she breaks that safe barrier she's built since Nordra and the stick. She speaks her desire.

"Stay," she tells him. She does not just say the word—she speaks it with meaning, with intent. She hurls the word like a stone. He stays, for the moment at least. But his gaze shifts, his arm drops from her back. One word won't keep him.

This is when she lies.

She studies his face, as she did long ago with Nordra, and

knows what words will convince him to stay. She can read his anxious doubt—his admiration of her nephews is intense, and he fears they think him a hanger-on.

Don't, Rin, she warns herself, but she feels so free, so wild; no fledgling on the nest but a falcon commanding the winds.

"Kif and Len never really liked you, you know," she says, one hand smoothing Wilem's tunic. His chest muscles flex under her hand.

"What do you mean?"

She glances up at him through her lashes and then back down.

"Oh, I'm sorry, I thought you knew how they are. Meaner than hungry dogs. They talk about you when you're not here, say you're boring and foolish. They were planning some cruel joke on you tonight, that's why I wanted to keep you away from them."

"But . . . they wanted my help pranking Jef."

She shakes her head sadly. "Kif and Len are waiting by Jef's house, but they mean to shove you into the dung pit." That was not a playful prank—that was the kind of cruel trick no kin of Ma would dare pull.

Wilem's brows pinch together. "Why?"

His sadness almost changes her mind then, but there are so many unspoken words beckoning her, filling the world with new risks, new chances and adventures. She's reminded of her brother Deet's report of drinking his first ale in the city, how it was bitter and made his stomach sore, but he did not want to stop drinking. Words are ale on her tongue and in her belly, heavy and foul. And irresistible.

She lies some more. "They're blind for not liking you. It makes me so angry. I didn't want to tell you, I wanted to keep you with me, keep you safe from their cruelty. You should stay with me, be my friend. I won't treat you like that. You're smarter than them anyhow, so let's play a trick on them instead."

"Sure, that's what we'll do." Wilem's eyes light with pained pride. "We'll show them."

Words are easy when she allows herself to use them without fear or shame. Now speaking is like that rare and perfect kind of sleep when she can control her dreams, guiding her own mind to what images she wants to see. She is controlling this moment. She is not a feeble stick of a girl after all. All this time wasted, acting as Ma's shadow, hiding inside others' behaviors, being small, dismissible. Now she feels power like a staff in her hands. Even the wrongness of what she does thrills her.

Why has she been so afraid of words? They are wonderful!

She steps closer to Wilem. "They mocked you, said you'd never kissed a girl. They said you would be too afraid to kiss me. I said you weren't afraid."

She moves even closer and puts her hands on his arms. It feels dangerous, the most dangerous thing she's ever done. But she feels crazy with words, she feels wild. She believes she can keep creating this perfect dream for herself, and it will never have a chance to fray and fall apart. She just has to keep talking.

"Kiss me, Wilem. Just kiss me, and prove everyone wrong. You'll show them."

Kiss me. They are not idle words. She can feel the strength of them, a command as sure as if she were his queen. And he obeys. He holds her arms, he kisses her lips, fast and hard. It does not feel good like a breeze combing through freshly washed hair. It feels like what it is—a hard, cold lie pretending to be affection.

"See? I did it! I'm not afraid." But there is a sadness in his eyes, as if he has been asked to give away something precious, like Nordra handing over her doeskin boots.

"Kiss me more," Rin demands. "Everyone thinks of you as that lonely boy with a boring brother. They don't really care about you. But I care. I'm the only one, Wilem. If you want Kif and Len to respect you, if you want to be more than just that boy, you need to want to kiss me. You need to be with me."

His eyes are hot. He leans to her again, meeting mouth to mouth. She grabs his hair and holds him to her lips, kissing awkwardly, trying to find in that touch the feeling she left up in the tree, trying to find the Rin whom Wilem called wild. And he is trying to please her. He is in pain from her words, she knows, and he is desperate for her touch to take away that pain. She allows his lips to move with hers, against hers, to feel that his lips are soft, his chin and cheeks rough. She touches her tongue to his, and the feel of it startles her heart. She grips his arms with her fingers, pulling him even closer, her lips strong, her mouth open, urgent, getting cross that she's still so hollow. She feels wild. But not loved.

Wilem stumbles back and looks at her, breathing through his mouth. He says, "What now?"

You should want to kiss me, *she thinks. You should want to stay near me. I shouldn't need to trick you for a kiss.*

She hates the mean, hard sensation in her heart when she thinks that, hates realizing that Wilem does not love her. So she just shrugs, wishing him gone. And he goes, looking as sad as a rain-beaten sapling with his head hanging down, heavy with her lies.

It is a relief not to be burdened with regret. Anger at his stupidity feels so much nicer.

A hot, sweet sensation fills her, burning and delicious, and she walks through the homestead for the first time knowing that she is better than everyone. There are ways to make them see that. She can read their faces as clearly as looking at the sky to tell the weather. She's always been able to see lies and truths in people's eyes, to guess what thoughts they hid, though since making Nordra cry, she forbade herself from speaking on it. No more shackles, no more rules. Now she is powerful Rin.

Is this who she has been all along? When she's not Ma's shadow, when she's not mirroring those around her or huddled up, abashed and afraid to speak, is she so bold, so pretty and fearless, so strong? Then why has she been hiding? The true Rin is wonderful.

Kif and Len return later, claiming that Wilem accused Rin of lying and kissing him.

"We told him to go wash his nethers with pine cones," says Kif.

"Our aunt Rin would do no such thing," says Len. "Don't know what's gotten into that pokey-toothed fool."

"Wilem is no good," Rin says. "I was shocked by the things he said about you. No one talks like that about Agget-kin."

"That little rodent!" says Kif. "I'll never speak to Wilem again."

What a pleasure to lie! Her feet do not touch the ground, her blood rushes through her as warm as sleep, her smile feels real. She might do anything to nourish that invulnerable sensation, might cling to it for days, or perhaps forever.

But the next person she sees is Ma.

"What did Wilem do?" Ma asks, stepping onto her porch in her sleep clothes, her fists on her hips. "Go on and tell me, Rin, and I'll thrash his tunic off his hide."

Rin sees her ma's round face, her white-streaked black hair, frizzy and incorrigible, pulling free from its scarf, her brown eyes that see everybody. Ma cares for every person in the world the same, except for Rin. She calls Rin her lily on a pond, her morning bird song, and everyone knows that Ma loves her daughter just a little more.

Rin's heart isn't floating anymore. Her hands and feet feel made of stone.

"Nothing. Honest, Ma, he didn't do anything."

"You sure, my honey-eyed girl? You sure? Don't protect him, now. I won't put up with naughtiness, not in my homestead, not to my baby girl."

Still Rin wants to cling to her strength, wants to keep those words that remake the world into whatever she likes. And she doesn't want to feel sorrow for what she did to Wilem—she wants Ma to hate him, shoo him away, punish him for not wanting to kiss her, for having to be tricked, for leaving so easily.

"You just tell me the truth and I'll take care of it," says Ma.

The truth. Rin cannot tell her that. "He didn't do anything. We were playing a game. It was just a misunderstanding."

Ma frowns, but nods and goes back inside. Kif and Len groan, discouraged the fun of war is already over. They leave her standing under a fir tree. It is spring, and the night air has a bite to it.

The warmth, the surety, the strength drain from her, leaving her chilled and discarded, a late-winter cellar root. She waits until Ma is asleep before crawling under the blanket beside her, huddled on the edge of the cot, her eyes wide. The memory of that delicious strength stays with her, like the scent of Wilem on her mouth. She enjoyed it. Even now she does not feel as bad as she should, and so she knows that makes her worse than bad.

She tosses in bed that night, the chill of her guilt settling over her. She cannot undo what she did. She cannot run far enough to get away from hurting Wilem, from lying and commanding. But even more, she is caged by the feeling that the true Rin— her deepest self, who was not simply mirroring others—was

*the girl who lied, who hurt and did not care. At her core, she is
someone Ma would not love. All night, wrestling in the dark
with sleep and with truth, she works to bury herself.*

<hr />

Rin slept inside the oak's thoughts. Its own memories of
weather and growth continued to hum, and like a pond, its
stillness reflected back herself. Suspended moments from
her life swirled, pelting her like rocks lifted in a windstorm.
She saw them the way a tree sees its years, rings circling each
other, all memory existing at once—*living in the Forest in silence, not tree and not girl; getting lost in the trees all day and finally
finding her way home, only to discover no one has noticed she's been missing; watching Razo leave the Forest for Tira, and feeling as if her insides
have been scraped out and dumped aside; realizing for the first time that
she is too big to curl up on her ma's lap.*

There, pulsing white, was seven-year-old Rin watching
Nordra play. Thinking with the tree made Rin's own thoughts
clear as snowmelt, and she saw that memory anew. *It is the
first time in her life she is without Ma and Razo. She feels so terrifyingly
alone, she scrambles for something to make her stronger, to make her all
right, and discovers an ability sleeping inside her—to see, to speak, to
command. That desire, that talent awakes, never to sleep again. The urge
is compelling, but Rin fears the loss of Ma's love and squashes it down.*

Rin turned inside the tree, tracing memories from the
years that followed Nordra and the stick, and saw how weakened she became, fighting something unknown inside, her

whole self out of balance, tilting. The tree-speaking gave her a place to lean, but it could not cure her.

Other memories pulsed hot, linked in a white chain from Nordra and the stick to the present—*saying anything to keep Wilem close; warning Cilie to keep away from Tusken; asking Razo to guard Tusken with his life; convincing the woman in the inn not to jump; telling that squat mercenary to let the girl go.* There were more to these moments than she'd realized, a force behind her words, a power in her voice.

With a rising horror, Rin's sleep-self turned to face the most recent memories—*standing behind a cairn of stones, Razo and Tusken in a cage; feeling pinned by Selia's words, subdued and help-less. Selia speaking. Rin speaking. Words harder than words should be, words like wind, words like fire.*

Rin quaked but forced herself to name it.

I have people-speaking. I am like Selia.

Only then did what was inside her become worse than the world outside. Rin opened her eyes, barely swallowing a scream.

in breathed in hard, shuddering gasps, taking in the waking world—the oak tree, the dark sky just stirred by light, Tusken asleep, and Razo staring.

"Are you all right?" he whispered.

She nodded. "A . . . nightmare."

"Don't blame you. You were sleeping hard there at the end. I poked you for a bit but you didn't wake. Kind of scared me."

Rin sat up and leaves tumbled from her head onto her lap. Her hand flew to her hair, and she was suddenly terrified that she'd been turning into a tree.

Razo smiled. "I decorated you while you slept. Made you a little crown. I stuffed one leaf up your nose, but you just sneezed it out and kept sleeping."

I wasn't really sleeping, Rin thought. *I was—*She felt a jolt pass through her as she remembered her dream thoughts. *People-speaking.* She tasted bile on the back of her tongue. Could she really have people-speaking? That "curse" as Enna had called it, that decay that turned people into monsters who forced others to do what they did not will?

Rin hunched over, imagining the huge gray worm of her nightmares curled inside her. All her life, believing she was bad, she clenched up, acted with caution, never sure what she was hiding from. Could she give it a name now? *People-speaking.*

Isi had said it was the most dangerous of all the speaking gifts, the one sure to corrupt the speaker. Would she turn into another Selia? She feared she'd already begun—with Wilem, she'd begun.

Razo was lying back on a branch. Tusken was asleep on his chest, his face nestled into Razo's neck. Looking at them fanned away some of the smoke of her panic. She did not matter, not now. But she'd walk across the ocean to keep Razo and Tusken safe.

Rin peered through the leaves. She could see the dark shape of Castle Daire. "Is it still the same night?"

"What? Of course it is, though near dawn. I think I dozed there for a bit, and I haven't heard anyone since I woke up. They must be running in all directions, trying to find us before Selia notices we're missing and gets so angry her face swells up like a frog's." This thought seemed to please Razo, and he closed his eyes for a moment, smiling. "All the same, they're bound to come back for the cage, empty or not, so I think now would be a good time to flee."

Rin climbed down first, hating the moment her body left

the cover of leaves. Her foot crunched on acorns, and she winced in anticipation of crossbow bolts. Razo lowered himself to a branch farther down until he could hand her the sleeping boy. She carried Tusken as they walked, pressing his body as close to her chest as she had strength in her arms.

He's all right, she told herself. *He's out of that cage. That woman didn't hurt him. We'll get him back to his ma again.* After a cramped, short night resting in a tree, her arms gave out much sooner than she would have liked, and she reluctantly handed Tusken back to Razo. Razo groaned with the boy's weight.

"You think he's all right?" he whispered. "The way he sleeps . . ."

"He always sleeps like the dead."

"Good boy. Shows real intelligence, I say." Razo rubbed his chin softly against the boy's head. "He wore himself out yesterday, fussing and crying, poor little man. It hasn't been a feast-day banquet, I guess I can tell you. But we did all right, Tusken and I. We're pals."

She had not recovered from the oak sleep yet—her head felt heavy on her shoulders as if filled with sap, her eyes unused to looking around. "Razo, the girls . . ."

"I know." His voice was tight.

"What are we going to do?"

"Rescue them, of course. Don't worry, I'm plotting. But first I need to be sure you and Tusken are safe."

Razo had changed these past couple of years, no question,

and not just his height. He reeked with confidence. Rin watched him as she might watch a squirrel if she was lost in the deep Forest, with a hope it would lead her to its cache of nuts.

"Finn left us in Hendric to ride for Geric, to warn him we were going to Kel. Maybe we should get Tusken to safety and wait for Geric to come—"

"Come siege Castle Daire? Start a war with Kel? And in the meantime, leaving Dasha, Enna, and Isi at the mercy of Selia? Not on your life. I'm going in there tonight and I'm going to get those girls out."

Rin's stomach did flip-flops like a fish on the riverbank. How could Razo sneak into a defended fortress and rescue three girls without meeting a sword point? But she did not dare argue. The idea of people-speaking throbbed and stung, making her conscious of her every word.

They did not talk, careful in their footsteps to keep quiet. Razo's face became strained and red, and he seemed scarcely able to hold Tusken. They reached a copse of trees that wore their leaves low, creating an enclosure nearly as solid as a wattle-and-daub house. Razo collapsed inside, muttering that he needed to rest for a few moments. Rin guessed he had not had much sleep or food those past days.

Razo lay Tusken gently on a patch of grass and rested his own head on a tree root, stretching his legs and arms and groaning as if in pain.

"We need to lay low until night offers us some cover. It

won't do our girls any good if I go barging at the castle in full sun and get shot down before I can even scale a wall."

"If you take a nap," Rin said, cautious with each word, "I can watch."

"I think I'd better . . ." Razo's eyes closed, and instantly came the low, grumbling snores she knew well. Tusken must have been used to the noise too, because he rolled in his sleep and nestled closer to Razo.

Dawn dripped through the leaves onto Rin's hands. She watched the two boys in their rest, her ears attuned to the sounds of the wood. Selia's searchers were out there. They would find them, kill Rin and probably Razo too, since he proved to be too much trouble, and take Tusken away. And beneath that worry, the slow, dark, greasy snake kept moving under her skin, that awareness of something wrong. After an hour or more, the anxiety became painful. Her heart beat so hard, it radiated sharp jabs through her chest.

I've got to keep watch, she told herself. *I need to stay calm. I need to protect them.*

But it was becoming unbearable. The anxiety of their situation beat at her, and she could not shut off the questions. *Am I a people-speaker? Have I always been? Am I going to turn into a Selia?*

The night before she had battled past the grimness that had blocked her from the trees' thoughts, and she had met the memory of what she'd done to Wilem and come out again. Perhaps she just needed more understanding and another encounter with trees to be at peace. She brushed her hand down the bark, alert to the silent hum of the tree. The crackle of bark and awareness of sunlight. A thrum that promised cool silence deep in the core.

She closed her eyes, succumbing to the question until she was inside the tree's thoughts, spinning again inside her own memories.

⚜

It's the morning after Wilem, and she feels as if she were tied in a knot only to pull loose by sunup. The events of last night are oddly hazy. She does not recall exactly what happened, and a tang of fear makes her fight against trying to recall. But there is a loose ache moving inside her, and she has an idea that if she just allows herself to speak freely, the ache will melt into relief—delight even. Some mysterious elation is still delicious on her tongue, making her insides rumble with hunger.

But there's Ma, humming while she works, smiling at her daughter. Guilt sinks inside Rin, and she's sure that she said something unforgivable, something that would make Ma not love her. So Rin stays quiet, helps prepare breakfast and clean up, and every moment that ticks by, she feels stretched farther away from that wild and brilliant Rin. Each time Ma touches her, speaks to her, Rin feels certain that she doesn't belong in this warm, happy house beside her good mother.

As soon as she can, she runs.

She runs away from the homestead and their neighbors, toward deepness. She falls into a fir tree, insisting herself into its thoughts, demanding its comfort. She expects the woody thoughts of trees to still her, but instead she is surrounded by what she's done. I lied to Wilem, I shattered his confidence, I filled him with sadness, and I did not even care. And I want to be that powerful again. *The memory catches her in its teeth.*

She's on her hands and knees, breathless. Scrambling back to her feet, she stumbles into an aspen grove, the round leaves chiming, the sunlight filtered to soft warmth. She tumbles against knotty white bark.

Take it away, *she begs.* Change me, undo me, make it not real. Make me someone else.

The tree does not hear her and obey, not as Wilem had. The tree simply reflects back to her what she is, what she's done. She is a girl with a desire to speak out and control, to raise herself above the rest. And knowing it was wrong, she still claimed that power and used it against Wilem. But she's never heard of people-speaking, doesn't comprehend what's happening, knows only that she feels wrong. That confusion and wrongness are a black loathing that suffocates her. She clings to the tree, and the sensation intensifies, burns spitting hot and smoky like grease in the fire.

She doesn't want to remember, she wants oblivion, and all the trees offer is the truth—who she is, what she's done. Feeling twisted and yanked and dumped on the ground, she rips apart her own memory so she won't have to look at it anymore. But hiding from what she did can't ease her wrongness.

I'm bad. Ma won't love me if she knows. I'm—

She pulls away from the tree, crouches over her knees, and cries for as long as the tears will come.

in's thoughts heaved inside her. She pushed away from the tree and hunched over, her belly and throat cramping. She pressed her hands against her eyes, against her chest, breathing until she could get herself under control, trying to keep quiet so as not to wake Razo and Tusken.

A rotting sensation throbbed in her gut, reminding her of what she'd done. But there was a little comfort too, just to have a glimpse of clarity. The trees of her Forest had not rejected her. It was the other way around—she had flinched away from them. These past months, she thought she'd thrown away the memory of what happened with Wilem and what she discovered about herself. But it had swelled inside her, the hidden thought becoming the loudest in her head. Ever since, when she'd tried to listen to the trees' calmness, the thought they reflected back to her was that pulsating secret that lurked just below the surface. She'd sought peace, but the memory of her mistake and the glimpse of her wrongness sickened her. Inside a tree's thoughts, she was surrounded by her own self. And after Wilem, that was a place she did not want to be.

I didn't know, she tried to comfort herself. She had not known such a thing as people-speaking existed; she had never met anyone like Selia.

Any child of Ma's should know better than to act that way, she thought. *I knew it was wrong, even if I didn't know why, and I did it anyway.*

That gray worm stretched, reminding her that she still wanted to be that wild Rin, still yearned to speak like Selia, to not be afraid of herself, to claim what she could do, and to let everyone see her shine.

Razo gasped and sat upright, his hands clutching his chest. He looked around deliriously until he saw Tusken beside him. The little boy snorted in his sleep and flopped onto his other side, his mouth open and drooling. Razo breathed out in relief, patting the boy's head.

"Thought he was gone. Dreamed she took him." He rubbed the heels of his hands into his eyes. "Ugh, that was an ugly dream. I won't be sleeping any more today. Did you hear anything out there?"

Rin shook her head, ashamed she had not been paying attention. Razo stole out, tiptoeing around their small glade, pausing to listen. He slipped back in and sighed as he sat, speaking low so his voice would not carry beyond their tree. "Now, you'd better tell me why you're being so naughty and hiding things from me."

Rin's heart was a startled jackrabbit. "Wh-what?"

Razo looked at her hard, his brown eyes glittering in the rising sunlight. "Well, I *was* teasing, going to accuse you of hiding all the food. But since you're acting guiltier than Incher with his pockets full of bread dough, why don't you just tell me what you thought I meant?"

"Nothing." She shook her head, shrugged, looked away. "I didn't . . . I mean, nothing . . ."

Razo's gaze was bright. "That won't do it, Rinna-roo. You're hiding something from me. Come on before I get my feelings hurt and start to cry." He let his lower lip quiver.

She smiled with a shrug. "Nothing really. I just . . . I'm realizing that I had—or have—some kind of understanding of trees. Sort of."

"Understanding of trees. Interesting. Go on."

He was not going to let her get away with shrugging it off. She could tell him this part but not her fears about people-speaking, of course. "Sometimes I can think more clearly when I'm close to a tree, like I'm thinking with it. And I can kind of hear them, be aware of where their roots are growing or their branches, feel the memory of past years and weather inside their trunks, and it makes me . . . makes me calmer to do it." She was silent a moment, listening for searchers before asking, "Can you do that?"

Razo blinked. "Am I still asleep? 'Cause you sound like you're talking in dream weirdness."

Rin cleared her throat. "Isi called it tree-speaking."

Razo slapped the ground, but even in his passion he was careful to keep his voice low. "Aw, really? Tree-speaking? That's not fair. Why does everyone—wait, maybe it's me. Do you think it's me? I mean, Enna and Isi, and Dasha too, now you. Maybe there's something about me that sort of sparks something in people, and wherever I go, people just start understanding everything because it . . . because I . . ."

"I think Isi could talk to horses and birds before she came to Bayern, and Dasha knew water-speaking when she was a little girl in Tira."

Razo considered this. "All right, all right. But all the same—" He considered it some more. "But . . . but . . . yes, all right." He considered again. "Fine. That's . . . you're prob-ably right. Fine. But did you know that I'm deadly good with a sling?" He nudged her with his elbow. "Huh? Did you know that? I'll bet you didn't know that. Huh? Huh?"

Rin swatted his arm away, trying not to laugh, or he was sure to get a big head.

"So, trees, huh? Well, fine, as long as that's all."

Rin let her face go dead serious. "Also, I can talk to bears and wolverines."

"You're joking now. You're teasing me now. I can tell." He stared at his sister as if he could see through her eyes to her thoughts beyond. Rin did not flinch. "You're not teasing, are you?"

She could not help the smile that teased the corners of her mouth. He sighed and leaned back.

"You *are* joking. Good. Or not. It would've come in handy about now, commanding an army of bears to go attack the castle."

"And wolverines."

"Right. And wolverines. But well enough. What good's bear-speaking anyway? I tell you, I'm honestly relieved not to have such a burden. Couldn't stand to have to talk to bears all the time. It's *I love berries and fish*, day and night. And their breath stinks."

"Not like anyone else I know."

"So you say." His look was suspicious. "You're still being dodgy. Are you hiding something else?"

"Only this . . ." She pulled a handful of grass from the ground behind her back and tossed it at his face. He answered with a clod of dirt to the chest; then they were scrambling for any ammunition, flinging sticks and grass and leaves and pebbles, then wrestling each other as if they were children again. Razo only grappled with one arm—to give her a fair shot, she thought. She was not sure how the wrestling match changed to an embrace, but moments later her arms were around his neck, and he was rubbing her back, promising her everything would be all right.

I'm scared, she wanted to say. *And I'm wrong inside too, like*

Selia. And I failed the queen. I can't trust myself, and I don't think I can go home again or I might hurt Ma and the little ones. And I don't want you ever to know.

"Thanks for that rescue back there, by the way," he said.

She nodded her head against his chest, feeling like a little girl. She remembered a time they'd been playing in the trees when she was six or so. He'd dared her to climb higher than she ever had. He'd never dared her to do something she could not do, so she had not questioned it. She had climbed and climbed and climbed, the sound of his cheers pushing her faster and higher, though soon the height was making her head feel swimmy and swoony, and her hands seemed too small to grasp another branch.

I can't do it, she had thought as her legs started to shake. *I can't go any higher.* And that was when she had fallen, smacking into branches as she went down. He had caught her at the bottom and had not said a thing as he'd held her and let her tremble from the pain and fright of falling.

The next day when Razo was elsewhere, Rin had climbed the tree again.

"I wish we could go home now," she said, homesickness so thick it filled her up inside, pressed out against her ribs and up into her neck.

She felt him nod. His muscles clenched and his jaw clicked, and she could sense how furious he was, how determined. No chance Razo would run when Dasha, Enna, and Isi were prisoners in that castle. But everything would be all right, because her big brother was here. She did not let herself stop to think why, instead of being relieved, she tingled with uncomfortable chill.

Rin squeezed her brother a little tighter, and he groaned painfully. She let go.

"Are you all right?"

He nodded. "Fine. I'm fine."

He scooted beside Tusken, resting on his side, and Rin did the same. She placed her hand on Tusken's back, feeling the slow rise and fall of his sleepy breaths.

"We should get moving as soon as he wakes," Razo said, idly rubbing his left side. "North, where the searchers won't expect us to be. Then you and Tusken hide out tonight, like you did last night, and I'll go to the castle." She must have looked worried, because Razo added, "Trust me, Rin. I've been in stickier spots."

That thought was not comforting. Her arguments and fears for his safety rose into her throat, but she swallowed them down, afraid of the damage she could do by speaking. Instead she asked, "Razo, who is Selia?"

Razo groaned and rolled onto his back, resting his head on his right arm. "Selia the soulless. Selia the treacherous snake. Selia the unkillable, apparently. She was Isi's lady-in-waiting back in Kildenree. When Isi was traveling to Bayern to marry Geric, Selia and half of Isi's guards rebelled and tried to kill everyone else. Isi escaped, but Selia had gone on into Bayern and pretended she was the Kildenrean princess.

Geric hadn't met Isi yet, you see. And ... well, it's a long story, but in the end, I myself was an indispensable part of how Isi convinced Geric and his father that she was the real princess. Ask Isi yourself. She'll tell you."

Rin nodded, to show that she was certain it was so.

"There you go. Now when you go home, you just convince Jef about that, will you? Anyway, all of Selia's evil guards were killed in a fight (in which I performed nobly), and later Selia was supposedly executed. She'd named the punishment herself—she was put in a barrel studded with nails and dragged through the streets until she was dead. Guess that didn't happen after all. Talked her way out of it, most likely. I wonder what dim-witted soldier or prison guard let her go and put a pig or something in the barrel instead. Hmph. Poor little innocent pig."

"And now she's come back and wants to kill Isi."

Razo sat up, looking around with mock terror. "The pig's come back to kill Isi? We're all doomed!"

"I meant Selia, you goat brain."

"Oh, right. Selia." Razo began stacking rocks on top of each other. "She wants them alive for now, or else she wouldn't bother kidnapping Tusken. Otherwise, you think I'd risk waiting till nightfall? She came for the boy on purpose, sneaked into Geric's camp, talked her way near Tusken and meant to take him alone. But I came along. Don't know how I managed. She was telling me to give her the boy and leave her alone, but I clung on. I believed every word she said and I felt like a fool for not obeying—she's gotten scary good with that people-speaking—but I'd promised you I'd take care of Tusken and I didn't let go."

"You managed to defy her?" Rin marveled, remembering the power of Selia's words the night before.

"Just in that. When I wouldn't put Tusken down, she seemed to change her mind anyway, saying two prisoners were better than one and it'd save her having to carry him. She told me to bring him along, and I trotted after her with Tusken in my arms like a good boy carrying wood for his ma and never so much as called out a warning to Bayern's Own. I tell you, when I think about it, I get an itch right here"—he pointed to the spot between his eyebrows—"that about makes me insane."

Rin recalled asking Razo to watch Tusken, keep him safe. Ordering him? Was it her own people-speaking that had helped him stay with Tusken? The idea did not please her—it filled Rin with shame. She tried to shut it off.

"Selia called Isi something odd." Rin closed her eyes, looking for the memory. "Princess. Something princess."

"Right. Isi was—" Razo put up his hand for silence, listening. Rin listened too. The wood croaked and shook and swayed—clicking of insects, moaning of trees, and silence that was heavy with air and sunshine—but she could hear nothing human. When Razo spoke again, his voice was even quieter than before.

"Isi was the Crown Princess in Kildenree before her

mother decided to marry her off instead of letting her inherit the throne. Don't know why Selia still calls her Crown Princess—just to mock her, I guess. She is rotten and wormy and so far gone I wouldn't be surprised to see her bite the head off a songbird for fun. Seriously, people-speaking might as well be a wasting disease."

Rin shuddered, wishing she could rest somewhere far away from herself. "What's it like when Selia tells you what to do?"

"Like she's cast a line and hook down my throat, and is pulling fish out of my belly, and all I can do is sit and watch. And gag."

Rin wrinkled her nose in disgust. "Eww. Was Selia always like that—controlling people with her words?"

"No, not like last night. She probably always had a way with people, could be very convincing and all. But when I first saw her, the king ordered her to be put in chains, and despite her fussing and screaming, the guards still carried her away. Seems like she's grown in her talent, hasn't she? Even now . . ." He scratched his head. "You feel it too? Even though she's not here and talking in my face, I still feel . . . kind of foolish not to like her. My head knows she's rotten, but I want to keep believing her."

"I was wondering—you know, just musing—when I asked you to take care of Tusken, if you felt at all like you do when Selia—"

"It's funny you should ask, because I'm always confusing you with Selia . . . Wait, which one are you again?"

"Never mind, I was just—"

"You were serious?" Razo squinted at her. "Why would you even ask me that? Rin, you and Selia are about as much alike as a pig and a raven."

"And I would be . . . ?"

"The raven, of course. Selia just sits around and squeals. Ooh, it's going to be fun to see my Dasha roast and drown her! I wish this day would hurry along already."

Razo thought he heard something, and he quieted to listen. But the noises of the wood seemed normal to Rin. She raised her hands to swat a leaf. A long thin touch of coolness ran across her bare wrist, though nothing was there. She kept sweeping her arm as if reaching for the sky and saw it at last, a single strand of a spider's web stretched between two trees. She felt it stay with her, lengthening as her arm moved, until it snapped and floated down.

Rin stared at the broken ends, twisting and drifting in and out of sight. If she had been with anyone else in the world, she would not have spoken aloud her fear, but to Razo she said, "They could already be dead."

"Not my Dasha. Don't let her fool you with her smiling and hopping around all the time. She's smart as a mongoose. And Isi and Enna aren't exactly thick in the head either. You'll see. They'll stay nice and alive as long as they can. You can bet your boots on that, Rinny-roo."

Rin snorted with disgust. "You tried that one before and it didn't work then either."

"Rinny-roo doesn't enchant you?" He mouthed it a couple of times, then shrugged. "You're right. I'll find the right nickname sooner or later. And the moment nightfall gives me some good shade for sneaking around, I'll find a way into the castle."

But how? And if he did manage to get inside, what good could he do? While Selia had been speaking, Isi could not manage to answer, let alone free Tusken. Then again, Rin could not imagine that Selia stayed with the three girls in the castle, speaking to them constantly. They must be jailed—and surely no jail could hold Enna, let alone Isi and Dasha.

"We need to get to them when Selia's not there," Rin said. "When they hear you and Tusken are safe, they'll break free."

"See, I tried to convince you that you're almost as smart as I am. But you always insist, 'No, no, Razo, you're the smart one. I'm just happy to be your baby sister. I'm just thrilled to—'"

Rin's water skin smacked him in the shoulder, and he stopped talking to take a long drink.

Tusken sat up, rubbed his eyes, and blinked at the world. Rin and Razo were immediately at his side. Rin stroked his hair, and he blinked at her several times, yawned hugely, and looked at Razo, who was grinning.

"Morning, Tusk! Look who joined us! See, I told you we'd find our Rinna-girl sooner or later."

Tusken lay his head against her shoulder.

"Win," he said happily. "Win, Win, Win . . ."

She hugged him and hugged him, relishing the tingling gladness that filled her. And thinking of Isi, she kissed him all over his face and neck and hands, and loved him as much as his mother might if she were there herself. He laughed and wriggled until he grew tired of the affection and rolled back to Razo and into his lap, the spot he had no doubt occupied for days.

"Ma?" Tusken asked, his fingers scratching Razo's un-shaven cheeks.

"We'll see her soon too," Razo said. "Maybe tomorrow. That cage game was getting old, wasn't it? Whoo-wee. But just you wait, little man, all the games we're going to play today—hide-and-find-me, and squirrel's tail, and if Uncle Razo is lucky, maybe even bathe-the-stinky-boy-in-the-nearest-body-of-water. How's that, huh? I told you and told you we were going to have the best time ever. Now I want to see if you've grown any more ribs this morning—better count them to make sure. One, two, three, four—no fair wiggling and laughing. You're making me lose count! I'll have to start over. One, two . . ."

The boy had endured days of cramped travel, not enough food, crying for his mother and father, and not understanding what was happening. And now all he wanted was to play. So as they walked north, they played chase, sometimes hopping on one leg for a stretch or running backward. Whenever Tusken spoke loudly, Razo pretended not to hear.

"What's that?" Razo said in an exaggerated whisper. "I can only hear you when you sound like this."

Tusken seemed to enjoy making whisper noises, and for the most part kept his voice quiet. When Rin found a hazelnut tree and stopped to pick clusters of the fruit for breakfast, Razo taught Tusken to climb.

"What a smart boy. Look how he's found a handhold. A Forest boy, natural as can be, no fancy folk weakness in our Tusken."

"Take care he doesn't fall and break an arm."

Razo scoffed, one hand resting lightly on Tusken's back as he climbed higher. "Really, as if I haven't been around plenty of children. We were scaling trees like this before we could walk, and we never—"

Tusken's hand slipped, and he gave a strangled call. Razo dove, catching the prince a few handbreadths above the ground and groaning in pain. He stared at Tusken and Tusken stared at him, his eyes wide and mouth open as if deciding just how loudly to wail before letting it all out. Tusken took a deep breath, then shouted, "Again! Again!" banging happily on Razo's head.

"Shh," Rin reminded the boy.

Razo forced a smile. "Right. Again. Um, how about we take a nice easy walk for a bit, toward that noise that just might be a stream? Huh? And wash out Uncle Razo's scrapes? That sound like buckets of fun?"

Razo moaned again as he got to his feet.

"Did you hurt yourself?" Rin asked.

Razo shrugged. "It's nothing, just bruised a bit."

He was lying, Rin could see. But they arrived at the stream and Rin let the idea drop away as they washed and drank. Razo feared it was too good a landmark for the searchers, so they left quickly, crossing the water on stones, carrying Tusken over the muddy banks to firm dirt that marked no prints. For some time after, Razo would not speak, giving all his attention to listening.

"We're mushroom hunting," Rin told Tusken. "We have to be quiet or we'll scare the mushrooms away."

Tusken nodded seriously. "Sss," he said, trying to make a *shh* sound. And he tiptoed noisily from tree to tree.

Talking to Tusken was a relief, and Rin wondered if young children were not affected by people-speaking, perhaps not until they were old enough to think about themselves more and care what others said. That was a good thought. Maybe after they rescued the fire sisters, Rin could travel from city to city and hire herself as a nurse-mary, caring for babies and young children, and . . . and never speaking to the parents and running off as soon as the children were old enough to be affected by her speech. She sighed with the ache in her chest. Imagining her future was like searching for a dropped needle with her eyes closed.

That was when a new idea began to poke at her. *You should sneak into the castle. Razo could stay with Tusken and then they'd both be safe. If you're caught or killed, no loss. Razo and Tusken could find Geric and save the girls some other way. You might even succeed. You've always been good at sneaking. Don't make Razo risk his life. Risk your own.*

She put a hand on her belly and felt how soft it was, imagined how easily a sword would part that skin, how simple it would be for a bolt to slide through her and end everything. And how Ma would ache to hear of it.

Razo's better at this sort of thing. I don't know how to fight or break into castles. All I can do is listen to trees. A tree isn't like fire, a tree can't end wars and stop bad people. A tree just . . . just is. I just am. And I don't know how to people-speak, not like Selia. She can stop the fire sisters from burning—I could barely get a boy to kiss me. I should take care of Tusken, and Razo should be the hero. He's smart, he's been out in the world stopping wars and doing big things. He'll be all right. There's nothing to worry about.

And she worried all day.

Chapter 19

They walked, and Rin watched the shadow of the sun, feeling its downward plunge tug on her, promising afternoon, and after that, night. The day seemed motionless, a kettle of water waiting to boil; and yet at the same time, it sped recklessly forward to the moment when Razo would leave and might not come back.

Rin's stomach was growling when they came upon a group of quail.

"Rin," Razo whispered, and understanding, she dug through her pack and handed over her sling, as his had been taken by Selia's men. She did not offer stones, guessing Razo would already have a pocketful. While Razo crept after the prey, Rin followed Tusken to a log to hunt for bugs. A few minutes later, she heard the crunch of a boot to her left and assumed it was Razo. She turned instead to meet the eyes of a soldier in a metal helmet and leather vest, his expression as startled as hers. Her heart banged once, as if just coming back to life.

Running to Tusken, she yelled, "Razo!"

At the same time, the soldier hollered, "I've got them! I've—"

She heard Razo's footfalls, his sling whirling. The soldier veered away from Rin and toward Razo, his sword out.

Rin scooped up Tusken without stopping and fled toward the thicker trees. She heard a dull thud, glanced back and saw the soldier stagger. The sword was still in his hand, though his eyes looked slightly dazed. Razo placed another stone in his sling as he walked backward, buying himself enough time and distance to get in another shot before the sword reached him. The soldier lifted his weapon and roared as he swung at Razo.

Rin stumbled on a tree root and looked where she was going again, clinging to Tusken.

"Wazo?" said the boy. "Wazo doing?"

"Nothing, just playing," Rin whispered, gasping through the fear for enough breath to speak. "Everything's fine. But we need to be very quiet, all right?"

She peeked back again. The soldier lay on the ground, motionless. Razo was stooped over him, holding the soldier's sword. Rin did not realize how hard she was squeezing Tusken until he started to cry.

"Sorry, lamby," Rin said between pants as she pushed herself to race faster. "Hush now. It's all right."

In a few moments, Razo was hurrying beside them, his

forehead damp with sweat. The soldier's sword hung from his belt, clanging against his knee as he ran.

"That one's down." Razo's tone was casual, but his face was full of pain, and he was breathing hard. "Don't know if there were others close enough to hear his hollering. Can't chance it. Let's go northeast for a bit."

When Razo did not offer to take Tusken from Rin's arms, Rin panicked, thinking that the soldier had gotten him with his sword after all. But she looked Razo over and did not see any blood, and he did not complain.

They ran hard to get some space between themselves and the soldiers, then changed course so there was no straight line to follow. Northeast they traveled, and then east, so as to confuse the searchers but still keep Daire close. Soon they slowed, taking care in their passage to leave no boot-print, no twig broken. Tusken sat on Rin's shoulders, and he fussed and screeched from time to time, anxious to get down. Their pace was plodding and Rin itched to just bolt, but Razo insisted they keep on with the trackless sneaking. After a time, Rin just could not carry the boy anymore, and she let him down to run alongside them.

There were no human sounds from the wood, and Rin had finally let herself breathe easy when Razo flipped out his sling and let loose a stone. Her hands clasped her chest as she searched for sight of the enemy. It was a squirrel.

"Sorry," said Razo. "I spotted dinner."

It was afternoon when they stopped again, Tusken so tired of walking he was likely to draw notice with his howls of protest. They chanced a small fire, finding a nice dense glade to hide in. Rin gathered wood and fished her small flint bundle from the depths of her pack, where it had lain unused and unneeded while she'd been traveling with the fire sisters. She made triple sure each piece of wood was completely dry, and Razo hopped around, arranging each stick to keep the fire burning clean with no smoke.

They roasted a squirrel and a quail on sticks, then ate the bland, hot meat and licked their fingers. It was not enough to fill their bellies, but in the Forest, Razo and Rin were used to not enough. Tusken ate his fill and curled up beside Rin. Soon his head nodded onto her chest and his breathing went slow and soft. Rin pressed her lips to the top of his head.

"Thanks for keeping him safe."

"'Course," said Razo. "That's what I do—keep people safe, and save people, and find murderers, and get a nice fat quail for lunch. Wasn't that a nice fat quail?"

Rin smiled. It was shocking to discover a smile on her mouth so soon after running for her life. Meat in her stomach, Tusken's sleepy breathing, and the trees all around filled her with a delicious and rare contentment that made her feel indulgent of Razo, so she said, "It was. And you do keep everyone safe and make everything better."

"Not always." He dipped the roasting stick into the flames, and the bits of fat left from the quail sizzled.

She had expected him to agree and preen a bit, and maybe even tell some rousing story of his good deeds in Tira.

"Come now, Razo, what have you ever done that was bad?"

He glanced over his shoulder, the direction they'd left the soldier's body some hours ago, and his face was tinged with pain. His eyes back to the fire, his voice went soft and simple, as if he were talking to himself.

"It should be a good thing to keep people safe, shouldn't it? It should be. Except . . ." He stirred the flames with the stick. "I guess I never talked to you about it. At that, I don't think I've talked to Dasha about it, or Finn. Or Enna. Never Enna.

"Well. Near the end of the war with Tira, Enna was dying from the heat of the fire inside her, I could tell that. Finn and I had been prisoners in a Tiran war camp, and everything was bad, bad, bad. The three of us were chasing the Tiran army, which was about to attack the Bayern capital. War was everywhere and nothing could get worse. Nothing seemed to matter except stopping the war, because any moment we would all die or the whole world would just crumple up and fall away. I don't like thinking back on it. But I do. Think about it. More and more since I met Dasha, for some reason.

"So Enna, Finn, and I were riding after the Tiran army. And we were almost too late.

"The Bayern army met the Tiran in the battlefield, and

both sides clashed. It was like banging two rocks together, the way they clashed—loud and hard and doing no good. People started to catch on fire. Is it so much worse in a battle to burn people than to hack them with a sword? That's what I can't figure. Death is death, right? It shouldn't be worse. But it was, so much. It was . . . it was bad, Rin."

His eyes flicked to her face then back at the fire. "I knew what was happening. Enna. She was setting them on fire, and they were screaming. The Tiran. She wasn't trying to torture them, she was just killing as many as she could, fast, to end the battle. To end the war. She was trying her best not to—not to let them suffer for long. I believe that. She thought she was doing good. But all those people . . ."

Rin watched him until she could not bear the sight. Razo's curse was to show exactly what he felt in his every expression. What horrors he must have seen. She'd had no idea.

When he spoke again, his voice was pleading, as if she'd accused him of murder and he was desperate to explain. "Back then the Tiran army was trying to kill us. All of us. In their square, they hanged straw men dressed like Isi and Geric—at the first chance, they would've hanged my friends for real, you see? And she'd been through some hell, our Enna had, prisoner to a Tiran captain for months. And he'd been a people-speaker to boot. So the lashing out— I'm not saying it was justified, though maybe it was, I don't know—it was understandable, that much at least."

He took a deep, quavering breath, as if he was at last

getting to the spot that stung. "While Enna burned, I stood beside her with my sword and I fought anyone who came her way. Finn and I did. We kept her safe while she burned those soldiers. And I never dare think too hard about it, because if I do, I wonder if I'm responsible too. If what I did, protecting her while she burned, if that means I helped kill them all, if I made a mistake so big that if I even think about it, it'll drag me down and suffocate me.

"Curse it all, there I've gone and thought about it! Why'd I do that? What is it about you, little sister, that makes me think about things I'd happily decided to forget? Curse you and war and everything, but that was a bad, bad time, and sometimes I feel like I'll never crawl out of it."

He wiped savagely at his face, then pushed his fingers into the corners of his eyes to stop the flow of tears. When they slowed, he met her gaze, expectant, pressing his lips together. He needed something from her. This memory of death and burning and guilt had been possessing him for two years—what could she say to all that? She wished that he'd let it stay buried, but the memory, the question, was out now, a bird hatched from an egg, angry with hunger and screeching. And he was waiting for her to speak, to make it better.

Her belly was full, Tusken was perfect contentment in her arms, the tree at her back stretched between sunlight and soil. Though inside she was still clenched up, flinching away from the idea of people-speaking, the fight in her was ebbing some, and she thought easing Razo's worry might be worth the risk. So she looked inside herself for something honest to say back.

"I'm surprised."

"Surprised that I defended Enna while she burned hundreds of soldiers?"

"Well, no. I'm just surprised that you thought you might've made a mistake."

Razo stared, then slowly his frozen incredulity softened and turned into an almost-smile. "You're yanking my boots now."

"I didn't think you were capable of making a mistake— you've always been the brother who can do no wrong." Though it was just the sort of thing she might say to tease him, she spoke the words earnestly.

Razo grabbed his knees and rocked back, grinning at the canopy. "I'd sock you one for the mean joke, but you're as serious as gravel in my socks, I can tell! You didn't think I was capable? But I'm the biggest . . . How can you have lived with me so many years and say I can do no wrong? Don't you ever listen to what our brothers say?"

"Yes. You're noodle-armed, you're too slow to catch a snail, you're short one leg, two arms, and a brain, you're—"

Razo forcefully cleared his throat. "Just so you know, for the future, that was one of those questions I didn't actually intend for you to answer."

"Anyway, you know the brothers are hard on you because they're jealous."

"Jealous of me."

Rin nodded.

"They're so hard because they're jealous of me. Of how perfect I am. How I can do no wrong."

Rin nodded.

Suddenly Razo was on his feet, moving his legs and back in a jerky motion Rin could only assume was meant to be a dance.

"Jealous of me. Jealous of me. Those big boys are jealous of me." Still not raising his voice above a whisper, he chanted and jigged and shuffled.

"They are, you know. You're the one who's traveled and fought and done and seen things, the one who always comes back and brings Ma enough coin to keep us all fed. You've always been the clever one, and clearly Ma's favorite. Of the boys, that is."

He sat back down, his face all innocent happiness. "I almost believe you, but it doesn't matter. You thought they were jealous. You thought I could do no wrong. You're better than roast chicken."

He smiled at her, so she smiled back, and her smile seemed to please him so much, he grabbed her hand that was not pinned under Tusken and shook it, then knocked her shoulder with his elbow, ruffled her hair, nudged her boots with his, making several small gestures of brotherly approval.

The conversation still felt half-formed, a crescent moon that was aching to wax round, and that empty space bothered her. She realized that despite the crowing and dancing, what he'd done while Enna burned would still bother him. On quiet nights it would sneak up and surprise him with the horrible sting of memory. And with that realization she knew what else to say. Habit bid her clamp down on the words, but her brother's sorrow made her feel angry and reckless. She let her energy warm in her belly and push the words up her throat and out.

"Razo, you had to protect Enna. She's your friend, and you were a soldier. She made the decision to do what she did, not you. Even if what she did was wrong, you couldn't have stopped her, and you certainly couldn't have stood back and let her be killed. You had to protect her."

"You think so?" His eyes were so serious, so hopeful. Even though speaking to Razo was almost as easy as talking with a child, it still cost her. Part of her recoiled from the people-speaking, but she fought back, needing to say one more thing to make it just enough.

"I know so. I don't think you ever need worry about that day again, Razo. You did right."

He nodded and closed his eyes. No jolting dance this time, no hurrahs and happiness. He put the back of his hand over his eyes and kept nodding, speaking to himself as if to a troubled animal. "Sure enough. That'll be how it was. No worry now. All right then."

He took a deep breath and when his hand fell from his face, his expression was calm, even pleased.

He pointed at her. "You're the one who can do no wrong, Rinna-girl. You're the family treasure. You're the reason Ma can keep smiling and none of our brothers have strangled each other yet and the homestead is the best place in the Forest. You are."

She shook her head, though she wished Razo could make her believe it.

"I want to go home." The idea filled her suddenly with hopeless longing. "I miss the little ones and the Forest, and Ma. Even our brothers. I miss it all."

He nodded. "We'll get you there. Maybe we'll be on our way tomorrow morning. You just stay here with Tusken while I sneak in and make the rescue." When he spoke, his hand strayed to his left side.

Rin glared. "You *are* hiding an injury from me, aren't you? Let me see."

She reached for his tunic, and he pushed her hands away. "It's nothing."

"Then it won't matter if I see."

She lifted his gray soldier's tunic and sucked in a breath at the sight. His entire left side was bruised deep purple, the edges turning green and yellow. Why hadn't she realized before that he was injured? *I could have*, Rin thought. *But I didn't want to notice.* If Razo was hurt, he might not be able to break into the castle, and she so wanted it to be him, not her.

"This is not good," she said.

"It's nothing, really. I tried to escape and one of Selia's soliders hit me."

"With what?"

"His fist." Razo shrugged. "He was a big one."

Rin touched the bruise, and he winced. "Razo, I think your rib is broken."

"No . . ."

"Remember when Deet fell out of a tree? That's how it looked, and he had trouble breathing. I've heard you panting as we run."

"It doesn't matter. Broken or not, I still have to go."

"I'll go." Rin spoke without thinking first, and it made her wonder if that was how everyone lived, talking all the time, speaking words before the thoughts had time to settle. "I'll go to Castle Daire."

Razo stared. "Were you always this eager to rush off after queens and break into fortresses?"

"Tusken needs his ma back. And I think I can do it. Sneak. They won't notice me. I'm a better choice than you."

"Ho there now, I thought you said I was perfect, that I could do no wrong."

Energy was rising up in her, and she knew instinctively she could make her words very convincing. Perhaps that was people-speaking, she thought. When she got warm inside like that, when words felt tangible before she even uttered them. She took a breath and concentrated on keeping her insides cool and calm. "You should stay with Tusken. Your injury could slow you down. I can sneak right past those guards, tell Isi that you and Tusken are free, and those fire sisters will—"

"Whoa, wait—fire sisters?"

She felt herself blush. "I mean, that's how I think of Dasha, Isi, and Enna."

"Fire sisters?" he said again, raising an eyebrow.

She shrugged. "It . . . the name sounded good in my head."

"Uh-huh. All right, go on."

"So as soon as the . . . the girls know, they'll be able to break out of the prison, and we'll come back and find you."

Razo sat back on his heels and stared up. Rin followed his gaze. The moon was hanging above them, white and ghostly against the blue sky as if anxious to bring on the night. Rin did not share that sentiment. Her hands were tingling cold in anticipation of Razo's decision. She did not want him to agree. She wanted him to insist that his ribs were fine and she should stay with Tusken. He should not allow his baby sister to endanger herself creeping into a fortress brimming with soldiers and murderous fire-speakers. Even if she did get inside, what could she do if something went wrong?

Then again, what would Razo do? If either of them were caught, it was over. Better he survive. He had Dasha and home—but she had nothing. Her family would not be safe with a people-speaker around. She would risk herself. It was her gift to give.

"I'm almost tempted to agree," he said at last. "But really, it's an idea more worthy of our goat-brained Jef than our smart-as-Ma Rin. You stay with Tusken and run to Bayern if I don't come back."

She almost did it then. Panic clenched inside her, all her energy gathered together, making fists of need, and she almost punched it all into words and told him, "Let me go, Razo. You'll be sorry if you don't. You know you tend to fail with these things even when you're not injured. You'd be safer with the child. Our brothers are mostly right about you—this is too important to gamble on your meager skills," and so on, until she'd found the hole in his confidence and tricked him into letting her go instead. The words were there, in her throat, on her tongue, insistent, demanding, real. She choked, and to keep the greasy black words down, she blurted instead, "I have people-speaking."

Razo blinked and shook his head as if she'd splashed water in his face. "Wait, whoa, what?"

"I have people-speaking. I'm like Selia."

"Is this like your bear-speaking joke? Because it really wasn't funny enough to keep it up."

She pressed her hands over her eyes. She'd already figured she could not trust herself to return home, but now that Razo knew what she was, that future seemed certain, the idea of home smoke in her hand.

"I'm a people-speaker, like Selia. I'm going to turn into a monster."

"Uh-huh."

"No, really. I am."

"Right."

"Listen to me!" Instead of words, sobs gathered in her throat. "I've had people-speaking my whole life. It's been inside me like . . . like an egg, growing until something foul could eat its way out. I didn't know what it was, but I always knew there was something wrong in me. With me. And I had to hold it in or I'd hurt people and Ma wouldn't love me. And now when I talk I'm afraid I'm going to say . . . I'm going to be Selia, I'm going to make people do things, and I can't be Rin, whoever that is anyway. I can't speak the thoughts in my head because by the time they reach my tongue they become infected with it, and I'm not sure when I'm speaking casually and when I'm letting that curse taint everything. No one should trust me, I'll need to be alone and hide away. I hate it. And I hate me."

She gulped her breath down and shut her mouth. She had not intended to say so much. People-speaking or not, she never should have spoken those last words aloud. Never, not to Razo, not to anyone. That part of her was a tight, ugly clump best left in the dark.

She stared at Razo, her chin trembling with the effort not to cry, terrified that he would acknowledge what she should not have said and try to console her with hollow words.

He was watching the fire burn. It took him a long time

to speak, and when he did, his words were measured and slow. "I'm not the smartest boy, I know that. Maybe that's not such a bad thing—smarts seem like a load of fancy clothes that you have to wear all the time, and they're heavy and rip easily even though you're supposed to keep them clean. A hassle, that's what that is. So I'm not so smart, and I can't say whether or not you have people-speaking, but one thing I know"—he looked at her, his eyes golden in the light—"you're nothing like Selia, and you're never going to be."

Rin laughed without humor and pulled her knees up, resting her forehead so Razo would not have to look at his sister's face.

His voice got hotter. "No, you listen to me now, Rinna-girl. You're never going to be. Never. Selia's the queen of Kel, is she? She's so smart and powerful and can just lock up Dasha and Isi and Enna, can she? Ha! She's a grunting piglet. And if it came down to a fight, you and Selia, I'd bet the last tree that you'd win without ever opening your mouth. Because you're Forest born, Rinna-girl."

Rin was crying then, so she kept her face down, hoping Razo would not notice.

Razo cleared his throat. "See? I know you believe you have people-speaking, but you haven't tried to talk me into sending you to the castle. You wouldn't do that, 'cause you're Rin. I'm your favorite brother and not so dumb for being not too smart, and I say, go on and rescue those girls. Show that Selia what it means to be Agget-kin."

She looked up then. "You're going to let me go?"

"No chance you'd ask if you didn't think you could do it. I don't like sitting here while you go off asking danger for an evening stroll. I think my sneaking skills are rather impressive and I enjoyed the idea of bursting into the prison and shouting, 'Tusken's safe, my girls. Break out of that stone box!' And Dasha rushing up to me and kissing me and—well, anyway, I think my plan sounds like more fun, but you wouldn't insist if you didn't mean it, and besides, you did manage to get away last night without being seen, and you were right about keeping us hidden in that tree. And if nothing else, Tusken's probably safest with me."

She nodded. Her middle relaxed in relief, even though the thought of stealing into that castle alone made her feel iced over.

"You *can* do this, right?" he asked.

She nodded again and thought, *Razo and Tusken will stay safe. I'll only have to risk myself.*

"All right." He rubbed his hands together and his tone became as serious as she'd ever heard out of his mouth. "You should head out in about two hours. There's only one entrance through the castle wall, and it'll be well guarded. I was going to try and scale the wall—you think you can manage that?"

Cold dripped over the skin of her back and down her arms. Could she? She'd try. If she could only get close enough to the girls to shout the news, then it would all be worth it. Rin nodded.

Razo sucked air in through his teeth. "I don't know, Rin . . ."

"I can, Razo. No problem. Really. I'm Forest born, aren't I?" He was not going to let her go. She scrambled for something else to say. "Besides, I have tree-speaking, so that will help."

"Oh, right, I didn't think about that. Good."

Would it help? She wondered if her knowledge of tree-speaking somehow endowed her to be better at sneaking, if it was just a matter of practice, or if she was just so boring no one noticed her. But tree-speaking was not like fire-speaking, not a weapon to be used. Isi said animals were living things and could not be controlled, not like fire or wind. Trees were living things too. She could not make them do things they would not normally do.

Razo was scratching a map of the castle in the dirt. "Castle Daire is a five-tower structure—a central tower with four towers around it. Once inside the wall, you'll see a main entrance into the central tower. It's nicely guarded, so I'd planned to find an entrance through one of the side towers. If there's a kitchen in one, it'll have its own little door— look for smoke or smell for grease. If they keep pigs, they'll be housed near the kitchen since pigs eat the scraps and bits. I've had pretty good luck getting in and out of kitchens. Once inside the side tower, you should be able to get into the central tower. Take the stairs down and you'll find the dungeon right enough. That's where Selia put me and Tusk, so I guess she'd put the girls there too. All you'll have to do is speak the words 'Tusken is safe' and the girls should do the rest. Now, are you really sure you can do this? That you want to do this?"

She was not so sure at all that she could, and she definitely did not want to. But worse would be waiting in the wood for days, not knowing if Razo was killed. Worse would be the searchers coming upon her and Tusken without Razo and his sling there to protect them. Worse would be hearing that Isi was killed because Rin had been too afraid. Besides, Selia would never endanger herself to save her friends, Rin was sure. And it felt very good to do the opposite of what Selia would do.

Rin nodded, and made her expression brave. She'd wanted to see if going out in the world could change her as it had changed Razo, if following Isi could make her more like the queen. Now it was time to leave the wood. No matter that Rin felt made of paper. She would see it through.

he sun was scraping the western curve of the sky when Tusken woke from his nap. Rin shouldered her pack, now slightly heavier with the roots and nuts she and Razo had gathered throughout the day.

"Win go?" Tusken asked.

She nodded. "I'll be back."

"I go." Tusken held up his arms. "I go, Win. I go."

"You'll stay with me, little man," said Razo. "We've got games to play."

Rin was on her knees, hugging Tusken. "Razo will keep you safe. I'll see you soon. And I'll bring your ma too," she added recklessly. She looked at Razo, who was burying the remains of their fire. "If I'm not back the day after tomorrow—"

"We'll inch our way to Bayern and send a message to Geric."

"And not try to come after me?"

Razo groaned but nodded. "Tusken's life is first priority. Don't worry about us, little sister. You just stay safe yourself. And when you see Dasha, tell her . . . tell her . . ."

His brow furrowed.

"They're smart," Rin said, echoing his earlier words. *They'll keep themselves nice and safe. They'd better.* "Two days."

Razo took Tusken's hand, and the little boy waved good-bye to Rin until she was out of sight.

"Keep him safe," Rin whispered. "Be safe, both of you."

She walked as quickly as her trembling legs would take her. Wound with worry and aching for the peace of trees, she kept one hand outstretched and let her fingers glance off trunks in passing. She tried to imagine how they were murmuring of deep water, the satisfaction when the roots were nestled in good soil, the urgings to dig ever deeper, the peaceful swaying of leaves as they rested in dim light, waiting for the sun to return again. She tried to pull that peace inside her and let it strengthen her core, imagined it surrounding her like the toughest bark, making her strong and fearless.

The afternoon cooled, and she could not hear anything over the crackling and clicking of cicadas, the storm of rasps and croaks. The wood teemed with insects so noisy her ears rang, though she could not see a one. What else was out there that she could not see?

She had to hurry, directing herself by slant of sunlight. Twice she thought she heard the rhythm of hoofbeats or footfalls, so she hid, then ran, losing time and direction. So little sleep, so much toil was wearing her down. When she began to stumble more than step, she stopped for a rest, curling herself into the leggy roots of a large tree, feeling as tiny and vulnerable as she had as a little girl climbing onto her mother's lap.

Evening sunlight grazed through the canopy, slashing at an angle into her eyes. She closed them, just for a minute, just to hide from the brightness.

Rin startled and opened her eyes.

Darkness. She felt odd, as if someone had dropped a heavy blanket over her head, and she could barely see or move. Her arms ached, her face was sore from pressing against the bark of the tree, her legs were cold from being scrunched up beneath her. She moved. That hurt. She sat upright, stretching her legs, and felt the painful pricking of blood rush through her. The lack of light was confusing and frightening. If she did not ache everywhere, she would have feared she was dead.

An owl called a warning, and only then did Rin understand that the world was dark because it was night. She had fallen asleep.

"No," she said. "No, no, no."

She lurched to her feet and began to run, her body still

waking up, her legs feeling like straw sacks. It was not long before she admitted that she had no idea where she was going. She tripped, felt against a tree, and stayed there, breathing hard.

Stop it, she scolded herself, taking her ma's tone. *Calm down and do what you need to do.*

She did not have time to panic. The girls were locked up. Razo had bet on her to succeed. Maybe it was not too late to find her way tonight, if she could just think it through.

She found herself remembering another time she'd been lost in a wood. After Nordra and the stick, after Ma had turned her back, seven-year-old Rin had gotten lost. That was the first time she'd opened herself to listen to the trees. After, she'd known her way home.

Rin wrapped her arms around the tree, closing her eyes and resting her head against its smooth bark. She did not demand of the tree what she wanted, as she had after Wilem. That was foolish, she realized now. And tree-speaking was an odd phrase anyhow—it was more like tree-listening. She could not tell the trees anything, only think through their calmness to understand her own thoughts better.

Her breathing slowed, she entered into the greenness, or perhaps it entered her, and there in the tree's depths she met again the tightening fear that she was a people-speaker.

Enough. She'd had enough of being chased away by what she'd done to Wilem and she felt angry enough to chew a stone to dust. *I know I'm bad. This can't shock me anymore. I need to do this task, and I need to be calm and able to think. I need a way to find where I'm going.*

Ignoring her own circling thoughts, she focused on the tree. With no sunlight to lure the tree up, the leaves curled slightly for the night, the center of the tree pulled downward. Her thoughts followed that motion into the roots, thousands of tips that touched other roots, leading to another tree, and another, the trees of the wood connected as if holding hands.

Her mind burned, her heart raced. All those trees, all connected. She followed the net of roots, finding a place where the trees stopped.

There. That was her direction, she hoped.

She had opened her eyes and was just about to push herself away from the tree when a horse cantered by.

Rin froze, not moving, her body still tight to the tree. The horse stopped. She closed her eyes and waited, her arms shaking in the effort to hold still.

Please, please, please . . .

The sound of hoofbeats continued on.

After that, she traveled cautiously, scurrying from tree to tree, weaving her way to avoid detection. When she discovered a spring, she took a little damp earth and packed it into her ears. The sounds of the night wood dimmed, and she missed the vibrant rattle of crickets, but she hoped the precaution would save her from the danger of Selia's voice.

Twice she scrambled up a tree to get out of the way of

horsemen galloping toward the castle. Once she dropped to the ground, huddled behind a trunk, as two soldiers passed by heading east. She inched closer and closer, until at last there was the castle. She could see the gates now, and she moaned at the sight, thinking she might as well try to swallow a pumpkin whole as get inside. The gates were shut. She'd fostered a delirious hope that she could sneak inside without trying to scale the wall, but that hope withered away.

Keeping her distance, Rin made her way around the castle, searching for a spot where she could climb. Soldiers moved everywhere like ants crawling over dropped meat. Her heart was thudding so hard it made her head hurt.

Calm, she told herself. *Be calm.* But just the narrowest thought of trying to scramble up those sheer walls under sight of armed sentries made her nearly whimper in fear. After circling the perimeter, she retreated into the trees. She'd taken herself so far the castle was out of sight before she realized that she was running away.

Rin climbed a tree, wrapped an arm around the trunk, and whispered to the tree, to the night, to herself, "Please. I need to do this. I need some courage. I need to bring Tusken his mother and keep Razo safe. And I need to believe I can do something of my own, because Razo's the only one who does."

The reality of her situation came down on her like a hard rain. She had to get in tonight. It would be a three-hour walk at least to get back to Razo and Tusken, and no chance Razo would send her back a second time. He would wait for the next night, then try to scale those impossible walls, an easy target for a crossbow. And in the meantime, what would happen to the girls? No, tonight. It had to be.

Anxiety was taking her farther away. Rin closed her eyes and opened herself inside, listening to the tree. For the first time in months, the dark remnant of the Wilem memory did not accost her. Instead, she was buoyed and floating on ideas of rain and soil, warm air hovering on a leaf. Soothed, she focused her thoughts into the first soft layer that ran with sap, down into the roots, and then out.

It was like a game, letting her thoughts pump through the network of roots and trees, her trail a dizzying maze of growth. Following the lattice of roots, she hunted for trees near the wall, hoping to approach the castle under shadow of the wood.

There she found a bundle of roots hunkered down under stone. Long ago, someone must have axed its trunk to make way for the wall, but the roots survived, sending up shoots, unfurling new, thin leaves to wave at the sun. Years upon years its shoots were cut away, but it lived on, and slowly its growth eased rocks loose, cracked mortar, made room to stretch.

Rin opened her eyes. A tree might have opened a hole in the wall.

She'd felt safe for the moment, and exposing herself

again to the night was almost painful. But she kept breathing, and picturing herself in the tree, imagining that she was that peaceful, with roots deep and branches high. And the panic held off for the moment, as if she were tucked away in her ma's house with the shutters closed against a storm.

She approached the back side of the wall from the northeast along a worn footpath. Guards walked the battlements, looking out. If they spotted her, she hoped a lone girl approaching from the direction of town would not warrant much suspicion.

Two guards met in the middle of the wall and spoke a few words, then turned their backs to each other and ambled forward, their eyes looking out. *Now*, Rin thought. *Go now!* She hesitated, then stumbled forward, took a deep-as-knees breath, and forced each foot to feel the ground beneath her before letting her weight pull herself forward. Best to be quiet, best not to draw notice, to be slow and easy as if she were nothing but a shadow.

"A night forest dreaming," she whispered to herself. "Nothing to ponder but years and rain."

She felt so aware of everything, the stick that might snap beneath her foot, the breeze about to rustle some leaves. The walk seemed to take days, but she reached the wall before the guards turned back again. She pressed herself against the stones, allowing herself now to shudder, cold prickles of sweat trickling along her neck and back.

She dropped to her knees and found it—a very old tree,

its stubborn roots still living, still growing, right through the wall. Rin yanked out a few stones, pushed her pack in before her, and crawled through, shoulders and hips scraping rock.

The castle courtyard was empty and dark and gray, a hollow skull. No cover, no trees to hide beneath. She sat by the arching roots of the old tree and listened to its thrumming thoughts, trying to pull that peace inside her. The tree did not mind that its trunk had been cut away, that it was not tall and beautiful as it once had been. It was still alive, and it would just keep on drinking water through its roots and shooting out new leaves as long as it could. The rhythm of water and sap, soil and growth circled through. Rin hummed it to herself like a song.

"Deep water flowing," she whispered. "Leaves curled and resting under the moon."

Her pace was casual, her steps quiet. She kept breathing, kept that silent hum rumbling through her, kept her body relaxed, walking along the inside of the wall, passing a stable, until the five joined towers of the castle were before her. But first she had to go around the garrison. Through the open doors and windows she could see the building was stuffed with soldiers, many spending the night on the floor. Others slept on the ground outside, while those awake sat playing quiet games of stones.

Move like you belong, she reminded herself. *Like you couldn't sleep and came out for the privy. Nothing to worry. No trouble at all.*

No one stopped her. She was in the moon shadow of the castle now.

She followed pig prints to one of the four smaller towers. Just as Razo had said, there was smoke on the air and a pile of kitchen scraps emitting rot.

And there was laundry drying on a line.

She slipped between two lines of laundry, stripped out of her Bayern travel clothes, and pulled on a white shift in the Kelish style with sleeves dangling from her forearms. Over that she donned a yellow sleeveless dress, tightening the lacing at the bodice. They were both a little short and the dangling sleeves felt cumbersome. She pulled a string loose from the hem of her discarded tunic to tie back her hair, then hid the dirty bundle under a slop bucket.

The kitchen door was narrow and low, meant to discourage invaders, she figured. It was also unlocked. Rin stooped and ducked inside. The kitchen fires were banked, and children her age and younger slept on the floor, waiting for dawn and the work day to begin. She tiptoed around their bodies and ducked through another door where the wall was as thick as her leg was long. Now she was in the large open chamber of the central tower. It was adorned as a banquet hall, with long wooden tables still scattered with the remnants of dinner. In the center of the chamber, stairs wound to the upper floors and deeper into the ground. She was so close. Over to her right was the huge wood door to the castle, shut and bolted, a dozen soldiers on the inside, standing, yawning, slumping. Her body yearned to hide, but she forced herself to keep moving casually through the chamber toward the stairway.

Someone was coming down the stairs—a thick woman with a square face, wearing a long-sleeved gray tunic with draping sleeves. Instead of a sleeveless dress over the tunic, she sported leggings like Kelish men. Around the hem of the tunic and sleeve, a pattern was worked in orange and red thread, loops with pointed tips. *Flames*, Rin realized. The woman was staring at her.

The stairs were there. There. Rin tried to lift her foot, to walk that insignificant length, to disappear into the darkness below. But the stare of that woman held her. Sweat was thick on Rin's forehead, itching down her back, across the palms of her hands. *I'm nothing, nothing, don't look at me. Please. I'm nothing.*

The way her mouth opened suddenly, the woman might have gasped, though with the mud in her ears Rin could not be sure. She flew to Rin, seizing her wrist. Rin made a small noise of pain.

The woman's voice was loud enough to push through the mud, though Rin did not understand the questions in Kelish. Rin thrashed and squirmed and tried to get free, but the woman's hand was strong. One of the guards charged forward, hefting his sword.

Rin grabbed the woman around the middle and pushed her hard to the ground. Though large, the woman was soft and awkward, and Rin managed to put her foot on the woman's throat and twist out of her hold in a dirty move forbidden at the homestead. But she was free, and she darted for the stairs, pulling in air to shout to the fire sisters and hope her voice carried. All she had time for was one breath before hands were on her, yanking her arms behind her back. The force of her capture knocked the wind from her chest, and she could not squeak a word.

It had been a desperate move anyhow. No chance she could have made it far. The horror of her failure engulfed her.

They took her pack and tied her hands. The woman noticed the mud crammed in her ears and scraped it out with her fingers.

She said something in Kelish that sounded like a question, and when Rin did not respond, she switched to the Bayern tongue. "Why putting dirt in the ears?"

One of the soldiers looked uneasy, speaking in Kelish and gesturing to Rin and toward the wood outside the castle walls.

The woman shushed him. "The queen asking questions next. You answering."

She had the soldiers drag Rin farther from the way to the dungeon, then ran up the steps to the higher levels of the keep.

The sweat that lay over Rin's face and under her tunic felt freezing cold, and she shivered. She thought if she could just see the soldiers' faces, perhaps she could figure out how to trick them into letting her go. But they held her arms at an angle, her back hunched so she could not twist enough to see. Her mouth was as dry as a fallen leaf, everything seemed hopeless. And Selia was coming.

in heard the Kelish woman's voice echoing down the stairs before she emerged, a shivering circle of candlelight descending before her.

"I not noticing her at first. I was seeing of her heat before seeing of her, Your Majesty."

Then, a second voice—Selia's. "What an enchanting mystery! Do you think we should keep her alive to figure it out? Or shall we kill her now?"

"She could be dangerous."

"Mmm."

The candlelight grew brighter, then in the circle of light Selia emerged from the stairs, flanked by the woman and two other men, also dressed in gray tunics with orange markings. Over her white nightgown, Selia wore a red velvet robe, the color of a very ripe berry, and her dark yellow hair was long and loose. Selia stepped daintily off the last stair, took in Rin with the soldiers, and smiled. Rin could not help thinking her lovely.

"My wonderful guards!" Selia extended her arms, as

if embracing the soldiers from a distance. "Flann, Imchad, Conall—you are so fine, so strong. What good work you do keeping my little home safe. How I adore you!"

"Thank you, Your Majesty," each one mumbled in voices that sounded sheepish bordering on lovesick. The other soldiers who remained at the gate watched intensely. A few shuffled closer, their faces eager, as if hoping Selia might notice them next. But her generous smile had turned to the woman beside her.

"And beautiful Nuala. Ever watchful, always brilliant. Your days of going unnoticed are long forgotten. You shine like a full moon."

Nuala bowed her head, red flush smeared over her broad cheeks.

Now Selia's eyes turned to Rin. Her gaze was uncomfortable, probing, and Rin flinched under it.

"Nuala, why are her ears smeared with dirt?"

"She had putting mud in her ears, Your Majesty. I cannot know why."

Rin thought Selia's followers must not realize the power of their mistress's voice.

Selia's eyebrows rose. "She did? Well, maybe she's a clever thing. Are you clever?"

Rin summoned all her strength and sent it into words. "Let me go."

Selia's eyes opened wide in pure surprise. "Pardon me?"

"You want something from Isi, from the *Crown Princess.*"

Rin fought to speak with confidence, to shine up her words and offer them like coins. But her chin trembled, and she was so aware of her own worthlessness she could barely squeak. "I can't give you what you want. You should let me go. I have nowhere to run. There's no point in keeping me around, just another mouth to feed. You'd feel so much better if you let me go."

Selia stared, then she leaned her head back and laughed. "Wonderful! So charming. It appears I have a little sister in talent. But is that your best effort, truly? How sad. Let me guess—you were afraid of yourself all your life, so you did not practice your skills; you shut them away. And now you are useless. Yes, Nuala, this one is terribly dangerous—if you are a beetle underfoot." Selia's smile was barely a twitch, yet it seemed the cruelest smile Rin had ever seen.

"She is not a threat?" Nuala asked, watching Rin with wary eyes.

"No, she is weak."

Rin shuddered. Never had any words seemed more true.

Then Selia's eyes softened, the cold smile melted from her lips. Her face was all benevolence. Even as Rin guessed that it was just another mask, a new tactic, the effect was profound, and she found herself thinking, *I wish I'd had a chance to wash before meeting her. I wish I looked a bit nicer. What can I say to make her like me?*

"I know who you are, Rin. Cilie has told me many charming stories. Eager to know you better, I was thrilled to learn you had escorted my old mistress to my home. So you may imagine my worry when I realized you were not among the girls. But all is as it should be again. You were so clever! We looked and looked for the longest time but could not find any trace of you and dear sweet Tusken. Truly ingenious. How did you elude my searchers?"

Rin blinked long and hard. She wanted to tell Selia. She should just tell her. Did it really matter if Selia knew about sleeping in the oak tree, or even about the tree-speaking? Surely she was about to kill Rin anyway. But there remained a thin, tough core in Rin's middle, pulled securely up toward the sky, down toward earth, and there within that single fiber, she could still think a little. *Keep silent, Rin.* At least she had some practice at that.

"Come now," said Selia. "None of it matters anymore. I just admire your competence." She studied Rin's face, lifting a finger to stroke her cheek. "No one appreciates you properly, do they? Your family? Yes, they do not see the true Rin, the clever Rin, the powerful Rin. Overlooked your entire life, tossed aside as if you were no more than any scrap of a girl. They don't know what secrets you hold, how you have fought to keep those secrets, all you have sacrificed to keep your family safe. And for what? For negligence? For dismissal? The way you have been treated is shocking."

Rin felt as if she could curl up at Selia's feet and fall asleep. Her thoughts relaxed too, drifting away from her control. *Selia would understand me. She and I have grown up with the same plague inside. She could teach me, and in turn I could help her change her ways. Only she could really understand . . .*

"I bet there are stories you could tell! I am near breathless in anticipation. Tell me. Tell me all of it, all the clever things you can do. How did you get them away without drawing notice? What did you do next?"

Selia put a finger under Rin's jaw and gazed lovingly into her eyes. Rin's legs trembled with eagerness to speak, her stomach tossed with joy. How wonderful it would feel to tell Selia about her sneaking, half in the green world, and her idea to hide in the very tree that held the cage. Selia would be delighted! Rin could see the path they had taken in her mind, their flight north, then east, and north again. *Silence, Rin. Keep silent.* The room seemed to tilt to one side; her head hurt. Maybe she could draw Selia a map . . . *No!* Why was everything so confusing? She tried to think like a tree, hide herself inside that wonderful bark of thought, sink deep in a sturdy trunk, close herself to all this confusion.

"You are fighting so hard!" Selia said. "That is sweet. You must think you have someone to protect, but there is no need. You should protect yourself now, and the way to do that is to speak. You are so good at speaking, better than you can even guess. No need to close yourself up any longer, little flower. Open yourself, claim yourself. Speak."

Rin wanted to, she really wanted to. But a tickly bug of an idea was irritating her, distracting her—Selia understood her. That meant that Rin's ability to read people was part of the people-speaking. When she guessed Ma's thoughts before Ma spoke them, that was people-speaking. When she detected the lie in Cilie's face, that too. And finding just the right thing to say to Wilem to keep him from running off with the boys. The ability to read people, know what they needed to hear, convince them to do as she wished. All of that. People-speaking.

Selia could see thoughts in people's faces, could read in their expressions what they wanted to hear, and told it to them. But the way Selia spoke was beyond finding the words to convince Nordra to give up the stick—Selia's words were webbing, thick and sticky, that clung and enshrined. Selia's words were weapons. Beside her, Rin felt weak as pudding.

"I have nothing worth saying," Rin muttered, and felt it was true.

Selia sighed. "Oh well, I was just curious. It does not matter now that I have the boy prince safely home with me."

Rin heard the gasp before realizing that it had escaped from her own throat.

Selia tilted her head, studying Rin's face, her expression amused surprise. "Oh my, you did not know that, did you? You thought Tusken and his little soldier friend were still out there somewhere? Look at her, Nuala, she is utterly shocked. She's trying to hide it, poor dear. And here we all assumed she broke into the castle in some fanciful attempt to rescue him!"

She smiled again at Rin. "Forgive me. I should show more

compassion. If you did not know, then . . . Well, I hope it won't come as a dreadful blow when I tell you that when my guards found the boy prince and his companion, they tried to flee, the poor dears, as if they had anything to fear from me! In the tussle, the dark-haired boy died. He tried to fight, but what good is a sling against a sword, especially with his boots on fire?"

Rin was on the floor. She did not think she had sat down, but suddenly the ground was there under her hand and backside, her body jarred as if she'd hit it hard.

"Did you know that boy?" Selia's voice dripped with concern. "I had no idea or I would have taken more care. My condolences, truly. I have lost loved ones too, and I know the pain. The deep, deep pain. But in good news"— her tone brightened—"the little one lives in excellent health! He is back in his aunt Selia's adoring arms. I have dressed him in silks and he sleeps upon feather pillows, his chubby little face still smeared with the honey sweets I fed him for dinner. Cilie is with him, my faithful lady-in-waiting, but he is most fond of me."

Razo is dead, Rin was thinking. It was all she could think. The thought crowded her head, her body, filled the room like smoke from a clogged chimney, and Rin could not breathe through it. *Razo is dead, and it's my fault. I failed him, I killed him. I fell asleep and lost all that time. The searchers found them, killed my brother, carried Tusken back to Selia. All while I slept. He's dead, it's my fault. I insisted on going myself, and now he's dead.*

Selia crouched beside her and placed something small and cold in Rin's hands. Her face was close to Rin's, so close she found herself watching Selia's pale eyelashes as she blinked.

"Tell the Crown Princess to name me the ruler of Bayern's eastern provinces. It *is* delightful to be a queen by marriage, but I'd so much rather have some land in my name. My provinces will still be part of Bayern. I'm not asking for the *crown*, after all. The eastern provinces aren't too much to exchange for the life of her child, are they? No, you agree. That would be greedy of her. And I will be a good ruler, and tie the kingdom of Bayern even more snugly to Kel. It will be a marvelous political alliance with both sides benefiting richly. I do not ask for something impossible, just a little piece of land, won fairly in this war game. All I require is her signature on a letter to Geric. He will honor what his wife signs, as long as I send it back with his son intact. If she refuses, I will keep Tusken as my own. I have always wanted a son. I do not think that will transpire—I believe the Crown Princess will sign, and then she will remain my guest until the king follows through on the transfer of land. Once that happens, everyone goes home hale and healthy! You see how reasonable I am."

Rin was nodding. She did not care about any of it— eastern provinces, political alliances. Trying to take it in felt like drinking dust. Razo should have come, not her. All along, she'd known she would fail, and sure enough, here she sat on a stone floor drowning under the news of her brother's death. But she nodded.

"Good. Very good. My hearth-watchers," Selia said, gesturing to the men and women in gray tunics, "will escort you downstairs to your companions. I apologize for the rough quarters, but alas, Castle Daire is not so grand as to boast of large guest chambers! Still, the sooner the Crown Princess signs her agreement, the sooner I can send that sweet little baby back to his father. Off you go, and tell the Crown Princess I will call on her tomorrow."

"She's a queen," Rin whispered.

Selia had begun to walk away, but she stopped where she stood, her smile rigid. "What did you say?"

Rin could not believe she had spoken at all. The words had slipped out; she had barely noticed them. Now she had to gather any energy left in her body to speak again, forcing the words out in a croak. "Isi. You call her Crown Princess. But she's a queen."

The change in Selia's face was astonishing. Her composure, her beauty disappeared as her face stiffened and turned red, her eyes glaring, her mouth quivering. Rin recoiled, sure the woman would strike. But just as suddenly, Selia's face calmed again, though now no smile graced her lips.

"All of this can end very well for you. How would you like to be the one to accompany the child back to his father? Yes, I can see that you genuinely care for him. You would love to be so honored, to have his well-being in your hands.

You could keep him safe. If the *Crown Princess* signs that document, you will be taking the little prince home tomorrow. And then I will not have a reason to cut your throat and toss you over the wall. Think on that. Come, Nuala."

Selia climbed the winding stairs, Nuala following. Selia's remaining hearth-watchers, those in the gray tunics embroidered with orange flames, took Rin by the elbows and walked her swiftly down steps so steep Rin feared she would drop to the bottom if she leaned forward just a bit. That was where she'd been trying to go all along, and now they took her willingly. Because it did not matter anymore. Rin had no good news to shout, and the fire sisters would not break free.

For some reason she was having trouble seeing. The torches on the walls swam with indistinct light, the steps beneath her feet seemed to curve and bulge. Only when she blinked and felt coolness streak down her cheeks did she understand that she'd been seeing through tears.

From the hiccups in her chest and the shake of her shoulders, Rin guessed she was crying hard, though a numbness consumed her so she was scarcely aware of her sobs. By the time the hearth-watchers unlocked a heavy metal door and pushed her through, she was nearly blind with tears. The room was completely black and stank like a privy hole.

She stumbled forward, and hands were on her at once, comforting hands. Rin kneeled, then crumpled, stone beneath her arms and head.

"What's happened, Rinna?" It was Dasha's voice. She was

stroking Rin's hair back from her forehead, and Enna and Isi were rubbing her back, grasping her hands, their touch desperate to ease whatever might be her pain. Rin covered her face with her hands. She had no right to their comfort when it was her fault.

"Razo's dead," she said through the sobs. The hands touching her stopped, frozen by her words. She forced herself to keep talking. "I got Razo and Tusken out of the cage. I . . . I left them in the wood. To come tell you that Selia didn't have Tusken so you could break out. But Selia's searchers found them. They . . . they killed Razo and took Tusken again."

That was all Rin could say for some time, but she did not need to talk. The three girls were sitting and lying beside her, holding one another, weeping, their arms and legs and hair tangled like the roots of close trees, sobs shaking them like leaves in a high wind.

For hours perhaps they lay there crying. Sometimes Rin noticed that her knees hurt on the stone floor or that her throat ached with thirst, but otherwise she felt a catastrophic numbness. She was aware of herself as if from a distance, watching and wondering how that girl Rin could cry so hard and not break apart.

"Rin," Isi said when she could speak again. "How was Tusken?"

Rin nodded, swallowing until she could find her voice. "He was happy. Playing with Razo."

"Good." Isi exhaled the word. "All right. That's . . ." Her voice caught and she stopped talking.

Rin was still clutching something in her fist, and she rubbed it between her fingers to see what Selia had placed there—a bead. Tusken used to wear it around his neck on a leather band. That proof of the boy's capture cut through the numbness and jabbed at Rin's heart, and she grimaced with the pain, an audible moan escaping her throat.

"She says she wants to send Tusken home." Rin told them of Selia's offer to let Rin take Tusken back to his father as soon as Isi signed her document.

"Was she sincere, Rin?" Isi asked. "Will she let Tusken go if I sign?"

Rin blinked, realizing that Isi wanted to know if she had detected truth or lie in Selia's face. "I'm not sure. I wasn't thinking. I wasn't watching her clearly. I'm sorry."

"Why the eastern provinces?" asked Dasha. Rin could not see her expression in the darkness, but there was a dry rasp to her throat.

Isi could only whisper. "If the king of Bayern were to die without a direct heir, the rulers of each province would vote to select a new monarch for the kingdom. The eastern provinces combined into one body would be the largest. If she convinced two other rulers to stand with her, then her vote would become the majority, and I can guess who she would select for the post. So. She plans to kill me. She most likely *would* return Tusken to Geric, but I can't imagine she'd leave them alone. Somehow, she'd find a way to kill them as well—but not through war, I think. Kel is not strong enough to invade Bayern."

"I don't understand that woman," said Dasha. "She had Tusken. Why lure you here as well? Why not just send you word of Tusken's kidnapping along with her demands?"

"She's crazy." Enna's voice was so full of sorrow, Rin scarcely recognized it.

Yes, Selia might be crazy, but Rin remembered her face and words the night before as she gloated, Razo and Tusken in the cage. Had it only been one day? To Rin it felt like weeks. "More than anything, she wants Isi to see her victory. Last night she was so happy Isi was there, she couldn't stop talking. I don't think she meant to talk that much. She couldn't help herself. Winning isn't enough—she wants to win in front of Isi."

Isi moaned. "I think you're right, Rin. Save us all, I think that's it."

"Cilie is here," Rin said. "Watching Tusken. She's Selia's lady-in-waiting."

Isi nodded. "Of course, and what a lovely irony— betrayed by another lady-in-waiting. Selia knew if some poor girl came to me with a story of abuse and abandonment, I'd take her in. Fool that I am. That will be how she gets to Geric and Tusken after my death—she'll get her followers into the palace. Geric and Tusken will be under constant threat of poisoning or accidents."

"And if they die," said Dasha, "Selia will become queen of Bayern."

Rin remembered the coldness in Selia's eyes when she spoke of taking Tusken as her own son, the delight she took in imagining Isi's pain. That little boy who loved to discover fat snails stuck to the undersides of leaves and holes in the shrubs perfect for climbing through—he was in that woman's clutches. He saw Razo die, and now he was alone and terrified. Rin's chest clenched.

"I want to kill her," said Enna. Despite the fierce crying of the past hour, her voice turned hard. "I want to kill her, Isi. Sometimes killing is justified, isn't it? I wish I didn't . . . I wish. But Selia is Selia, and she killed Razo, and I want to—" Above their heads, a ball of fire popped, briefly illuminating the cell, four walls of stone and a heap of straw in the corner. The light extinguished, leaving behind a scratch of smoke in the darkness.

"Tomorrow," said Isi. "I'll talk to her tomorrow. I'll figure it out, Enna, and you won't have to kill her. Because if she touches one hair on my boy's head"—Isi paused as if trying to find enough breath to speak—"then she'll answer to me."

It must have been day by then, but it still seemed to be night in that dark room below the castle. Crying had made Rin's eyes sting, her body throb, and she lay side by side with the fire sisters. She was not sure whose arm was on hers or whose hair tickled her face, but there was an exhausted relief just to be close, and she slept a little.

Hours later, the shaky glow of a torch peeped through the door's small, barred window. One of the hearth-watchers appeared—a middle-aged man with an uneven beard and shifting eyes.

"Crown—," he began, then changed his mind. "Bayern queen, Her Highness Queen Selia asking for you. You for coming alone."

Isi sat up, her arms resting on her upright knees. "I want to see my son."

"I for taking you. The queen will deciding." He put such emotion into the word "queen" that Rin knew he was in love with Selia.

For a few moments, Isi did not move, but when she rose, it was with purpose. Enna stood beside her.

"I'll go with you."

The hearth-watcher shook his head. "Alone, the queen is saying."

"I'll be all right," Isi said, low enough that her voice did not carry through the door. "She doesn't want me dead— yet. I've still some value until the land matters are settled. If I can talk to her, maybe I can find out more about Tusken, bargain a way to see him. If I can just see him, I think I can take care of her fire-speakers and get Tusken safe."

"Let me go with you, Isi." Enna was pleading now. "I can do better against her this time, I know I can. Please. I don't want you alone with that viper."

"I think it's better that way, Enna. If you or anyone else comes too, Selia might use you to get to me. She'd threaten you, hurt you, and she knows I couldn't stand it. For now, she needs me, but to her, you three are expendable."

As expendable as Razo, Rin thought.

"If she sends food to you, don't eat it," Isi went on. "And the moment you get word that Tusken is safe, don't hesitate— get out any way you can."

Rin shook her head. Strong as Isi was, Rin was not so sure she could withstand Selia's assault.

"Still, Isi," said Enna, squinting at the door. "I don't like the thought of you without a friend at your side. I don't trust her."

Isi forced a casual expression. "Who, Selia? Come on, she's a pussycat. Besides, what's the worst that could happen?"

Enna stared back at her, and then at once they both laughed. It was so sudden, and yet sincere, Rin wondered if the darkness of the dungeon had already turned them mad. But there was a light in their eyes, an intelligence, that made her believe they laughed because they needed to.

Enna shook her head. "Send her my warmest regards, and if the opportunity presents itself, I mean my very *warmest* regards."

The sound of the laugh stirred something in Rin. Her

core firmed, and she felt a surge of hope. So when Isi rose to the door, Rin sprang up beside her.

"Where is Tusken?" Rin demanded of the man—a hearth-watcher, she saw by his clothing. "Tell me where she's got Tusken."

The hearth-watcher shook his head, his expression startled.

"Tell me where Tusken is," said Rin again, finding any energy inside her and pushing it into words. She was flailing, she knew, but she had to try. The man just kept shaking his head, so Rin tried, "Let us all out. Don't take Isi to Selia—take her out of the castle. Let her go into the wood. Get Tusken and let him go too. Let us all go."

The man's eyes narrowed at Rin. "The queen waiting," he said with malice. Again, from the way he spoke of the queen, she could see the adoration quivering in his expression. This was a man who would die for his mistress, and she guessed he was so full of Selia's voice, Rin's weak whimpering could not tempt him away. She had no other solution, no way to save Isi or Tusken, no idea at all. Sadness doused her, and buried under thoughts of Razo she crumpled to the floor.

Dasha and Enna seemed confused by Rin's outburst, but Isi whispered, "Thanks for trying, Rin." To Enna she said, "Keep them safe," and she smiled before the door clanged shut.

They waited.

No one brought food, poisoned or otherwise, but Dasha filled their cupped hands with water she pulled from the moisture in the air. Rin drank greedily. The water was clear and tasteless, as if it had come from fresh rainwater. Apparently the floor of the dungeon had been sticky with damp at first, but Dasha had dried it all. So they huddled on the straw while Rin recounted her time with Razo and Tusken. Enna got more and more angry, but Dasha seemed to crumple. Even in the scatty light from the torch, the heartbreak on Dasha's face was as visible as noon sun.

She really did love him, Rin thought. *She loved him in her way as much as I do.* That knowledge made Razo's death feel a hundred times more real, and Rin had to look away.

"Say something hopeful," Dasha said. "I can't stand all this . . . just give me one light thought."

"I think it's my birthday," said Rin.

Enna croaked a half-laugh. "That is really sad, Rin."

"Happy birthday," Dasha whispered.

If Rin were home, one of the brothers might smoke a beehive and bring home a dripping comb. Honey on bread was enough for a celebration, but some years Ma made cakes, and of course the children would decorate her with flowers and sing the song of years. Then Ma would put Ulan or Sari in charge and take Rin for a walk to their favorite copse of aspen, where they'd sit and chat for hours. Honey and flowers and songs were nice—but that walk in the woods with Ma, that was her birthday.

Rin folded herself over her legs, too dried out to do anything but ache.

Enna paced and occasionally struck the door, cursing Selia and her various body parts, and then Razo's stupidity for letting himself be killed. Once she was standing by the door and said, "I think they're nearby. I'm not so good at hearing the wind as Isi, but I think that's her. There's another room down here, and a draft came from under its door."

After that, Enna would not leave the door, straining for any breeze, any hint of where Isi was and what was happening.

A long time later, a door nearby slammed open and they heard Selia's voice shrill and angry.

"What did you do? What did—no! Curse you, idiots!" And she screamed an angry, piercing scream like a pig at slaughter. When they heard her voice again, she was closer, as if in the narrow corridor just outside their door. "Fine. Fine, fine, fine. Too late now. Get rid of it. Throw it at her friends, tell them that Tusken is next if they lift a finger against me. Do you hear? Tusken is next!"

The three girls were on their feet, watching the door.

"They can't have meant . . . ," Dasha began. "She was not talking about . . ."

The door to their dungeon opened just enough for them to see the hands of two soldiers holding a body, yellow hair fallen over the face. They dumped her on the ground.

She did not twitch. She did not groan. The guards slammed the door and fled, but Rin, like Dasha and Enna, had eyes only for Isi. Dasha and Enna knelt at Isi's side, but the terror in Rin kept her still. She already knew, could already see that something had departed out of Isi. She was looking at a hollowed log. The girl on the floor was dead.

asha's fingers were on Isi's neck, then hovering above her lips. She spoke in hurried gasps. "She's . . . she's not breathing. I don't see a wound, but her hands are ice cold, and she's not—"

Enna shoved Dasha out of the way and crouched beside Isi's body.

"Isi, get up," she said, almost conversationally, then her voice deepened into a demand. "That . . . that *thing* can't kill you. You're Isi, you're my yellow lady, you can't just stop. So get up!"

Enna shook Isi, and the queen's lifeless head rolled on her neck, her hair falling over her face. Rin backed away until she hit the wall. How did these things happen? How did living become dagger-sharp and dangerous, and everything so murky and cold, no way home, no light, just wandering and wandering and being locked away and killing and dying and pain? The weight of the whole world hung above her head, threatening to crush her, promising to make the end of everything.

She wanted to be far away. She could not run, she would not let herself scream, and in desperation she sought out the one thing she could to survive the moment—she tried to remember the calm of a tree.

She was standing straight, her feet grounded on the earth, her head reaching for light. She let her chest fill with the memory of a tree's thoughts, the thrumming of sap, the contentment of soil and light. Peace rushed up from her toes, strengthening her legs, making her skin feel as hard as bark. When she opened her eyes again, the whole world seemed changed. Still, timeless, a breath held, as if she were both awake in the human world and asleep inside the green world. Dasha was bent over Isi. Enna was sobbing, laying her head on Isi's neck. But Rin the girl, Rin the tree in her serenity, understood that everything was going to be fine.

She looked over Isi's body, but she saw it like a tree—it was not chopped down or burned to ash, not broken into bits. It was simply uprooted. The leaves were beginning to wilt, the roots drying in the air, but it had not been long— perhaps only moments before. Dasha had said Isi's hands were ice cold. In Rin's pocket of stillness, her thoughts cleared of emotion, she realized that was strange. If Isi had stopped breathing moments before, her body should still be warm. This was not a normal death, then. Something might be done. It was out of her power, but . . . She looked at Enna and seemed to see a mass of white and orange swirling around her—wind and fire, breath and heat, dancing together, ready for action. So Rin reached out her hand, gripped Enna's shoulder, and tried to be to Enna what a tree was to Rin. A source of peace, a place of clear thought. Just an idea of it, that was where to begin.

Rin found the words to speak. "She's only just stopped breathing, she's cold and airless, only just."

Enna breathed in, a great slow gasp as loud as wind rushing through a cave. Her sobbing stopped. She looked back at Rin and blinked. Where despair had clouded Enna's eyes, an idea glimmered.

Enna placed her opened hands on Isi's chest and belly. Her eyes closed. Rin closed her eyes, too. She was still touching Enna, and the deep, tough thread of her core understood what Enna was doing—setting tiny flares of heat inside Isi, in her heart, in her blood and muscles, filling her everywhere with gentle taps, warming her body, the work as intricate as threading a tapestry. And she pushed air into Isi's nose, into her lungs, in and out too, the rhythm as natural as breathing, the movement swirling the hair over her face.

While Enna's wind tried to force her to breathe, subtle strokes of heat worked at Isi's heart, making her chest rise and fall in spasms—*ta-tum, ta-tum, ta-tum* . . .

The peace in Rin was starting to fade, the surety that everything would be all right trickling down her length, dripping from her fingertips. Rin opened her eyes. Isi was still, her eyes open but unlooking. And terror began to scratch at

Rin, to shake her limbs. Tusken's mother was dead. Tusken would have no Ma. Rin's grip on Enna's shoulder weakened.

But Enna did not stop. "You do not get to die, Isi. *She* doesn't get to kill you, Anidori-Kiladra. You are too strong to die. Listen to me!"

Keeping one hand on Isi's chest, Enna grabbed Dasha and pulled her close. "Do what I'm doing. She needs water too, and more fire. Easy with the heat, just enough to wake her up."

"I . . . I . . . ," Dasha stuttered.

"Do it!" yelled Enna.

Rin did not wait to be commanded too. She sat by Isi's head, held her face in her hands, smoothed her hair as if her hands were wind going through leaves. She tried to find that peace again, to feel it rise out of the earth and into her core, to let it flow into Isi. She did not know if it would help, but the terror was so thick if she did not try something, she would harrow her way out of the dungeon herself. There was this body—this still, cold body before her, this husk that used to be Isi, and she could not bear it. So she reminded herself of who Isi really was, the truth of Isi. The words formed in her throat, and she decided to speak them aloud. If people-speaking could add any good or truth to the world, then she demanded of herself that it do so now, convince Isi of who she was, help bring her back before she slipped completely into that unknown of beyond.

"Mother of Tusken," Rin whispered, "wife of Geric, queen of Bayern, daughter of Kildenree, friend of Enna, friend of Dasha and Finn and Razo. And Rin."

And Enna was saying, "Take a breath. Take a breath, Isi. You don't get to die. I can feel you in there still. Just wake up!"

A breath. A gasp. Rin pulled back, as surprised as if she'd suddenly found herself holding a snake.

The hair over Isi's face stirred. Her heart was beating so loudly, Rin could hear its murmur. Isi's chest rose. The three girls bent over her, their hands on her arms, on her cheeks, their breath held as if not to make any sound louder than Isi's heart.

Dasha swept the hair off of Isi's face. The queen's eyelids closed and opened. And closed.

"Anidori-Kiladra Talianna Isilee," Enna said, her face drenched from crying. "If you're really alive, you'd better say so right now or I'll kill you myself."

Isi's eyelids barely parted. She opened her mouth, then coughed dryly. Dasha's fingers flinched, and Rin guessed the Tiran girl was moving water in the air to wet the queen's throat and mouth.

Isi's voice croaked. "Just now, stuffing the queen of Kel into a barrel of nails sounds like a mercy."

The three girls laughed, then sobbed, hugging one another, repeating Isi's words again and again, wiping their running noses on their hems. Isi just smiled and curled up.

They were all exhausted from laughing and weeping and almost dying, and they lay down, bundled around one another. Rin slept with her head on Dasha's side, one hand on Isi's hair. Enna slept closest to Isi, her arms wrapped fiercely around her friend to keep her warm.

in woke with hope clawing up from the pit of misery in her chest. If they could get to Razo's body, maybe they could fix him as they had done for Isi. Dasha could give him water, and Enna could give him heat and breath so he lived again. *If only . . . if only . . .* She closed her eyes and imagined Razo breathing in, sitting up, and asking, "What happened? Did I fall asleep? Where's Tusken, and why are all you crazy girls staring at me like that?"

She clung to the hope because she sensed it was about to blow away. Isi'd had no serious injury and she'd stopped breathing only moments before. Fire and wind could not heal a burn or a sword wound, could not bring back a boy dead for a day. *My brother is dead.* The thought pressed on Rin, pushed against her eyes, filled her mouth. She thrust away that knowledge, desperate to keep it from burying her, at least not until Tusken was safe.

Isi stirred and seemed to want to wake, but Enna

kept shushing her and insisting she sleep on, until at last Isi protested that she was thirsty enough to drink Enna's blood.

Then Enna popped right up and said brightly, "Good morning, Your Majesty. I believe the rooster has crowed."

Dasha said there was not much water left in the dungeon air. She pulled as much as she could, letting fat drops splash into their cupped hands. Rin sipped the warm liquid from her hands, licking her fingers, feeling the air around her crackle and dry up. Their bellies all groaned in chorus, and to distract them from hunger, Isi told them about the day before. She and Selia had talked for hours. Selia had tried to persuade Isi to sign the document, but Isi had insisted she would not sign anything without seeing Tusken first.

"I was a little better at resisting her people-speaking than last time, especially when she was trying to provoke me to do what I didn't want to do. Her ability to dissuade me from action was still quite strong. After a time she got frustrated and wanted her pet fire-speakers to hurt me without really hurting me, just to cause me pain. They were poking me with heat. It stung. I didn't attack back, but I did wash away their heat with wind. Nuala, her favorite of them, retaliated and pulled all the heat out of my body. I think it was a mistake. I think she was just clumsy and took too much. But that's what did it . . ." Isi put a hand on her chest and stared at it for some time.

"Do you want to tell us?" Dasha asked, her voice more concerned than curious. "What was it like?"

"It hurt." Isi took a breath. "It hurt a lot, as if she'd put her fingernails into me and was yanking out something essential, like, oh, all my internal organs."

"Lovely," said Enna.

Isi's eyes were haunted. "The yanking kept going, and I couldn't . . . while Selia was talking at me, I couldn't concentrate enough to call a wind. Then a huge pulsing numbness exploded from my belly and radiated through my whole body, and . . . I don't remember much of anything until I heard Rin's voice, and then Enna shouting at me. You were none too gentle."

"What am I supposed to do when my best friend dies on me? Pat your cheek and say good for you?"

Isi squinted at the dark wall as if she were trying to make out someone's face from a distance.

"You remember something else," Rin whispered.

"Do I?" Isi smiled, surprised. "I wasn't sure. It's like I have a memory of a memory, barely the scent of it. I think . . . there is a place that still remembers. Where all things know all the languages. I think I was there, or almost there. I felt something . . ." She frowned in concentration. "I think I was bursting with the first words of *all* the languages. A good feeling. For a moment, I was looking forward to learning them all."

Isi's gaze shot to the door. "Someone's coming."

"Quick, pretend to be dead," said Enna.

Isi lay on her side, her back to the door. Dasha and Enna knelt beside her.

"What's your plan?" Isi whispered.

"Surprise," Enna said. "I guess."

Rin did not think. She bound to her feet and pressed herself against the wall, closest to the door's opening. She'd stopped moving just as a boy of about fourteen years, his chin and cheeks red and pocked, peeked through the bars in the door.

Enna and Rin met eyes, then Enna leaned down and whispered something in Isi's ear.

"I am just a page," he said, his Kelish accent less pronounced than most Rin had heard. "So do not hurt me, please. Her Majesty wants—*aah!*"

He cried out as Isi twitched. Enna and Dasha pretended shock.

"Can it be?" Enna exclaimed. "Is it possible? Does she . . . *live?*"

Isi twitched again.

"*Aah!*" said the page.

Dasha stooped over Isi's body. "There's something strange. I can't feel a pulse, and yet she moves! Come look! Hurry, you'll want to report this to your queen."

The page opened the door, barely peeking through. Three soldiers were gawking over his shoulder. Isi trembled again, and they recoiled, but when she stilled, they opened the door a little more, peeking closer, their attention wholly on Isi.

It was not much space, but it was enough for a thin girl with a lot of sneaking practice. Her whole mind, her whole body, pulled in thoughts of that tree by the wall—no trunk, a few scrawny branches thrusting leaves up to the sun, its roots still living, still drinking and growing, still breaking stone.

Go like roots under soil, she told herself. *Moving, though no one sees; living, though no one notices.*

She bent her knees and eased through the opening, ducking beneath the page's arm, twisting to avoid the guard. She did not look back as she left the dungeon behind.

Rin fought to keep her legs from shaking and her steps careless. Trees were never afraid. Finding Tusken was as important as roots finding water, as leaves cupping sunshine. She flowed through the underground corridor, up the twisting stair. Some thoughts she tried to keep small and quiet in her head—the knowledge that if she was discovered again, Selia would cut her throat and toss her over the wall. It did not matter anymore, not since she saw Isi die, not since Razo died. If life and death were so sudden, so arbitrary, then nothing mattered. Except Tusken.

Climbing from the lower stairs into the central chamber was the worst part. Only a handful of soldiers, Nuala, and Selia had seen Rin. Dressed in Kelish robes, walking with purpose, she hoped others would dismiss her. But climbing up from the dungeon would certainly make her look suspicious.

She hesitated near the top, listening. There were footfalls, conversation, but perhaps not near. She took a deep breath, reminded her body what it felt like to be calm, to feel breezy, to walk with casual purpose.

She climbed the last stair. The guards at the gate were looking out, not in. Workers were coming and going from the kitchen, but did not glance her way. She circled the first floor of the central tower, picking up a discarded bucket to aid her look of errand runner. The spotty-faced page came up from the dungeons and continued upstairs. She turned her back and pretended busyness sorting plates on a table, hiding in plain sight until she could no longer hear the slap of his boots.

She passed by the four chambers of the side towers, their doors all open in the summer heat—kitchen, kitchen storage, armory, and a rest chamber for the guards. None seemed likely places to keep a kidnapped prince.

Rin started toward the central winding stairs up to the second floor.

"...have much to account for, Nuala. Let me see for myself if the little sausage lives."

Selia's voice. Rin stopped, pressing her back against the rounded wall separating her from the stairs. Cold sluiced through her limbs, and she held her breath, listening to Selia and her hearth-watchers descending into the dungeon. Rin closed her eyes, trying to remember the rhythmic whooshing of life inside a tree.

The lick of sunlight on a leaf, she told herself. *Deep water flowing.*

With trembling stilled and breathing slowed, Rin left her wall and climbed the stairs. She'd already begun to ascend when two more soldiers came down after Selia's party. Rin's face burned red in surprise, betraying herself in her panic. It was too late to hide the blush, to pretend innocence and normalcy.

They stopped her, demanding something in Kelish. She tried to moisten her mouth, but people-speaking was useless when she could not speak their language.

Then again . . . She could not risk saying a word, but if guessing a person's thoughts and desires was part of people-speaking, she was not completely powerless.

The soldier who had spoken was handsome—very handsome, with bright blue eyes and a square jaw, firm shoulders and chest. By comparison, his perfectly normal companion seemed dull.

Rin ducked her head, putting a shy hand over her mouth, pretending her blush was caused by embarrassed affection. Recalling the mannerisms of her oldest niece Minna whenever she met new boys, Rin glanced up at the handsome soldier through her lashes, back down again, and up, as if she would never tire of the sight of him. She licked her lips, smiling the sweetest, most innocent smile. And then, she giggled, covering her eyes, hiding playfully behind her hands.

The second soldier groaned impatiently. Clearly the handsome one got this reaction a lot from girls. The first spoke again, his tone exasperated, but there was no real fire behind it. He was flattered, she could tell, and now there was a danger he might corner her into a conversation. So she giggled again, peeking at him through her fingers, and fled up the stairs.

She stopped at the top just out of sight, her hand on her chest to keep her heart from thudding through, listening to hear if they would follow. One soldier called up after her, but the second said something in a teasing tone to his companion, and they continued down. Rin exhaled and took in her surroundings.

The central chamber on the second floor was fitted with large tables, carved wooden chairs, tapestries twitching in the breeze that arched in through the tall, thin windows. Compared to the bustle of downstairs, it was as quiet as a meadow morning. It took some time for Rin to make her way through all four side chambers. One of the doors was locked. She could hear voices on the other side, and she waited for someone inside to emerge. Her legs hurt, as if she'd been standing for days. Selia was down in the dungeon even now. She would notice Rin's absence. Soon they would search, and no girlish giggles would protect her.

Some minutes passed when two disheveled-looking women emerged from the fourth door and blinked at the day as if just waking up. They hurried downstairs, letting the door swing closed behind them. Rin stood behind it, grabbing the door before it shut and slipping inside. Another sleeping chamber, this one crammed with beds and pallets, and completely empty of life.

The winding stair to the third story of the central tower seemed to stretch into the clouds, and she imagined it the trunk of a tree, leading her out to its branches. The idea made the castle seem less hostile.

At last it opened into a large receiving room, not as grandly furnished as Isi's in Bayern, but neat with rugs and tables and lounges. It was empty. Two of the side doors stood open and Rin moved through those chambers, finding no one. She tried the door of the third—locked. The fourth was closed but unlocked. It was a bedchamber, this one with only one large bed. The narrow light from the window dropped a slit of yellow across the floor, neat as the slice of a blade. The contrast of concentrated brightness against the dim room was blinding. Rin squinted through the glare and spotted a bump on the bed, a shape like a sleeping child.

She leaped forward, her hands out to pull him in to her chest, to cuddle him and kiss him.

"Tusken!"

The shape that gave beneath her touch, soft and square, was a pillow under a blanket. The room was empty.

Rin slammed a fist against the wall and sank to her knees. She was exhausted, starving, her whole self teetering on the edge of despair. Perhaps Tusken was not in the castle itself but in an outbuilding—the garrison perhaps. Or even in the town of Daire to the northeast of the fortress. Wherever he was, there would be hearth-watchers guarding him, and soldiers too. How could Rin possibly get him free? Or even run back to tell Isi without getting charred to bits?

It did not matter, she decided. They had killed Razo. They had killed Isi and would again, and that was wrong. Being with Isi had not changed her the way she'd hoped, but she knew Isi would not quit searching. Rin would check that last locked door, then the garrison, and walk to town if she had to. Keep moving. Throw herself into the fray and hope for the best.

Rin inhaled deeply, letting breath fill her center, and eased her way out the door.

She made sure the door shut silently behind her, then turned. Selia was entering the chamber, surrounded by seven hearth-watchers and several soldiers. Behind Selia, with her head bowed, came Isi.

o. Rin had been so sure Enna and Dasha would not allow Isi to be taken alone again. But Selia must have proved the stronger. Rin ducked behind the nearest chair, but it was too late. She'd been seen.

Nuala yelled in Kelish, and fire erupted on the rug beneath Rin's feet, encircling her in a flaming ring. She screamed, tossing her arms across her face to shield her eyes from the blaze. The fire extinguished just as suddenly as it started and soldiers were around her, hands seizing her arms, shoulders, waist, and hair. She whimpered in pain.

"I won't allow it," Isi was shouting. "If you hurt her, or hurt me again, I will fight back. And you don't want to fight me, Selia. I'm not the same girl you left in the Forest those years ago."

"Easy," said Selia. "No one need fight. Let us talk as friends. I did say no harm would come to anyone as long as you cooperated. When this girl sneaked out of her safe cell and violated my home, she forfeited her right to my protection."

"Selia—," Isi started.

Selia lifted one of her pale, thin-fingered hands. "But to show you my compassion, I will pardon her. For the moment. You see she still lives, the fire that could have been her death doused and gone. Her safety as well as Tusken's depends on you, Crown Princess. But just to be safe, since she's proved to be a slippery little thing . . ." Selia motioned to one of the soldiers, a thick-set man with auburn hair and white temples. He clamped iron cuffs around Rin's wrists, one hand gripping her upper arm.

Rin winced as the cuffs bit into her skin and wondered why they did not just kill her. But she remembered Isi telling Enna, *Selia might threaten you, hurt you . . . use you to get to me.* Rin's stomach squelched as if full of sour milk.

"Your Majesty?" It was hard to use that title on Selia, but she managed to squeak it out. She was cuffed and held, but not gagged, and she reasoned she had nothing much to lose. "May I speak with you?"

Something in Rin's aspect might have intrigued Selia, or alarmed her, because she strolled a little nearer, keeping the soldier who held Rin between them.

"You have something worth telling me?" Selia raised an eyebrow.

Rin cleared her throat, then spoke softly, sure Selia would

not allow her to keep talking if her hearth-watchers over-
heard.

"When you're muddled and lost in a crowd of people,
you can't see yourself anymore. All you can see is them. So
many faces and voices, so hard to remember which one is
you, because it's easier to see all of them than to see yourself. It can feel like drowning."

Rin was breathing so hard, she was getting light-headed.
Though Selia cut her eyes at Rin, she did not interrupt. Rin
continued.

"You need to be up a little higher, just to keep ahold of
yourself. You *should* be a queen. That is what you were meant
for, right? A queen—one woman who is lifted above, who
has the right to speak and everyone must obey. Who is not
lost in the crowd. No one would question the way you hold
yourself up, the way you speak out, if only you were a queen.
It's not fair that a queen is decided by birth, is it? A queen
should be chosen, a queen should be the one everyone loves
and wants to follow. That's you."

Still Selia listened, though her gaze was not something
Rin enjoyed enduring. Rin's breathing was becoming more
sure.

"I understand that, Selia, and I think you know I can
sympathize more than anyone. But I also understand the
rest." Here her voice dipped even softer. "The hate that
chokes your soul, the shame of cheating to get what you

want, of tricking people into loving you, of pushing your-self up so high you can no longer touch and hold the people who loved you. Everything you've accomplished doesn't feel as good as it should, does it? You hurt so much. And you think that hurting Isi in turn will make that go away at last. It won't. When Isi is dead, when Tusken and Geric are dead, when you're crowned queen of Bayern, the pain will still chase you. Let Isi go. Let Tusken go. Be queen of Kel. This is your best chance at being happy."

It was alarming to witness the struggle of emotions on Selia's face—anger, curiosity, fear, wonder, and beneath it all, horrifying pain. Her face was blotchy red, her chin quivered, her eyes blinked too fast. Unexpected tears stung in Rin's eyes as this woman who had killed her brother became so terrifyingly human. Rin's heart ached for the pale-haired girl from Kildenree: homeless, wandering, unhappy, and searching all her life for relief. *She could help me,* Rin thought, *and I could help her. I could.*

Then Selia straightened, her nostrils flaring. She breathed in and her struggle ended. She came very close to Rin, lean-ing so her lips touched Rin's ear as she whispered, "You understand nothing. You are a worm quivering on a stone. You are a crushed beetle. And if you'd had any real talent at understanding, you would have seen that I don't care to be understood."

Selia put a hand on the soldier's upper arm and whis-pered, "Hurt her."

His elbow slammed into Rin's gut, and she doubled over, groaning.

Isi started. "No!"

"Whoops!" Selia said. "I said, *don't* hurt the girl. So sorry, Crown Princess, an error. We should get on with these negotiations to avoid any more mishaps."

Rin's gut wrenched, her wrists smarted where metal rubbed against her skin, her head ached from her rough capture. Speaking had not helped. Selia would force Isi to sign the document and then she would kill her. Rin sensed that familiar pit of despair open beneath her, felt herself barely balanced and slipping. *Useless, hopeless, failed again, Razo's dead and nothing matters . . .*

The windows were open, and the breeze that trickled inside carried the first cool murmurings of autumn. Autumn was Razo's favorite season, mostly because he liked nuts, and nothing pleased him more than scavenging for his own food—except perhaps eating it. Despite her nauseating pain, Rin wanted to smile. Ma said that giving in to despair was like eating poisonous berries to keep from feeling hungry. Razo never despaired.

You're Forest born, he'd told her.

Rin kept her eyes on Isi, set her jaw, and breathed deeply.

Selia was sitting on a carved chair with deep red cushions, several paces from Isi. The seven hearth-watchers surrounded Isi, and two soldiers with swords drawn and bows on their shoulders stood behind Selia's chair. Selia was smiling at Isi, speaking in her usual calm, pleasant tone.

"Spark a single flame, and Tusken loses a finger. Hurt one of my people, and Tusken loses a limb. I'd prefer to keep him alive for my purposes, but truth be told, I don't need *all* of him. That leads to a question—how much fun can a child have without legs or fingers? I can't imagine you would be so cruel, Crown Princess, but I really don't know."

"I won't hurt you." Isi's face troubled, her voice heightened as if she were trying to speak from the bottom of a well. "But understand, if you kill me or hurt Tusken, an army of your hearth-watchers and soldiers won't stop that girl in the dungeon. If you had truly killed me, Enna would have seen to you and all your followers. The moment she so much as suspects I'm hurt, she and Dasha will tear this castle—"

Selia tsked. "Really, such talk."

"I will protect myself. If you—"

"Please, show some pride. There is no need to grovel for mercy. Yesterday was a mistake"—she glanced at Nuala, whose broad face was bright red with chagrin—"and will not happen again, so long as you behave. I regret the tactics taken to encourage your participation, and I regret your placement in those foul dungeons. An oversight on the part of my steward. You are my guest, an honored prisoner of war, and from now on you will be treated as such. Your son will go home and your friends as well, if only you will sign your name here."

Selia gestured to the ornate table before her, the only barrier between the two yellow-haired women. A document lay beside a quill and pot of ink. Rin observed Selia, trying to tell if the woman was lying. She seemed to mean what she said—she was willing to send Tusken home if Isi signed. But there were mysteries behind those words that Rin could not guess.

"Sign, Crown Princess. Sign your name. So simple a thing! You acknowledge that I have won this move in our war game, and thus allow the boy to return to his father. I swear on my own life that I will not kill him, and he will not come to any harm, save if you break my rules." She picked up the paper, wafting it in the air, her eyes shut as if it created a most refreshing breeze. "Just sign your name, my dear. Just sign."

"Fine." Isi spoke rigidly, as if she had practiced her words in advance. "I will put my signature to that document, decreeing you lady of the eastern provinces on Tusken's eighteenth birthday, so long as he is alive and well on that day and living with his parents in Bayern."

Selia barely flinched, but Rin's eyes caught it. "A marvelous idea! Well thought. Sign first, and I swear upon the life of my mother that I will add that clause as an addendum."

"I . . ." Isi shook her head, a tight, small gesture. "Write the addendum first. And I will sign it, after I see my son."

Selia clicked her tongue in disappointment. "Crown Princess, Crown Princess, now why would I hazard my most valuable possession? As much as I trust my voice soothes your more suicidal instincts, I just don't know what you might do if Tusken were in this room. I need to keep him away from you so I can return him safely to his father."

Isi glanced once at Rin before speaking again, her face taxed as though she spoke with effort. "That was clever. What you did. Escaping execution in Bayern."

"Yes, it was, wasn't it?" Selia smiled at the window as if at a pleasant memory.

"How did you do it?"

Selia looked at Isi with sympathy, and Rin knew she guessed that Isi was trying to get her to reveal some weakness. "It is a marvelous story. I will tell you all about it after you sign."

Isi pressed her lips together, breathing in through her nose. "I guess you made an offer to your prison guard, though I can't think of many things you had to offer . . ."

Selia sat up straighter, her eyes twinkling. "Oh, is that what you imagine? You have no idea what I'm capable of."

"I know you're capable of escaping death by my hands, but I've done the same from yours," Isi said, her face still down. "I know you're capable of marrying the king of Kel, just as I married the king of Bayern. So far I haven't seen you do much that I haven't done as well."

Selia stood, her lips trembling. She must have known that Isi was baiting her, must have read those intentions in her old rival as easily as she talked her into submission. But she could not seem to help speaking.

"I am capable of everything, Anidori. Everything! It was all me. You should feel flattered by the lengths I go to get your attention. Even the war was my gift to you."

Isi scoffed, but Rin knew it was just to provoke Selia more. "You started the war?"

Selia's smile was condescending, making sure Isi knew she realized her intentions, though she was willing to speak all the same. "After your botched execution, I left Bayern and went south to Tira. I adore Ingridan and genuinely considered marrying the prince there, but he has no true power. Shame. Tira was a lovely place and so enchanted by war, much to my delight. After some prodding on my part, the Assembly was swooning in rapture at the idea of invading Bayern."

Isi gaped, genuinely shocked, and no reaction could have pleased Selia more. She laughed, clasping her hands to her chest.

"Yes, that was me! It was a wonderful plan, until... Enna, was it? Yes, Enna started burning. As you can imagine, I was intrigued by the idea of a person setting fires out of nothing. I spent some time in Yasid and uncovered writings on how to learn the way with fire, bringing them back to Tira. There was a disillusioned Tiran war captain by the name of Ledel who was embarrassingly fond of me. He was thrilled to try and learn the fire way, to teach a band of soldiers too, and simply gushed over my idea of using it to restart the Tiran and Bayern war. I left him to it and journeyed on to Kel, just in case he failed, which he did, poor dear. But no matter, by then I was courting the king of Kel. I have decided war is much too unpredictable. This way is superior, because here we are."

Isi did not try to hide her shock and anger. That was wise, Rin thought. Selia would see through it anyway.

"You didn't explain how you freed yourself from the barrel of nails," Isi said. "I imagine it's too shameful to repeat."

Again, fury flashed in Selia's face, and Rin winced, expecting at the very least thrown chairs and tables. Selia's eyes were hot, but she remained in control, speaking in fixed, measured phrases.

"It was so ordinary as hardly worth the trouble to mention. I made friends with my guard. I invited him to free me and put some animal in my place. I suggested he be the one to bury the dead animal so no other knew. So devoted he was to me, he did not speak of it all these years, but of course I could not trust him to remain silent forever. And if anyone suspected I was still alive, getting my hands on you and Tusken would prove so much more difficult. Even that loose end is tied up now, thanks to you. I had my hearth-watchers burn that little town in order to lure you out. Geric came instead, but as I'd hoped, my one-time collaborator rode along."

"Brynn. You had your fire-speakers kill him."

Selia examined her fingernails. "Was that his name? Of course I had to wound Geric as well so you would come trotting to his rescue. With both you and Geric out of the palace, your darling son would be much easier to carry away. So I thought. But not as easy as if you actually brought him along for the plucking! Many thanks for that, Crown Princess."

Isi squeezed her eyes shut.

Selia eased into her cushioned chair with a forced calm, the remnants of anger disappearing. "Well. You see how utterly useless it is to fight against me. I have friends in five kingdoms, I have knowledge and understanding you can only guess. And I will win. Submit to me." She spoke the words like a mother to a baby, encouraging her to rest. "I know you are exhausted; it will be such a relief. Submit to me, and then you will rest and all will be well."

Isi inhaled deeply, lowered her head, and knelt. With deliberate show, she bowed her body to the floor, her forehead pressed to the rug, her arms stretched out.

It caused Rin an almost physical pain to watch Selia's satisfaction then, her glory in victory. Rin knew how Selia felt—strong, unique, special, sure that others could not comprehend it, but at the same time, frantic that they know. Rin was sickened now to remember her own rush of elation when she realized how much she could affect Wilem's actions. She had glowed with the heady sensation that she understood everyone—she could do whatever she desired. How that desire had burned!

Rin was still doubled over from the slam to her gut. Perhaps she'd been wrong to stifle her desire to speak all those years. If she had not fought it, she would be stronger now. She might stop Selia, instead of cowering shackled in a corner, Razo dead, Isi prostrate.

Seeing Isi beside Selia set them into sharp relief. Selia spoke like a queen, ruled and commanded and moved like a queen. But Isi *was* a queen—even captured, even prone on the floor. It stung a little, to see in Isi what Rin wanted but could not be. But it was liberating too, just to recognize real power. Knowing Isi, Rin did not believe she could ever be tricked into buying Selia's crooked kind of queenship.

I don't want to be Selia, Rin thought. *Maybe I'm weaker for that, but so be it. I don't want to be her.*

Selia gazed at Isi for some time, then sighed as if regretful to end the moment. "That's incredibly sweet, Crown Princess, but the submission I requested included your signature on the paper. No more questions. No more stalling. I will see you sign."

Isi returned to her knees, her eyes glancing at the paper

on the table. Her lips were white and trembling, but still she said, "And I will see my son."

Selia spoke as if to a naughty but adorable child. "Here, I will compromise. That is what a good queen does. I will show you some token of his well-being, all right? Nuala, go request something of the boy's from Cilie."

Nuala hurried to the winding stairs, her head bowed. Since her careless and failed killing of Isi, she had lost her self-assured bearing. It made Rin wonder what Selia had done to the woman. Or surely Selia need only speak a few words to tear the confidence from her previously proud follower.

The sounds of Nuala's footfalls climbed down. So Tusken was not behind the locked door. In the garrison then? Rin wondered if Isi would strike now that they had a better idea of her son's location. But Selia kept talking, her voice sliding over Rin, slithering into her ears, filling her head. Isi's eyes were closed as if struggling against the noise. She plugged her ears for a moment, but Selia's voice was high and became even louder, and she soon gave up.

Rin did not bother trying. Her middle still ached as if she'd swallowed herself, and she stared at the thick clamps around her wrists. While she looked, the single metal link joining the two shackles glowed red, then faded. Rin blinked. Again it glowed red, then orange before fading. Isi was working on her chain, sending heat into that ring to weaken it. Trying to help her escape. The thought made Rin sad. For once she did not want to run away—she wished to stay and help.

The ring glowed yellow, then white, the heat burning through the cuffs to Rin's wrists, and Rin pulled her hands away from each other, the cuffs biting into her skin, the link thinning, lengthening just a little. One of the hearth-watchers muttered something to another, both alert now and looking at Rin. The heat vanished, and Isi ducked her head. The hearth-watchers looked at Selia and whispered to each other, as if trying to decide whether to interrupt Selia. But no fire had erupted to cause alarm, and Isi sent no more heat, though they watched her now with hawk eyes.

Nuala returned with Cilie. Isi's former waiting woman hurried to Selia's side, taking in the sight of her mistress with wide, hungry eyes. She handed something to Selia, and when Selia touched her hand to take it, Cilie's eyes wetted with joy. The display enraged Rin. That pig-eyed woman had betrayed Isi and conspired to kidnap Tusken so she could be Selia's lap dog? Rin should have pummeled her when she had the chance.

Cilie curtsied deeply and began to walk out of the room backward, never looking away from Selia.

"Wait, Cilie."

Cilie froze. Selia's tone had not been pleased.

"How is the boy?"

"He's well, Your Majesty."

"Are you sure? You aren't with him at the moment."

"I left him with many protectors and only just to answer your summons."

"I ordered you never to leave his side, did I not?"

Cilie's eyes went wide at Selia's icy tone. She stared, unblinking, unmoving.

"Did I not very specifically tell you to never leave his side? Why, here is his worried mother. What must she think of me, seeing that the caregiver I assigned to Tusken would leave him so readily?"

Cilie's mouth opened and closed, until she finally stammered out, "I was only . . . you called me—"

"I asked for tokens, not for you. You could have stayed. I need to show his mother how seriously I take this, Cilie, so she can rest assured her son is in safe hands. You failed me. I hope it is only a part of you that is unreliable and not your whole being. You are made up of pieces, Cilie. You would be better off without them all. Give me one."

Selia opened a drawer in the table, pulled out a pair of long, thin scissors, and handed them to Cilie. The girl's eyes were wide, her lips trembling, and she stared at the scissors as if at her own death.

"My lady, Your Majesty, I don't—"

"Do you question me?"

Cilie broke into sobs and fell to the ground, petting Selia's skirt. "No, please, I will do whatever you ask, mistress. Whatever you want of me."

"You have such lovely hair. Haven't I always told you so?"

"Y-yes, yes, you have."

"Give it to me."

Cilie's hand flew to her head. Rin had seen Cilie brush that hair for an hour at a time, her beautiful thick hair that framed a plain face, wide cheeks, and small, close-together eyes. Beautiful hair that all of Isi's waiting women had envied, that the palace women had admired whenever she'd walked past. Fat tears began to drop from Cilie's eyes, but she did not blink.

"My hair?" she whispered.

Selia nodded matter-of-factly. "A fitting sacrifice, I think. But I am all benevolence. If you wish, you may choose some other piece."

The scissors trembled, but Cilie did not hesitate as she lifted her left hand and let the silver blades slide over her smallest finger. Her right hand squeezed, and the scissors bit through bone.

If Cilie screamed, Rin did not hear it. Everything in Rin went out like a smothered candle. Suddenly she was crumpled on the floor. The soldier still had a firm grip on her arm. He hauled her back on her feet, and her brain seemed to roll around in her head like seeds in a dried gourd.

Cilie's face was white and she looked up at the ceiling as Nuala approached her. A flare of heat struck the stump where Cilie's finger had been and the bleeding stopped.

"You may go, Cilie, but take the scissors with you back to Tusken . . . just in case." Selia's gaze rested on Isi as the waiting woman gripped the scissors in her undamaged hand and, trembling, crossed the room to the stairs.

Selia examined the object Cilie had brought from Tusken, her smile adoring, then she held it up—a cut lock of hair in Tusken's unmistakable tawny hue.

Isi's breath shuddered with a tense sob.

Rin bent over, her head feeling airless after her faint. Close by her feet lay a shard of ceramic, perhaps from a broken pot. Rin could imagine Selia throwing things in a rage. It was too small to use as a dagger, but she palmed it anyway.

"So you see, he is quite well and whole." Selia rubbed the lock against her cheek. "Just missing a bit of hair, that is. He is such a good boy. I don't think there will be any need to use those scissors on him. No, I'm sure there won't. As long as his mother behaves."

Rin fingered the shard and daydreamed about throwing it at Selia. With her wrists clamped, she could not get enough of a swing to do any damage. She did not think even Razo would be able to hit a target with his hands cuffed. So what would Razo do? Something ridiculous, she thought, something to get a laugh. Make sport of Selia. Pull a prank.

Selia's droning was making the whole room seem dark and cramped, and Isi looked ready to collapse into a heap. Rin had to do something.

In a low, quick movement, she tossed the shard across the room. It struck the wall under one of the windows with a distinct *clack*. Everyone looked toward the noise.

Selia frowned. "What—"

Rin made a startled scream.

Selia turned her slow, icy gaze to Rin. "You interrupted me."

"I'm sorry, I just can't believe what I saw. A huge stone cairn walked by, and one of its littlest stones fell through the window."

Some of the Kels looked at the window nervously. A hearth-watcher made a sign over his chest as if to ward away bad luck.

Selia snarled. "What are you talking about?"

Speaking was making Rin giddy. "Maybe the gods sneaked out of the wood, and the cairns are looking for them. Selia, have you seen any gods running about your castle? We could go look in the kitchen—they might be hungry. Or maybe they're out playing stones with your mercenary army. The cairn is probably on its way to join them—I bet cairns are naturals at playing stones."

"You have lots of pieces too, girl, and it's time you earned your right to be here. I think I'll start taking pieces of you until your timid royal friend signs."

The soldier yanked Rin's arm up and held a knife under her finger.

"No, don't!" Isi yelled.

Rin's whole body clenched, and she found herself standing on her toes, trying to get away from that sharpness. The soldier looked at Selia for permission.

"Yes, I think I will," said Selia. "I'm going to carve her up piece by piece for you to watch, so you can imagine what will happen to Tusken. I wonder what he'll think of his nurse-mary then. She'll have trouble carrying him home with her fingerless paws. Cilie is surely back with Tusken now—I wonder if he's noticed her missing finger. I wonder if he knows he could lose his own so easily."

Distantly, Rin knew she should be terrified, but her mind was reeling with a realization. She had been looking at Selia as she spoke—really looking to understand. The laugh, the prank, had made Rin feel more like herself, like Forest born, like Agget-kin. Made her forget to be afraid, forget that she'd let Razo die and would soon be killed too. She'd been so certain she would fail, she had not questioned the failure. But now she watched Selia speak and saw what she had not looked for before.

Selia is lying. Realization flowed through Rin, so hot and sure that she barely noticed the sharpness of the knife against her finger. Selia's guards had not caught Tusken, had not killed Razo. They must be out there in the wood, safe, hidden. Alive. Far from this viper's hissing voice, far from soldiers and hearth-watchers and cages and dungeons. Of course she was lying. Rin could see it now etched in every line of her face, in the darkness under her eyes that belied her forced calm, in the twitching corner of her mouth.

Razo must be alive! And Tusken . . .

Enough, Rin thought. *That's just plain enough.*

Isi was standing at the table. She picked up the pen.

The soldier's knife bit a little harder against Rin's finger, teasing the skin almost to bleeding. There seemed to be no energy left in her that had not been doused by grief and exhaustion and doubt. But she found some, hidden pockets of will she did not know she had. She did not hesitate as she gathered all that energy together, pushed it into words, and sent them at Isi, quick and strong as a crossbow bolt.

"She lies," Rin said. "Razo lives. Tusken is safe."

In one moment, Isi's aspect completely changed—her eyes widened, her back straightened. The pen dropped from her hand.

All she said was, "Rin, get down."

Chapter 25

The knife under Rin's finger became red hot, burning her skin before the soldier flung it away. Rin dropped to the floor, though her guard still kept hold of her arm. The other soldiers and the hearth-watchers leaped toward Isi, but a windstorm had begun. Then the room exploded.

First fire burst through the roof, so hot and quick the timber burned up in an instant, raining chunks of ash and stone. Now the room was open to the day. Wind gushed through the hole, a stiff cord of air, strong as a rampaging bull. It struck the soldiers and hearth-watchers, shoving them into a heap in the corner. The shriek of wind was loud enough to silence Selia's voice.

The air began rippling, so dense Rin could actually see the deadly columns of heat shooting from the hearth-watchers toward Isi. But Isi's wind thickened, pouring past Rin in great syrupy gusts. The wind ravaged through the waves of heat, breaking them apart and sending them swirling away. Sometimes the heat crashed against a wall and found a tapestry, and fires burst to life. But just as suddenly the fires died as if the wind had sucked the air out of them.

Rin spotted a soldier coming up the stairs, not caught in the corner with the others. He was making his way around the room, behind Isi's back.

"Isi!" Rin yelled, just as the soldier hurled a heavy metal box. Wind gushed between them and the box was knocked aside, missing Isi's head but thumping against her leg. She faltered, and the wind died for just a moment, but it was enough. The hearth-watchers jumped to their feet and split apart, and the soldiers ran forward with swords. Heat and steel were coming at Isi from every direction, seven fire-speakers and three warriors, all looking at Isi, all set on her death.

And Selia was still speaking, now in a high, piercing noise that barely cut through the wind. "Stop fighting, Crown Princess. It's useless! You'll get your little friend killed!"

Rin's guard still gripped her wrist. She wished she was in the dungeon, locked away in darkness where she would not have to see the queen of Bayern die. If only Enna were here instead of Rin—Enna would wipe out the entire room instead of cowering on the floor.

Isi kept pushing back the hearth-watchers and soldiers with her wind, occasionally letting small fires ignite a sword handle or scorch someone's boots. But they were gaining ground, and the closer they stood to Isi, the harder it was for her to blow away their shooting heat in time. The hem of Isi's skirt was smoking, her face was strained, her eyes sad. Rin believed Isi was holding back somehow—for fear of hurting them, or from the heavy strain of Selia's voice. Or perhaps knowing that Tusken was safe took the will to fight out of her. She defended herself with wind but she did not attack back with fire, and she left Selia alone.

Rin's hands tightened into fists. It was not right. Selia should not win. She had not been playing fair. Anyone who had ever so much as met Ma knew that you play fair or you do not play at all. People-speaking was no excuse for being a bully.

Rage crackled inside her, at Selia, at Isi. At herself. Why did she have to be so weak? The anger roiling through her limbs did not feel weak just then. And she thought of that tree, hacked away and assumed dead, yet still growing through stones, taking a chunk out of a fortress wall. Wind tears down trees, and new ones sprout again. Fire destroys forests, and they grow back. People chop them down to build their walls, and the trees reclaim the land. The thought made her feel wild—dangerous. If Isi could not take care of Selia, then she would.

Rin stood, meeting eyes with her guard. She had failed completely with the guard in the cell. She had asked too much—she could not wield such power as Selia, to make others believe the impossible. She did not have the will to speak lies or commands—it reminded her of what she'd done to Wilem, made her feel dark and greasy and used up. She could only tell what truth she had. What did this soldier want more than anything? To please his mistress. Rin could see that yearning in the faces of all her followers.

"Your mistress is very powerful, but so is the queen of Bayern. I'm holding you back. You could show Selia your devotion better if you didn't have to guard me. Why don't you join the fight?"

He blinked.

"I'm not going to run, I promise. I've nowhere to run. You can't help your mistress holding me. Let me go and I won't leave this room. Besides, I'm still shackled. What harm could I do?"

Her words seemed to make sense to him. He released her, drew his sword, and moved toward Isi.

Rin covered her mouth with her hands. *It worked. It worked.* She wanted to shout out in relief and weep in shame. Both would have to wait. She sat, grabbed the cooled knife off the floor, and holding it with both hands, sawed at the metal link. It was thin and a little misshapen from Isi's heat, but still intact. She twisted and bent, the effort making her sweat. Isi was at the center of a maelstrom, soldiers and hearth-watchers pressing in from all sides, Selia bellowing threats.

Come on, Rin thought. *That's your queen out there. Show Selia that Isi's subjects are stronger of their own will than her pack of fire-singed babies.*

Rin angled the knife again, scratching the link between blade and floor. The knife blade bent, slipping into a groove in the metal, a brittle spot that gave. Rin twisted her hands and her cuffed wrists separated.

Selia was screaming commands, and the anger in Rin bunched and quivered, eager to scream back. *No, not like Selia,* Rin told herself, pushing her anger to merge with her quiet places. Her thoughts twisted into ideas of aspens at the end of winter, done with resting and ready to move again. The burst of spring in a previously sleeping tree was as dramatic to Rin as the explosion of fire. She felt ready to spring.

With her thoughts stilled, her core strong, she was able to think clearly. She had to keep moving. Go forward. Stop Selia. There was a roomful of soldiers and hearth-watchers who would try to stop her. She could not let them.

Rin faced Selia and took a step. Isi's wind tangled in her skirt and whipped her dangling sleeves. Rin thought of how trees move in the wind, making small circles, bending. Roots moved too, so slowly that a root never bruised itself on a rock or scraped another root.

Warm, dark, wet soil, she thought. *Open sky above.*

Rin took another step.

No tree nearby to cling to, so instead she sank into herself as if into a tree's thoughts. But her eyes were open, she was still Rin, still aware. As she had done on her walk to the cage, Rin felt as if she existed in two places at once—safe inside the green world of a tree's thoughts, but still aware and moving in the human world. And this time panic did not eat at her. She felt perfectly balanced, half in, half out, and alive in both.

Everything seemed slowed, like a drip of sap fixed by cold weather. She had the time to see what was happening— the wind about to sweep back a lock of Isi's hair, a bead of sweat dripping down a soldier's cheek, Selia's mouth opening to cry out.

She was aware of Selia speaking to her, the words rising in pitch. Orders to stop, to obey. They slid off her like rain off a leaf. At Selia's command, the four soldiers turned to Rin. The sounds of their boots seemed loud and distant at once. Rin took another step. One soldier aimed an arrow at her and released. The arrow was zipping toward her chest. In the time it took to lower her foot midstride, she watched the arrow, saw the gleaming point growing in size as it came nearer. She began to lean to one side, as those tall pines lean with the wind to keep from breaking. Rin would not break. On her chest she could feel the narrow push of air coming at her before the arrow. She kept leaning. The cold spot of air moved along her collar bone, her shoulder. Her body tipped just a little farther, and then the arrow itself whisked past. With a crack it lodged into the wall. Rin righted herself, faced Selia, and took another step.

Now she could feel new movements coming at her, the cool breath of air changing into heat. She could see the air ripple with bursts of fire-making heat from two hearth-watchers. This time she crouched, bringing her head against her chest, until she felt the tops of her hairs sizzle and heard the heat whoosh away into nothing, having found no fuel to turn into fire. Another blaze, and she leaned, just enough, rolling to her side and back onto her feet. Outside herself, she could feel the sting of pain across her leg. But such a little thing did not matter—a tree is not disturbed by the loss of a few leaves, the snap of a twig.

She took another step. Selia was yelling, but Rin did not hear a word. Another arrow came. She could see at a glance that the angle was wrong and would only scratch her shoulder, so she ignored it, the sliver of pain feeling as distant as home. Another column of heat and she bowed beneath it, and then the opposite of the heat—a cold tug as one of the hearth-watchers tried to pull her own heat out of her. But the tug could not find her or hold her, perhaps unsure if she were girl or tree, and she slid out of its pull. Now she was at the table, the false queen close enough to touch.

Selia's mouth was wet with rage, her eyes wide, surprised that her voice and her followers were failing. Her lips formed the word *stop,* but Rin had chosen not to hear.

I'm Forest born, she thought.

She pulled back her arm and punched Selia in the nose.

Rin meant to jab her in her throat to stop the talking, but Selia jerked away, and Rin's fist hit her nose instead. All the same, it had been a nice, firm strike, just as Razo had taught her. She had never punched a person before, and was surprised at the give beneath her knuckles as Selia's head moved back from the force. There was a tiny crunch under Rin's fist, a burst of pain in her knuckles. Selia bent over.

A hush of silence. Rin could feel everyone staring, the whole room twanging with tension.

"Ow," Selia said with a pathetic whine. She cradled her bleeding nose, stomping her foot for the pain.

Rin looked at the soldiers and hearth-watchers—they gaped, frozen by this action, surprise and confusion on their faces, as if they had believed Selia was untouchable, as if they had not known her body contained any blood at all.

Rin twisted to see Isi, who was a few paces behind, her stare as bewildered as the others. Why wasn't anyone doing anything? Rin had not thought through her actions farther than the strike, but clearly that was not going to be enough.

The stunned pause lasted only a moment before Selia began to screech so loudly it made the insides of Rin's ears stretch.

"Dem," Selia sputtered through her bloodied hands, gesticulating madly at Isi and Rin. "Kih dem!" And the hearth-watchers and soldiers sprang for Isi again.

"You need to stop talking!" Rin shoved Selia, knocking her down. She kneed her in the lower back, grabbed a fistful of hair, and yanked with all her strength. Selia shrieked wordlessly. This was dirty grappling that would earn a paddle with Ma's wooden spoon back home but Rin was enjoying it. When Selia tried to squirm out of her hold, Rin kicked the back of her knees and kept hold of her hair.

Rin looked up at the scene. All seven hearth-watchers and four soldiers had their eyes on Rin, straining to get to their mistress. The soldiers no longer held weapons, the bows burned to ash and the swords too hot to hold, but they were bullying their way through Isi's windstorm while the hearth-watchers attacked the wind with heat and tried to set fire to Isi herself. The hearth-watchers fought as if especially crazed, their expressions grotesque in their delirium to pro-tect Selia. The attack pushed Isi back until she was standing directly in front of Rin and Selia.

Selia bawled as Rin pressed her shackled wrist against the back of Selia's neck, shoving the woman's face to the ground. Rin could not let Isi lose. She stared at the door, wishing Enna and Dasha would come bursting through.

The reminder of her own uselessness struck her like a blow, and Rin's grip on Selia loosened for just a moment. Selia lurched out of her hold and sprang to her feet. Rin reached to tackle her again but hesitated, her attention straying to Isi. Selia was insignificant beside the true queen. Letting Selia flee to her hearth-watchers, Rin put her hands on Isi instead.

Tell her the truth.

"Isi, you're stronger than the lot of them. Isi, you're the queen. Selia's nothing. Her lies can't shackle you. Tusken needs his ma, and so does Bayern. You have a right to live."

Isi's eyes widened.

Rin nodded. "You can end this."

Selia positioned herself behind Nuala and the others. "Kih hah!" she yelled thickly, her hands over her nose and mouth.

But Isi shook her head once. Outside, a sizzle of lightning, a gush of rain. And in the chamber, everyone fell, clutching their throats and chests as if desperate for air. Then the wind struck.

This was a storm that could uproot trees and tear houses from the ground, and it ravaged inside that one small room. It pushed at the people on the ground, rolling them over and over, sending them sprawling back into the corner. The furniture followed, tables and chairs and sofas banging against them, trapping them against the wall. As the small ornate table took flight toward the others, the document Isi had not signed rose into the wind, its corners flapping as if it were a white bird on the wing. It dissolved into flame and ash.

Rin should have fallen over too. But she felt the wind weave around her, pass through her fingers, arch over her as if she were made of leaves. She bent and flowed and did not fall.

The soldiers and hearth-watchers were packed into the corner, chairs and tables pinning them down and back. But Selia had slipped away. She sprang for the stairs.

Isi's wind slammed the door to the stairs shut, then fire

poured into it, burning any escape. Selia fled to one of the four inner chamber doors, screaming hysterically, but then that door was blazing too.

The fire in the door to the stairs extinguished, and someone from the stair side kicked through, shattering the charred wood like glass. Through the rising smoke rushed Enna and Dasha, looking for a place to attack. From behind them soldiers clambered up the stairs, shouting a battle cry in Kelish, the high lilt bringing goose bumps to Rin's arms. Before the soldiers reached the landing, they dropped their flaming weapons and tripped over their now-sodden clothes. *That was Enna and Dasha's doing,* Rin thought, but as the soldiers stumbled into the chamber, it was Isi's wind that shoved them into the others.

"Watch them," Isi said, pointing to the heap of people and furniture in the corner.

Enna and Dasha nodded, and water began to flow over the hearth-watchers, down their heads, soaking their clothes, making a pool on the ground around them. Enna stood on one side of the cage of furniture and Dasha on the other, hands twitching as if ready to attack at any provocation, eyes roving over Isi and Selia, trying to determine if things were settled yet.

One of the soldier's hands strayed to a dagger in his boot. Enna kicked him in the ribs. "Try it and this fire-haired Tiran fiend will drown you where you sit."

The hearth-watchers recoiled, wiping at the water oozing

down their faces, blubbering anxiously, some reaching for their mistress.

Rin jumped to her feet and put herself between Selia and the now-open entrance to the stairs, her hands in fists. The look of terror on Selia's face almost made Rin laugh. Half-hysterical, Selia began circling, frantic for an escape. Selia's clothes and hair were whipping around her body, and if she was yelling commands to her trapped followers, the wind circling her face swallowed the sounds.

"You are never going to touch my family again," Isi said, her voice cold and firm. She still had not moved from the center of the room. "You will let me bind your hands and mouth and you'll come quietly with me back to a cozy Bayern prison, or ..." Wind nudged a barrel that had been pushed aside in the windstorm and rolled it to rest at Selia's feet. "Or I'll fetch some nails and a couple of horses, and we can take care of this right now."

Selia kicked the barrel away and swatted at the wind as if at bees. Her lips were moving, chanting something, and she flung herself about. Her running seemed frantic and without thought until suddenly she was at the narrow window, just wide enough for one person to fit through. Selia clawed her way onto the sill.

Rin heard Isi gasp with surprise, and wind swept through the window, trying to push Selia back into the room. But she did not pause before flinging herself out.

The wind hushed. With hurried bursts of steam, water

gathered over the fires and fell in puffs, so in moments the room that had been filled with burning and whipping chaos was calmed to silence.

Enna and Rin ran to the window while Isi turned a glare at the soldiers and hearth-watchers buried under furniture. Rin doubted that through the clutter and wind they'd seen what had just happened.

"I am not feeling jovial at this precise moment," Isi said. "So let me make this clear. You move to attack any one of us, and you're a bonfire. Nod your heads if you understand me."

There was some general head nodding. The hearth-watchers were searching the room with their eyes, looking for Selia. Some began to wail in Kelish.

"Dasha, if they so much as twitch . . ."

Dasha nodded. Her eyes never left her captives. "I am in such a mood. I feel positively unhinged. Did you know I could fill your lungs with water? It's a trick I long to show the first of you who twitches aggressively."

Enna was leaning out the window, craning to get a view. "Um, Isi . . ."

Isi waited until she was near Enna, her back to the captives, before asking quietly, "The serpent got away, didn't she?"

"Actually, no. She . . . no. Her life heat . . . it's gone. There's no chance she lived through this one."

Rin put a hand on Enna's shoulder and stood on her toes. She could just see Selia's pink skirt fanned out above her bare feet. The fall had knocked off her slippers.

"I have to see," said Isi, "or I won't sleep again for worrying that she's sneaking into Tusken's room."

Still, she hesitated a moment before getting close enough to lean out the window. While she'd been attacking, she'd seemed regal, impervious. Now she looked very human again, slight even, and sorry.

Isi's voice dipped low. "Do you think she died quickly?"

"I'd been rooting for an excruciatingly slow and terrifically painful end for our fair queen of Kel, but yes, I'd say she hit those stones headfirst and was gone before her feet caught up."

Dasha, too far from the window to hear the exchange, looked inquiringly at Rin. Rin nodded her head, yes, Selia was dead. Dasha's shoulders relaxed.

"It makes you wonder, though," said Enna, still staring out the window, "what she was thinking there at the end. Seemed like she was shouting something, and I can't help wondering . . ."

"I heard it." Isi leaned her elbow on the sill, wrenching her gaze from Selia's body up to the afternoon horizon. "She said, 'I will die a queen.'"

Rin shuddered.

"Sick in the head," said Enna. "I've said that all along. Sick. In. The. Head."

"How did you get out?" asked Isi.

"A page told us he heard fighting upstairs, so we couldn't just sit there. Dasha had been sending water into the masonry

around the door for the past couple of days. Loosened a
rock. A few good kicks and we were free. I was going to try
to burn through the lock, but the whole door is metal . . ."
Enna shrugged. "I still think I could've done it, but I admit,
she was clever working at it the way she did."

One of the hearth-watchers spoke in Kelish and the wailing turned into rejoicing. Another pointed at Isi and said,
"She is gone now, you are never for finding her. And she will
coming for us and we are being her chosen again!"

Enna whispered, "Doubt that."

Isi headed for the burned-out door. "Rin, come with me
please. Enna, Dasha, can you . . . ?" She inclined her head
toward the heap of prisoners.

"Yes, of course," Enna started, "but—"

"She's going to get Tusken," Rin explained as she ran after
the queen. She did not dare say anything about Razo until
she was sure. "We'll be a few hours."

in sped after Isi, leaping down stairs and sweeping past sentries. If a soldier challenged Isi, his weapon blazed in his hands. To the gate guards, Isi said, "Selia, the so-called queen of Kel, is dead."

Rin could see the guards knew it was true. Selia's body must have been spotted and news was spreading around the keep. Their eyes were hot with sorrow and mistrust. But Isi did not flinch.

"I am Queen Anidori-Kiladra Talianna Isilee of Bayern, friend to King Scandlan. In his name, I reclaim Castle Daire for Kel. I will hold this fortress for your sovereign, and any who oppose my authority or that of my three companions will be stripped of his rank and cast in the dungeon to await the king's verdict. Send your quickest messenger to Bressal to inform Scandlan of his bride's fate and request his presence here. Now please fetch me three horses."

Nobody moved. There was a significant amount of staring going on.

Isi sighed. She pointed to the young page with the skin spots who was peering around the corridor. "You. Are you capable of riding messenger to Bressal?"

He nodded, his eyes bright. Isi turned a questioning look at Rin, and she nodded too—he seemed trustworthy.

"I don't have time to write a formal letter. Just be as straightforward as you know how. Tell King Scandlan what you've seen here, and tell him I respectfully request his presence. Now climb on a horse." She pointed to the soldier closest to the gate. "And you, unlock this girl's shackles, then prepare three horses, fast movers saddled to ride."

Isi did not have people-speaking. Her words did not affect Rin as Selia's had, slide into her head and make her itch to believe and obey. But when Isi spoke, Rin had no doubt she was in the presence of a queen. Neither, apparently, did the gate guard. He fumbled for a key from his belt to click open Rin's wrist clamps then fled toward the stables.

Rin breathed through a smile as she and Isi followed, a rush of elation making her limbs tingle. It had been frightening in the moment, but now she felt swept away and flying. Isi was amazing, Rin had done ... something, and it had felt so good. Hope was thick in her chest. With relief came the awareness of her injuries: burns on her leg and the insides of her wrists, a scratch on her shoulder from an arrow, and bruised knuckles from punching Selia. There did not seem to be a spot on her body free of ache.

Soon they were mounted and riding north, a third horse trotting behind on a lead rope.

"Can you hear what all horses think?" Rin asked, between hurried bites of the bread they'd borrowed from the stablehands' supply. Her stomach groaned pathetically.

"No, I can only speak with my own horse. I was present at his birth and formed that initial bond. But having communication with my horse has helped me to understand all of them, at least in part. Not their language, but their meaning."

"So can you tell whether or not this horse is plotting my death?"

Isi laughed. Perhaps Isi thought Rin was joking, but Rin could not help notice that she did not answer the question.

As they got closer to where Rin had left Razo, Isi gripped her reins, her focus dead ahead. Rin's middle was icy with anticipation. She let her hands graze tree branches and trunks as they hurried past. Two days in a stone dungeon had felt like two years.

Isi's gaze whipped to the side, and Rin looked, hoping to see Razo's face. Instead a stranger on horseback cantered through the trees—a soldier, his weapon raised. He yelled in Kelish but his sword turned red hot and fell from his hand, then wind knocked him out of his saddle and onto the ground. Two companions flanked him, and they too were soon on their backsides in the bracken.

Isi stayed mounted, tall above them. "Do you speak the

western tongue? Good. Then hear this: your search is off. I am Queen Anidori-Kiladra of Bayern. Your former mistress is dead, your king is coming to Daire. Go back to the castle and await his arrival."

Their eyes darted to their cooling swords, as if planning a new attack. Isi sighed.

"Will you tell them, Rin?" Isi's question and look were so direct, Rin had no doubt of Isi's meaning. She guessed that Rin was a people-speaker. And that made Rin want to scratch up a blanket of moss and pull it over her head.

She took a breath to steady her shivers and studied the soldiers' faces a moment before speaking.

"Did you love your queen of Kel?"

The soldiers' attention was wholly hers.

"You did love her. But she was not made for a long life. You felt that, didn't you? That this couldn't last. That her reign had to be brief, a fire that burns too hot. She's dead. You were true servants to her, but your service is over now. Time to go back to the castle, to mourn and await the king. You'll have a new service, and it'll be even more important than your time with the queen of Kel."

Rin could see they believed her words, but they had to decide to act on them. One by one, they picked up their fallen weapons, mounted their horses, and rode south.

As soon as the third soldier was gone, Isi nudged her horse forward.

"So, Rin . . ." Isi seemed anxious as she scanned the trees, eager to talk just to relieve her nerves. Rin tensed for a question about people-speaking, but instead Isi asked, "What do you think of Kel?"

"Kel? Nice, I guess, but they need larger dungeons."

Isi smiled. "You seem different now. More ready to speak."

"Sorry," Rin said, her face hot.

"Oh no, please don't be sorry! I admire you for sharing your thoughts. It's hard for me to talk casually, I worry so much about saying the wrong thing, offending. I've often wished along with understanding birds and horses I had people-speaking, a talent that could bring me closer to people."

"Closer? But look what it did to Selia."

"She was overcome by it. Selia might have learned another language herself if she ever held still to listen. But she was too busy talking. To be more aware of other people, to see through lies and fear and really comprehend a person—that should be a noble gift. People-speakers like Selia, they let their desires lead them, burn them up. They don't have balance. Though I don't know what could balance people-speaking."

"Nothing," said Rin.

"Balance with any gift of speaking is essential, but especially, I think, with people and nature. With nature-speaking, you have to be the master. Change the wind or fire, change the water or trees, don't let them change you. Animal-speaking is different—I can't control my horse, can't order him the way Enna and I command the wind. I just listen. I'm just happy to understand. Same with the birds. I speak with them, but they aren't a tool I can use. By understanding, I'm the one who's changed."

"Trees are more animal than nature, then."

Isi nodded, her expression surprised. "I guess that's so—trees are living things, like animals. The living things have no master, the living things change the person who understands them."

Then I'm the one who's changed, Rin thought, but she said, "People are living, too."

"I don't imagine Selia gave that much thought. People-speaking tends to warp, makes the speaker want to be the master of people, to control, not to listen. But if there was someone who was careful and didn't try to control everything, just understood, just listened . . . if there was someone who could do that . . ."

Someone like you, Rin thought. This queen was the kind of person who could be a people-speaker and not devolve into Selia, who could know all the languages and contain them. Rin did not think that even if she lived beside Isi for the rest of her life, she could learn how to be like the queen.

Isi seemed about to say something else when her attention snapped forward. She nudged her horse into a gallop.

"Tusken? Tuksen!" She dismounted, not bothering to tie up her horse, and rushed forward. "Tusken? Ma's here. Tusken, honey boy?"

There was a two-year-old shriek, and Tusken came streaking out of the brush with arms wide. He rammed into his mother, and she laughed as she fell to the ground, Tusken on top of her.

"Ma!" he yelled. "Ma, Ma, Ma, Ma!"

Isi held him and held him, burying her face in his neck, rocking him and squeezing him and kissing his head, rubbing her tears into his hair, all the while saying, "Oh, I love you, I love you so much, and you're all right, you're all right."

Razo sauntered out of the trees, hands in his pockets, seemingly unworried, though Rin could see he'd been near frantic before they came. "Knew you'd do it, though you took your time, eh, Rinny-binny? I was going to strike out for Bayern tomorrow—"

Then Rin was hugging him. Relief and joy swelled inside her till she thought she would burst.

"Uh . . . ," Razo said, patting her head as if she might be crazy.

"You were dead," she mumbled against his chest.

"I was? Well, I wish someone had told me. Would've been nice to relax on my back for a while. Um, how'd I die?"

"Selia said you were fleeing from her soldiers and your sling was no match for a sword."

"Ha! Then she's never seen me sling."

"Isi died too, but just for a minute."

Razo shook his head. "What've you girls been up to? I hate it when I miss all the good action."

Rin hugged him tighter, enjoying the feel of his ribs rising and lowering with a breath, the heat of his heart coming through his chest, and considered that a brother, a living big brother, was the best, safest, greatest thing in all the world.

Razo groaned and Rin released him, remembering his broken rib. "Sorry."

He shrugged. "A little pain is the least I deserve for dying on you."

"That is so true."

It was not long before Tusken had enough of holding still in his mother's embrace. He squirmed away, took her hand and said, "Up, Ma. Up."

"Can't keep him out of the trees," said Razo. "He's a Forest boy at heart, no question there. Isi, you'd best come stay with my ma or Finn's ma at least, let Tusken get in some climbing. Those showy little shrubs you have in your gardens are a good joke, but this boy needs a real challenge." Razo pointed to a towering evergreen. "You should see him go!"

"Razo," Rin said sternly. "You didn't let him climb that tree, did you?"

Razo's expression froze, mouth wide. He glanced at Isi, then back to Rin. "No. No! Of course not. Because that tree's way too high for a two-year-old. Right? Way too high. We just . . . just looked at that one. In an admiring sort of way. From afar. And climbed those bitty squatty ones over there, is all."

But Tusken had dragged his mother by the hand to the base of the monstrous evergreen, reaching for the lowest branch and saying, "Up. Up."

"Razo," Rin hissed.

"Well, what was I supposed to do?" he whispered back. "The boy's a climber. He's got the balance of a bird and the hands of a squirrel, not to mention stubbornness equal to our Enna."

They rode unchallenged through the gates of Castle Daire just as the sun grazed the western horizon. Some of the soldiers even saluted. Rin tumbled off her horse, grabbed Razo's hand and half-dragged him, making for the winding stairs. But Isi said, "No, they're outside," so Rin veered toward the courtyard, passing from the dark stone castle back into the luminous sunset. She could not move quickly enough. Her heart thrummed with excitement.

Half of the courtyard was soaked in yellow light, the leaves in the kitchen garden rimmed with gold as if trying on autumn tones. A group of people stood in the distance, but for all the rich light, Rin could not tell orange hair from black.

"Dasha!" she yelled. "Dasha!"

A face looked up. Then two. They started walking toward her, then running. Dasha was in front, her eyes set on Razo, her face caught in an expression of desperate hope.

"Razo," she said, panting as if she had been running from

very far away. "Razo, it had better be you. If it just looks like you, I am going to kill you. It had better—"

He'd reached her by then. They embraced, and he swung her around, her legs lifting in the air, her tunic swirling. She laughed high and so pleased Rin thought she could break glass with that sound. Then Dasha was kissing Razo's face and crying and smiling and declaring all his perfections.

"Well, this isn't half-bad," said Razo. "I think I'll die more often."

Rin was so happy she could not help bouncing on the balls of her feet.

Enna was staring, at Razo, at Rin, at Isi with Tusken in her arms, her eyes so wide as if she did not dare believe what she saw. "But what . . . ?" she said. "But how . . . ?"

Isi said, "Selia lied. He was never caught."

Enna leaned her head back and laughed at the sky. "Of course he wasn't! What could kill Razo?"

Dasha embraced him again and squeezed until Razo had to admit that he was injured. "Love the lips, not the ribs," he said, and pulled her into a long kiss.

From the midst of the group of people just beyond the garden, a fire was blazing, its smoke black and ugly against the golden sky.

"What's happening there?" asked Isi.

Enna grimaced. "The hearth-watchers. It's their funeral pyre."

Isi's eyes flashed to Enna, her expression full of frightened disbelief. Rin had to wonder too—had Enna killed them?

"Not me," Enna said, her smile sad that she would need to assure them. "Not me, Isi."

"No, of course not. But what happened?"

"Later," Dasha said, still smiling up at Razo, holding his arm around her waist. "Right now let's go eat and celebrate and gaze at Razo some more. And sleep. In a bed! How would that be? No one will threaten our peace tonight unless they fancy a swim in dry air. We can talk about the unpleasant parts in the morning."

Unsure whom they could trust among the castle servants, Isi dismissed the kitchen workers and steward for a couple of hours. Isi and Tusken sat on the kitchen floor, playing with pots. Dasha and Razo tried to cut vegetables, but stopped so often to tickle each other or whisper or kiss, Enna finally wrenched the knives away and did it herself. Rin helped, and they all dined on a good Forest meal. As they ate on the floor, Razo recounted his past days with tense narrative and plenty of dramatic pauses. Isi in turn told some of their time in the castle, but before she could recount her confrontation with Selia, Tusken had fallen asleep in Isi's arms, so she declared it well past bedtime.

The six of them took up residence in Selia's sleeping chamber, housed in one of the four side towers on the third floor. The bed was round like the room and large enough to fit most of them. After all her longing for a bed, Dasha said she'd grown used to the ground, and she and Razo curled up on the rug, their arms around each other. Razo was snoring in moments, and Dasha giggled with delight. The fire sisters agreed to take turns at watch, in case any of the castle servants or soldiers thought to get rid of their Bayern guests before King Scandlan arrived. Isi insisted on first watch.

"I wouldn't be able to sleep for some time anyhow. I can stay happily occupied just staring at Tusken till dawn."

"You'd better wake me before then," Enna said, yawning.

Rin lay beside Enna, her arm curled over the edge of the bed, and thought there was no chance she would be able to fall asleep. Her burns sang out, her bruised middle groaned, her mind was afire with things Selia had said. But the sounds of Razo's snores were oddly lulling, and the occasional murmur of Tusken in his sleep made her feel dreamy with contentment. Despite lying in the bed of the woman who'd tried to kill them in a castle where she'd been a prisoner, Rin was not afraid, not with Isi keeping watch. So she closed her eyes, feeling as safe as if she'd crawled inside the trunk of a great old oak, and dreamed of the soft breath of leaves.

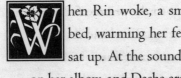hen Rin woke, a smear of sunlight draped the bed, warming her feet. She rubbed her eyes and sat up. At the sound, Enna stirred, Isi leaned up on her elbow, and Dasha arose from where she had been keeping guard at the door.

Dasha gestured with her head toward the antechamber, and Isi nodded.

Isi extricated herself from the sleeping Tusken, stacking pillows around him so he would not roll off the bed. Dasha threw a blanket over Razo, so deeply asleep he did not twitch. The door had been burned through, allowing Isi to still keep an eye on her son from the other room, and the girls gathered half-charred cushions and rolled-up rugs. They made themselves comfortable sprawled in the center of the chamber, looking up through the rip in the roof at the sweetly blue sky. Rin found it strange, lying there in the wreckage as if in a copse of aspens with the chores done early and nothing to do until dinner.

Isi spoke first. "I find it very valuable that the Tiran

ambassador observed all this. It might prove uncomfortable with King Scandlan if the queen of Bayern were the only witness to the mysterious death of his bride."

"I was thinking the same during my watch this morning," said Dasha. "There is a grave risk Scandlan will hold Bayern in blame."

"Hold Bayern in blame . . ." Enna scowled. "What about that fact that his wife kidnapped the prince of Bayern and imprisoned Bayern's queen, and the Tiran ambassador too?"

"A man who would marry Selia might not be able to see a situation clearly," said Isi.

"Then I'll help him see it clearly," Enna said. "That hussy is the reason Geric's scarred, Brynn's dead, we spent an inhospitable amount of time in a dungeon, and I'm still not married to Finn."

Rin noticed Isi flinch at the reminder of Brynn, but she said nothing about it, asking instead, "What did you do with her body?"

"It's in the crypt. I wanted to make a nice fire for it, but Dasha thought the king should see the evidence." Enna sat up, her face brightening with a new idea. "Isi, can I go find the corpse and kick it in the shins?"

"No!"

"Fine. I wasn't serious anyway. Not really." She rolled onto her side and muttered against her arm, "It's just that I never got a chance to kick her in the shins."

Dasha was staring at Enna. "That's just . . . that's creepy, Enna."

Enna sat back up. "You know what's creepy? A woman who can convince everyone to do what she wants, and what she wants is to be queen of the world and take a little boy from his mother, and the only friends she has are so out-of-their-mind in love with her that they'd burn themselves alive rather than go on without her. *That's* creepy."

Dasha nodded. "Good point."

"Is that what happened to Selia's hearth-watchers?" Rin asked. "They burned themselves?"

Dasha and Enna looked at each other, as if waiting for the other to speak first. Finally Enna groaned again and threw her hands into the air.

"They were as insane as their mistress, obviously. Dasha was keeping them nice and soaked so they couldn't burn us, and I was . . . uh, nudging them along, trying to get them out of here and down into the dungeon. One of them got too close to the window and . . ." Enna frowned. "I didn't realize how they'd react to her death, or I would've used stronger tactics to keep them away from the window. But when one of them saw the body, she started to wail, 'The queen is dead.' She was crazed, I mean, tearing-out-her-own-hair crazed, then she flung herself at the window and was gone. Dasha and I were . . . we were so surprised—"

"It happened really fast," Dasha muttered.

"Four of them threw themselves out the window before

I could get enough wind coming through it to keep them back. The others weren't happy about that. 'We have to join our lady,' and such stuff, and moaning, and hitting their heads, and then . . ."

Enna paused, then looked at Dasha, as if to say, *It's your turn.*

Dasha winced. "When they couldn't jump out the window, they burned themselves up. Between my water and Enna's wind, they couldn't throw heat away from their body, but it would seem they could still pull it in . . . and keep it in. They died really quickly, but it was . . . not nice."

Rin shuddered and looked into the pulsing blue of the sky to keep from imagining it.

Enna said, "Please can we not think about that anymore? For a while, huh? I was really enjoying the morning for once. Razo's alive and Tusken's safe and . . . and can't we think about something pleasant?"

"I have a question." Dasha examined the print of the rug under her hands as if the pattern was more interesting than her own thoughts. "You did not tell us all last night, Isi. How did you overcome Selia?"

"I'm not entirely sure. I wouldn't have by myself. After Rin said Tusken was safe, I wasn't afraid to fight those fire-speakers, but Selia . . . her voice still nagged me, and I just couldn't get myself to attack her. Then Rin . . ."

Isi looked at Rin as if asking permission, and Rin shrugged.

"Rin did it for me. She moved . . . it's hard to explain. She walked across the room as casual as anything, but nothing could touch her—not arrows, not fire. It was mesmerizing."

Dasha and Enna stared at Rin, waiting for an explanation.

"I have tree-speaking."

"Oh," Enna said, nodding, as unruffled by that declaration as if she'd just mentioned she had a flea bite on her ankle.

"So . . ." Dasha looked up, her brow creased. "So you spoke to the trees and—"

"No. I mean, there were no trees around. I don't actually *speak* to trees anyway. But I listen, and maybe because of all that watching and listening over the years I just know stuff about trees that made me realize that something else was possible."

She described falling into the memories of the oak tree and realizing that trees do not comprehend time. They just exist, everything slow and careful, past and present intertwined. So for a few moments she'd walked half in the green world, seeing everything at once, moving like a tree that sways in the wind to avoid breaking.

"It seemed the right moment, the right thing to do," said Rin. "But to be honest, I don't really understand what I did, or if I could do it again."

"Don't leave out the best part," said Isi, explaining the rest.

"Wait—you punched Selia in the nose?" Enna stared at Rin, her wide mouth turning into a huge grin. "You are my girl! So why didn't we wake Rin for a turn at watch last night? She can handle anything if she stopped Selia."

"But I can't. I couldn't do enough. Then I saw in Isi . . ." She blushed, embarrassed to describe what she thought. "I saw how powerful she is. And I tried to speak the truth of it to her, so she'd know all that she can do." The words did not make sense outside her head, so she shrugged again. Besides, adding more detail might bring up people-speaking, and admitting that part was about as enticing as cutting off her own finger.

"So, Isi . . ." Enna peered at her friend with one eye. "How much exactly can you do?"

Isi winced. "Some. When Rin said Razo was alive and Tusken was safe, it was as if half of the chains binding me just fell away. But I was . . . hesitant, I still couldn't do enough. I guess Selia's talking had hammered away at me, so that I didn't think I had anything left. But then Rin spoke again, and I just understood. Not that I was strong, but that everything else was, the wind and the heat in the air, if I could just allow them to speak to each other through me.

"And there was another motivation. Just as I was about to attack again, I heard on the wind that you and Dasha were coming up the stairs. I didn't want you to have to do anything. Not that I think you actually could kill anyone, you're so bad at it. But just in case."

Enna smirked, but there was understanding in her eyes, a softness.

"You are . . ." Dasha's eyes were wide. "Isi, you and Rin completely incapacitated four soldiers, seven fire-speakers, and an extremely powerful people-speaker?"

"Not me," said Rin. "I just watched. And knocked Selia. Isi did the rest."

Isi glanced at Enna, her expression a little nervous. "Is that all right?"

Rin understood the uncertainty in Isi's voice. Enna had always been the strongest one. She'd stopped the invading Tiran army, she was so dangerous the best soldiers stood down when she was in the room. It was Enna's place to be powerful, while Isi was the queen. And Isi did not want to take that away from her friend.

Enna stared up at the charred roof, then a chuckle growled out of her throat.

"What?" said Isi. "What? Share your humor, Enna. I could really use a laugh right now."

"I was just thinking . . . if Geric thinks you're, you know, especially attractive when you're angry, how'll he react when he hears about this? You should probably tell him at a time when you two are conveniently alone and sentries have been given orders not to disturb . . ."

Isi blushed and sputtered and looked as if she would order Enna to hush up, but when she opened her mouth all she could do was giggle.

Enna said, "Rinna-girl, we need to find you a suitor."

"No thanks," she said, and she meant it. She could not

trust herself to get as close to someone as Isi was to Geric, not with the canker of people-speaking inside her. No loss, she assured herself. One time her brother Sten imitated the sound of a squirrel emitting gas, and all six brothers had laughed to tears. Honestly—to tears. It made Rin wonder about the sanity of her brothers' wives, since they chose such boys as mates.

"Conrad told me he thought you were nice," Isi said.

"Ha," said Rin.

Enna elbowed her. "You'll change your mind soon enough. Just make sure you choose a good Forest boy."

"No, no, trust me," said Isi, "one of the Gerhard clan is the way to go. I wonder if any of Geric's cousins—"

"Sorry, I have to agree with Enna here, Your Majesty," said Dasha. "Forest boys are far superior to your city stock, no matter how fine the breeding."

"That's right," said Enna. "They're not dull and worried about dirtying their fine silk tunics. Not that Geric's that way *necessarily*, but Forest boys are ready for anything, well-tumbled and apt to climb."

Dasha was nodding emphatically. "And they love their mothers, the truest of sons, which is so sweet."

"And just smart enough—not bookish and silly with big words, just as smart as you want them to be."

"And they are loyal, completely loyal and faithful and true and—"

"And they know how to cook a mean stew—"

Dasha raised one finger. "Ooh, and skin a squirrel! Because . . . you never know when you might need to skin a squirrel."

"Right. And they know how to love."

"It's all true."

"Every word." Enna really looked at Dasha. "You're agreeing with me. Great crows, we see eye to eye, on this matter at least. Pinch me, someone, so I can—*ouch!* What're you doing?"

Dasha batted her eyelashes innocently. "You did say to pinch you."

Part Four

The Forest

y the next day, Isi had put Castle Daire in order—meals had a schedule, watch rotations were precise and well manned, and the roof over Selia's antechamber was ringing with hammers and the shouts of workmen. Isi kept Rin beside her as she interviewed each member of the household, watchful for those who were full of Selia's voice and might, for instance, consider crushing poisonous berries into Isi's dinner.

In the afternoon, Rin was in the courtyard practicing slinging with Razo and Dasha when a sentry announced approaching horsemen. The three ran out as a small group of Bayern soldiers gained the wall's gate.

"Ho there, you lazy brigands!" Razo shouted. "What have you been doing these past days, polishing your boots while the girls and I take down a tyrant?"

Two horsemen galloped ahead of the rest, and Rin recognized Geric and Finn.

"Does anyone smell roasting meat?" said Razo. "Oh, wait, it's just Geric's face."

Dasha nudged his arm and spoke low. "It is not seemly to talk that way about a king before his men."

"Men? It's just Finn."

The king's head was no longer bandaged except for a thin band over his left eye, but the skin along his left side was red and puffy.

"Is Tusken here? And Isi?" shouted Geric.

"They are, Your Majesty," Dasha answered. "Both here and well."

Much of the pain in Geric's face seemed to go away. "What's happened?"

Razo rubbed his hands together, gleeful with the news. "You'll never guess, King Scarhead—*oof!*" He rubbed his arm where Dasha had just elbowed him, then cleared his throat. "You'll never guess. So I'll tell you. You have to be really ready, though. Are you ready? It was . . . *Selia.*"

"What?" Finn stood up in his stirrups.

"Selia?" Geric leaned forward on his horse, gaping. "But . . . the Selia who was dead?"

Razo beamed. "Well, she's dead now. Some folk you have to kill twice. Like me, for instance. It seems—"

But the castle gate was opening, and in a streak of yellow and blue Isi was running, and Geric was dismounting and running too. He grabbed Tusken first from her arms, hugging him and tossing him in the air.

Finn leaped from his horse to greet Enna, and she entwined herself into him, their arms around each other, their faces close. Though they did not kiss, Rin thought that the way they looked at each other was even more intimate.

It's too bad Finn doesn't have a brother, Rin thought, then stung with the thought.

"Let's get married," Enna was saying with yearning in her voice. "Please, let's get married right now."

Finn put his face into her neck and whispered something that made her hum.

I don't really need my own Finn, thought Rin, feeling her face go hot. *It's no loss.*

Still, over the next few days, Rin let the thought wander through her mind from time to time. Sometimes she imagined a boy who was nice, who was curious about what the trees thought, who might hold her hand and walk with her under the Forest canopy. The way Enna talked about Finn sometimes made Rin want to climb a tree and never come down. But other times she felt a curious flutter tickle her heart, and a longing seize her belly. A nice boy who would like to be Agget-kin too, and build a seventh house in the homestead, where she could embrace her ma again, play with the little ones, live under the trees she knew, be Rin and be at home.

It never took long for the hope to snap. The memory of Selia was like seeing herself reflected in watery glass.

King Scandlan arrived a few days after Geric. He had thick lips constantly parted in confused amazement, and eyes that were lined and sad. He went straight to the crypt, where he knelt beside Selia's body and wept. Like a thunderstorm she must have come in, brilliant and frightening, and made the world seem beautiful in a new way. And then she'd left him in silence. Rin could see that Scandlan was not soothed by the quiet after the storm.

She sat on the steps that led to the crypt, her arms around her knees, listening to the echo of the king's throat-cracking sobs. The smell was all of dungeon.

She stood, poised to go down to the king, words and the sounds of words scampering in her mind. She had things to say.

An image of Selia handing scissors to Cilie burned in Rin's mind. She fled back upstairs.

But she found herself hovering about all day, outside the king's chamber, near his table at supper, watching him. A king, a man of greatness, ruler of Kel, brought to his knees by Selia. By a people-speaker. Fascination and horror battled inside Rin. She could not look away. And still the words danced.

The day after his arrival, Isi, Geric, and Dasha counseled with Scandlan in one of the side chambers on the third floor. Rin played with Tusken in the central chamber, the roof now solid above them. The door slammed open, and the king of Kel stormed out.

"She was my wife," Scandlan said, his lips quivering. "I know she would not do the things you say she did. You break into my fortress, kill my queen, and expect me to throw a banquet!"

Isi and Geric watched him go.

Dasha sighed. "He is haunted by Selia. After seeing what those hearth-watchers did to themselves, it makes me wonder . . . did her people-speaking leave permanent damage? Maybe those who were closest to Selia will never recover."

"That would be a tragedy for anyone," said Geric. "But for the king of Kel, it's dangerous."

Rin shuddered, as if she could feel the taint of people-speaking slide through her, a thick black snake tense in her throat. Dasha might be right. Cilie sat in the dungeon now. When she'd heard of her mistress's death, instead of trying to escape, the abandoned waiting woman had taken a knife and cut off her own hair.

Lord Forannan and Lady Giles, the original denizens of the castle, returned from their brief exile in the town of Daire. That night they organized a feast for their sovereign, enlisting twelve town men to perform the hummers dance. The men wore sacks over their heads painted with grotesque faces, red eyes wide, red lips in exaggerated smiles and sneers. One sack face was blank.

The dancers' wooden swords sliced and dove as the men jumped and rolled, rocked and swung in complicated maneuvers, almost touching and always escaping. Women sat to the sides, beating drums in a hard, throbbing rhythm, and the dancers hummed a tune more animal than human.

Rin watched Scandlan. His gaze followed the dancer with the blank face, his own eyes wide and red lips parted as if painted on. The drums beat faster. The dance grew more intense, the men blinded by their sacks still moving together, ducking from the slice of wooden swords, sword against sword whacking in time, one, two, three, and again, their shirts stained with sweat, the drums even faster and dancing so quickly it seemed impossible they would escape the touch, but again they ducked, rocked, spun, and escaped, one, two, three, faster and hotter, drum beats so tight it seemed one continuous bang, men moving so quickly they seemed always about to fall, when someone yelled and eleven swords turned as one, pointing in. The faceless dancer was caught inside the circle of swords.

The drums stopped. The humming stopped. The faceless dancer fell.

Scandlan rose so quickly from the table he knocked his plate to the floor. He did not pause at the crash, but fled from the castle.

Rin followed.

The music started again behind her as she crossed the threshold into the yellow-hot heat of the last of the summer evenings. Scandlan stood atop a battlement overlooking the wood, his arms crossed over his chest. Soldiers approached him, but the king shooed them away.

He's a king, Rin thought. But this time she did not allow that thought to chase her away.

She climbed the steps slowly, her legs shaking as if from exhaustion. Then she stood behind him, watching quietly, and even from the simple slump of his shoulders, she understood so much about him it hurt. In some way he'd always known Selia was bad for him. But she'd been so brilliant, so tempting, a rare fresh fruit when all the world was winter. It did not matter that she had tricked him or overpowered him. Because even now that she was gone and he knew for certain just how wrong he'd been, he still missed her. He missed how she'd made him feel. His pain seemed a cousin to Rin's own defiant confusion after Wilem—her feverish yearning to feel powerful again, and her shame for that desire. She rubbed her arms as if brushing off the trails of a spider's web.

The king sat, resting his head against the battlement wall, and words swirled through Rin. So many possibilities. She knocked away most of them, ones that gave her advantage, that might woo him to admire her, even those that could trick him into thinking well of Bayern. She could see so much pain in him, her own skin stung. It became a challenge to find the words that might have been her balm those months ago.

Don't, she warned herself. *It's dangerous. A misstep could hurt him, or worse—cause a war.* But she knew—not just what could make it feel better now, but what was true. She was not skilled enough to manipulate him as Selia had—besides, that was the last thing he needed. But the words tinkled like chimes, ready and lovely.

"Your Majesty?" Rin sat beside him. "My name is Rin.

I'm . . ." *I don't know what I am. I used to be of the Forest, but I'm not anymore. I'm here, that's all.*

"You are Rin. Of where? Nowhere? That is a curious name."

She nodded agreement.

"How old are you?" he asked, squinting. His mastery of the western tongue was nearly perfect, his accent smooth.

"Fifteen. No, I had a birthday . . . sixteen."

He nodded. "You have the look of my daughter. She hates me, of course."

It was a strange thing for him to say, Rin guessed, and from that she knew that his pain was so hot that he ceased to be wary, lost the careful walls of diplomacy he must usually build. That made it easier to speak, as if they were peers comforting each other.

"My father disappeared when I was two," she said, wanting to share something in return. "Sometimes I've thought I'd give about anything just to have a memory of him."

The king nodded, wasting no words on feigned sympathy. Rin pulled her legs under her and decided she would tell a story—a true one. That is what Isi might do.

"When I was seven or eight, my ma decided that instead of spending all summer roaming the Forest and gathering food to last us through the winter, we'd start making things to sell and so buy more grain and other kinds of food we couldn't scavenge. It seemed a fine idea at the time, a way to make everything just a little nicer. We carved wooden bowls and canes and mud shoes. In the fall, my ma went to marketday in the city, sold our goods and bought a wagonload of food stuff. Once home, she discovered half the bags were nothing but chalk dust. She'd been swindled. Well, there were about twenty people in our family at the time, and chalk dust wasn't going to get us through winter. So she cried for a minute, 'cause sometimes that helps us get through the worst bits. Then she called us all in the yard and said, 'This week we scavenge like the squirrels. I've got a prize for the body who brings us the most.' And it was a game. We flowed all over that forest, hunting with slings, finding mushrooms and late berries, roots and sprouts. We had a good time—maybe even more fun than we'd had making bowls."

The king was looking at her curiously. "Did you find enough?"

"Our bellies shrunk a bit and we chewed on pine bark till our teeth hurt, but nobody died that winter. The next spring my brother and I added water and grass to the chalk dust and patted it all over Ma's house. It was pretty, sitting all white like that. Pretty as a bird." The memory struck ache into her heart.

The king nodded.

"That swindler, he tricked my ma and got away with it too. But he didn't even slow her down. It's good to cry a bit, 'cause that helps us get through the rough parts. And the winter is tough, there's no doubt. But we just hang on until spring when that ache will be all but swallowed up."

His eyes narrowed, and for a moment Rin feared he would yell or throw her back in the dungeon for speaking presumptuously to a king. But then his eyes softened, and his sigh was full of ache.

"You are young. You cannot understand these things."

She was certain she was using people-speaking even before she pushed those words out, but she spoke anyway, because it was true. "A heart's a heart, in a child or a man. You are tougher than you feel right now. Your roots are deep, your canopy's spread wide. You're going to show everyone what it means to be a king."

He blinked a few times, and a tear sped down his cheek. He wiped it away. "I will show them, will I, Rin from Nowhere?"

"Yes, sire."

"You speak boldly for fifteen years."

"I'm sixteen now."

He smiled just a little. "For sixteen years, then."

She shrugged. "I'm just trying to speak truly."

"Then speak on."

Now it was Rin's turn to be startled to tears. She nodded too, wiping them away and leaning back against the wall beside the king. Rin did not think he had people-speaking, but those words still entered her like arrows, and she felt stunned and downed by their command. *Speak on.*

So she did. She told more stories about home, the culture of pranks among her brothers, the games of the children. How it felt to climb a tree so high you inched about the canopy's shadow and turned your face like a leaf to the sun. How it felt to get lost inside one of Ma's hugs. How the night Forest sounded, chewed to bits by crickets and thrumming with bats and breeze.

After a time, silence fell between them, but she stayed, Rin beside the king of Kel. She let his words sprout inside her while the sun dragged the evening down into the west and the world merged with night.

in did not approach Scandlan again but she detected a change. His eyes were still sad, his shoulders slumped as if something was reaching up for him and pulling him down by his beard. But he did not weep openly anymore, and he met Geric's and Isi's eyes when they spoke.

Speak on, he'd said. But fear crouched inside Rin, tense. What if Selia had begun like that, speaking to comfort, hoping to help? How long did Rin have before she began to act as she had with Wilem? How long before she turned into Selia?

The next evening Rin did not speak a word through dinner, sneaking out of the castle after everyone drifted off to bed. She spent the night in the wood, nestled beneath the great oak, where she could see the three stone cairns keeping their hulking vigil.

Without fear, she let her thoughts melt into the tree's core, felt that good tightness, and claimed what calm seeped into her chest. It was balm, but not healing. The timber could not take away the curse of people-speaking or even offer words of advice. She slept fitfully that night, a root arching behind her back, and dreamed that she was exhausted and could not sleep.

The next morning Rin ate a handful of hazelnuts and decided to live in Daire's wood for the rest of her life— hunt in the winter, scavenge in the summer, build herself a hut of dead wood and never speak again. The decision was still new and daunting when she heard a voice calling her name.

"There you are!" Razo strutted through the trees, his hands in his pockets. Some time ago, he'd asked Isi's thread-mistress to add pockets to all his tunics because he liked how casual he looked with his hands resting. Of course he had not told Rin that outright, but she guessed. "I've been looking all over for you, Rinty-minty-moo."

Rin could not help smiling. "Rinty-minty-moo?"

"Not my best?" Razo squinted up at the canopy, his lips mouthing the words *Rinty-minty-moo*. "Hmm. I'd been pleased with it in my head, but now I think it's safe to say that was my worst one so far. Don't worry, I'll find the perfect nickname for you yet."

He sat beside her and stared up into the gaudy patterns of the oak leaves, a quiet flinch the only sign he was remembering when those branches hid them from death.

"It occurs to me that you've been acting odd—that is,

odder than normal. But being me, I didn't figure out what it was until you didn't show up for breakfast this morning—which, by the way, consisted of cherries and cheese and cold beef with jellied fat. Surprisingly tasty. Anyway, I figured it out." His tone deepened, his frown serious. "Rin, I know you're worried about hurting people. Because of, you know . . . how badly you *smell*."

Rin could not contain an angry gasp.

Razo laughed. "That was a priceless expression! Let me just absorb that for a minute in memory so I never forget . . . all right, that'll do. Anyway, I mean because of the people-speaking, of course. And you shouldn't worry." He picked up a thin stick and rubbed it between his fingers, making it spin. "I'm going to tell you something I've never told anyone just to prove to you I'm telling the truth. There was a time when I didn't like to be home, because I felt all squished in the family, like I was just one too many Agget-kin. Like I wasn't really one of the brothers.

"Sometimes"—he winced, and the stick spun faster—"sometimes I didn't even want to be around Ma. But then I went to the city as an animal worker, met Enna and Isi and Finn, became a scout and a spy for Bayern, met Dasha, and don't know if I mentioned how I stopped a war in Tira? Did I ever tell you about that? Maybe once or twice? Anyway, I like being home now. And it wasn't the homestead that changed. So I'm saying, it's all right if you change some. Stay out in the world longer if you need it. You'll figure it out. And then you'll go home again and it'll be just right. You'll see. Besides, there's nothing Jef could use so much as a people-speaker to convince him how loud he snores."

Razo left, walking backward while he said, "We leave in the morning. Isi thinks Scandlan is suddenly better, and Enna's determined to marry Finn now or we'll all feel the pain. In the morning, Rinn-a-round. If you disappear, we'll look for you till we find you, and just imagine Enna's mood after that delay."

He turned and jogged off.

Relief bloomed in Rin's chest until it almost hurt. She did not deserve to be so relieved—she scolded herself for not feeling glum and coming up with a new plan to flee. This solved nothing. She still did not know how she was going to live with that disease, how to keep people safe from herself. But at least, for now, she would not be alone. Her brother would not allow it.

Back at the castle, Enna declared that if it were not for Finn's mother, waiting for her only son's wedding back in Bayern, she'd have Geric marry them right there in her traveling tunic and leggings, not so much as a flower in her hair.

"But how can I break a mother's heart?" she said.

And so the party took leave of Scandlan. Formal farewells between the sovereigns lasted a good hour, and Rin waited in the wagon with Tusken, singing a song about colors. The Kelish king walked Isi and Geric to their horses, and after they mounted, he kept coming through the Bayern party and straight to the wagon. Straight to Rin.

He stared at her for several moments in silence—and so, Rin felt, did everyone else. She resisted pulling a blanket over her head.

"Rin of Nowhere," said the king. "What was the prize?"

She blinked. "The prize, Your Majesty?"

He nodded. "Your mother said there would be a prize for whoever scavenged the most before winter. Who won? What was the prize?"

"Oh!" She almost laughed, she was so startled by the question. "I don't think anyone remembered to ask about a prize. We just scavenged as if it was a game. Maybe the prize was that no one starved."

The king nodded. He smiled a little bit, just with his eyes, before turning back to the castle.

Speak on, Rin, he'd told her.

The thought was intimidating, sitting in the midst of hundreds of soldiers. It made sense to her now why she felt so uncomfortable in crowds. People-speaking gave intense meaning to words and expressions, and trying to truly see every person in a large group made her head hurt. She thought of what she'd said to Selia and felt its truth—it would be more comfortable to sit up high and command than to stay low and watch.

The wagon lurched forward and Tusken tumbled onto her lap, his noise of surprise turning into a giggle.

"Did you fall, Tusk? What a brave boy to fall and laugh!"

He laughed some more, and Rin remembered how easy it was to talk to that little boy. It was a start at least.

With no hurry (except for Enna's), Geric's party took the main trade road, checking on the rebuilding of Hendric's inn and the village of Geldis, stopping at castles in the major towns. Rin kept to herself, caring for Tusken when she was needed. Razo was often nearby.

Before Rin could come up with a plan for her future, Bayern's capital edged into view, the city's walls lining the horizon in sturdy gray. It was late morning, and Rin was riding a horse named Careful, or so Isi had called him. Tusken was sharing a horse with his father and doing something that made Geric laugh as if he too were a little boy. Enna and Dasha were trotting together, and Rin could tell they were jabbering about something silly the way their voices climbed up in pitch, though both set their jaws as if determined not to laugh.

Razo rode near Isi and Rin, trying to convince the queen that what her son really needed was to spend his summers in the Forest.

"He's got no playmates, and that's just wrong. Who'll teach him to take a punch without crying with no older brothers? I'll tell you who—Agget-kin. I've got twenty-two nieces and nephews, Isi. Twenty-two. You ever fallen face-down on an ant hill? That's what it's like to live there—but in a good way."

Rin whispered, "Actually we've got twenty-three," and Razo slapped his forehead.

"I went and forgot baby Linna again, didn't I? Don't you dare tell Jef or he'll have me changing her dirty squatters as penance. How could I forget Linna? She screams like a kestrel."

Isi smiled. "You have a Rinna and a Linna in the family?"

"Names like that are common in the Forest," said Razo. "We've got a Rinna, Linna, Winna, Minna, a Tin, Kin . . . let's see, who else?"

"Finn," said Rin.

"Right, if we're talking about Forest folk outside our family. I know a Shinn, Kinna, Vinna, Nin—I'm forgetting some—and then of course there's Enna, Genna, Senna, Hen, Gren, Lenna, Brenna . . ."

I rhyme with half of the Forest, Rin thought. She wondered if Isi's name held resonances of Kildenree, Dasha's of Tira. If it was common everywhere to resonate with your birthplace. *I belong in the Forest.*

She was not so sure it was true, but the desire for its truth burned, red coals in her chest that she did not want to die out.

"I should visit your family," said Isi. "Meet all those *-innas* and *-ennas*, and let Tusken climb a few challenging trees."

"Now that's some sense," said Razo. "I have a feeling about that boy. Soon he'll be leaping from branch to branch like a squirrel, mastering the sling and preferring moss to pillows."

Tusken heard Razo's voice and shrieked for him, so Razo trotted up to the boy and his father, shouting, "There's a dangerous brigand! I'll teach you yet!"

Isi watched him go, then bowed her head, her gaze on her hands. Isi had been so relieved to have Tusken safe, so happy that Razo was alive, only now was Rin seeing past those brighter emotions and noticing the sadness that roiled beneath the surface. Geric wore a reminder of Selia's cruelty on his face, but Rin supposed he was not the only one left with scars.

"You're unsettled," Rin said quietly. "Selia's changed you, shaken your confidence."

Isi did not look up. "Her words don't go away easily."

Unbidden, some of those words rose up inside Rin— *You were afraid of yourself all your life. And now you are useless. Weak.*

"Not everything Selia said was a lie," said Isi. "She was right about my being a coward. I let her punishment stand, but I was too afraid to witness her execution. And since I hid and hesitated, she survived and went on to make war. How many people died due to my incompetence?"

"Selia said the Tiran were eager for war. It might have happened anyway."

"Perhaps. But she was right—I flinch from duties. I go at being queen like a horse on a lead rope."

Rin started with a new thought. "You don't want to be a queen, do you?"

Isi shook her head, a little shyly. "My husband is king and I know my responsibility. I hack away at it, do my best, and hope no one notices the blunderer in the crown."

"No." Rin shuddered, the untruth in that so cold it chilled her. Fighting back, she gathered in warmth, let it roll around in her, ready to speak truth. "You aren't playing at being queen, Isi. You *are* a queen. Everything you say and do and think and fear—all of it makes you a queen, and the greatest queen I could imagine."

Isi shuddered too, as if a warm cloak were suddenly lifted off her, but she seemed lighter for it. "Thank you." She looked at Rin curiously. "What did Selia say about you?"

"That I'm weak."

"She was wrong."

Rin shook her head. She was still unsure if any of her words were harmless or if people-speaking laced them all. With the queen especially, she wanted to be cautious.

"You should know," Isi said after a time, "it can be over-whelming to know only one speaking gift. Ever since our conversation in the woods—was it just weeks ago? Feels like years—I've been contemplating what gift you might learn to balance trees. But then I realized . . . perhaps you already know one."

There it was. Rin was sitting firmly in the saddle but felt herself tumble a long way down.

"Do you want to tell me about it?" asked Isi.

Rin did not answer. Shaking her head would have been a lie.

"You were born with it, perhaps?" Isi's voice was soft. "But maybe by the time you were old enough to understand something of what you could do, you realized it was dangerous. Maybe you often want to speak but stop yourself." Isi waited, but Rin stayed silent. "A few times you may have used it in earnest and been frightened by what you could do."

Rin shut her eyes against her own embarrassment. "When I'm careless, the longing begins to sweep through me again and assures me I can be anything. I can do anything. All I have to do is speak. Sometimes I believe I could become that person, and *this* me is only a shadow of who I really should be."

"That may be true."

Now Rin looked up. "True? But—"

"You can allow yourself to be powerful, Rin. That's not a bad thing."

Rin shook her head, truly wordless now.

"You saw Selia. You know what not to become. So, what will you be? I have a feeling that discovery will be an adventure to make these last weeks look like a stroll through the wood."

They were entering the city gates, and conversation hushed with the relief of arrival and the hurrahs from the gate guards. Rin let her horse fall back and rode alone up the long, twisting streets of the capital.

What will you be, Rin?

ll who had journeyed were given three days' leave from duty. Most spent it sleeping, Rin and Razo included. Enna spent it planning. On the fourth day, Enna and Finn were married.

It was not a day too soon. Rumor was that the palace kitchen-master had resigned his post due to Enna's aggressive planning style, only to be cajoled back by Isi, and the thread-mistress had on three occasions faked a wakeless slumber to avoid the bride. But at last the court gathered in the great hall, lords and ladies alongside soldiers and Forest born. Pine and fir boughs entwined the pillars, filling the hall with the deliciously sweet scent of evergreen, transforming the chamber into its own forest.

Isi stood on the dais dressed in bright yellow, and with her pale skin and yellow hair, she had an inhuman beauty, like an image stamped on a gold coin. She spoke lovingly about the couple before Geric performed the ceremony. Gilsa, Finn's mother, was positioned beside the king and queen in a place of honor. She wore what were no doubt her best woolens, a bright yellow top with deep blue skirt and a red scarf in her hair, but must have shunned the idea of dressing in finery. The way she glanced at the crowd with a carefully concealed eye roll, Rin felt certain that Gilsa would not have cared if Finn and Enna had married in Kel. She was just looking forward to grandchildren.

No one stood for Enna's family on the dais—she had none. Her mother and brother had both died in the past few years. Rin wondered that she had not thought of that before. How lonely Enna surely would be, if she did not have Finn.

Enna and Finn held hands before the dais, directly on a square of sunlight cast by a window high in the ceiling. Enna wore a long red gown with Kelish lacing at the bodice, a style she fancied at the last minute. Her hair was wound together and pinned up, twining posies making a band of white across her crown. Rin barely noticed Finn's black tunic and jacket, because whenever she looked at the Forest boy, her eyes naturally traveled back to Enna again. He stared at her as if she was so stunning, so perfect, nothing else needed to exist. His gaze made Rin want to stare at Enna too and reason out her perfections. Did love make him blind to any faults until his Enna was a lie? Or did love imbue him with a specific kind of people-speaking, so that only he in all the world saw her truly?

Rin felt a tiny crack in her heart as she realized no one

would ever look at her as Finn looked at Enna. Rin must keep herself silent and apart.

Geric pronounced the final words. Finn held his hands to Enna's face, his fingertips light on her cheeks, and leaned down to kiss her. Enna blushed, a thing Rin never thought she'd see. The whole room cheered till the pine boughs swayed.

"Hurrah, hurrah, hurrah for the woman and the man," the crowd shouted in the traditional chant.

"It's about time," Razo muttered at Rin's side.

Dasha wiped a tear and shouted loudest of all. "Seven children, seven hearts, seven lives of happiness!"

Rin grimaced and figured it must be something they said in Tira.

"Seven cats too!" Razo shouted.

"With seven fleas!" said Rin.

Dasha bumped against Razo. "Oh stop it, you two. It is a perfectly normal wedding wish."

Rin and Razo laughed.

The crowd poured out of the palace and into the gardens, where a path lit by small white candles led to tables laden with sweet things. Razo and Dasha hooked arms and began to stroll in a manner that suggested Rin's brother had been more affected by the romance of the ceremony than he'd let on. Rin left them, making her way through plants heavy with growing, shrubs pulled low by their leaves, waiting for autumn to relieve their burdens. She felt a little autumnal herself, wearing a brownish red dress with fancy thread work around the sleeves. She patted her head, feeling the nice clean crown of braids Dasha had put in. A shrub had lost a few yellow leaves, and Rin swept them up and stuck them in her hair.

"Hello, Rin—Rinna." A boy Razo's age with a face thick with freckles stood suddenly before her, his ever-present orange cap in his hands.

Rin sighed. "Hello, Conrad."

And she kept on walking. *Not Conrad!* she thought. She glanced back. He was looking after her, twisting his cap in his hands. *Well, maybe . . . no. No. Not Conrad. Not anyone.*

The misty autumn evening welcomed her, pulling her deeper into the garden. She walked and walked, through the ordered garden, the fountains of late roses dipping their branches into the grass. Then she saw it—the elm tree, the trunk's girth as wide as all six of her brothers wrestling in a knot. It seemed so out of place beside the garden trees and flowering shrubs, an ancient, gnarled grandfather waiting patiently for a visitor. It had changed in the few weeks Rin was gone, looking shabbier and a little unloved now, many of its leaves brown and ragged around the edges. She knew the tree did not care—autumn was part of circling time, a reason to shed and exhale, prepare for sleep. But Rin mourned the loss of its lustrous summer glory.

She guessed the elm had stood on that hill since before

the castle was built. Some early king or queen must have taken a fancy to it and ordered it be spared the ax, the gardens and stables growing around it. Rin wondered if she could drown in the memories of such a thing. Just then, the thought was appealing.

She placed a slippered foot in the crevice of trunk and branch and climbed into its crossing limbs. Like diving into a deep pond with arms still at her sides, Rin lay her head against a branch, closed her eyes, and fell into the tree's thoughts. She did not leave a thread of thought behind her to hold on to, did not worry about finding her way out again. She just let herself plummet through dry, woody memories and left herself behind.

Her fears encircled her like rings in a trunk, and she existed in the core of it, spinning, facing them, seeing them—speaking a serpent's words, turning into a monster, becoming Selia, harming those she loved, spending forever alone. She spun and spun, fighting to face herself, trying not to fear so she could see her own face clearly. But she spun so quickly, the rings were a wall higher than any fortress, and she had no hands to climb. She wanted to scream at the tree, demand solace.

No, Rin. Listen.

She stopped fighting, leaned against the wall of rings, and decided to be comfortable inside confusion. As she waited, listening to the pulse of sap, what had felt hard and rough melted into softness. Walls lowered and she began to see again. It was a memory of Isi riding toward the capital, telling Rin she needed balance.

Rin looked at herself as if she were a tree, saw the circles of her tree-speaking and people-speaking growing side by side since she was a child. After she broke her own rules with Wilem, the rings of tree-speaking thinned, and the rings of people-speaking thickened, turning dark and ragged.

She turned in the elm and saw Selia, her face full of fierceness and need, slaving for her own desires, clawing her way to a crown, words leaving her mouth like cast stones.

Rin turned and saw the elm, passionless, calm, rumbling of deep soil and sunlight on leaves.

Nothing can balance people-speaking, Rin had thought.

The elm creaked in contentment, its trunk settling a little deeper into the soil.

Rin imagined herself thick with the voice of the trees, her center calm, her hands outstretched, words leaving her mouth like falling leaves. Bright autumn leaves, rich in golds and reds. She saw Scandlan, Razo, and Isi gathering her fallen words and weaving them into crowns.

The tree-speaking pulled her down and center, roots deep, content and sturdy in the soil; but people-speaking branched her up from herself and out toward sunlight—and people.

Finally she turned and saw herself, a thin, quiet girl with haunted eyes. An uprooted thing that longed to anchor herself and grow. She had been Ma's shadow, and Razo's and Isi's—but there she was now, ready to let herself be changed. She was not a queen—not Isi, and not Selia. She would be the Forest girl who listens to people the way she listens to trees and speaks truths the way leaves fall.

Rin was glowing with joy there, spinning inside the tree, weightless and without worry, whirling through images of good things, tree branches filled with people, people she loved crowned with leaves. She spun and glowed and maybe laughed until she felt ready to stand, to stretch, to look on the world with her own eyes.

And with that decision, she came crashing back and found herself sitting upright on a branch, her heart pounding, her breath coming into her lungs like blows of a hammer. She smiled, then began to giggle, throwing herself out of the tree and onto the ground. Her fancy dress was wrinkled, stuck with leaves and flecks of bark, her woven crown of braids coming loose at the ends. She felt pretty.

And new, too. Remade. Ready to move again. Listening was the start, she decided. Doing was the next step.

She patted the tree in thanks for letting her share its thoughts and come out again. By the light in the east, it was nearly morning—hopefully just the next day, she thought. Her limbs quivered with cold and exhaustion, and she was thirsty enough that the trough near the stables looked enticing. But she could not help giggling some more as she stumbled toward the palace.

She stopped in the castle to change into her old Forest clothes and pack her few things. The waiting women were asleep, the door to Isi's chamber shut. Rin glanced once at her bed and thought longingly of rest. But her heart was pumping hard with life, and she could not bear to lie down and close her eyes again, to say good-bye to the whole world even for as long as a nap.

She meant to search out Razo, but no sooner had she left the antechamber than she bumped right into him, his upright hair matted on one side.

"You're up early," she said.

Razo swept his fingers through his hair, encouraging the tips up. "When I couldn't find you after the wedding, I bribed a few sentries to wake me if you turned up. Where were you anyway?"

"Sleeping in a tree."

He snorted. "Of course. And now . . ." He looked pointedly at her pack. "Sneaking off again?"

"I'm going home."

He exhaled. "That's all right then. Be sure to give Ma a hug from me and do something spooky to Jef—could you tell a tree to bend down and wrap its branches around him while he naps? No? Shame. But do something good, and make sure you tell me all the details when I come back. Dasha and I . . . you know, we're going back to Tira for the winter, so I won't see you till spring."

She nodded. There was a burn of sadness against her

heart at the thought, but the burn did not consume her. She was Rin, Razo was her brother, and that would not change through autumns and springs.

He rubbed the top of her head. He did it fondly, but in the process pulled more hair loose from her braid, and she shoved him back before he could make a complete mess of her.

His eyes brightened with a sudden thought. "Maybe you could come with us! You'd love the boat ride, and Ingridan is . . . well, it's amazing. You'll see."

"Maybe sometime. But I can't leave Ma waiting any longer." She was not ready to explore the wide earth yet, not when home still felt mysterious. Besides, she aimed to visit the capital now and then. She might help Isi unstitch the words Selia had stuck inside her. And she could not imagine leaving Tusken for good. But she still felt like a shadow of a girl, sitting at the feet of the fire sisters, half-formed and callow. Home was a good, safe place to learn some and grow some.

"You going to want a horse for the trip home?" Razo asked.

She looked at him without humor.

"Oh. Right. But I don't know if you should make that walk alone."

"Razo." She lifted her palms up. "I'm Forest born."

Razo nodded.

"Will you let Isi know I went home for a bit? I'm no

waiting woman—she knows that, and she expects me to go. I could tell. But I'll miss that Tusken. Hug him for me? And invite them both to the homestead before winter." She spoke lightly, aware of a low heat she could draw up and pour into the words, make them stronger than what they were, but just then she found it easy to resist.

"I swear on my life." Razo gave her a quick kiss on the top of her head before turning away. She was halfway down the stairs when he called after her.

"I finally thought of the right nickname for you. What do you think about Rinna-girl?"

She smiled. "Perfect."

Rin took three days to get home. Autumn was young, breathing freshness into every gust. Instead of feeling bone-frozen and homesick for sunshine, Rin was enlivened by the weather. It made her shiver and remember that she was alive.

She took her time on the journey, listening to the pines and firs of her home. She was startled and delighted to discover how much of what she heard from the trees was just her own self echoed back. When she was filled with self-loathing for what she'd done to Wilem, that was all she heard from the trees. And in the same way, when she brimmed with sweet calm, she was not borrowing the tree's peace but actually tapping into her own. Hers was the core strong, roots running deep, branches reaching high. Hers was the radiating peace.

After realizing that, she just had to run for a while, skipping over ferns, weaving around firs. Running again, but this time toward home.

On the third day, she slowed to greet an aspen, running her hands over the papery bark and hard black knots, a contrast she found more beautiful than sunsets. She let her thoughts go in and down, listening to an aspen for the first time since she'd left home. Now she was not seeking the calm but listening for their silent green voice of life. She startled and opened her eyes. This was not an individual sapling. Every aspen in the Forest was part of the same tree. How could that be?

She touched that delicate bark again and listened. Aspen roots were part of a network that stretched over the entire Forest, thousands and tens of thousands of saplings growing up out of the same shared roots. And that root system was ancient, older than the elm, older than anything she could have imagined. Memories of fires hummed deep in its fibers, flames that had wiped out everything growing, except the aspens. Safe underground, the roots had lived to sprout new trees. Windstorms and mudslides, fires and droughts and axes, nothing had been able to kill those aspens. The tough roots survived, new trees bloomed, and the Forest kept on.

"So it is," Rin whispered.

She was not that lone elm in the garden, not some far-flung cedar clinging to a wind-battered hillside. She was from a forest as old as the stones of the earth, pines protecting each other from wind, firs entwining roots and sharing rainfall, aspens sprouting from the same source.

"Rin!" Her nephew Incher spotted her from his perch in a tree. Without another word, he leaped to the ground and ran off.

After weeks away, to have home suddenly near made her heart flutter like a trapped bird. Her first instinct was to run off, so she took a breath and found true things to speak to herself.

You are allowed to be powerful. You are not Selia, and you are not dark loathing. You have a strong core, reaching down deep, straining up high, but with eyes to see and a mouth to speak. You don't control the trees or the people. You are the changed one.

By the time she could see the bough-heavy roof of her ma's house, everyone was running toward her. All five brothers, five brothers' wives, twenty-two nieces and nephews (the twenty-third carried), and Ma, white-shot black hair frizzing free of her headscarf. There was no way Ma could outrun the likes of long-and-lean Jef or Hinna of the forever leaping legs. So perhaps she flew, because Ma did get to Rin first, her hands reaching for her girl, and then Rin was inside her mother's embrace.

It was like being lost in the rings of an ancient tree, how

she seemed to be falling and yet warm and still and as secure as could be. There was no fear, no wincing away from
herself. There was just Ma and Rin. And moments later,
everyone. Hands slapped her back and rubbed her head, children hugged her legs, bread was stuffed into her hands and
offered to her mouth, kisses and hugs and demands for news
of Bayern and Razo even as others shouted all the news of
the Forest.

"Rin, you're not to touch a spoon or a rag for a week at
least, you hear me?" said Sari, Brun's wife. "We women have
been talking about it ever since you left and not liking a bit
the way things were."

"That's just so," said Jef's wife, Ulan. "We've been treat-
ing you like an old lady instead of the girl you are, and it's
not right. So you just take it easy for a time till we figure
out how to treat the new Rin."

"But I wanted—," Jef started.

"Not a word, Jef," said his wife. "You let her relax a time
and just be. That's what she needs. I mean, is that what you
need, Rinna?"

Everyone looked at her now, question in their eyes, waiting for her response, and she could see that they did want to
know.

"I don't mind helping out still," said Rin, "as we figure
things out."

Rin wanted to start the next day fresh and feeling like
herself, whoever that was, to let home seep into her and

nudge loose that scared little girl, to balance the dizziness and get her feet under her again. Part of that would be telling the truth to her nephews and finding Wilem, asking for forgiveness and trying to explain. That thought was chilly and hard, but good too in its way, because she knew it was right.

"I missed you lots," little Hinna said, rubbing her face into Rin's side.

Rin laughed. It tickled. "I missed you too, Hinna."

Ma still had her arms around Rin's neck, and she asked in her ear, "Are you staying, my girl?"

"I'm staying."

Ma sighed, her breath scented with juniper berries.

Rin checked inside herself—strong in the middle, a core that stretched from her belly to her throat, hands touching others like leaves brush leaves, body close to Ma like the roots of great trees wrapped together.

I'm Rinna-girl, she thought, *and I'm Agget-kin. I'm a tree-speaker and a people-speaker. I'm Razo's sister and Dasha's, Enna's, and Isi's friend. I'm many things, some that I don't even know yet.*

All the hands and voices pulled her into the clearing of the homestead and onto a seat by the fire. A hearty lunch stew filled bowls; laughter and excited chatter bounced off the trees. Rin was silent. She tried to read her own self as she often had others, and she saw much fault. How could her family know her when she never expressed a wish or an opinion? When she feared herself and hid behind her ma?

Slowly, carefully, she could change that. It no longer seemed a hopeless task. With her ma beside her, nieces and nephews hugging her legs, the voices of her brothers and their wives falling over her like rain, she was deluged in home. She felt so aware of her family, they seemed a part of her own body. They loved her, she knew. That was a place to start. Now it was her turn—it was time to let her family meet Rin.

The End

Acknowledgments

Many thanks to the following:

- Dean Hale and Victoria Wells Arms for their usual spot-on feedback and inspiration
- Deb Shapiro, whose publicity fu is strong
- Barry Goldblatt, a knight in shining armor
- LittleRedReadingHood.com, where my fan base begins
- My blog readers—squeetusers, who did a lot of buoying-of-Shannon's-spirit through this tricky book
- Melissa Bryner Whiting, whose reaction to *The Goose Girl* first sparked the idea for this story
- Bonnie Bryner, Kayla Huff, "Big" Maggie Thatcher, Kindra Johnson, and Nikki Mantyla for loving my children while I wrote
- The King's English, the Salt Lake County Library, and all those lovely book people everywhere who get excited about matching the right book to the right person
- Bryant, Thatcher, Gabe, Kira, Mari, Livie, Tessa, Ellie, Max, Levi, and Maggie, the children in my family, who were very much in my heart as I wrote this book. May good stories surround you, comfort you, keep you safe, and make you feel at home.